Face Off

CHELSEA CURTO

Proofreading by Kristen's Red Pen

Copy editing by Britt Tayler at Paperback Proofreader

Cover by Chloe Friedlein

For the girls who don't only like to read about sports, but like to play them too.

(And for the girlies who love to see the six-foot-four NHL captain get on his knees and beg like a good boy–Maverick Miller is for you).

AUTHOR'S NOTE

As someone who's been an athlete my entire life, it's been a joy to watch the rise in attention the women in sports are finally getting. This enthusiasm for female athletes didn't exist ten years ago, and to live in a day and age where the NCAA women's basketball championship earned more viewers than the NCAA men's basketball championship is unreal.

I'm in my sports romance era, and when planning a hockey series, I knew I wanted to write a story with a twist.

When I first started dreaming about Face Off and the idea of a woman playing professional hockey, the PWHL (Professional Women's Hockey League) wasn't in its complete existence yet. Instead of creating a league for Emmy, I decided to let her play with the boys.

Trust me.

I know women don't play in the NHL (minus Manon Rhéaume who played in an exhibition game with the Tampa Bay Lightning).

This book is a work of fiction. It stretches the borders of believability to make it work, but the representation of women in sports is important to me, hence the woman in the NHL.

I also know hockey teams have more than nine players.

For readability, I've limited the number of people mentioned throughout the book so it isn't confusing to keep track of everyone (and I've included a roster as well so you know who is who)!

Lastly, some of the characters briefly mentioned in Face Off are from my other books in a different series. Dallas, Maven and June are from Behind the Camera (a single dad x nanny sports romance). Reid is also a character getting his own book in that other series. I wrote Face Off in a way where reading the other series isn't necessary (I hope!), but if you have any questions, please don't hesitate to DM me on Instagram (@authorchelseacurto).

CONTENT WARNINGS

Face Off is a romantic comedy full of laughs, spice and swoon, but I want to share a few content warnings that some readers might want to be aware of.

-explicit language
-multiple explicit sex scenes between two consensual partners (including light choking with permission)
-on page alcohol consumption
-a reformed playboy with a history of being a womanizer (there is NO OWD, and he's not with anyone after he meets the FMC)
-hockey fights (including blood and punching)
-mention of a hockey injury (off page)
-mention of parental abandonment (brief)
-mention of life in foster care (brief)
-mention of childhood cancer (brief)
-sexist comments made by side characters (brief, and including a non-consensual comment not made by any of the main characters)

As always, take care of yourselves and protect your heart. If you have any questions about any of the things listed below, please know my DMs are always open (@authorchelseacurto on IG).

DC Stars Roster

Maverick Miller - right winger
Emerson Hartwell - left winger
Liam Sullivan - goalie
Hudson Hayes - defenseman
Riley Mitchell - defenseman
Ethan Richardson - center
Grant Everett - right winger
Connor McKenzie - center
Ryan Seymour - defenseman

Brody Saunders - head coach

ONE
EMMY

I'VE BEEN around a lot of penises in my life, but the one six inches away from my face is the last one I ever wanted to see.

"Grady." I throw my arm over my eyes in a desperate attempt to shield myself from his flaccid dick. "We made it two seasons without this friendship turning weird, and you pick my last day to act like a creep? And in a sacred space like our locker room of all places?"

"Someone stole my boxers." Grady Whitlock, my best friend and one of the only reasons I've survived my stint as left winger with the San Diego Iguanas of the ECHL, the NHL's AA league, has never been the shy type. "You know I'm not like that."

"The proximity of your balls to my mouth says otherwise. I think I might have nightmares."

"Hang on." There's a string of mumbled curses followed by the zip of a duffle bag and the rustle of clothes. "Okay. You can look now."

I open one eye and sigh in relief when I find myself staring at dark jeans and not a scrotum. "Thank god. Who stole your boxers?"

"Probably Andrew," Grady grumbles. "The fucker has

had it out for me ever since I beat him in last week's practice shootout. Sorry, Em."

"I forgive you, but only if you never show me your junk again," I say.

"Maybe we can hypnotize the memory out of you."

"That, or I'll take a sledgehammer to my skull. You're going to have to find someone else to flash, buddy. My flight is in three hours, and then I'm out of here for good."

Grady frowns. "This place isn't going to be the same without you, Emmy."

"Getting called up to the big leagues was the last thing on my bingo card for this year, and I'm this close to freaking out." I pinch the air with my thumb and forefinger. "Come to think of it, can you show me your dick again? It's veiny, but it's way less terrifying than thinking about the future. Me? An NHL player? Are they *sure*?"

"Ah." He rubs his jaw and smiles. "We're in the deflecting stage, I see. People call what you're experiencing *emotions*, Emmy. You should embrace them. They don't make you weak."

"I know that." I wave him off, but a string in my chest pulls tight when I look at him. "It's all very sudden."

He walks toward me. When he's close enough to reach, he cups my cheeks with warm fingers and calloused palms. "You can do hard things, Em. This transition isn't going to be easy, but it's the opportunity of a lifetime."

Dammit.

I was really hoping to sneak out of here without our conversation turning deep. Grady has this way of drawing big, scary feelings out of me and forcing me to wear my heart on my sleeve, and I'm not sure I can handle that today.

I fidget with a loose thread on my shorts. My palms are clammy as I tug on the long, frayed strands of denim, and I swallow down a deep breath.

"Am I out of my mind to take this offer? For giving up the

sure thing I have here? You know I hate sitting still, but it feels like I'm jumping into the ocean without a life vest."

"Think of it as the next step. A redirection," Grady says, always the voice of reason in our locker room. "You've worked so hard for this. It was only a matter of time before an opportunity came knocking."

Call me selfish, but I *have* worked hard for this.

Really fucking hard, and now I have a chance to play for the DC Stars, our NHL affiliate team.

The Stars used to be a powerhouse who made it to the playoffs a record-setting twenty-four years straight. They're in a slump now, and they can't seem to break out of it.

They're coming off their eighth losing season in a row. A Stanley Cup Champion banner hasn't been unveiled in a decade and a half, and things aren't starting well for them this year, either.

An early season injury left their elite rookie winger with an ACL tear, and they've been rotating AHL guys through the empty roster spot without any success.

I learned all of this during a call with my agent and the Stars head coach. After nearly half an hour of flattery and reciting a list of my accolades that stretch back to high school, Coach Saunders extended me a contract offer because he liked how I played and admired my tenacity.

I kept waiting for someone to tell me it was a joke. A giant misunderstanding that should've happened to a different Emerson Hartwell, but the punchline never came.

And now here I am, with my bags packed and my heart in my throat as I lean forward and hug the man who's become a brother to me.

I've never been one for tears, but my nose stings and my vision blurs when Grady squeezes me tight. He smells like day-old sweat, but I don't care. I don't know when I'll get to see him, and I want to savor this moment.

He pulls away and gives me a serious look that tells me

he's about to go into protective mode. "Do you remember our rule?"

"No fornicating with teammates," I laugh. "Don't worry. I learned my lesson last time."

"That includes Maverick Miller. He doesn't believe in rules. He's got a girl in every city, and he's been pictured with models and actresses every other week. There's a rumor floating around that some big-time reality dating show offered him the lead, but he turned them down."

I roll my eyes. "I've dealt with those kinds of guys my entire career. I don't care how pretty or famous he is. I'm not touching that with a ten-foot pole."

"Good." Grady kisses the top of my head and ruffles my hair. I swat him away, and his attention bounces to my cubby. "I never thought I'd see your locker empty. Where did all your shit go? There used to be nineteen hairbrushes and enough plants to supply oxygen to an entire town."

"Fuck you." I put my hands on my hips. "Don't talk about Fernie and Freddie Ficus like that."

"Their leaves were in my space. I'm glad to see them go." Grady reaches in the front pocket of his jeans and pulls out a folded piece of paper. "This is for your new locker, if you can find any room for it."

I unfold the crinkled note and choke on a laugh. It's a photo of us we took on my first day with the Iguanas two years ago. His arm is slung over my shoulder. I'm leaning into him. We're wearing matching grins and matching jerseys, and I remember it like it was yesterday.

"Look at us," I say. "We're babies. You had all your teeth."

"And you thought bangs were a good idea."

"Never again." I bite my bottom lip. "You don't think the Stars called me up for a 'diverse hire' thing, do you? So they can be the first team with a woman on their roster?"

"Fuck no. They called you up because you're the best skater in the ECHL *and* the AHL. Because you can go toe-to-

toe with any guy in all three of the leagues. Who gives a shit if you have tits and wear a sports bra?"

"I wish everyone had the same attitude as you. Look how long it took me to win over the guys here—an entire season."

"That's because you're prickly, not because you're a woman. You're my little cactus." Grady pinches my cheek, and I glare at him. "If your new teammates want to talk shit, make them back it up when you scrimmage. Kick their asses then gloat humbly. If you're feeling extra feisty, bring up their positions in the standings." He stares at me, and his expression turns softer. "They're going to make a movie about you one day."

"This is getting weird. I've never had someone tell me so many nice things in a row without trying to get laid," I joke.

"Yeah, yeah. You need to work on accepting a compliment every now and then." He clicks his tongue. "Tell me about this person you're going to be staying with. Is she safe?"

"Piper Mitchell wouldn't kill a bee if it stung her. We were friends in high school, and she works for the Stars in their broadcasting department."

"Teenage you had friends?" he asks, and another laugh slips out of me. "That must have been a sight."

I flip him off and look around the locker room I've called home for two years, my heart hammering in my chest.

"It's the end of an era, isn't it?" I ask.

"And the start of a new one." Grady lifts his chin toward the door. "You know I hate goodbyes. Get out of here before I chop up your plants and feed them to the birds."

"You'd never." I hug him again, and a piece of me roots itself to him with the embrace. "Be good, Whitlock. Keep your dick in your pants."

"My confidence is taking a nosedive today. Is it really that bad? God, maybe that's why Sabrina didn't call me back after Saturday night at the bar."

"Because your penis hangs to the left? I doubt it. It's probably because her name is Samantha, not Sabrina." I pat his shoulder. "Look at you turning into a fuck boy."

"Dammit." He tips his head back and stares at the ceiling. "I really liked her. The bar was too loud. I couldn't hear. That's on me for not asking her to repeat herself."

"There's always next time." I scoop my bag off the floor. "I'm rooting for you."

"Hey. No sleeping with your teammates just because you're cold and bored and suffering from Mid-Atlantic seasonal depression."

"I promise I'll behave." My phone buzzes in my pocket, and I check my notifications. "I should go. My ride's here."

"Love you, Emmy. Have the time of your life," Grady says.

"Love you too, asshat." I poke his side and pull away. "There will be a ticket waiting for you at will call if you make it out east."

I head for the door that leads to the practice facility's lobby and glance over my shoulder. This is the biggest step I could ever take in my career, and when Grady smiles at me, I know I'm going to be okay.

TWO
EMMY

A MONSOON GREETS me on my ride from the airport to Piper Mitchell's apartment, and I'm drenched by the time I make it to the entrance of the upscale residential building.

The ride up to the eleventh floor is quick, and I wrestle my suitcases down the hall to Piper's door. I knock twice, and it flies open.

A five-foot-three blonde with bright blue eyes greets me with a hug that knocks the wind out of me, and for the first time since I touched down at Reagan International, I smile.

I never had a lot of female friends growing up. I gravitated toward sports and made it my mission to get picked for the boys' teams. All my spare time was spent training, clearing my schedule for practice and trying to prove myself. It was exhausting.

Not like the other girls, the guys on my recreational hockey team would say after I took an elbow to the face in a game. *One of us*, they cheered when I wiped blood from my nose.

I'd laugh it off, but deep down, I *wanted* to be like the other girls.

I wanted someone I could talk to about first kisses and bad dates. Period cramps and hot substitute teachers.

It's been hard to recreate that girlhood as an adult, though. People like to tell me I'm difficult to get along with. Closed-off and too snarky. It's how I've always been, ever since I can remember. I'm not angry but unsettled, which is why I'm always chasing the next big opportunity. Why I'm looking for the next place to go.

That usually translates to leaving before any real connections are formed, and the cycle continues.

Piper was different.

She snuck her way in when we were partnered up in English Lit our sophomore year, and it stuck.

If she's the sunshine, I'm the storm cloud.

One of us is the people-pleaser and the other is the people-avoider.

Two total opposites who found a friendship that works.

We lost touch in college—I was busy keeping my grades up to maintain my athletic scholarship. She was busy with broadcast journalism and falling in love with the legacy-student-turned-tech CEO who, as it turns out, ended up being a massive douche.

They split up last year, and we reconnected through Instagram DMs that turned into weekly FaceTime calls.

I'm not a big believer in soulmates, but I think Piper might be mine.

She found me when I needed her the most and made me feel lovable. Capable.

When I called her and told her I was coming to play for the Stars, she invited me to stay with her. It was like no time had passed in our friendship, and she was so excited for me, you would've thought *she* was the one who made the team.

"You're here," Piper exclaims.

"I'm here, and I'm soaked. I'm going to ruin your floors," I say.

"Who cares about the floors?" She lets me go and motions me inside. "How was your flight? Do you want to take a shower before I give you the tour and help you settle in? Are you hungry?"

She's talking a mile a minute, and my jet-lagged brain is slow to catch up.

"Do you mind if I rinse off?" I look down at the puddle forming at my feet. "The guy in the middle seat ate an onion sandwich, and I think the stench followed me."

"An onion sandwich?" Piper leans forward and sniffs my shirt. "That's disgusting. What comes on an onion sandwich?"

"Bread and onion. That's it," I say. "My poor rideshare driver gagged the whole way here, so I'm definitely losing my five-star rating."

"The decency of the traveling public has gone out the window. Thank god we fly on charter planes. If I had to see someone walk into the airplane bathroom without shoes on, I'd track down an air marshal and make sure they landed in jail." She tugs on my arm and guides me down the hall. "I'll show you your room so you can get cleaned up, then we can do the whole tour."

"Holy *shit*, Piper. I know you sent me photos, but this place is massive." I glance at the floor-to-ceiling windows in the living room. The DC skyline winks back at me, and I'm officially impressed. "This would go for millions in California."

"It's great, isn't it?" Piper grins at me over her shoulder. "If that fucker was going to cheat on me with his secretary and then say the divorce was my fault, you bet I was going to drag him for everything he was worth."

"How have you been holding up?" I ask.

"I'm fine," she says, but her smile is strained in the corners. "I had no clue how much he was limiting me until I was away from him, you know?"

I do know, and I hate that my sweet friend now does too.

"I'm sorry you had to go through that, and I'm sorry I wasn't there to help."

"Don't be. I'm on the other side of it, and things are going well." Her megawatt smile is back in place, and she stops us in front of a door. "This is your room. There's a bathroom attached, and I have towels set up for you. There's even a towel warmer."

"Gosh you're fancy." I hesitate before I lean forward and hug her again. "Thank you for taking me in."

"You don't have to thank me. This is going to be fun. There's no rush to settle in. I'll be in the living room when you're ready."

With a wave and a flip of her hair, she saunters down the hall and hums a tune that sounds suspiciously like "Goodbye Earl."

Thirty minutes later, I sit next to Piper on the couch and accept the beer she hands me. We knock the bottles together in a celebratory cheers, sit back and relax.

"I can't believe you're here, Em. And not only are you here—you're signing a contract with the Stars."

"How many people know about the signing? Did a memo go out?"

"No. I only found out when the broadcast team was given your stat sheet so we could do some research on you. I have a feeling it's going to be released to the media very soon, though. There's always someone who tells someone who tells someone else, and the next thing you know, it's plastered all over ESPN. Maverick knows, of course, so when it gets leaked, we can blame him."

Maverick Miller.

I've watched his highlights, and I know he's an incredible hockey player.

He's the former NHL Rookie of the Year. A First Team All-Star five seasons in a row. A recent Ted Lindsay Award winner, voted as the most outstanding player by the members of the NHL Players Association.

He might be an athletic phenom, that once-in-a-decade number one draft pick you go all in on because you know he's going to win you a Stanley Cup, but his social media is littered with posts that scream *look at me.*

I did a deep dive on him on my flight over, and I wish I hadn't.

There are pictures in VIP sections at clubs with an obnoxious silver chain around his neck. Other photos of him lounging in a suite at a DC Titans football game and throwing out the first pitch for the DC Dolphins baseball team.

I'm all for flaunting your wealth and showing off what you've earned, but he's the league's golden boy. The one modeling in magazine spreads wearing suits that cost eight thousand dollars and the guy who gets everything handed to him on a silver platter.

I heard a story that he wanted to use a public gym during the off season, and they shut down the building for two hours so he could get a workout in.

I bet no one's ever told him no.

It's difficult to play with people like that. There's ego involved, a *me* not *we* attitude that makes the locker room tense and uncomfortable.

I've seen it firsthand, and I don't want to be a part of that environment again. If that's how the Stars are operating, I'm not going to last more than a week.

"Miller," I say, and I hide my curiosity with a sip of my beer. "We have a morning skate planned for later this week, and I don't want to go in without knowing more about what he's like off the ice. My friend says he's a fuck boy. Is that true?"

Piper blushes. "I don't know anything firsthand, but on the road, he's been known to sneak someone back to his hotel room after curfew. The women are always very enthusiastic."

"That has to mean he's an asshole, right? Someone who doesn't have his priorities figured out."

"Not at all. Maverick is kind of like a puppy. He's full of energy and bounces around everywhere. Everyone loves him, and the work he does for charitable organizations is admirable. He also wears his captain hat well. It's why he's still here, even through all the losing crap: he believes in these guys, and he loves DC."

Interesting.

I can't say I've pictured the guy getting his hands dirty and doing charity work, but I tuck that away for later.

"Why have the Stars lost so many games? They haven't had a winning season since Miller was drafted. A guy that good should turn a whole organization around."

"I've only been here a few years, so I don't have the whole story, but I've heard rumors about toxic coaching. Sounds like he wasn't utilized to his full potential in his first couple of seasons. They'd leave him on the bench down the stretch in the third period, and he'd get frustrated. He also led the league in time spent in the penalty box his first two years with us."

"He has a temper?"

"It's not a temper—he wouldn't hurt a fly. He's very loyal, and he doesn't like seeing his teammates taken advantage of. Coach Saunders came in, and the dynamic has shifted. Coach is a lot easier to get along with while still having that authoritative personality. The guys finally believe they have what it takes to succeed after being told they weren't good enough for so long," Piper explains.

"And there have been injuries," I say, and she nods.

"Yeah. It's such a bummer about Finn Adams. He was having a solid preseason, and he and Maverick meshed really well. But accidents happen, and that means you get the chance of a lifetime, Emmy. Are you excited?"

"Being the first woman to play a regular season game in

the NHL would be…" I pause and rub my thumb up the neck of my beer bottle. "There aren't words. I'm so proud of myself, but I'm also terrified. The attention that comes with being a professional athlete is overwhelming, and even more so when you're playing without a dick in a male-dominated sport."

She giggles. "God. You're going to piss so many people off. The Chads and Joshes are going to lose their minds."

"It's always men with those names, isn't it? It wouldn't be the first time they told me to get back in the kitchen." My lips twitch in amusement. "Enough about me. When are you going to land an official spot on the Stars broadcasting team? I know you've been filling in here and there."

Piper shrugs. "Maybe next season. Someone is thinking about retiring, and I'm next in line. It's a waiting game, but I'm happy with what I'm doing right now—player research. Team development stuff. Becoming very familiar with everyone's career highs. The stats I can recite would be a cool party trick."

"I hate talking to the media, but I'd be happy to do an interview if it was with you."

"You're going to be the first person I talk to when I finally have a microphone in my hand. There's no escaping me, Emmy Hartwell."

"Wouldn't dream of it."

We stay up late talking about the team and the players and what our lives have been like since we last saw each other. I feel that same sense of calm with Piper that I do with Grady.

The assurance that even when everything feels overwhelming, there are still people who believe in me.

THREE
MAVERICK

SOMETHING IS TOUCHING MY ASS.

Which is weird, because I thought I went to bed alone last night.

I open an eye and groan at the sunlight filling my bedroom. It's too early. Too bright. And my head hurts too damn much.

"Christ," I mumble into my pillowcase. "I'm never drinking again. I'm too old for this shit."

"That's not what you said last night," a high-pitched voice says from somewhere behind me, and I scream.

A full-on scream like I'm in one of those theme park haunted houses and someone in a Michael Meyers jumpsuit is chasing me.

What the hell?

My memory of the last twelve hours is hazy at best. I remember going to a club after we beat New York 3-0. Strobe lights and free-flowing alcohol. Laughing with a couple of my teammates and a brunette grinding against me to the beat of EDM music.

I lift my head and look over my shoulder. A blonde woman

smiles back at me, way too perky for this early in the morning, and there are bite marks all down her neck.

"What time is it?" I ask, because I do *not* remember inviting her to stay.

"Ten." She leans forward and drags her tongue over my ear. Her hand grips my ass, and when her finger slides between my cheeks, I roll off the bed with a thud and take the sheets with me.

"Christ on a mother fucking cracker." I rub my elbow. "That's my good arm."

"Why are you running away? You wanted to play last night," the blonde says.

"Listen, I'm down to try anything once, but that was definitely the alcohol talking. Drunk thoughts are not the same in the morning, and they should not be repeated. Especially when they involve my ass."

"That's no fun. Come back to bed," she says.

"Kind of busy at the moment."

The world tilts a little bit as I lie on the floor under a pile of overpriced silk. It's nicer down here, and I think this might be the way I die: with tequila in my blood, my vision blurring around the edges, and my ass thoroughly groped.

I take a deep breath and glance up at her, ready to launch into my usual speech.

It's not you, it's me.

It would never work—I'm hardly home.

You deserve a man who can drop everything and be by your side.

The sex was great, but last night is all it'll ever be.

"Look, Bailey. I had a great time with you, but I—"

"It's Bethany," she says, and she crosses her arms over her bare chest.

I whimper at her cleavage, and now I remember why I let her palm me through my jeans on the ride home; her tits are fan-fucking-tastic.

"Right, sorry. Bethany." I sigh like this is the most painful thing I've ever had to do. It kind of is; my head won't stop throbbing, and I'm going to need three Advil just to get through the day. "I have a meeting with my coach in an hour, and I have to pull myself out of this hangover."

It's not a total lie. I *am* hungover and I *do* need to see Coach Saunders, but I also want her to leave as soon as possible.

"Can I give you my phone number? Maybe we can get lunch sometime. Or dinner. Oh! My sister is getting married next month. You could come as my plus-one," she says. "Her fiancé is a big hockey fan."

"I'm not looking to date right now," I toss back, trying not to cringe.

A fucking wedding?

We're entering the stage five clinger zone, and I have to get out of here.

"But—"

"We agreed it was only for the night, right?" I stare at her, and she's pouting. Full on *pouting*, with her bottom lip sticking out like a kid who didn't get their way.

"I thought maybe I could change your mind. You told me how much you liked it when I—"

"Mav?" A voice booms from my living room, and I groan again. Too many loud noises. "Where are you? I brought breakfast."

"This has been fun, but it's time for you to go…" I hesitate. What the fuck is wrong with me that I can't remember this woman's name? "…Becky," I inject all the confidence I can muster that I've guessed right.

"*Bethany*," she huffs.

Swing and a fucking miss.

"Bethany," I repeat, pretending like I'm trying to make it stick.

"Fine. I'm going."

She grabs a dress and a pair of sky-high heels off the floor and storms out of my room buck naked. I hear murmured voices out in the living room, then the door to my apartment slams shut.

"I handled it," Hudson Hayes, my teammate and one of my best friends, says, appearing in my room. "Lovely girl. She's not a fan of you anymore, though."

"Sorry, man. I didn't mean for you to be on clean up duty."

He runs his hand through his blonde hair. A sheepish smile breaks across his face, and he lifts a shoulder in a shrug. "What are friends for?"

"You said something about breakfast?" I ask.

"I did. Pancakes from that place up the road. Thought I'd stop by and see if you were hungry."

"*Fuck.*" I groan and try to stand. My feet get caught in the sheets at my waist, and I topple back down. "I love you."

He laughs, and his attention moves to the bed that's missing half its pillows. The box of condoms on the night-stand and the underwear *Bethany* left behind.

Fuck yeah, I'm getting good.

"You really need to find some new hobbies, Mav," he says.

"I'm young, Hud. There's plenty of time for hobbies." I reach out a hand. "Help me up?"

"I swear to god if you drop that sheet and I see your tiny dick again, I'm going to be pissed."

I check to make sure I'm wearing boxers. They might be on backward and inside out, but I'm covered. "Tiny? Go get a ruler. Let's settle this right now. You know I'm the biggest guy on the team."

"I don't carry around a ruler. Do you?"

"No. I guess I need to start keeping one in my pocket so when this argument comes up again, I can provide clear evidence of size ranking. You would lose so bad, Hayes."

He rolls his eyes and pulls me onto my feet, heading for

the kitchen. It's even brighter out here, and I regret not closing the shades last night. I straddle one of the barstools at the island, and my mouth salivates when he puts a plate of flapjacks in front of me.

"Are you going to Seymour's later? He's throwing a pool party and grilling burgers to celebrate our weekend off. His girl is also making brownies," Hudson says, sitting next to me. I swear there's a drop of drool hanging in the corner of his mouth—the man loves food more than he loves hockey. "Should be a good time."

"Can't." I shove half a pancake in my mouth, and the carbs soak up the last bit of alcohol in my system. "I'm meeting with Coach today. He wants me to skate with the new guy."

"Which one?"

"Some dude from the west coast. Coach sent me his footage, but I haven't gotten around to watching it. I've been busy playing catchup."

The guys know I spent the summer coaching the junior Stars hockey camp. As much as I'd kill to spend my first weekend off in months drinking beers and eating burgers, we're two weeks into the season, and I'm already in over my head.

"Are you talking about Emerson Hartwell?"

I knock over the salt shaker and grab my phone. I ignore the Instagram DMs flooding my inbox and pull up the email from Coach, double checking the name. "Yeah. Hartwell. Know anything?"

Hudson hums and takes a bite of his breakfast before answering. "I think Emerson Hartwell will be exactly what we need this season. More than any of the other players we've rotated through the last couple of weeks."

"I really thought this was going to be our year." I rub my eyes and sigh. "The guys in the locker room are finally proud to wear their jerseys, and Coach is getting more confident in his play calling every game. Then Adams went and tore his ACL in the fucking Bahamas, and our playoff dreams went out the door. Rookies shouldn't be allowed to go anywhere without a chaperone—I don't care if it was only for a weekend. He needs an adult watching him at all times."

"Chin up, Cap." Hudson reaches over and clasps my shoulder. "We've been through this before, and we can go through it again. The younger guys are going to be looking up to us now more than ever, and we have to show them that patience pays off. It'll all work out."

Hudson was drafted by the Stars the year after me. We clicked right away, and it's been a comfort to suffer through all this shitty bad luck with someone who gets it.

"I wish you could look into a crystal ball and read the future. It would bring my stress levels way the fuck down," I say.

"Think of it this way: things can't get worse. Anything better than last place in the league standings is a vast improvement."

"Wow. We're really grasping at fucking straws, aren't we?"

"Glass half empty, half full kind of thing. Our team psychologist would be proud," he says.

"Of you at least. I'd get another lecture about how my coping mechanisms are shit."

"Because your coping mechanisms are shit."

"It could always be drugs, Hud. Consensual sex never hurt anyone." I look at the time and sigh. "Shit. I gotta go. Coach is going to chew me out for being late."

"You're not going to watch Emerson's tapes first?"

"Don't have time. It'll be fine." I jump off the stool and give him a thumbs up. "Thanks for the nourishment, Dad."

He laughs and flips me off. "You can walk your one-night stands to the door from now on. And no more pancakes for you either."

I grin on the way to my bedroom to get changed for the arena.

I've played with thousands of guys over the course of my career, and I hate to be the realist, especially after hearing Hud so optimistic, but I doubt Emerson Hartwell is going to be what turns our team around.

No fucking way.

FOUR
MAVERICK

I LOVE BEING at the rink, but on a Friday when the sun is shining and the temperature is hovering around eighty without a cloud in the sky, I'd much rather be with my teammates by the pool enjoying one last hurrah before late fall rolls in.

I park my Mercedes in the arena garage and twirl my keys around my fingers. My head is still pounding, and I hope this session is quick. An introduction and a few laps around the rink should be enough to get to know this guy and make Coach happy.

"What are you doing here, Mav?" Bill, the security guard who's worked for the Stars for nearly two decades, closes his newspaper and looks at me. "Thought you kids were all off today."

"Captain duties," I explain. "We're bringing in another guy to try to fill the left winger position. I'm meeting him now."

"I sure hope this season is the turning point." Bill shakes his head, and I can feel the years of disappointment in the movement. "I was sorry to hear about Adams. That kid is going places."

"Me too, Bill. Maybe we'll have a shot next year."

"I have a lot of respect for you," he says. "Other players would've demanded a trade years ago, but you've stuck around. With you and Coach Saunders changing the mindset around here, I think we might come out on top one of these days."

"Thanks for your support, sir." I reach out my arm and we shake hands. "I better run. I'm already a few minutes behind schedule."

Bill waves and goes back to his newspaper as I head for the players' entrance. It's tucked away from the doors the fans use so we can slip into the locker room unnoticed.

I turn the corner and stop in my tracks.

There's a woman hanging around security screening in a spot the general public isn't allowed. Her elbows rest on the metal railing, and her head is tipped toward the ceiling like she's lost in thought.

I've never seen her before.

She's not one of my teammates' girls or someone I've slept with, which means she snuck in here without anyone noticing her.

I grin.

I've always liked rule breakers.

Her eyes are closed and her red hair is up in a high ponytail that hangs halfway down her back. The black pants she's wearing hug her curves so well, there's nothing left to the imagination—I can see every line of her body.

God damn.

She's hot as sin.

Exactly the kind of woman I could get into trouble with.

I'm staring, but it's hard to look away. There's this energy about her that makes my palms sweaty and my heart pound in my chest like I've been running for miles.

It's not the hangover, either.

It's *her.*

My lips curl into a smile.

"Hey," I call out, and her eyes flutter open and cut over to me. Bright green, and dangerous enough to make me think she could eat me alive. "Can I help you with something, sweetheart?"

She scoops a duffle bag off the floor and slings it over her shoulder like it's as light as a feather. Her hips sway as she walks toward me, and she's got to be pushing at least 5'10". The hem of her shirt rides up above her belly button, and I notice the muscles spanning across her stomach.

Fuck me.

I'd be shocked if I didn't have heart eyes right now. Athletic women are my goddamn kryptonite, and this one clearly knows her way around a gym.

"Yeah, actually," she says. "I'm looking for you, Maverick Miller."

Guess it's my lucky fucking day.

I grin, flashing her the trademark smile that gets me any number I want. "Well, here I am. Fans aren't allowed back here, but we can head to my place after my meeting if you don't mind waiting an hour."

She stops in front of me and lifts a perfectly shaped eyebrow. I wait for the agreement that usually follows, but she doesn't say anything. She just stares, and I blush when her mouth pulls up into a smirk that almost makes me drop to my knees.

The goddess sets her hand on my chest, and I take another good look at her.

There are freckles all across her nose and cheeks. They look like little constellations, clusters of stars I'd like to draw into pretty shapes. Her shoulders are sculpted, and she's wearing lipstick, a dark shade of red that nearly matches her hair.

She drags her nails down the front of my shirt in the cruelest form of torture I've ever experienced. I puff out a strangled breath, and my throat goes dry.

"Does that line normally work?" she asks, her voice sultry and low.

I think this woman is going to kill me.

"Hundred percent success rate," I croak.

"Even when you have a hickey on your neck?"

I touch the skin under my silver necklace and shrug. "Yeah."

She stands on her toes and brings her lips to my ear. I smell vanilla and something flowery. Her breath is warm, and I wonder what she would feel like underneath me.

"It's a shame it's only going to be ninety-nine percent effective now. The only thing I want to do with you, pretty boy, is kick your ass on the ice," she whispers.

I swallow and try to get my bearings. She's so close, and I fucking love it. "You think I'm pretty?"

"You would only hear that part, wouldn't you?"

"Is ice play some sort of kink of yours?"

"God, no." She takes a step away, but I want her to come back. "I don't know if I should be flattered or insulted you're hitting on me."

"Flattered," I blurt. "Definitely flattered."

When she laughs, it doesn't sound like she thinks I'm funny. "For being the captain of an NHL team, I thought you would've done your research."

What the hell does that mean?

The woman turns and heads inside the arena like she's been here a thousand times. I'm left gaping after her, confused and soothing the sting of rejection.

It takes a second for my brain to catch up. When I float back to earth, I realize I should probably chase after her and ask what's going on. I fly through security and follow the swish of her ponytail as she heads into the team's administrative offices.

By the time I tumble into the boardroom, she's already sitting at the long oval table and those pancakes are feeling like a brick in my stomach. Coach is across from her, grinning from ear to ear, and I've never seen the fucker look so happy.

"You're late, Miller," he says, and he doesn't bother to glance my way. "Sit down."

"Sorry." I slide into the chair closest to the door. "What's going on?"

"What do you mean what's going on?" Coach Saunders frowns. "Why aren't you in your skates?"

"My skates? I'm just—" My eyes flick over to the redhead. She's watching me, and that smirk is still in place. "It would be great if someone could bring me up to speed."

"You're kidding," Coach says. "You didn't watch the videos I sent you?"

I wring my fingers together. "The Emerson Hartwell tapes? No, I didn't."

"Who's going to be the one to tell him?" the woman asks Coach.

"Someone please tell me," I practically whine, and he motions for her to continue.

"I'm Emerson Hartwell," she says, and I burst out laughing.

It takes a minute to get myself under control. My stomach muscles cramp up, and when I finally settle down, I have to wipe a tear from my cheek.

"Yeah. Okay," I say. Another round of giggles hit me, and I wonder if I'm still drunk. "And I have an ocean front property in Iowa."

"Wow." The woman looks over at Coach, unimpressed. "This guy is leading your team?"

"*You're* Emerson Hartwell?" I ask. "But you're a—"

Her eyes narrow, and heat flickers behind the green. It's like her claws are at the ready, waiting for a fight. "Please, finish that sentence."

"I thought Emerson Hartwell was a dude," I say, which is clearly the *wrong* thing to say. The scowl on her face tells me she's definitely going to eat me alive. "And you're... *not* that."

"I'm not a fan who wants to go to your apartment either," she tosses back.

My cheeks turn bright red. I hate being embarrassed, and right now, I want to crawl into a hole.

"I made an assumption," I say. "Big deal. Usually when a woman is looking for me, it's to give me her number or... well, to come back to my hotel room. It's not because she's a professional hockey player."

"Classy," Emerson draws out.

"Miller," Coach says, and my head whips in his direction. "My office. Now."

If this man told me to jump, I'd ask how high. So I hustle out the door and follow him down the hall.

Brody Saunders isn't much older than me.

He's a guy in his late-thirties who got injured early in his hockey career and turned that misfortune into some solid scouting and assistant coach stints before landing the head coach position with the Stars a few seasons ago.

There's a level of mutual respect between us—he was a bullet on the ice when he played center, and he knows what he's talking about.

He asks my opinion on lineups and plays, and we've always gotten along. But from the way he's looking at me right now, I think he might murder me then leave my body out for the vultures.

"What's happening, Coach?" I ask. I lean against the door and kick my foot up. "Is she serious, or are you all fucking with me? Is this one of those hidden camera shows?"

"What's happening is your head is so far up your ass, I

ought to take away your captain title. What the hell have you been doing this week, Miller?"

"I've been busy," I admit, and the skin at the back of my neck prickles. "I haven't been able to—"

"To, what? Give me five minutes of your time instead of spending all night at the club?" Coach demands, and my shoulders curl in.

"You know we were at the club?" I ask, choosing to dodge the insults to my character.

"Hard not to, when TMZ is posting pictures of you with your hands on every woman in this goddamn state. You're in charge of this team, Maverick, but you're not acting like it. You're acting like a rookie who can't handle responsibility, not a thirty-year-old man."

I hang my head. "Sorry, Coach," I mumble. "It won't happen again."

"It's not me you should be saying sorry to. You disrespected Emerson, and you're wasting our time. Time that should have been used to get to know each other on the ice, but instead, I'm playing mediator like you're preschoolers."

"Are you serious?" I glare at him. "I'm not saying sorry to her. She was rude to me first and made me look like an idiot when she could've told me who she was from the get-go."

"I don't care who did what. If you don't want to act like an adult, I'll dock your pay for every minute you stand here and act like a child." Coach Saunders points at me. "Ball is in your court, Miller."

"Missed opportunity not saying 'the puck is on your stick,' Coach."

"Don't start with me."

I grind my teeth together. There's no way I'm going to win this argument. He's is a stubborn motherfucker—once he has an idea in his head, he runs with it.

"Fine," I say.

"Good. You better be on the ice with her in ten minutes,"

he says. He pushes past me and leaves me standing in his office, annoyed as hell.

He told me I had to skate with her.

He didn't say I had to be *nice* to her.

If she's going to dish it out, I'm sure as shit going to give it right back.

FIVE
EMMY

GRADY:

How did it go with Maverick?

ME

.....

No comment.

GRADY:

That bad?

ME

If you see me on the news, know I acted in self defense.

STUDYING hours of Maverick Miller's game film did not prepare me for meeting him in person.

He has this overwhelming presence about him. Dark hair and even darker eyes. Six-foot-four with broad shoulders.

Tattooed arms and long legs. The hint of a smirk and the cut of a dimple on his angular cheek, sharp enough to cut glass.

He walks with a confident swagger and the roll of his shoulders is boastful and proud, like he *knows* he's that hot.

His good looks irritate me more than his cocky attitude.

I knew he would be a little arrogant, but hitting on me and not having a goddamn clue who I was threw me for a loop.

It's not that I expected him to know everything about me.

He's a professional athlete with half a dozen endorsement deals. Captain duties and a personal life that stretches to a hundred different women in a hundred different zip codes. Probably some in other countries too, and maybe one in Antarctica, just to prove he can.

But I expected a little more respect when I met him. Less eye-fucking and more professional courtesy. Now we're off on the wrong foot, and it's his fault.

The door to the boardroom opens, and I sit up straight. Coach Saunders slides back into the room and gives me a hesitant smile.

"I'm sorry about that, Emerson."

"You can call me Emmy," I say. "And I'm sorry too. I wasn't an innocent party in that exchange, and I apologize for acting so immaturely. It's not the first impression I wanted to give you."

"Emmy, you could hit someone with a car in the parking lot and I'd find a way to have you on my team." His smile turns softer. "I'm glad you're here."

"So am I. Thank you so much for this opportunity. I know you've gone through several players while trying to find the perfect fit, and it means a lot to wear a Stars jersey."

"I want you to know I didn't bring you here to check a box or any bullshit like that," Coach Saunders says. There's a fierceness in his tone that wasn't there before, and I feel horrible for initially assuming exactly that. "We want the best hockey players on our team, and that includes you. I figured a solo session with Maverick would be beneficial before your first practice with the whole team, but now I'm second guessing myself."

I grab the bag with my skates and pads off the floor. "We'll be fine."

"I hope so. I want this to work out, Emmy. There's a restroom down the hall where you can change, and the rink is just past it. I'll touch base with you after and see how things went."

I give him a smile I hope doesn't look as forced as it feels. "Can't wait."

I stand on center ice in the famed Civic Center, awestruck. Exhilaration like I've never felt before pounds in my chest, and I have to remind myself to breathe as I take off around the rink.

All the tension I've been holding onto this week melts away the longer I move. Packing up my apartment. The cross-country flight. A new team and a new normal.

I skate faster and harder until my muscles relax. Until it's easier to breathe and the cool air fills my lungs.

After my sixth lap, I finally relax..

"Hey," a deep voice calls out, and I glance over my shoulder. Maverick is standing on the edge of the ice in his practice gear. His hands are on his hips, and he makes the stick next to him look small. "What are you doing?"

"Skating," I say innocently, just to piss him off. A muscle ticks in his jaw, and I give myself a point. "Is that allowed?"

"This is my rink. We're going by my rules."

"Funny. I didn't see your name on the building, hot shot."

"All I heard in that sentence was hot."

"How do you plan on skating with that inflated head of yours?"

"I'm captain."

"Congratulations. Since you like to tell people what to do, what do you have planned for the next hour? Are you going to waterboard me?"

There's that dimple in his right cheek, and I hate the fucking thing. "Sounds kind of fun. Is that one of your kinks?" Maverick smirks.

"You're awfully interested in the sex life of someone who will never get in bed with you," I say. "Do we need to get HR involved?"

"I love a good challenge. My determination is one of my best qualities."

"Right up there with annoying as hell, probably."

"I promised Coach I'd play nice, so we'll do a 1v1 tag up," he says.

I scowl. "A peewee drill? You can't be serious."

"Come on, Red." Maverick gives me a wicked grin that warms my skin. For half a second, I can see why women fawn over him. He moves across the ice like it was made for him, heading for the goal. "You don't think I'm going to waste my time until I know you can actually play, do you?"

"This could've been avoided if you had just watched my tapes." I sigh. "But okay. I'll bite."

Maverick tracks my position as I move toward him. He watches me line up at center ice. He follows my hands when I adjust my grip on my stick, and for one fleeting second, I think I see admiration in his eyes before he blinks it away.

"I don't have all day, Hartwell," he says with a lazy drawl. "Unless you want to talk more about biting. Then you have my attention."

"Any last words, Miller?" I drop the puck and tap it with my blade. "There's still time to walk away, sweetheart."

He laughs.

It's manly and low, filled with gravel. If he wasn't so obnoxious and full of himself, I might find it sexy.

He leans forward, and his grin stretches wider. "Good luck, Hartwell. You're going to need it."

Maverick doesn't play goalie, but from what I've seen in videos of scrimmages and dick-measuring shootouts with teammates, he favors protecting the left side of the net over the right.

He doesn't know I know that, though, and I use it to my advantage.

I move from side to side, taunting him. He watches me, a predator tracking its prey.

When I shift back to the left, he reaches to the top corner of the goal, falling for my fake out. I take advantage of his misread, winding up and hitting the puck as hard as I can to the right, a slapshot that sails straight into the net.

"What was that?" I ask. "Did you say something about luck?"

"What the fuck?" Maverick looks at the puck then at me. "Again."

"If you say so."

His stance widens and his broad body takes up every inch of space to play defense. I set up like I'm going to do another slapshot, but I change my grip at the last second.

The blade cuts around the puck. I shift my weight from my back foot to my front foot as I move with the motion.

My hands follow through, an upward trajectory resulting in a wrist shot I used to spend hours perfecting with my dad on the lake behind our house.

Maverick stares at me. I think he might be seconds away from kicking me out of the rink, and I brace myself for whatever wrath he's about to unleash.

"Do it again," he barks out, passing the puck my way.

So I do.

He blocks my third attempt, a sloppy backhand I fumble from a stationary position. I score on the fourth and fifth tries, two more slapshots I net despite Maverick's best efforts to stop them.

Again and again we go. Ten minutes stretches to twenty, then thirty. Neither of us say anything, but every now and then, he lets out a grunt that's just as deep and low as his laugh.

My arms ache. Sweat rolls down my cheek, and my sports bra is soaked. My breathing turns labored, and even Maverick seems winded when he lifts his chin and looks at me.

"Stop," he says. He pushes his fingers into his side and leans on the goal post. "We're taking five."

"Can't keep up, Miller?" I ask, skating toward him warily. My heart thumps in my chest, and his eyes drop to the pulse point on my throat before he drags his gaze back up to my face. "I thought you'd be quicker on your feet."

"Given I play forward and not goalie, I'm not sure how much quicker you want me to be. My save percentage is forty."

"Means I scored on you sixty percent of the time."

I haven't gone head-to-head with anyone in ages, and it's invigorating to push myself. To feel that slow rise of exhaustion hug my bones and tire me out.

"AHL?" Maverick asks, and his voice echoes in the empty arena.

"ECHL," I answer. "San Diego Iguanas."

"Record?"

"Kelly Cup. Two seasons in a row." I pause and give him the curve of a smile. "Better than what your team can say."

"Glad to know you're keeping tabs on our team, Red."

"Some of us like to be prepared when meeting people we're going to be playing with."

The laugh that slips out of Maverick is easy and light. He pulls off his gloves and unbuckles his helmet with long, nimble fingers. He shakes out his sweat-soaked hair, and I catch the heart tattooed on the back of his hand with the letter J in the center.

I wonder what girl he kept around long enough to ink his skin for. Maybe it was a drunken dare in Vegas.

"We're done for today. I've seen enough," he says.

"You don't want your ego to take another bruising, do you?"

"I'm looking out for you, actually. Coach is going to put us through the fucking ringer at practice on Monday, and I'm going to mop the floor with you."

"Any other peewee drills I should study? Maybe a refresher on how to tie my skates correctly?"

"You rely too heavily on your dominant side, and you're weak on the right. It leaves room for someone to steal the puck from you." Maverick lifts the hem of his jersey and wipes his face. The muscles on his torso are nothing short of what I imagine Adonis looked like in his prime. Even with his gear on, I see a deep cut V. Chiseled lines and sharp edges. My stomach swoops low at the sight, and I squeeze my eyes shut. "Hudson Hayes is going to make you look silly. He's our—"

"Defenseman," I finish for him. "I told you I like to be prepared." Hudson Hayes is a former all-American and a Frozen Four champion. He has two rescue dogs, and he spends almost all his time on social media posting about the local shelter where he volunteers. "Can't wait. It'll be nice to have other people around. Someone to back me up when I give you hell and you don't like it."

Maverick's smirk is a dangerous thing. I ignore how it makes my heart race and turn my cheeks pink. I tell myself it's just from the exertion of the last half hour, not his pretty face.

He moves toward me. When he's six inches away, just close enough for me to fist his practice jersey if I wanted to, I have to crane my neck to look at him.

His smirk turns into a pleased smile, glad to have the upper hand, and I've never hated my height more.

"Are you going to think about me between now and then, Hartwell?" he asks, and I hate that I haven't skated away.

"Only about ways to destroy you," I answer, voice impossibly soft as I unbuckle my helmet and his eyes gleam with delight. "You better make sure you eat your vegetables on Sunday night, Miller. What you saw today doesn't touch my A game."

"I have no problem with that. I love to eat." He licks his lips, and the implication behind his words is obvious. "Sleep tight, Red. You have no idea what you're in for."

"Do you have stupid nicknames for all the people you antagonize, or am one of the lucky ones?" I ask.

"I only have them for the ones who try to pretend they don't like it. But it's obvious you're blushing."

"Someone really needs to knock you down a few pegs, pretty boy." I elbow his stomach and give his shoulder a light shove as I push past him. He stumbles on his feet and falls onto his ass. I look down at him with an innocent smile. "Oops. I tripped."

"Glad to know you still think I'm pretty." His grin is proud as he stretches out on the ice, a long-limbed starfish. "Game on, Hartwell. I hope you're ready for war."

"I always win, Miller," I say as I skate toward my bag, glad to leave him behind.

SIX
MAVERICK

PUCK KINGS

ME

What is wrong with you all?

CONNOR

I didn't do anything

EASY E

Neither did I. It was probably Grant.

G-MONEY

Fuck off. I'm innocent!

CONNOR

Yeah, right.

ME

Why didn't anyone tell me Emerson Hartwell is a girl?

HUDSON

*woman

ME

Fuck you.

SEYMOUR

Who? What?

LIAM

Why the hell am I still in this chat?

Liam Sullivan has left the chat
Easy E has added Liam Sullivan to the chat
Liam Sullivan has left the chat
Easy E has added Liam Sullivan to the chat

EASY E

You're stuck with us, dude.

LIAM

Goddammit.

EASY E

Is she hot, Mavvy?

Cap?

O Captain my Captain?

G-MONEY

WTF? Who leaves people hanging like that?

EASY E

This is literally worse of a cliffhanger than Back to the Future II.

The rooftop pool at Ryan Seymour's apartment is packed with people, and I don't recognize half of them. I squeeze past a group of girls who won't stop giggling, and I give them a polite wave when they tug on my shirt.

My hamstrings are killing me, and I've been nauseous since I left the rink. The two bottles of Gatorade I chugged at my apartment didn't give me any of my strength back, and I feel like I'm crawling through hell.

"Hey, Mavvy," Grant Everett, our second line right winger, calls out from a pink pool float. A leggy blonde is next to him, and she has her hands on his chest. "You're a little late."

"Where's Hayes?" I ask. He jerks his chin toward the dessert table, and I roll my eyes. "Shocking."

I head over to Hudson. Just as he's about to lift a brownie to his mouth, I knock it out of his hand.

"Hey," he exclaims, turning to glare at me. "What's wrong with you? You're wasting food."

"What's wrong with me? What's wrong with *you*? When were you going to tell me Emerson Hartwell isn't some guy from BU or Michigan or wherever the fuck she went to college, but a woman who's been playing in the ECHL for years?"

Hudson snatches up another brownie and shoves half of it in his mouth. "Don't blame me. It's not my fault you didn't watch the tapes Coach sent."

"Did *you* watch the tapes?"

"Obviously."

"Great." I collapse onto a wicker lounge chair that probably cost Seymour, our left defenseman, two grand. "I'm such an idiot. I can't believe I fucked this up."

"What did you think of her?"

An hour with Emerson Hartwell, and I don't know if I should be turned on or pissed off by her talent. I grab a beer from the cooler to my right. I pop the top off and take a long sip.

"She's something," I say after a minute.

"Oh no." Hudson sits next to me. Millie, his golden retriever, runs up and nudges his hand. He scratches behind her ears and sighs. "What did you do?"

"I might have called her a fan," I admit. "Asked if she wanted to go back to my place and acted like a total douchebag."

"You didn't."

"I did." I rub my jaw and take another sip of my drink. "I mean, she was standing there looking hot as hell, and I—"

"Not relevant to the story. Keep going."

"She's just as guilty—she talked shit about me to Coach. Went on about how I must not know how to lead a team, all because of a mix-up when I ran into her near Coach's office —*loitering* without a visitor's badge, I might add. I felt really stupid."

"And you think she didn't? She's a female athlete who's probably had to put up with that shit her entire playing career. The guy who's supposed to be her new captain treats her the same way, and there wasn't a lick of respect. I'd be pissed too," he says.

"She could've told me who she was," I argue.

"You could've watched the tapes instead of spending time with what's-her-name last night," he throws back. I hang my head because he's right. "She's a good skater, isn't she?"

Good doesn't begin to describe what I saw today.

Hartwell's hockey skills are on a different planet, and I think I might be a little bit in love with her. I've never seen anyone play like that, and I have no fucking clue how she's not already on an NHL roster.

She moves like a figure skater and has the strength of a weightlifter.

Her attention to detail is unmatched. I saw the way her eyes anticipated my defensive moves before I got into position, and I'm going to dream about the way she hits the puck until my dying days.

It's effortless. Smooth like butter, and everything I adore about the sport.

I regret not watching those damn videos, because I would've shown them to my camp kids a few weeks ago. Given them a lesson on what hockey should look like, because she's the gold fucking standard.

"Yeah." I take a long pull from my beer. "She's good."

"Why is your face red?" Hudson asks. "Is Maverick Miller *blushing*?"

"I'm not blushing. I'm hungover, sore and tired. Leave me alone."

I'm also distracted by the hot redhead who did, in fact, kick my ass on the ice. But I'm not going to tell him that. He'd give me shit, and I've taken enough punches today.

"The media is going to go wild when Coach makes the formal announcement after practice on Monday."

"She's feisty. She can hold her own." I glance across the pool and watch my teammates. Six of them are playing chicken with women on their shoulders. The others are checking out Seymour's new grill. They look like kids in a candy shop when he turns on a burner, and I hold back a laugh. "We'll need to have a talk with the guys."

"About what?"

"About not hitting on her and treating her with respect. Coach is going to be on our asses."

"You hit on her," Hudson points out. "Isn't that the pot calling the kettle black?"

"She rejected me." I lift a shoulder and finish off my drink. "That was a first."

He bursts out laughing and Millie startles, then howls along with him. "She did? Please tell me what she said."

I groan and toss the empty beer bottle into a nearby recycling bucket. "'The only thing I want to do with you, pretty boy, is kick your ass on the ice,'" I repeat, and I rub my hand across my chest. I can still feel the sting of embarrassment there. No one has ever turned me down before. "And then she did just that."

"Oh, *hell.* I can already tell she's going to be my new favorite person."

"You're not allowed to gang up on me."

"Why not? It's so much fun."

I roll my eyes and scan the party, locking gazes with a woman. The yellow string bikini she's wearing matches her hair, and she gives me a flirty crook of her finger. I know it's an invitation, but that usual rush of adrenaline I get from interacting with a woman is noticeably absent.

"I'm going to head out," I say.

"Are you taking that blonde with you? She hasn't stopped checking you out since the minute you got here. I'm pretty sure she took a picture of your ass."

"I have a nice ass."

"As someone who's forced to stare at it for significant stretches of time, I can confirm you do have a nice backside. Make sure to wrap it up," he says, giving me the same lecture he gives all of us. "Be smart and don't do anything that's not consensual. You know the drill."

"I do, but I'm out of whack. It's not happening tonight." I stand up and pat Millie's head. She licks my hand, and I smile. "Besides, I told Dallas I'd babysit for him, and after today, nothing sounds better than watching a Disney movie with my niece."

"Emerson did a number on you, didn't she?" Hudson grins. "I've never seen you leave a party early, and especially not alone."

"I don't know what she did, but I don't like it." We knock knuckles, and I give him a nod. "Enjoy the weekend off, H. Come Monday, I think everything is going to change."

"Honey, I'm home!" I call out when I walk into Dallas Lansfield's apartment twenty minutes later.

"Uncle Mav!" June, Dallas's daughter, shrieks as she runs down the hall. I lift her in my arms and spin her around. "I'm so glad you're here. Can I paint your fingernails? Mommy got me a new polish."

"Of course you can, June Bug." I kiss the top of her head and hold her close to my chest. "How are you, princess? Did first grade treat you well today?"

"Lucas pushed me down at recess and Ms. Wilson put him in timeout." June grins smugly. "When she wasn't looking, I pushed him back."

"That's my girl. Proud of you, Squirt. Where are Mom and Dad? Did they leave you to steer this ship by yourself?"

"No." She giggles. "They're getting dressed. Daddy is wearing a tie and Mommy is wearing a dress. It's very pretty."

"Absolute knockouts, those two." I walk down the hall and into the living room, plopping down on the couch and putting her in my lap. "How does pizza sound for dinner?"

"Pepperoni, please!"

"We're definitely doing pepperoni."

"Ice cream too?"

"Obviously, kid. Maybe we'll eat ice cream before our pizza, and we won't tell the bosses. It'll be our secret," I say.

"What will be your secret?" Dallas asks. He stands in the entryway in a gray suit, his hair slicked-back. "Don't corrupt my daughter, Miller."

I grin at my best friend of nearly a decade. "Wouldn't dream of it. You look nice, man. Where are you going tonight? Somewhere with the Titans?"

Dallas is the kicker for the NFL team in town, a Super Bowl champion and one of the fans' favorite athletes. He almost gave up his career when he became a single dad six years ago, but he found a woman who loves him and his daughter equally. He's able to balance playing and parenting a lot easier now.

"Dance lessons. Maven is determined we learn the tango for our wedding reception, but I keep stepping on her toes." He checks his reflection in the mirror and fixes his tie. "Then we're going to dinner at a new French restaurant. She's been craving macarons, and apparently this place is really good."

"Craving, huh? Something you need to tell me?"

"Nope," Dallas says. "Not yet at least."

"Bummer. I'm counting down the days." I stretch my arms out on the pillows and sigh happily. "Stay out as late as you want. We're off until Monday, and I can take June back to my place if you two want to… you know."

"You're really pushing for this, aren't you? Make one of your own," he says.

"Nah. I like being Uncle Mav, and I need some more nieces. Maybe a nephew too. Enough kiddos so I can have a full hockey team."

"Daddy? Can I skate with Uncle Mav?" June asks, and I grin victoriously.

"See? She already has it in her system. Bring her to Family Night at the arena and let me take her for a spin on the ice," I say.

"Absolutely not," comes from the hallway. Seconds later, Maven Wood, Dallas's fiancée and one of my favorite people in the world, appears in the living room. "Our kid is not getting anywhere near a puck. Neither are any of the ones who might come after her."

"Damn, Mae." I look her up and down and whistle. "You are smoking."

"Thanks." She grins and spins in a circle to show off her dress. I'm used to seeing her in game day clothes and a beanie as our team's official photographer, but the woman can pull off anything. "And speaking of smoking, I hear you got torched on the ice today."

"Really?" Dallas's gaze bounces between us. "I thought you were off today?"

"What the hell? None of my teammates know what happened yet, and I hope I can keep it that way," I say.

"Word travels fast, Mav. Emerson is Piper's new roommate, and Piper and I are close. She told me Emerson was beaming pretty brightly when she got home. I would too if I made Maverick Miller look like a scrub. And here I thought you were the highest paid athlete in the NHL." Maven tosses her hair over her shoulder, and my mouth twists in irritation. "I guess not."

"She did not make me look like a scrub."

"Can someone fill me in? I don't like being out of the loop," Dallas says.

"Emerson is the Stars' new left winger," Maven explains. "She's insanely talented. Gorgeous, too. A little rough around the edges, but I liked her from the five minutes I spent with her."

"No wonder Miller is out of sorts. You know how much he loves an athletic woman," Dallas says.

"That's my fu—freaking dream girl," I whine, making sure I don't drop any f-bombs in front of June. "We had a horrible first meeting, and now I have to play next to her with my tail between my legs."

"You do remind me of a dog," Maven says.

"You look like one too," June adds, and I blow a raspberry on her cheek.

"Pretty sure I wanted to bark when I saw her for the first time," I say. "It's fine. Everything's going to be fine. I'm either going to charm the pants off of her so she has no choice but to like me, or I'm going to annoy her so much, she's going to demand a trade."

"Definitely a trade." Dallas and Maven exchange a look. "Gorgeous, you said?"

"Oh yeah." Maven nods and grabs a tube of lipstick from her purse. "Hottest woman I've ever seen."

"Why does she have to be a hockey player? Why couldn't I have met her in a bar? Or in an airport? Or at some charity gala where I could throw a million dollars at whatever environmental cause she's passionate about so she'd fall in love with me?" I groan. "This is so unfair."

"Your life is so difficult. Truly, I'm not sure how you get through the day," Dallas says.

"Some best friend you are," I huff. "I'm suffering here."

"You'll be fine." He drapes his arm around Maven's shoulder and brushes his lips across her forehead. "Ready, honey?"

"Hey. Knock it off you two. There are kids around," I say, covering June's eyes. "There's a time and a place for that."

"Yeah and you're one of the kids." Maven sticks out her tongue. "Maybe you're jealous. You want what we have."

I burst out laughing. "Christ, woman. You've lost your mind. That's never going to happen. You know I enjoy staying out late with women I won't see again and fu—"

"Don't you dare finish that sentence in front of my daughter." Dallas glares at me. "Or I will break your fingers."

"Sorry." I hold up my hands in apology. "I'm keeping it G-rated from here on out. Starting with our date with Anna and Elsa. Are you ready, June Bug?"

"Yeah!" June lifts her arms in the air and cheers. "It's time for *Frozen!*"

"Third time this week. Bring it on, snowman."

I turn on the TV and lean back, letting June get comfortable, and I don't think about Emerson the rest of the night.

SEVEN
EMMY

UNKNOWN NUMBER

Morning, Hartwell. Happy first day of practice.

ME

Who is this?

UNKNOWN NUMBER

Some people have referred to me as pretty.

I think hot was thrown around too ;)

ME

Does using winking faces in your texts normally work on people?

UNKNOWN NUMBER

IDK. I've never had to work to get someone to like me.

ME

I'm happy to be the first.

UNKNOWN NUMBER

Are you more of an emoji woman?

I'm partial to the smiley face with the party hat. That guy seems like a good time.

ME

You're so weird.

How the hell did you get my number?

UNKNOWN NUMBER

Captain privileges.

I have all the guys' contact info in my phone in case of emergencies. You're inking a contract today. Figured it was time to add yours too.

ME

Why are you bothering me?

UNKNOWN NUMBER

Is it really bothering you if you're messaging me back? Seems like you might be enjoying this.

ME

I'm going to block you. And probably knee you in the balls.

UNKNOWN NUMBER

Can't wait ;)

THE MAKESHIFT LOCKER room the Stars created for me is an old utility closet that smells like dirty mops and glass cleaner.

It's not ideal, but it's only temporary until Coach Saunders can find a better solution. For now, I get to stare at a pile of used rags while I dress.

"Hey," Piper says, and our gazes meet in the mirror. "Are you okay?"

I inhale a deep breath and hold it for a count of three. "Yeah. No. I'm not sure."

"Want to talk about it?" She tilts her head to the side, and I know it's a gentle coaxing. That she's saying *I'm here*. "We have time."

"I'm panicking." I run my hands over my pants, and I tap my fingers against my thigh. I didn't get any sleep last night, and I've been vibrating with nerves since the sun came up. "This is going to be a lot."

"It is."

"I think I'm making a mistake."

"You're not."

"There are going to be interviewers and cameras everywhere. I knew this was going to happen, but… I like my life of solitude. I like only being semi-recognizable. Just good enough for people to know my name but not spot me out on the street when I'm getting froyo at eleven o'clock at night. That's going to change after today."

"That's what all trailblazers experience."

"I'm not a trailblazer."

"You are, Emmy. I know you don't like to boast about your accomplishments, but it's okay to own it." Piper braids my long hair into two pigtails and adds a tiny ribbon to each side. "Besides, how hard can it be to play on an NHL team? Boys do it."

"Yeah. Boys do it. Thanks, Piper." I reach over my shoulder and squeeze her hand. "I mean it. Thank you for being here."

She loops her arm around my chest and hugs me. "There's nowhere I'd rather be."

"Do you know when we're doing the signing?"

"After practice. Coach Saunders decided to put together a

panel of players to join you in talking with the media. Maverick will be there. Hudson Hayes, too. I'm trying to corral Liam Sullivan, our goalie, to come, but he has a giant stick up his ass. He doesn't like interviews." She fixes my left braid. "You won't be alone, so you'll be able to deflect a little bit."

"Until Maverick makes me look like an idiot in front of everyone." I pull away from her and stand up. "I can't believe what an ass he was during our first meeting. He thought I wanted to sleep with him."

"Definitely not a meet-cute," she agrees. "And, to be fair, most women want to sleep with him. You're an anomaly."

I snort. "In his dreams."

"At least things can only get better from here. The press love Maverick. He does a good job of telling them just enough information to keep them off his back. Don't worry about him," Piper says.

It's hard not to worry about him when he's the best guy on the team. When he's the biggest, fastest, most intimidating specimen in the NHL whose opinion also happens to carry the most weight in the locker room.

He might drive me up a wall—and I'm going to have to change my phone number—but Maverick Miller is the key to keeping my position on the Stars.

I don't have to pass to him.

I don't even have to *like* him.

I just have to keep things professional so the people who write my checks think we get along well enough to keep me around.

"You're right." I grab my stick and shuffle toward the door. "It's going to be fine."

"Look at you." Piper claps her hands together, and I think she'd find happiness even on the gloomiest, rainiest day. "You're going to do great. It's the same practice you've done hundreds of times. Worry about the media after, and tonight, we can stuff our faces with Mexican food."

"And wine?" I ask, and she grins.

"Bottles and bottles of the stuff. I haven't gotten tipsy since the night I signed my divorce papers, and I'm overdue."

"Wasn't that a year ago?"

"Yeah." She shrugs. "I don't like to drink alone."

My stomach drops to my feet. "Shit. I've been a horrible friend."

"You have not. You've been busy living out your dreams, just like I thought I was living out mine. We're here together now, and that's what matters." Her smile is kind and full of encouragement that I feel deep in my soul. "Give them hell, Emmy."

My first day of middle school, I ate lunch in a bathroom stall by myself.

I'm worried today is going to go the same way.

The core group of these guys have been playing together for years. They might suck, but they make it obvious from interviews and photos they love each other.

It's hard to wiggle your way into a team's already tight-knit circle of trust without coming across as trying too hard.

I'm purposely the first one on the ice so I can shake out some nerves, and I take four quick laps around the rink. By the time the rest of the team shows up, that lingering self-doubt that's pounding in my chest starts to quiet down. I pull off to the bench and grab my water bottle, not wanting to look like an overeager showoff.

A few of the players nod my way. The guy decked out in goalie gear—Sullivan, his jersey tells me—gives me a grunt for a greeting that sounds like he's either pissed off or in pain.

Piper was right—he does seem to have a stick up his ass.

Grant Everett, a five-foot-ten guy who barely looks legal to drink, asks if I could sign a towel for his sister after practice.

I'm so flustered by the number three pick in last year's NHL draft wanting *my* autograph, I miss my mouth when I try to take a sip of water and drench the front of my practice jersey.

I recognize Hudson Hayes across the ice, and when he gestures for me to join him, I make my way over to the corner of the rink where he's stretching.

"Hey." He pulls off his glove and holds out his palm. "I'm Hudson."

"Emerson," I say, and his hand dwarfs mine when we shake. "But you can call me Emmy."

"Nice to meet you, Emmy." His smile is warm and kind, and I already like him. "How's DC treating you?"

"It rains too much here. I've barely seen the sun since I landed."

"You're telling me. You moved from California, right? I'm sure this is a big change."

"Mhm. San Diego by way of Michigan, with a few stops in between."

"Lansing, I think?"

"Someone did their homework. You could teach your captain a thing or two."

"Probably more than that," he jokes, and a soft, surprising laugh slips out of me. Guess I don't need to be specific about which teammate I'm talking about. "Does the gender-neutral name throw people off?"

"All the time. When I took my SATs, the proctor tried to kick me out of the room because he thought I was impersonating someone. I got a whole lecture on how identity theft is a felony, even as a teenager. It kind of makes me want to legally change my name to Emmy, but seeing people's reaction when they're wrong is hysterical."

"You mean like dumbass hockey captains who try to hit on you?"

This back-and-forth is exactly how it felt when I met Grady the first time. A full-on grin bursts across my face at the thought of my best friend, and I wonder if Hudson could be that to me too.

"Exactly. I wish I had video footage of that day," I say.

"I could probably track some down. There are security cameras all over the arena. We could use it as blackmail." Hudson grins back at me. "Let me know if Mavvy pisses you off too much. I have no problem putting him in his place."

"Mavvy? That is an obnoxiously cute nickname, even if his pretty-boy charm doesn't work on me."

"You sure about that?" a low voice asks from behind me. "Maybe the charm is working, because you still think I'm pretty."

"Your selective hearing is something else." I turn around, and Maverick is standing there with his helmet and stick in his hands. "Maybe I'll call you a troll instead. Or a leech, since you can't seem to leave me alone."

"The compliments keep getting better and better," Maverick says. "I can't wait to hear what you think up next."

"Did you need something?" I ask.

"Just wanted to say good luck today."

"Since when are you nice to me?"

"I'm nice to everyone." He puffs out his chest, and I swear he grows another inch taller. "I know we got off on the wrong foot, but if we're going to be around each other for the next seventy games this season, I figured I'd be civil. It's going to be hard to win if your hands are around my neck and cutting off my air supply."

"You're not into that? I'm surprised."

"I might be. Want to find out?"

"Dream on."

"Says the woman who won't stop talking about me when I'm not around." His grin stretches into a proud beam and his eyes crinkle in the corners. "Are you obsessed with me or something, Hartwell?"

"He can be delusional," Hudson says. He skates over to

Maverick and clasps a hand on his shoulder. "If you ignore him, he tends to find someone else to bother."

"So he's a pesky gnat. Got it," I say.

A whistle blows. The coaching staff stands on the red line with clipboards in their hands, and my heart moves to my throat.

"Huddle up," Coach Saunders calls out, and we all head over.

"Don't suck too badly," Maverick tells me, knocking his stick against mine. "Having you on the team wouldn't be the worst thing in the world."

"Thanks," I say weakly, but all my confidence leaves my body.

"Hey," Hudson says, and his smile matches the one Piper gave me earlier. "You're one of us now. We've got you."

His words buoy me toward something I can't quite describe. Gratefulness, maybe? Appreciation? The start of a friendship and letting myself think I can get comfortable in a place that feels so unfamiliar?

The sensation strengthens when Maverick nods his head, his eyes locked on mine, and adds, "Yeah, Hartwell. We've got you."

EIGHT
MAVERICK

I'VE NEVER SEEN the media room so packed, and they're all here for Hartwell.

Every chair is filled. There's a wall of bodies in the back, and more people keep filing in. I don't know where the hell they think they're going to go.

Microphones are set up in a neat little line at the table at the front of the room, and cameras from the largest sports networks point to the spot where my teammates and I will be sitting. Nearly everyone has a phone in their hand, ready to record an answer to their question.

"Fucking hell." I step back into the hallway. "That's insanity."

"What?" Emerson asks, and I gesture to the door.

"Take a look."

She pokes her head around the corner and her shoulders lift to her ears when she spots the sea of people. She moves away from the glass and takes a deep breath, the door slamming behind her.

"Holy shit," she curses.

"Thinking about what I look like shirtless, Hartwell?" I joke. "I'm flattered."

A smile—the tiniest, faintest smile I've ever seen—pulls at her lips, and I'm the proudest motherfucker in the world.

I want to set off a confetti cannon. Hang a banner from the rafters of the Civic Center that says **I MADE EMERSON HARTWELL SMILE**. Put it on a T-shirt and wear it around town.

I think she'd actually strangle me if I did that, but it makes me want to do it even more.

"Is it always like this for you all?" Emerson asks. "The media room back in San Diego has one chair."

"Who's the lucky guy?"

"Doug from the *San Diego Chronicle*. He writes down all of his quotes in a notebook and has no idea how to use a microphone."

"He sounds like a gem. Our media room never looks like this. The last time I remember seeing it so packed was after my first game as a rookie, but even then, it didn't turn to standing room only. You're hurting my ego by outshining me, Red."

That earns me another half smile from her, and I want to collect them all. Shove them in my pocket and keep them for myself.

"I can't believe I'm saying this, but I'm glad you all are going to be here today," Emerson admits. "I don't want it to be all about me, and it'll be nice to share the spotlight. I'm sure that won't be a problem for you. You probably have cameras at the foot of your bed."

"The flattery continues. Keep it up, and I'm going to develop a complex."

"If this is you without a complex, I don't want to know what you'd be like with one."

I grin. "Can I ask you a question?"

Emerson lifts her chin and looks up at me. Her green eyes almost sparkle under the shitty fluorescent lights, and I see a little bit of brown mixed in there too. "Why?"

"So we can get to know each other. If I'm going to be playing next to you, I need to know how you take your coffee. Consider it a very lengthy, very drawn out game of Twenty Questions. Better yet, let's make it Five Hundred Questions. Every time we're together, we get to learn something new."

"You say that like I plan to be around you more than the required amount of time. The less I see you, the better, Miller."

"I can be very persuasive," I say.

"You say persuasive, I say obnoxious."

"Tomato, tomahto."

She sighs and puts her hands on her hips. "I hate games, but I know you're not going to stop bothering me until I agree."

"Look at you. You're already learning things about me."

"Fine. What do you want to know?"

A lot of things, I think, and that's a first.

I never make small talk with women. I don't have to.

Everyone knows what they're getting into with me—sex. An orgasm or four, depending on how the night goes. A good time before we go our separate ways, and absolutely nothing deep and meaningful.

But for whatever reason, I'm really fucking curious about Emerson Hartwell.

I don't care that she's not going to end up in my bed later tonight.

I don't care that she'd probably hit me over the head with her stick if given the opportunity.

I just want to know something about her.

The name of a childhood pet. Her Mount Rushmore of hockey players. If she's an early bird or night owl.

Fucking anything.

I'm willing to bet she doesn't give out personal information willingly, and, just like with her smiles, I'm fucking greedy for more.

"Who's the asshole who made you believe you shouldn't be proud of your accomplishments?" I ask. On the other side of the door, Coach Saunders rattles on about the future and next steps for our team. I should probably be listening and getting ready to be hounded by the media, but I tune him out and focus on the freckled redhead in front of me. "Did they give you a reason not to celebrate everything you've achieved?"

A muscle in Emerson's jaw works. Her eyes flare with heat, just like they did the first day we met, and, *fuck*, I like that fire she's got in her.

"Why do you care? We're not friends, and we've only been teammates for three hours. I'm not going to drop to my knees and worship the ground you walk on just because everyone else does, and I don't understand why you want to get to know me."

Why wouldn't I want to get to know her?

She might be a little rigid, but she still seems really fucking cool. It's obvious someone fucked her over in the past, and I hate that she's so hesitant to even let her teammates learn things about her.

"My selective hearing only picked up dropping to your knees," I say, trying to make a joke, and she rolls her eyes. "Do you remember what Hudson and I told you before practice? I know you don't give a shit about me. I know we're not friends, but loyalty is kind of my thing. I take care of the people in my life, Hartwell, which now includes you. If someone told you that what you're doing—what you've done—as an athlete isn't deserving of recognition, I'd like to know names so I can kindly tell them to fuck off and stop messing with my left winger's head on what should be the biggest day of her career."

"I'm sorry," Emerson says, and it's the softest I've heard her speak. She breaks her gaze away from mine and digs the toe of her shoe into the carpet. "That was aggressive, and I'm sorry."

"You've got a lot of bark behind your bite, Hartwell. I can't wait to see you take it out on the puck."

"Says the guy who follows people around like a lost dog."

"I'm just looking for an owner I guess."

"Maybe someone should take you back to the pound." She studies my face for a second before sighing and adding, "I had an ex-boyfriend who used to tell me I only got opportunities handed to me because I'm a woman, not because I'm a good player. Because I..." she trails off and swallows. "Anyway. Once you hear the same thing so many times, you start to think it's true."

My hand flexes at my side. I narrow my eyes. Irritation rips through me, and I have the urge to hurt someone really fucking bad.

"You dated this guy?" I ask, and she nods. "I don't know jack shit about relationships, but putting your girlfriend down because you don't like watching her become more successful than you doesn't seem like someone I would want to be around."

"We all do dumb shit when we're young and in love. Play stupid games, you win stupid prizes. Mine happened to be an asshole who liked to make me feel small while he was the one with the tiny dick."

I choke on a laugh. "How tiny are we talking?"

Emerson holds up her fingers barely four inches apart. "That tiny."

"I need to send you a fruit basket and offer my condolences."

"I'm allergic to strawberries."

"Noted. You gonna give me a name?" I ask.

"Nope," she answers.

"I have friends who could track him down. They could hack into his computer if you ever feel like retaliating."

"Who the hell are you friends with?"

"Stop wanting to know things about me," I say smugly. "I'm going to think you like me, Red."

"If your ego gets any bigger, there's not going to be any room for us in the hallway."

"You could stand closer to me, if you want."

"I think I'd rather die." She looks down at her shoes and holds a foot up. "Should I put on flats? I don't want to look too tall in the photos."

"Too tall?" I wrinkle my nose. "Is there such a thing as too tall? I love tall women."

"I'm definitely going to put on flats then."

"Stop." I touch her elbow then pull back when I realize what I'm doing. "Sorry. I'm not a judge on *Project Runway*, so my opinion on fashion has little merit, but I like the heels. And if you like them too, who cares what anyone else thinks?"

"I read your *GQ* article from last summer. You seemed to have a lot of thoughts on fashion," she says, and she covers her mouth. Her eyes widen, and a pretty pink color pops up on her cheeks when she realizes what she just told me. "Shit. Pretend I never said that."

I break out into a slow grin and lean my elbow against the wall above her head. "Well, well, well. Are you reading up on me, Hartwell? Writing my name in your diary?"

"I was using the photos as a dartboard. Your face was the bull's-eye."

"Did you hit your target?"

"Right between the eyes. Every time."

"Atta girl," I say, and the pink on her skin changes to crimson as it moves down her neck. "That makes me—"

"Am I interrupting?" Hudson asks. His eyes bounce from me to Emerson, and he smiles. "Glad to see you two can get through a conversation without someone getting hurt."

"The day is young," Emerson says, and she slides away from me.

"Where were you?" I ask Hudson. "You're late."

"Sorry. Ethan has this spot on his ass he thinks is skin cancer, and he wanted me to check it out. He was going to ask Lexi, but she might've ripped it off his body for bothering her."

"Who's Lexi?" Emerson asks.

"Our head athletic trainer. You'll meet her soon," I tell her. Then, to Hudson, "How the hell would he have skin cancer on his ass? Is he walking around naked?"

"It's Easy E. I wouldn't put it past him," he says. "I've seen his dick more times than I've seen my own."

Emerson snorts, and something sharp slices through me at the sound.

I don't like that he's making her laugh. I don't like that she thinks he's funny, and I liked it better when it was just the two of us.

The applause on the other side of the wall breaks up my pissy mood, and the door to the media room swings open. Piper gestures us inside, and she glances over Hudson's shoulder.

"Where is Liam?" she hisses.

"Sorry, Piper. He said something about a bird and a cage." Hudson blushes, and he scratches his right ear, his nervous tic he does when he's uncomfortable. "I know it's a lie, and I'm sorry I have to be the one to tell you."

"That man." Piper huffs and grabs my arm, yanking me toward the table. "Too late now. You all are up."

"Hey, Red," I say, making sure to keep my voice soft enough so the reporters can't pick up on it. "If you need a break, tap your nose and I'll start talking about tiny dicks or something."

"Bonding over genitalia doesn't mean we're friends, Miller," she says.

"Wouldn't dream of assuming anything of the sort, Hartwell."

NINE
MAVERICK

THESE REPORTERS ARE PISSING me off.

We've been here for an hour, and they won't give Hartwell a second to breathe.

As soon as she finishes answering one question, another is thrown at her like we're in the middle of a goddamn tennis match. I'm exhausted just listening to her, and I can't keep up with how quickly she pivots from talking about her college career to what she's most looking forward to this season.

I get it—she's a hot commodity.

The story everyone wants to read about.

But *Jesus Christ.*

Can't they let her stop for half a second to take a sip of water? She keeps reaching for the bottle in front of her, but she hasn't had a chance to open it.

"Emerson," a squirrely looking guy calls out from the second row, getting her attention. "This all must seem like a lot of unnecessary production for a hockey team who hasn't won more than twenty games in the last couple of seasons."

I narrow my eyes when I recognize who's talking to her.

It's Simon Buttecker, the same asshole who once wrote a scathing article on Hudson's defensive weaknesses the day after his mom passed away from cancer. The piece of shit who called him out for being *distracted* during games, as if Hudson was on the beach in Saint Tropez instead of visiting his sick mother in the hospital every chance he fucking got.

Nothing good comes from that fucker's mouth, and I brace myself for whatever bullshit he's going to spew Hartwell's way.

"Maybe," Emerson says. "But the Stars still generate over a quarter of a billion dollars in revenue every year. My ECHL team didn't make a profit last year, so I think a little fanfare is fine. Plus, it's nice to feel important. Who wouldn't want a red carpet rolled out for them?"

Everyone in the room laughs. Simon sits up straighter, getting ready to go for the kill. "You're coming into the NHL as the first woman to play a regular season game with a team. How do you think you're going to stack up against the men in the league? Do you think you'll get minutes, or just spend time riding the bench?"

My fingers curl around the lip of the table and my eye twitches. Hudson stiffens beside me, and the grin he was wearing disappears from his face.

"I hope I'm going to do well," she says, giving off no hint that she's irritated by his question. "I've always relied on my speed, and I'm going to use that to my advantage when I'm playing against athletes who are larger than me. As for how many minutes I'll get, that's for Coach Saunders to decide. I'm honored to be here, no matter if I'm on first line or fourth line."

I had a little bit of media training when I was a rookie, but eventually it boiled down to not being a dick and never throwing anyone under the bus. It's obvious Emerson went through something more intense, because she's way more cordial than I would be.

"Your stats are impressive." Simon pauses, and his grin is lethal. "For a female athlete. I noticed your assists—"

"Hold up," I say, and every head in the room turns to look at me. I crack open the water bottle that's sitting in front of Emerson and shove it toward her. "We're not going to do that."

"Do what?" Simon asks, and he's lucky there is a barrier between us.

"Throw in the *for a female athlete* one-liner. You've been around since I was a rookie, Buttecker, and I've never heard you tell me my stats were good for a male athlete. If you're going to cover us this season, you're going to recognize Hartwell is an NHL player. Full stop."

"In that case, I'll amend my statement. Her stats are impressive, but she'd be last in the league in all categories."

"She hasn't played a game yet and you're already throwing her under the bus?" I ask, grabbing the microphone. "Pardon my language, but that's not going to fucking fly around here. Treat my teammates with respect, or I'll make sure we remove your press access for the foreseeable future. You can watch games on channel 5, not from the cushy media box, asshat."

I take a breath and wait for Piper to drag me away from the table. Revoke my interview privileges for three months like she did with Connor when he dropped half a dozen vulgarities on live television after an embarrassing 7-0 loss last year.

I didn't know there were so many ways to tell someone to fuck off.

Instead, she grins and flips off Simon from the side of the room where he can't see her and motions for us to keep talking.

"Uh, maybe we can get back to the excitement surrounding Thursday's game," Hudson jumps in, always one to defuse the tension. "We're playing at home. We've won two in a row, which is far from impressive, but, hey. It's better than losing fifteen straight like we did my rookie season."

Everyone laughs again, someone asks him a question

about the number of young players on our roster, and the conversation continues.

I spin to face Emerson to gauge her reaction from the last few minutes. She looks unbothered, but I'm starting to think that's just how she is.

Cool. Composed. Not giving a shit about what's said to her. It rolls off her like waves, and I wish I had the ability to be so nonchalant—I'm over here gearing up for a fight.

"You good?" I ask. "Sorry for interrupting you."

"I'm good," she says. "I'm normally better about holding my own, but I'm exhausted. I thought I was used to how quickly my life moves, then I got here, and it's like everything is zero to a thousand in two seconds."

"Welcome to the big leagues. We have ten more games than you all played in ECHL and four more teams. There's more traveling and longer stretches of time on the road. You have to take care of yourself first, and that means telling these people to wait a damn minute with their questions so you can have some water."

"I'm going to cut this off here," Coach says. "It's been a long day for my players, and Emerson needs to sign her contract."

"You read it over with your agent, right?" I ask out of the corner of my mouth, and she nods once. "Good."

She crosses and uncrosses her legs. Plasters on a smile when Coach sets a stack of papers and a fancy pen in front of her and rolls her shoulders back like she's about to get down to business.

"I want to thank the Stars organization for this opportunity. I know there are people out there who might think I don't deserve a spot on this team, but I've always thrived on criticism." Emerson uncaps the pen and twirls it between her fingers. "It's my motivation to keep working hard, so thank you for the fuel."

I look over her shoulder as she signs the first page of her

contract. Her signature is all pretty cursive and swoopy letters, and I wonder if she ever took a calligraphy class.

"Stop breathing down my neck, Miller," she mutters, turning to the next page with a flick of her wrist.

"Sorry. My penmanship looks like shit compared to yours, and I'm fascinated."

"You don't have a girl's handwriting inked on your body?" Her eyes bounce down my tattooed arm then back up. "I'm shocked."

"I don't. Can I use yours?" I ask. "I'll put *pretty boy* right over my heart."

"You never stop, do you?"

"Nope. Twenty-four-seven job, Red. But at least I made you smile again."

"You did not make me smile." Emerson flips to the next page and signs two more times. "You're imagining things."

"Is that why you're biting your bottom lip?"

"I'm biting my bottom lip so I don't snap at you."

"It's okay if you don't want to admit it. We can pretend you're smiling for the camera. Look. There's one over there." I wave and grin at the long lens pointed at us. "Say hi."

"You're exhausting."

"Nicest thing you've said to me all day. Hey. What are you doing tomorrow night?" I ask, dropping my voice.

"Not you." Emerson stands up and nods at Coach, shaking his hand as they pose for a set of photos I know are going to be on the front page of every sports website tomorrow morning. "We aren't friends, remember?"

"Like I could forget in the five minutes since you last reminded me," I tell her when the media starts to pack up their things. "We do this team dinner every Tuesday night at my place. Everyone brings a dish and we hang out for a couple of hours. Some people play video games. Some people drink. Some break out the stack of puzzles I have in the living room. There's no hockey talk. It's chill. You should come."

"You like puzzles?"

"Is that your question of the day for our game?"

She rolls her eyes for the hundredth time, and her irritation makes me grin. "I guess."

"I love puzzles. I did them a lot when—" I clear my throat and switch directions. "My niece loves them too, and when I'm watching her, we always put one together."

"Thanks for the invite, but I told you I intend to spend as little time with you as possible." Emerson looks down at me with something I'm going to pretend is a hint of regret. "It's better for all of us."

"Wish I could do the same," Hudson chimes in. "You're smart to keep your distance, Emmy."

My insides coil into a tight knot when he calls her that. Like they've been best friends for years and I'm the outsider trying to break into their circle.

"The invitation is there," I add. "This week. Next week. A month from now. You don't forfeit it just because you don't come tomorrow."

"Noted. See you at practice on Wednesday," she says, slinging a black purse over her shoulder and walking away.

"Put your tongue back in your mouth," Hudson says, and he smacks my shoulder. "And stop staring at her ass."

"My tongue is exactly where it belongs, fuck you very much." I scrub a hand over my face and lean back in my chair. "And I wasn't staring at her ass. I don't want to lose a hand, and that woman wouldn't hesitate to use a buzz saw on me."

"She seems like the stabby type, doesn't she?"

"Yeah," I laugh. "That's going to work well for us on the ice."

"You think she has a shot? Simon's a dick, but he asked what everyone's thinking."

"She has a shot. It's like you said—things can't get any

worse around here. Maybe Hartwell will help light a fire under us. God knows I've tried and failed."

"Are you on her side now?"

I shrug. "I'm captain. I do what's in the best interest of the team. If that means getting along with the woman who would rather feed herself to the lions than spend time with me, so be it."

Hudson scoots closer and drops his voice. "I heard what you almost told her about the puzzles. You never go there with anyone."

"It almost slipped out unintentionally," I say. "Besides, I don't think Hartwell is just anyone."

"Watch it, Cap. Don't go falling in love with her."

"Easy, Hud." I stand up and flash him a grin. "You know falling in love isn't in my DNA. The same woman every night? Sounds fucking horrible."

"We have women in the NHL now. Anything is possible."

I clasp his arm and squeeze his shoulder. "Anything except me settling down. That's impossible."

TEN
EMMY

"YOU CAN DO HARD THINGS," I tell myself in the mirror. I've repeated the mantra fifty times, and I'm not any closer to believing it. "This is just another game. Pretend it's a scrimmage or morning skate. It's no big deal."

Except, it is a big deal.

It's my first game in a Stars jersey, and I'm nervous as hell.

I've played hundreds games since graduating college and god knows how many before that, but this is the most important one.

This one dictates my future as a professional hockey player, and as someone who's never imagined my adult life without the sport, it needs to go perfectly.

It's been a frenzy since I signed on Monday. Every time I log into social media, I have more and more followers. I'm pushing a quarter of a million on Instagram, and overwhelmed is an understatement.

Messages and comments flood in from people who are cheering me on and asking where they can purchase my jersey. *Good luck* and *make us proud*.

For every comment of support, though, there are a dozen hoping I fail.

She won't last a month.

Can't wait to see her cry LMAO

Man, get this shit off my television.

What happens when she gets a cramp? Is she going to be out a week?

#FreeMaverickMiller

I screenshotted a handful of them and posted them on the wall in my locker room, right where I can see them when I dress every night.

I've always wanted to silence the haters, but I really want to prove the internet trolls wrong.

I want to play so well they come crawling back with their tail between their legs. I want them to be so embarrassed they beg for forgiveness.

But I'll never give it to them.

I'm not doing this only for myself. It's for all the girls out there who have ever been told they can't. That they're not good enough, and they'll *never* be good enough, so why bother trying?

It's a giant *fuck you* to anyone who's ever made us feel two inches tall—in sports, in life, in a relationship—because we deserve so much more.

My phone buzzes, and I glance down. I usually ignore my devices this close to puck drop so I can go through my pregame warmups without any distractions, but Grady's name pops up for a FaceTime call. A pep talk from my best friend is exactly what I need right now.

"There's my star," he says, and his face takes up the whole frame. Light brown hair, green eyes that match mine, and a smile that's nothing but kind, it feels like he's in the room with me. "Look at you in your uniform."

I prop the phone against the mirror and take a few steps back, spinning so he can see the full jersey and my name on the back. "This is the first time since this whirlwind started that I feel very, very legit."

"Signing a million-dollar contract didn't do it for you?"

Grady teases, and I stick out my tongue. "We're in Duluth tonight, and I had the hotel set up a projector in the conference room so the guys and I can have a watch party."

"I doubt I'm going to play very much. I'm still learning the lines, and Coach said he's going to gradually work me in."

"Who gives a shit? You're going to be in an NHL game, Emmy. We want to cheer you on, no matter if it's ten seconds or ten minutes of ice time."

My heart swells three sizes with his support. "You're too good to me, Grady. How's everything going in San Diego? I saw you scored a hat trick two nights ago."

"First one of my career." He grins proudly and sits back in his hotel room chair. "Things are good. We're still adjusting to you not being here, but we'll figure it out. How are the Stars treating you? Do you miss us?"

"You know I miss you all. The guys are nice. There's a lot of youth on the team, and sometimes I feel really freaking old when they start talking."

"You're thirty, Emmy, not two hundred."

"Yeah, I know. Hudson Hayes is my favorite. He reminds me so much of you."

"I swear to god if I get replaced, I'll raise hell," Grady says. "He might be taller than me, but I could take him."

"You could. It also helps that he's the nicest man in the world, and he probably wouldn't hit you even if you hit him first," I say.

"What about Prince Charming? I heard him stick up for you during your press conference."

"Don't get me started on Miller." I sigh and flip my braid over my shoulder. "He's hell-bent on us becoming friends, and I don't know why."

"He wants his squad to do well, Emmy, and camaraderie with his teammates, even the cactus-like ones, is important to him."

"Thanks for the reminder that I need to water my plants."

I grab my helmet off the floor and hold it against my hip. "I should get going. Showing up late to my first game will probably earn me a stern talking to from Captain Know-It-All."

"Have fun tonight. Remember how much you love the sport, and it'll be a blast."

"No pressure whatsoever. Thanks for the pep talk, Grady." I wave. "I'll text you tomorrow."

I click off my phone and take a deep breath, buckling my helmet under my chin. I grab my stick off the wall and slip into the hallway, surprised to find it empty. The noise from the arena echoes down the tunnel, and I smile at the voices of fans filing in to their seats.

"Hartwell," a voice barks out.

I look over my shoulder and see Maverick leaning against the wall in all his gear. One ankle is crossed over the other, a lazy slouch to his tall frame.

"Yes?" I ask, turning to face him.

His eyes sweep me up and down, from my jersey to my skates, and even from here, I can see his dimple pop. He motions me forward, and my feet move on their own. I trudge toward him, wondering what he has to say, and I brace myself for the worst.

We're sending you to our AHL affiliate.

You're headed back to California.

Finn Adams had a miraculous recovery, and we don't need you anymore.

"You good?" he asks when I get close.

"I'm fine. What did you need to tell me?"

"Need to tell you?" Maverick pushes off the wall. He looks down at me and frowns. "What would I have to tell you?"

"Some bad news or something."

"What the hell are you talking about?"

"I don't know." I shrug and slip my hand under my jersey to fix my shoulder pad. "Why else would you be looking for me?"

"Uh." He wrinkles his eyebrows. "To wish you good luck. Today is a big day."

"Oh." I pretend to inspect my gloves, not wanting to look him in the eye. "Really?"

"Yes, really. You and your self-doubt, Red. We're going to have to work on that," he tuts. "Do you want to hear about my first game?"

"I know you're going to tell me anyway," I say, and I am curious.

Maverick laughs, and it unknots the string of tension in my spine. "I spent thirty minutes before puck drop barfing in the bathroom. My coach at the time couldn't find me, and when I finally dragged myself out to the ice during player introductions, my pants were on backward. But the worst part came eight minutes into the first period."

"What did you do?" I ask, unwillingly captivated.

"I scored on the wrong goal." He giggles, a high-pitched noise that almost makes me smile. "Sent the puck straight at my own goalie because my nerves got the best of me. The ESPN headline the next day was *Miller's Mishap*, and I hid my face for a week."

"Shit."

"I know."

"How did you survive with all the attention?"

"It was tough, but I persevered. I'm not a quitter, Hartwell." He grins, and there's an unexpected swoop low in my stomach. "All that to say, you're going to be fine. I'm not sure how much Coach is going to use you tonight, but as long as you skate the right way down the ice, I think we can consider it a success."

"The bar sure is low," I say, surprising myself with a laugh. Maverick's grin grows brighter, and I narrow my eyes. "Stop it."

"Stop what?"

"Stop smiling at me."

"I forgot how much you hate it when I'm nice to you, Red." Maverick knocks my helmet with his knuckles, and a fire flickers inside me. "Are you ready to get this party started?"

"Yeah." I nod. "I'm ready."

I received a standing ovation when I took the ice for the first time, and I didn't miss the way Maverick encouraged the crowd to cheer. I played three minutes in the first period and four in the second.

When I'm not in the game, I study the Stars' transitions. I'm sloppy tonight, and I don't want to make the same mistakes again.

Maverick spends more time on the ice than anyone, shaking his head when Coach tries to replace him with Grant late in the third period. Watching him fly past me, a blur of blue jersey and white helmet, is nothing like seeing him at practice.

He's a beast on the ice, determined to help his team win and ready to sacrifice his body in the process. I knew he was competitive, but in a game environment with the clock ticking down, he's lethal.

It's easy to see why he's one of the best players in the league. Nothing is half-assed, and I admire the way he makes skating look *easy*.

"Hartwell," Coach says, and I lift my chin. "You're in."

"There are two minutes left," I say, and I buckle my helmet with a shaky hand.

"And?"

"And… and nothing," I say, knowing better than to push back on a coaching decision.

Coach Saunders nods, and I stand up. When Presley

Donohue, our left winger on the second line, glances toward the bench, I make my move, tumbling onto the ice and taking off with the offensive attack.

"There she is," Maverick calls out. He shoulders a defender into the glass and grunts. "You looked a little bored sitting for so long."

I catch a pass from Hudson and cross the blue line, my eyes scanning the ice. I spot Ryan Seymour open to my right, and I send the puck toward him.

"Maybe I was bored from watching you," I say.

Maverick's laugh wraps around me as he skates past, a towering mass of man charging toward the goal. Seymour passes back to Maverick who toys with the defense for three seconds before rearing back and netting a perfect snap shot that sends the hometown crowd into a frenzy.

"Still bored? That one was for you, Hartwell," he says, adding a wink.

"Such a showoff," I say, joining the guys huddled around him.

"Think you can score one more?" Ethan asks, his arm slung over Maverick's shoulder. "I've won every face-off so far tonight. I can win another so you can really bring this home, Cap."

"Let seventeen have it," Maverick says, nodding my way. "We'll set her up for a shot."

"*What*? No way," I say. "Coach is about to take me out and—"

"No, he's not," interjects Riley Mitchell, Hudson's defense partner. "He never takes out players in the last minute, especially if it's after a goal. You're in until the final buzzer, Emmy."

"You're fine," Hudson says gently, and he nudges my side.

"Unless you don't think you can handle it," Maverick adds. "Grant can step up."

"*No*," I blurt out, and his smirk tells me he was trying to egg me on. "I can do it."

Our huddle breaks, and Ethan does win the face-off. The puck goes to Hudson then Maverick, a cruel game of keep away from the opposing team as they charge for the attacking zone.

"Red," Maverick calls out, and he taps the puck my way. "Let's go."

I catch it and take off, my blood buzzing with excitement.

I've always lived for these types of moments in sports. The game winners in front of a crowd that cheers my name. Gatorade dumped on my head and a dogpile on the ice after a victory. With twenty seconds on the clock, the dream is close to becoming a reality.

Hudson angles a defender toward the boards, and I know this is my chance. Another defender appears on my right, just as I pull my blade back, and there's no way for me to score without the puck being stolen from me.

I see Ethan open on my left, and I pass to him, watching him score time expires.

"Yes!" he yells, skating toward me. He wraps me in a hug and laughs against my helmet. "What a pass, Emmy."

"An assist in her first game," Hudson says, hugging me next. "Helluva way to start an NHL career."

"That was awesome," I pant.

"Way to go, Red," Maverick says, nice and low. "I thought you had the goal."

"I dumped it so I didn't give up a breakaway." I shrug. "There will be more opportunities for goals."

"Damn right." He pulls on the end of my braid and grins. "Are you proud of yourself?"

"Yeah." I match his smile. "An assist is awesome, and, on the plus side, I didn't *own-goal* myself like someone else here."

"I mean, shit. I think you might be a better player than me, Hartwell."

"I know I am, Miller." I skate toward the bench where the rest of my teammates are cheering for me. "And I can't wait to prove myself right."

ELEVEN
EMMY

BANE OF MY EXISTENCE

Congrats on third line, Red.

Working your way up!

ME

How do you know these things before they're announced?

BANE OF MY EXISTENCE

Magic!

Kidding.

Coach told me about the changes in our weekly meeting, and said I was all for it.

ME

Glad to know I have your approval.

Can't tell you how much it means to me.

BANE OF MY EXISTENCE

Is that sarcasm?

Sure sounds like it.

Red?

Cool. I'll just go fuck myself then!!!

MY ENTIRE BODY HURTS.

Muscles I didn't know existed ache, and I'm embarrassed by the whimper that escapes my chest when I try to prop myself up on an elbow to read my book.

A sharp sting up my thighs triggers a groan after two pages, and I use a wrinkled grocery receipt as a makeshift bookmark. I press my thumbs into my calves and the balls of my feet. My eyes roll to the back of my head when I rub, the pressure so glorious, I might cry in relief.

"Are you okay?" Piper's voice slides under my door. "You sound like a dying cat."

"That's an insult to cats everywhere." I groan again. "You can come in, but only if you promise to massage my legs."

"That's all it takes?" The door swings open, and she shuffles across the carpet. "Gosh, you're easy."

"What's that smell?" I sniff and try to place the scent. "Are you baking?"

"I am." Piper grins and jumps on my mattress. She wiggles her way up next to me and puts her head on my shoulder. "I made a marble loaf cake. I figured we needed a little something to celebrate your first two weeks with the Stars."

"Are two weeks worth celebrating?"

"Everything is worth celebrating," she tells me, sounding like the perfect one-liner for a motivational poster in the locker room. "I even added chocolate chips."

"Oh, hell." My mouth waters, and I realize the last thing I ate was my breakfast after practice this morning. The one day off between games slipped away from me, and the setting sun tells me it must be close to dinnertime. "You spoil me."

"And I do it gladly." She loops her arm through mine and taps the back of my hand. "How are you feeling? You've been a total badass on the ice. Press has been positive, ratings and viewership of Stars games are up, and even people like Simon-freaking-Buttecker are talking about what you bring to the team."

"I'm…" I shrug, hesitant to use words like *good.* It feels like a curse to say it. Like I'll break this rare bubble of happiness I'm in if I give it a name. "Three games in five days. Two were on the road, and I've never been so sore or tired in my life. But…"

"But?" Piper waits, knowing I have more to add.

"But things are going well."

"They are, aren't they? And I'm so proud of you." She pinches my cheek, and I smile. "What are you doing tonight?"

"Not moving more than a foot to my left or my right. Wishing I had a little robot that could bring me water and food so I could live in this bed and never leave. Coach is sadistic—what kind of person schedules a full practice between games?"

"A guy who might finally be on the brink of a winning season," she says matter of factly. "Do you think you could throw on some jeans and a sweater?"

"For what? It's almost six, Piper. My social window is closing."

"Dinner with me, Maven and Lexi. We're going to this restaurant around the corner. Their food is to die for, and I promise we won't stay long. A drink and a burger, then we can come home so you can get some good sleep before the game tomorrow night."

I open my mouth to say no like I usually do, but the word doesn't surface.

It gets stuck somewhere in my throat, and for the first time in months, I want to spend the evening with the people I'm still getting to know. A night out with my new friends sounds like fun.

"Okay," I say. "I'd like that."

"Yes!" Piper squeals and throws her body on me. I laugh when she hugs me tight. "Make sure to wear a jacket. It's chilly tonight. Damn winter is just around the corner."

"What are the vibes of this place? Heels? Sneakers?"

"Casual for sure. There's a jukebox in the corner, and we try to go weekly when we don't have a road game."

I wonder what it would be like to stick around somewhere long enough to have a routine. To have the guy at the bagel cart recognize you when you come by on Sunday morning and the barista at the coffee shop up the road know your order by heart.

"It sounds perfect," I say.

The tables at Johnny's Place are small and cramped together. The four of us barely fit in the tiny leather booths, but after one drink, it matters less. I'm relaxed as my shoulders fall away from my ears and warmth settles in the center of my chest.

"You all are coming to family dinner on Tuesday, right?" Piper asks, her cheeks pink and her hair out of the ponytail it's been in all day.

"You all go to family dinner?" I ask, surprised.

"Of course we do. It's the highlight of the week. Every Tuesday at six, and the only time we've missed in the last couple of years was for Hudson's mom's funeral. The boys all bring food, and it's fun to hang out with them outside the arena." Her eyes cut over to me. "Why haven't you come yet?"

"I don't know." I rub the back of my neck and shrug. "I didn't know if I'd fit in."

"You'd fit in. Even Liam comes. He sits in the corner and doesn't talk to anyone, but he's there," Piper assures me, and her attention turns to Maven. "You missed last week, Mae."

"Because this wedding is taking over my life and we had a cake tasting." Maven's engagement ring flashes in the dim lighting, and she spins the diamond on her finger. "We should've just eloped at the courthouse."

"You're engaged?" I ask. "I mean, obviously you're engaged. That ring is huge. Sorry. I should know this, but I—"

"You've been a little busy too, Emmy." Maven's smile is kind. "Do you watch football?"

"Here and there. More so when I was on the west coast."

"My fiancé, Dallas, is the kicker for the DC Titans."

"She was his nanny," Lexi whispers loudly, and she punctuates it with a tipsy giggle. "She used to work for the Titans, and fraternizing isn't allowed between players and other members of the team. Then she got a job with the Stars, and now she and Dallas are going to live happily ever after."

"Oh, Dallas is a dad? How old is his—your—daughter?"

"Almost seven now. Maverick is her uncle."

"Wait." I push my drink away and rest my elbows on the table. "Miller has a brother, and he's *also* a professional athlete? What are the odds?"

"Not blood related. He and Dallas are best friends, and when June came into his life unexpectedly, Maverick jumped in to help. They—and their other friend Reid—raised her together. The three of them are so precious with her." Maven laughs and grabs her phone. "A couple Halloweens ago, we dressed up like the characters from *Frozen* because June was obsessed. Maverick walked around town in a carrot costume for hours and didn't complain once. I think he's the only person on earth who can wear bright orange clothes and still get a woman's number."

"Oh." I rub my hand over my heart. A dull ache forms behind my ribs when she shows me a photo of their outfits.

Beaming faces. A little girl in Maverick's arms, and so much joy there. "That's—I had no idea."

"He'll drop everything to be Uncle Mav. I think of all his accolades, that's the one he's most proud of."

There's a beat of silence before Lexi breaks it with, "We're going to talk about how he's hot as hell too, right?"

Piper bursts out laughing. "So hot. I'm so glad I'm not the only female in the organization anymore. It's cruel to be around these men and not have anyone to talk to about them."

"All the sports team-adjacent men in this city are hot," Maven says. "What the hell is in the water?"

"Yeah. Like your godfather," Lexi adds. "A silver fox. Aging like fine wine."

"I'm missing some context," I say.

Piper scoots closer to me. "Maven's godfather, Shawn, is the head coach for the Titans. He's ridiculously attractive."

"Okay, can we stop talking about my family and instead figure out who's the hottest guy on the Stars?" Maven asks. "You can only pick one."

Lexi taps her cheek, deep in drunken thought. "This is tough. Ethan is hot, but he's not my type. He's loud and messy and owns three motorcycles. That's a disaster waiting to happen."

"What about Grant? That man is always trying to get your attention," Piper says, and Lexi rolls her eyes.

"He can try all he wants. I'd never go for him. He's ten years younger than me and barely knows how to be an adult."

"Riley is cute," Maven adds. "And he's one of the quiet ones."

"You know what they say about quiet ones," Piper giggles. "Hudson is attractive, but he's a relationship guy. After my divorce, I want to experiment and figure out what I like. Mess around with a few different people at the same time and just have *fun.* I've only ever been with my ex-husband, and everything was so vanilla between us. After reading some of the books on my shelf, I have these… I don't want to call them cravings, but there are so many things I want to try."

"Oh, honey." Maven reaches across the table and squeezes her hand. "There are so many better men out there."

"Hear, hear." Lexi lifts her drink. "What about Liam? You know what they say about goalies."

"What do they say about goalies?" I ask.

"Something about being flexible and passionate and neurotic. I feel like he'd be dedicated to the point of obsession. He'd lay you out naked and mark your body with a Sharpie so he knows where you like to be touched."

"Okay, but that sounds hot as hell." Maven giggles. "A road map to orgasms."

"No one's ever been obsessed with me," Piper says.

"It's worth the wait," Maven says. "Trust me."

"Who would you pick, Emmy? Hottest guy on the team?"

"I'd like to be exempt from this question. I've seen these dudes when they have bloody noses and smell like roadkill."

"Maverick, though." Lexi sighs. "You *have* to think Maverick is hot."

"The tattoos?" Piper asks.

"His height?" Maven adds.

"I've heard he's a *real* ladies' man in bed. Totally selfless. I ran into a woman in the elevator leaving our hotel at an away game last year, and she said he made her come five times in one night," Lexi says.

My face burns. I wish my glass wasn't empty, because I'm going to need something sinfully strong to get through this conversation.

"Is five times even humanly possible?" I ask. "That sounds like an exaggeration. Are you sure he didn't start that rumor himself?"

"When you're with the right guy, anything is possible,"

Maven says. "Five times. Six times. I'm not sure there's a limit."

"Miller is…" I hum and trace the rim of my glass with my fingers.

I'm stalling, because I don't know what the hell he is.

He *is* hot.

Gorgeous and strong and an incredible athlete. An absolute pest who won't go away, but I can't help but be curious who he is behind closed doors.

Large hands that could rest on my thighs and nudge them open. A firm chest to lean against as he slipped a long finger inside me and a boyish laugh when I shuddered against him. Gentle encouragement and praise.

"You gonna finish that sentence, Red, or just leave me hanging?" a deep voice asks.

I whip my head to the right.

There's Maverick Miller, holding three beers in one of his hands and grinning at me.

TWELVE
MAVERICK

I SPOTTED Hartwell the second the girls walked in.

That hair is hard to miss, and I think even in a crowd, I'd be able to pick her out. She's impossible to ignore and goddamn sexy in her tight jeans and that cropped tank top showing off her shoulders.

Our table is on the opposite side of the restaurant, but I've been watching her.

Studying her like I do my opponents; the way she swirls her drink around before she takes a sip. The laughter that's half a beat late, like she's not sure she's allowed to find the conversation funny. How her teeth sink into her bottom lip.

Fuck.

Those damn lips.

Plump. Painted pink. Kissable to the point of being a distraction.

And fuckable.

Now that I'm standing in front of her, I start to imagine what she would look like with my cock in her mouth.

I wonder what it would feel like if she left lipstick marks on my shaft while she sucked me down until I hit the back of her throat.

"What are you doing here?" Emerson snaps, and I'm yanked out of the fantasy of her on her knees. That fiery hair wrapped around my hand. Wicked green eyes blinking up at me with a drop of drool on her chin. "Please don't tell me you followed us."

"Ladies," I say to the group, ignoring her because I know it will piss her off. My gaze bounces to Maven. "You and your fiancé are on the same wavelength. He suggested Johnny's without knowing you were here."

"I love that man." Maven sighs, all happy in love and shit. She peers around me, no doubt looking for Dallas. "Who's watching June?"

"You don't see her at the bar? She's behind the counter slinging handles of vodka."

"Maverick Miller."

"Just kidding around, Mae. She's with a babysitter. Reid had a bad day, and he needed to get out of the apartment. I should call him over here. So many beautiful women, his mood would pick right up." Emerson scoffs, and I look down at her. "I'm still waiting to hear what you think of me."

"You really don't want to know what I think of you," she tosses back.

I love when she's sassy. All tough girl and independent woman who doesn't take shit. It's kind of fun to be put in my place.

"Yeah, I do." I lean my arm against the wall to my right, and I don't miss the way her eyes linger on my tattoos for the quickest of seconds. I wonder which one is her favorite. "I'm a big boy, Red."

"I've heard you're small. Average at best."

"You don't strike me as someone who listens to gossip. C'mon. Give it to me."

"I need a drink before I dive into a deep psychological deconstruction of the parts of you I dislike. Do you all want another round?" Emerson asks the rest of the women, and she gets three nods.

"Please," Maven says.

"And french fries!" Piper adds. Her eyes glaze over, and she's past tipsy and barreling toward drunk as a skunk. "So many french fries."

"With extra salt," Lexi chimes in, and she stirs her empty drink with her straw. "Buckets of salt."

"Got it." Emerson slides out of the booth and stands. Her heels make her taller than she is on her skates, and I whistle when she comes up only a few inches shorter than me. "What?"

"I told you I liked your heels the other day at the press conference. That's still true."

"Flattery isn't going to get you very far, Miller."

"What about a few feet forward to the bar so I can help you carry the drinks and food back here?"

Emerson blows out a heavy sigh. "Fine. But only because I know the sooner I give you what you want, the sooner you'll leave us alone."

"I'm easy to figure out, aren't I? Let's top you off before you destroy me."

The bar is tiny, and when we sidle our way up to the counter, there's no way around touching each other.

"Sorry," I say when my arm brushes against hers. I shuffle backward and stand behind her so she can have some space. "Not a lot of room in here."

"It's okay." She looks at me over her shoulder. "Thank you."

"For what?"

"Offering to help."

"I just wanted to steal a fry—I'm still starving after practice this morning. Are you having fun tonight?"

"Yeah." A small smile dances across her face. She tucks a piece of hair behind her ear, and I spot three piercings I never noticed before. I see sparkly, dangling earrings that make me think she likes to spoil herself and buy nice things. "Piper invited me, and I'm glad I came."

"Even with the interruption?" I ask.

Emerson bites her bottom lip again, and it really shouldn't turn me on as much as it does. "Even with present company."

"They're all really good people. I've known Piper the longest, and it's been cool to see her work her way up to the broadcasting team. I hope she's the lead sideline reporter one day."

"I'll be shocked if she isn't. Every time I get home, she asks two dozen questions about practice and my thoughts on how the game went."

I haven't spent any time with Emerson outside of the rink. She didn't show up to the team dinner last week and she doesn't hang around after practice long enough for us to shoot the shit with her. On the flights to our away games, she sits up front with the girls, away from the chaos the boys get into and leaving me no time to get a good read on her.

Her soft laugh and the way she doesn't run away tell me she might be enjoying this conversation, and that gives me the encouragement to keep talking.

"What's your drink of choice?" I blurt.

"Is that your question of the day?"

"Yeah. Then you can ask me yours. I know you've got one ready to go. I can practically see the wheels spinning in your head."

"If I'm at home, I prefer red wine." Emerson turns to the bar, trying to get the bartender's attention, but he doesn't see her. "If I'm out, I like to have a martini, but this bar doesn't strike me as somewhere that has good olives."

"Don't underestimate this place. I came here once after a loss, and I was craving something sweet. Johnny—who's a real person and the only cook in the building—handed me a plateful of giant chocolate chip cookies twenty minutes later—*freshly baked*. I'm still not sure where he got all the ingredients, and it's probably better for everyone if I never find out."

"That's the Maverick Miller effect."

"I haven't heard about the Maverick Miller effect. Please, enlighten me."

"Your charm. It makes people do things for you because of who you are."

"Nah." I run my free hand through my hair and shrug. "That's not who I am here. I'm just Maverick, the guy who can't throw a dart to save his life and puts quarters in the jukebox so it plays shitty songs on repeat. I eat frozen mozzarella sticks and pretend like I don't know why "Funkytown" is playing eight times in a row."

"It could be worse. You could play "Achy Breaky Heart" instead."

"Don't tempt me with a good time. You sure you don't want me to run out and get you some olives? I will. There's a grocery store that stays open until midnight a few blocks up the road."

"Are you always this accommodating?" Emerson asks.

"Not really. Must be a you thing. A captain/teammate dynamic. I take care of my people, remember?"

"And tracking down olives is part of that caretaking?"

"It is. Top of the list, I'm pretty sure."

"It's fine. Really." Her eyes drop to the beers I should've brought back to the table ten minutes ago. "You're a beer guy?"

"If I'm with my friends, yeah. If I'm at a club, I'll drink something stronger. Loud noises and all of that."

"Interesting."

"Was that your question?"

"No," she says. "I was throwing your question back to you. That's how this game works."

"I see." I rub my lips together to stop myself from smiling. "I didn't realize there are rules now."

"There are." Emerson spins around so she's facing me, and there's even less distance between us now. I can smell her perfume. See the freckles across her nose and a small, jagged white scar above her eyebrow. "Is your tattoo for June?"

She surprises me when she reaches over and taps the back of my left hand. The touch jolts me, and I feel like I've been short-circuited. Shocked awake and buzzing with energy.

I smile and put my hand over hers. I guide her fingers over the curve of the heart and the hook of the J, and I hear a quiet hitch in her breathing.

"Have you been looking into me, Hartwell? I'm flattered."

"Maven told me. I didn't ask. I thought it was for some woman you got drunk with and married in Vegas."

"I'm not the marrying type, and definitely not one to tattoo a woman's name on my body." I keep my hand over hers and trace the heart, slower this time. She hasn't pulled away yet, and I'm going to enjoy this for as long as I can. "Except for June Bug. Dallas didn't know she was coming into his life, and when he did, he panicked. Reid and I stepped in to help, because he would've done the same for us. I know she's not mine, but she *is* mine. I'm going to take care of her for as long as I can. Spoil the shit out of her. Love her and help teach her life lessons—the good and the bad. She can run away to my apartment when she's pissed at her parents, and I'm absolutely going to interrogate her first boyfriend until I'm sure he's a decent guy."

"You'll also dress up like a carrot and look like an idiot."

I throw my head back and laugh. "Maven showed you those photos?"

"You had a stem on your head." Emerson steals her hand back, and I miss her touch. "And orange shoes."

"Damn right I did. And I'd do it again."

Ralph, one of the bartenders, finally makes his way over to us and jots down Emerson's drink orders and the basket of fries. I pull out my wallet and ignore her argument when I drop three twenties on the counter.

"I can pay for this," she tells me, and I shrug.

"I know you can, but I wanted to."

"Thanks."

"My pleasure." I stare at her collarbone then the spot where her shirt dips toward her chest. "Do you have a tattoo?"

"You already used your question up."

"I did, but, per your rules, I'm obligated to get an answer to the question you asked me."

Her cheeks flush a dark red, and she licks her lips. "Yes," she says slowly. "I do have a tattoo."

"Where is it?"

"Someplace you'll never see."

"That makes me want to see it even more," I say, and I imagine where it could be hiding. On her ribs. At the jut of her hip or her lower back. "Is it—"

"Excuse me," a voice says, interrupting us. I turn, and a blonde woman smiles at me. "You're Maverick Miller, aren't you?"

"Depends. Did I do something wrong?"

"No." She flashes me a flirty smirk. "But I'm hoping you're in the mood to be a little bad. My friends are leaving, and it's too early for me to call it a night. Want to come back to my place?"

"Sorry," I tell the blonde with a grin. "I'm kind of in the middle of something with my baby's mother right now. The kid is half alien, half potato, and we're trying to figure out where they got these genes from."

"Ooookay," the woman says, and she wrinkles her eyebrows. "That's weird. I didn't know you had kids."

"Are we classifying tiny extraterrestrials as kids? I guess we should. It's inclusive and better than calling them skin dogs—since we all call dogs fur babies, you know?—or something like that." I point my thumb over my shoulder. "I better get back to it. Janet here thinks the UFO has her eyes, but I'm pretty sure he looks most like me."

"I'm so confused," the woman tells me. "You're not Maverick Miller, are you?"

"No way. That guy is way better at hockey than me. All I bring to the table are alien children."

"Don't forget the potato part," Emerson adds, and I almost lose it.

"Ew. I knew my friends were wrong. You're not nearly as hot as him." The blonde looks me up and down and scoffs before storming away.

"Wow. Talk about a blow to your ego," Emerson says.

I face her again and steal a french fry from the basket that just arrived. "I'll get over it."

"Does this happen a lot?"

"What, alien babies?"

"No. Women coming up to you and thinking they'll go back to your place."

"Everywhere I go."

"And you always say yes?"

"Most of the time. Why not? Everything is consensual. I use protection. They know I'm not going to get down on one knee and propose, and, honestly? It's nice to think about something other than hockey."

"Will your dick fall off if you don't sleep with someone tonight? How will you survive?"

"Your compassion knows no bounds, Hartwell. Thanks for your concern, but I'll be fine. I'm more worried about you. Birthing a life form that looks like a potato spud was probably really traumatizing."

"Almost as traumatizing as standing here and talking to you for the last ten minutes." She puts her hands on her hips and stares at me. "You're frustrating. That's what I think about you."

"Good frustrating or bad frustrating?"

"I haven't decided yet. You're cocky and flashy, then you go and do sentimental things like tattoo your niece's initial on the back of your hand. It's confusing."

"Have I been that flashy guy tonight?"

"No," she admits quietly. "You haven't."

"Did I go home with that girl?"

"No."

"Then that should give you an insight into who I really am." I grab half of the drinks and hold them close to my chest. "Get a water for Piper, too. That woman is drunk, and we have a game tomorrow night."

"Good call. My legs are killing me—I'm not going to be able to help her home."

"I'll call you all an Uber."

"We live four blocks away."

"Better than walking and hurting yourself. Let's get you back to your friends before they start to worry I kidnapped you."

"Or before any more of your alien babies find their way into the world. That's a terrifying thought. One of you is more than enough." Emerson glides by me. Her hip brushes against mine as she passes with arms full of alcohol and food. "And for the record, if you tried to kidnap me, you wouldn't get very far."

"I'm going to win you over one day, Hartwell," I call out. "Just you wait."

She might flip me off after she distributes the drinks to her table and ignore me the rest of the night, but I see the smile she's fighting to hide.

Point: me.

THIRTEEN
MAVERICK

ME

Rise and shine!

REDHEADED ASSASSIN

Are you texting me while someone is sleeping next to you?

ME

You saw me leave the bar alone.

REDHEADED ASSASSIN

I don't know what you got into when you went home.

ME

Just a bag of Oreos. I ate six.

Oh. By the way. Coach wanted me to tell you you're on first line tonight.

REDHEADED ASSASSIN

Don't fuck with me, Miller.

ME

I'm not forking with you.

Ducking

Jesus Christ, Siri. Fucking!!!

REDHEADED ASSASSIN

Are you serious?

ME

Isn't that the opposite of not fucking with you?

REDHEADED ASSASSIN

You're going on my shit list.

ME

Shit list? Sounds positively titillating.

Tell me more about your disdain for me.

REDHEADED ASSASSIN

Look at you using big words.

ME

You know what else is big?

REDHEADED ASSASSIN

This was fun while it lasted. Blocking you now.

ME

I was going to say the round of applause you're going to get tonight!!!!!!

Hartwell?

Red?

Damp it.

"THERE'S nothing like playing for a sold-out crowd, is there?" I ask Hudson as we stand in the tunnel and wait to take the ice. "It's amazing what winning a couple games will do."

"Brings out the whole city." He fastens his helmet and moves his hips in a circle, ignoring my snicker at his stretches. "When's the last time we filled the upper bowl?"

"It's been ages, hasn't it? Definitely didn't happen last season."

"I think it was when they gave out those shirtless calendars of the team to all the fans in attendance. Remember the line to sign your photo after the game? You were here until midnight." Hudson bursts out laughing at the memory. "The woes of being attractive."

"Says the man who has two million Instagram followers who go crazy when you post a shirtless photo of you and your dogs." I flex my fingers under my glove, wincing. "My hand hurt so bad that night, but half the ticket sales that night went to charity. It was worth it. Maybe we should do that again."

"Smile, boys," Maven says, interrupting us to snap a picture. I sling an arm over Hudson's shoulder, and we both grin. "We should do the calendar idea again."

"Is your man joining tonight?" I ask her.

"Yeah, up in the boxes," she answers. "June too."

"Oh, shit. My favorite girl is here? How did you convince him to let that happen?"

"It wasn't me. June batted her eyes and Dallas had no choice but to say yes."

"What a deviant. She could ask for eighteen ponies and I'd give them to her," I say.

"Are you going to come say hi after the game? She'll want to see you."

"I'd love to, but I have a commitment. How about ice

cream when we all get back to the apartment later? I'll bring it by."

"We'd love that. You're such a good neighbor." Maven pinches my cheek and hustles down the hallway toward the rink, her large camera tucked safely against her chest. "Have a good game, boys!"

Hudson pouts. "I want ice cream."

"Get your own," I say, and I flick his ear. "And get your head in the game. It's almost go time."

"You feeling good this afternoon, Cap?"

"I'm feeling fantastic."

Adrenaline courses through my veins like it does before every game, but today is different.

I'm riding the high of a few stellar performances over our last couple of games. The pieces are sliding into place, and we're getting close to the point where magic happens on the ice.

I fucking love it.

It's exciting to love playing again. To look forward to every game and know that my teammates are going to give every ounce of their effort because they want to win just as badly as I do. I've never gotten to experience that pinnacle in the NHL before, and the last two weeks are the closest I've ever been.

"They're going to be chanting your name soon, Mavvy," Hudson jokes, grabbing his stick off the wall. "Where's Emmy?"

"No clue. I haven't seen her since morning skate. Maybe she's doing an interview with Piper."

"Speaking of Piper, she looked queasy when she shoved me into the press room an hour ago. Is she okay?"

"Probably hungover. She was at Johnny's last night with Maven, Lexi and Hartwell. When I left, Piper was on drink number four."

"Wait a minute." He frowns. "You hung out with Emmy outside of practice and lived to tell the tale? I'm impressed."

"We didn't hang out." I take a sip of my sports drink and swish it around my mouth. "We were at the same place at the same time. Alien babies were involved. I turned down an invitation for sex, and the best part? I didn't get a beer thrown in my face."

Hudson blinks at me. "That sounds a lot like hanging out to me."

"It wasn't. More like the universe having a laugh."

"And you turned down a night with a woman? You never do that."

"Alien babies, Hud. Aren't you listening? There were more important things happening."

"You didn't miss anything, Hudson," Emerson says, appearing at my side in her jersey. "But it would've been more fun if you were there."

"Ouch." I put my hand over my heart. "I thought you enjoyed our chat, Red."

"We have very different definitions of enjoyment, pretty boy." She fixes her hair and tosses it over her shoulder, two white ribbons fluttering behind her. "Why aren't you all warming up?"

"Because it's your first start." Hudson drapes an arm around her, and I see the way she smiles up at him. She doesn't look at me like that. "And, per Stars tradition, it deserves a minute of celebration."

"I had three pieces of marble loaf cake when I got home last night to celebrate two weeks on the team," she says, and his eyes go wide. "We really don't need to do a first start ritual or anything."

"Where the hell did you get marble loaf cake?" he practically whines.

"He has an unhealthy obsession with food. Dessert especially," I explain to her. "Come to the team dinner on Tuesday and see for yourself."

"Team dinner means more time with you, Miller, and I'm

at my capacity as of late. Piper made the loaf," Emerson tells Hudson. "I'll sneak you a piece at practice tomorrow. I'm a dessert fiend too. If you ever want to do a food crawl around the city so I can find all the places with the best slices of cake, I'm down."

"My kind of woman." He shakes her shoulders, and a real laugh falls out of her. "Are you ready for tonight?"

"I guess. I'm still kind of in shock that this is my life. I'm waiting to wake up from a dream and have it all taken away," she says.

"You're going to be stuck with us for a while," I say, desperate to be a part of their conversation. I don't like that he's making her laugh and I don't like how close they're standing. "We have months to go."

Emerson's eyes meet mine. "There are worse people to be stuck with, I guess."

I touch my gloved fingers to my temples, concentrating. "Probably the highest compliment I'll ever get from you. I need to commit it to memory."

"Is he always this weird?" she asks.

"Always," Hudson says.

The grin I give her earns me an eye roll, but I don't care. At least she's looking at me. I lift my chin toward the rink and the flashing lights. The thumping music and the screaming fans. "You deserve to go out first."

"Liam always goes first," she says.

"Not tonight."

"Are you sure?"

"Positive." I give her a gentle nudge. "Go on, Hartwell."

Emerson takes a deep breath. Collects herself before she nods and shimmies out of Hudson's grasp. She walks across the mats, and without another look back, she disappears onto the ice.

"I want to say I can't believe she's doing it, but I actually can," Hudson tells me, and we watch her wave to the crowd. He bumps his shoulder against mine. "I'm proud of you."

"For what?"

"Not holding a grudge just because she made you look stupid. Being mature and welcoming. Keeping your dick in your pants."

I laugh and elbow him in the ribs even though he can barely feel it through his pads. "I do have some self-control, motherfucker."

We follow behind Emerson, and I barely make it out of the tunnel before I dig my blades into the ice and brake hard into the boards.

"What's wrong, Cap?" Connor asks, skating past me.

"You good, Mav?" Grant knocks his knuckles against my helmet, and I stare at the crowd.

"Holy shit," I whisper.

Half the arena is women, which isn't anything new. What's different are the signs and jerseys they're holding. None of them are for me or the boys.

They're all for Emerson.

"Wicked, isn't it?" Ethan grins. "I've never seen anything like this."

I look for Emerson and find her talking to Coach near the bench. She's nodding along while he draws a play on his whiteboard, totally chill and totally un-fucking-fazed.

I guess she senses me watching her, because she glances up. Our gazes meet again, and I stare at her.

It hits me then.

Right near center ice and in front of twenty thousand people.

A thought I've been having more and more lately these last few weeks, but becomes solidified right now: this woman is fucking incredible.

Special.

Changing the future of the sport and inspiring girls and women everywhere, all while wearing ribbons and mascara.

Simon Buttecker is going to be *pissed*, and that makes me giddy.

"Circle up," I bark out, and my teammates huddle around me. "Every win is important, but we have to leave everything out there tonight. The media crucifies us on good days, and they're going to go after Hartwell's first start hard. Let's not give them any ammunition. Lock it up. Focus. We've gotta play strong for all sixty minutes."

"Hell yeah, Cap. I love when you get fired up," Riley says, and he looks over his shoulder. "Emmy! Get over here."

She joins the group, slotting between Connor and Seymour. If she's nervous, she doesn't let on.

"What's going on?"

"We wanted to tell you we have your back," Grant says smugly, like this pep talk was his idea. "I'm bummed you're not going to be on my line, but I guess Mavvy is an upgrade."

"Debatable," she mumbles.

"Hands in," I say, and everyone stacks their hands on top of each other. "Together on three. Count us off, Hartwell."

"One, two, three," she says.

"Together," we all yell at the top of our lungs, and I know we're going to be on fire tonight.

"The fuck is your problem?" I scream as I skate past the ref who's been giving me shit since the puck dropped.

I got hit with a cross-checking penalty earlier, and now I'm being sent to the sin bin for slashing like I'm some high schooler.

We're getting obliterated in front of the home crowd, and all that momentum we had before the game has left the building.

The refs won't give us a break. We can't find a rhythm. Our transitions are sloppy, and we're a half second late on every breakaway.

It's excruciating to watch.

There's a whistle signaling another penalty. It's followed by a chorus of boos, and I crane my neck to see who's the lucky one to join me.

"Assholes," Hartwell curses, throwing her stick next to mine as she collapses on the bench beside me.

"Pleasure seeing you here, Red," I say, and she snorts. "What are you doing time for?"

"Closing my hand on the puck, which is bullshit because I dropped it the second I had possession. I know the rules." She stretches out her legs and groans. "Why have a replay system in place if you're not going to use it?"

"I like when you get feisty." I hand her a bottle of Gatorade, and she takes it. "I'd ask how you're enjoying your first start, but I think I know the answer to that."

Emerson rubs her jaw. Her right cheek has a nick on it, a small cut from a stick to the face. "All these people are here to see me, and I'm playing like I've never been on the ice before. It's embarrassing."

"We all have bad days," I reassure her. "The good news is we still have the third period ahead of us. You know how quickly things change."

She takes a sip of the orange drink, and I watch the bob of her throat when she swallows. A drop hangs to the corner of her mouth, and her tongue sneaks out to lick it away.

That's distracting.

"It's a lot harder to shift that momentum when nothing is going our way. Jesus. What is all that banging?" Emerson asks. She looks behind the penalty box and snorts. "The girls are trying to get your attention, Miller."

I follow her line of sight and see a group of five women wearing my jersey right against the glass. They've cut the fabric to show off their stomachs and cleavage, and I give them an awkward wave.

"Do you ever wonder what it would be like if we went to someone's office and held up signs that say 'can I hold your stick? or 'put a baby in me, Miller' while they were working?" I ask Emerson. "Probably a lawsuit waiting to happen."

"Kind of like the alien babies," she says under her breath, and I grin.

"Hey." I tap her skate. "Sounds like someone had a good time last night."

"With my new friends, yes."

"But you enjoyed yourself while I was in the area, so we're getting somewhere."

"The bar is low, Miller." She sets the bottle down on the ledge of the box. "You're back in thirty seconds."

"Thanks for keeping an eye out for me, Red. I'm going to pretend it's because you care, not because you're trying to get rid of me." I scoop my stick off the ground and check to make sure my helmet is tight. "Chin up, buttercup. We've got time to turn this shit show around."

"If you ever call me buttercup again, I will end you," she says, her arms folded across her chest and an evil gleam to her eye.

"Atta girl," I say when I jump back on the ice, grinning when her cheeks turn as red as her hair.

FOURTEEN
EMMY

I'VE GIVEN everything to hockey.

I've missed out on birthdays and family events because of practice and games. I've sacrificed blood and sweat and tears. Pushed my body to the brink of exhaustion time and time again, only to come up short on the biggest night of my life.

I've never been this angry or disappointed in myself.

I stare at my reflection in the mirror and sigh. My legs throb and my feet burn. New blisters sprouted up on my toes between the first and second periods, but I taped them and pushed through the pain.

As the adrenaline wears off and the reality of the last couple of hours settles in, everything hurts.

My calves.

My forearms.

My heart.

I re-lace my skates and stand, shuffling to the door of my locker room with a new wave of determination. I crack it open and peer out to the hallway, and I'm not surprised to find it empty.

The game ended ninety minutes ago. The arena lights are

off. The music has long quieted down. There are no more boos or cheers.

It's totally silent.

I step toward the rink, unable to stay away.

Whenever I lost a game as a kid, my dad and I would trudge out to the pond in our backyard. The bitter Michigan air nipped at our noses and our fingers turned red with cold, but we didn't care. We'd replay the game in slow motion and break down where things went wrong or right. Debate if I should've made the extra pass or taken the wide-open shot.

It was cathartic to work out my frustrations. To send them out in the world instead of holding them inside.

By the end of the night, once the moon was high in the sky and the stars began twinkling, everything was better. A weight lifted, so I could let the past go and start fresh for the next game.

My dad might not be here to decompress with me tonight, but I know what I need to do. The only thing that is sure to clear my mind and get me back on track before our road game later this week.

It's an important matchup against our division rival in Milwaukee, and I can't allow myself to fuck up again.

I don't bother with gear and pads, skating around the rink in a pair of leggings and a long-sleeved Stars shirt. I shiver at the temperature, but I welcome it.

Some people like to talk about the feelings they're keeping inside.

I prefer skating.

I always have.

There's a puck at center ice, and it feels like it's waiting for me. A consolation prize to make up for some of the worst playing in my career.

I tap it with my stick, a hit that crosses the blue line, and I take off after it with a grunt.

Pretending like I have two defenders in front of me, I fake

left then right, just like I did in the second period. I pull back and slap the puck as hard as I can, my aim on the net ten feet in front of me.

I miss.

The puck ricochets off the post with a loud *plink*, and I narrow my eyes.

"Dammit."

I go through the play six more times, relaxing as the tension leaves my body with every goal.

Satisfied, I move to my next big mistake of the game: a missed pass from Hudson that resulted in a turnover and a scored point by our opponents.

I know exactly where I went wrong—I was too slow. A half beat late, and I need to practice my speed.

I lean my stick against the boards by the bench and skate toward the opposite goal as quickly as I can. My hamstrings and quads scream as I reach the goal line, and I take a deep breath.

"Again," I tell myself, knowing the only way I'll be able to hang with the men in this league is to match their speed and intensity.

I don't know how long I stay out there.

It could be minutes or hours.

I go back and forth, from one end of the ice to the other, only stopping when my lungs burn like they're on fire.

"What the fuck are you doing?"

The deep, rumbly voice echoes across the rink, and I know exactly who it is.

I'm still caught off guard when I turn around and find Maverick watching me. The ends of his messy hair are wet and he's wearing a matching long-sleeved Stars shirt with gray joggers that hug his thighs. There's an angry look on his face I've never seen before, and I falter.

Shit.

I thought he'd be the first one out of the garage after our

loss. Speeding away from the scene of an athletic massacre in whatever fancy car he drives—I bet he rotates them depending on the day.

But he's here.

Watching me with a dark glint to his eyes and wrinkled brows. Storming his way around the rink until he's in the player's box and glaring at me.

I swallow.

In the couple weeks I've been around him, he's always been the joker. The team's funny guy, giving out goofy smiles and one-liners like they're party favors.

He looks *pissed* right now, and if he wanted my attention, he has it.

"Don't worry about it," I say.

"I'm going to ask this again: what the fuck are you doing?"

His voice is rougher this time. Some low timbre I've never heard from him before, and it makes me shiver. Makes my nipples pebble under my sports bra, and I've never hated him more.

"Don't worry about it," I repeat. I try to grab my stick, but his large hand folds over the top of it, preventing me from moving anywhere. "I get it, Miller. You're stronger than me. Congratulations."

"The game ended two hours ago," he says, brushing off the compliment he'd usually make a big deal about.

I give up on the stick and drop onto the wooden bench. It wouldn't hurt to take a break. "And?"

"And you should be home by now."

"So should you," I challenge, and he turns quiet. Loses a little of his gusto. "Please don't tell me you were fucking someone in the locker room."

"No." Maverick sits close to me, taking up too much space with his long legs and broad shoulders. He drops his elbows to his knees and stares out at the ice, a far-off look in his eyes. "I was giving a Make-A-Wish family a tour of the arena."

I stop breathing. "What?"

"Yeah. I saw you when I was showing them the VIP suites and promised Rachel—that's her name—I'd get one of your jerseys signed for her."

"I am such an asshole," I whisper.

"Why are you out here?" His gaze cuts into me. "And without a fucking helmet? Come on, Hartwell. You know the rules."

He told me something. I can tell him something back. Information for information, a fair trade. "I played like shit today."

"We all played like shit today. Liam gave up three goals, which is more than he's given up in the last few games combined," he says.

"I especially played like shit. And on my first night starting? The media is going to have a field day."

"Welcome to the NHL. Everything you do is scrutinized, and even on your best nights, people find a way to shit on you. After my first hat trick, all they could talk about on ESPN was how I was selfish and should've gotten my teammates more involved."

Quiet hangs between us.

This isn't our usual back-and-forth, and knowing that Maverick is peeling back a layer of my story makes me uneasy.

I want to run—I normally run.

But I can't move.

"It's something my dad and I used to do," I tell him. "It helps me move on from a bad game."

"What helps you move on? Running yourself ragged? We have a road trip in two days. We just got off a stretch of three games in four days, and there have been full practices on either end of that. When the hell are you getting your rest?"

"I don't like to sit still. It's better this way. I can come back stronger."

"Christ, Red." Maverick laughs, but it's not humorous. "The only way you're going to get better is if you take care of yourself. That includes not skating around like a bat out of hell after a grueling game."

"I appreciate your opinion, but this is something I have to do. I've taken care of myself for years just fine."

Maverick hums, like he wants to say something else.

He pops onto his feet instead, and I think that might be the end of it.

"Then I'll join you," he tells me.

"What?" I stand too, staring at him. "That's not necessary."

"Yes, it is. It's part of my captain duties—no one gets left behind."

Maverick disappears toward the locker room, and I sigh. There's no use trying to fight him—he won't stop until he gets what he wants.

He's only gone five minutes, but when he returns, he looks just as mad as when he left.

"Why the hell is your locker room a supply closet?" he asks, and he hands me my helmet.

"It's a temporary fix until the building development team comes up with a more permanent solution."

"Well, that's bullshit." He buckles his helmet and moves onto the ice. "You deserve a space just like us. Where's your shower? And massage table?"

"I shower at home, and I don't have a massage table."

"That's going to have to change real quick." He motions me forward. "Come on, Red. I'm not getting any younger."

"What are we doing?"

"I don't know. Whatever it is you've been out here doing by yourself for god knows how long."

I give in and join him. "Can you play defense? I want to practice a breakaway."

"Sure. Whatever you need."

I don't know why his agreement makes my heart skip a beat. Why it puts a heavy pressure on my chest, but it does, and I shove the feeling away.

We spend the next forty-five minutes going through different parts of the game. Quick bursts of speed. Slower glides as I work on maneuvering the puck around him. Physical moments that end up with him pinned against the boards and his laugh warm on my neck.

"I'm going to take a second." I lean on my stick, panting hard. "A timeout."

"Take as many seconds as you need." Maverick unbuckles his helmet and sprawls out on the ice, flat on his back. "You're making me feel ridiculously out of shape."

"Whose fault is that, pretty boy?"

"I'm going to blame you, Red. I had plans to eat ice cream with my niece and bitch about the game from the couch, but this is fun too. I love when my ass is frozen and sore." He puts his hands on his stomach and sighs. "If I die here, tell June I love her."

"How was your tour with Rachel?" I find myself asking, and before I know what's happening, I'm dropping onto the ice next to him. "I didn't know you do things like that."

"I don't advertise it, because I hate when people have the resources to help and they only do good things when there's a camera in their face." His eyes flutter closed and he exhales. "But I love it."

"Will you tell me about her?"

His smile is soft, and that weight on my chest is back. "She was born and raised in DC and grew up as a Stars fan."

"Talk about some recent disappointment."

"Seriously. She got sick a couple years ago, and her health has started to deteriorate the last few months. Hockey is the thing that makes her happy, though, and her family still gets out to the games. They have season tickets in the upper bowl, but her wish was to sit right behind the bench and get a tour. I upgraded them for the rest of the season, and she really liked seeing the arena without anyone in it."

My eyes sting. A lump settles in my throat, and it won't go away. "That's really generous of you."

"What good is being rich if you don't spend the money on people who deserve it? It's also really fucking humbling. Of all the things she could've done, she picked hanging out with me. She has all these dreams and aspirations. She wants to work for NASA and also find a cure for cancer." His voice cracks, and I feel it too. "I'm just a fucking hockey player."

"You're more than a hockey player," I say, and he opens his eyes to look at me. I think he can see straight into my soul. "You're her hero, and there's not an honor higher than that. Just think: one day she's going to be at NASA or some prestigious research hospital, in a room with really smart people, and she'll tell them all about how she got to spend time with you. That sounds like my idea of hell, but I'm glad she likes it."

Maverick's smile shows off his dimple. "She likes me a lot, but she loves you. Gave me your entire stat line from college and the ECHL. I know you think you played like shit, but guess what? She still wants your autograph. She's still going to be here next week cheering for you and wearing your jersey."

"I have this tremendous opportunity, and I don't want people to think I'm disappointing them," I say. The words won't stop, and for once, I let them out. "I don't want to let anyone down."

"You're a woman in the NHL, Hartwell. You're breaking fucking barriers. There's not a damn person out there who thinks you're a disappointment."

My skin prickles like it always does when someone tells me nice things. "It's tough to remember that sometimes. I'm hard on myself."

"No shit," Maverick draws out, and I snort. "Was that a laugh, Red?"

"No. It was a chortle."

"The fuck is a chortle? Is that a Pokémon?"

"I don't know. Not a laugh, though. And definitely not at something you said."

"Admit it. You think I'm funny."

"You're mediocre at best."

"Better than being the worst." His grin is smug. "You want to grab some food?"

"I'm fine," I say, but my stomach picks that moment to decide to make an embarrassing loud noise I try to cover with a cough.

"You're such a bad liar."

"Why do you want to grab food?"

"Because you're hungry and tired and you've made your fucking point. Do you like sandwiches?"

"I love sandwiches."

"Good. You've had enough ice time today, and I'm cutting you off."

"And if I don't agree?"

"I'll throw you over my shoulder and carry you out of here," he tells me without hesitation.

"I don't think you could lift me."

"Is that a challenge, Red?"

Warmth pools in my stomach and between my legs.

It feels wrong to imagine his arm around my thighs. His hand near my ass and my chest pressing against his back.

But *fuck*, I like the thought of him showing off. Being the big, strong man and not leaving me a choice.

I like it more than I should.

"I'll walk out on my own," I say, and I tuck my chin to hide the blush creeping up my cheeks.

"Good." Maverick pops onto his feet and offers me a hand. "Shower first, then we can go."

"I'm not supposed to be in there, remember?"

"It's just me here, and I'm not sitting next to you when you smell like *that.*"

I let him pull me up. "I'll be quick."

"Take as long as you want. Do you have a car?"

"No. I do Ubers or the Metro."

"I'll drive us. It's not that far."

I dust ice shavings off my leggings. "Why are you being so nice to me?"

"Because I'm a nice guy, and I can see how today is getting to you. I don't want you to sink into some funk just because of one loss. I'm also really fucking hungry, so the faster we get there, the better."

"Fine." I give him a small smile, and he answers with a beam of his own. "Show me where these showers are."

FIFTEEN
EMMY

THIRTY MINUTES LATER, I'm sitting across from Maverick in a red-checkered booth in a diner that's so small, I could probably touch both sides of the wall if I stuck out my arms.

I look at the paper menu on the table that tells me the restaurant has been around since the 1930s, and my stomach rumbles again.

"Do you come here a lot?" I ask.

"Once a week since I got drafted by the Stars." Maverick scoots half an inch to the left to avoid hitting his head on the low hanging light overhead. "It's kind of like Johnny's. I can throw on a hat and a hoodie, and no one will know who I am. If they figure it out, they don't care. They're just here to eat good food."

He did throw on a hat on the quick drive from the arena then had the fucking audacity to turn it backwards on his head when he parked his Mercedes in the gravel lot out front.

I've always considered myself a feminist, but there's something so goddamn sexy about a man in a backwards hat that has me ready to drop to my knees for the patriarchy.

I clear my throat. "What do you normally order?"

"It's cruel to pick a favorite. The grilled cheese is delicious.

You can't go wrong with the club or meatball sub either. And, if you're really feeling wild, the burger with a pretzel bun is better than any orgasm I've ever had."

The comment makes my heart race. I stare at the list of side items, trying to distract myself from thinking about Maverick Miller and his orgasms.

Potato salad.

French fries.

Coleslaw.

Right there, Red.

Atta girl.

"A grilled cheese sounds great," I almost shout.

"That's what I usually get. The pickles on the side really bring it all together." He glances to his left and smiles at the woman with graying hair and an apron around her waist approaching our table. "Hi, Mama Darla."

"There's my sweet boy." She wraps her arms around his shoulders and kisses the top of his head. "How did the game go?"

"Not great, but there will be plenty more." His eyes bounce over to me. "Mama D, this is Emerson Hartwell. She's our new left winger, and a first timer at The Nook. Thought she might need some comfort food to cheer her up after today."

Darla's mouth drops open. "Oh, heavens. Some of the boys come in here after games or on their days off, and I was hoping I'd get to meet you. My granddaughter is a big fan."

"That's very kind. Thank you."

"Would you—is it okay if— " Darla fumbles with the order pad in her pocket and hands it to me. "Could you sign something for her?"

"I'd love to. What's her name?"

"Lydia. She has red hair just like you."

"Another fire girl." I write out a quick note to her, adding a heart and my signature. "There you go."

"Thank you, darlin'. This means a lot. Now. What can I get y'all to eat?"

When she leaves, Maverick gives me a sly look.

"See?" he says.

"See what?"

"Mama D doesn't care you had a bad game and neither does Lydia. You just made her day."

"You might be right."

"I'm sorry. Can you say that again? I didn't quite hear you."

"You might be right," I repeat, louder this time.

"Hartwell thinks I'm right," Maverick announces to the mostly empty diner. "I'm on top of the world!"

I slide down the booth and hide my face. "I'm never spending time with you again."

"Not a single person looked up from their newspapers." His knee knocks against mine under the table and I pull my leg away. "You could act like the biggest idiot in the world and no one would know."

"You would know," I say, and his grin is sharp.

"We could keep it our little secret—kind of like you and this sweet side of yours. You show everyone your tough exterior, but I'm starting to see what's underneath."

"What are you talking about?"

"Signing an autograph. Calling Lydia a fire girl—which she is. She's eight and an absolute hellion. Asking about my arena tour with Rachel. You're nice, Hartwell, and I'm not sure what to do with that information."

I ball up a napkin and throw it in his face. "Fuck you."

"There she is. That's more like it." Maverick puts his hands behind his head and gets comfortable. "Do you want to ask your question of the day first, or should I kick us off? We're not in a team setting, so our normal rules apply."

"You can go first," I tell him.

"What did you want to be when you were growing up?"

"Of all the things you could ask, you go with one about my childhood?"

"Patience, Red. I've got 495 questions left. I'll get to all of them eventually. I'm not in a rush."

"That's assuming you'll still see me 495 days from now. I could get traded. Or sent back to the AHL or ECHL."

"You could also get hit by an anvil falling from the sky when you walk out of your apartment tomorrow morning, but consider me optimistic." Maverick stares at me, his eyes locked on mine. "I'd find a way to track you down."

Awareness blooms in me with his attention. With the proximity of his body to mine and the careful way he's watching me like he can't wait to hear what I have to say.

It's a line, I tell myself.

A ruse he uses on all the women that come in and out of his life.

I'm not special.

But maybe you'd like to be.

I lean back, needing some distance from him.

He's distracting when he's this close. I keep wanting to look at the fading bruise on his cheek. Examine the tattoos on his arm and ask what they all mean. Learn which one is his favorite and trace it with my fingers.

I sit on my hands.

"I wanted to be a vet," I say. "My dad's distant family has a ranch in Colorado, and one year when I was younger, we went out to visit in the summertime. I saw all the horses and cows and the six dogs that lived with them, and I wanted to find a way to work with animals. A vet seemed like a logical choice. That winter, I picked up a hockey stick for the first time, and I never looked back. The veterinary dream went on the back burner to make room for being a professional athlete, and here we are."

"A ranch in Colorado? I've only ever been in cities and can't imagine that much open space. It sounds like heaven."

"It is. We moved around a lot when I was a kid. My mom kept finding jobs in different places, and my dad worked for the postal service, so he could have a career anywhere. I remember pulling up to Rolling Green Ranch and thinking, *This is a place I'd never leave.* I'd lay down some roots and stay there forever—and I've never thought that way about anywhere else."

"What makes it so special?"

"It's one of those places that's so stunning, it's hard to describe. Do you know what I mean? There are mountains and trees everywhere. Sunsets made of colors I haven't seen anywhere else. But saying that seems silly, because it doesn't do it justice. Even a picture doesn't fully capture its beauty."

Maverick nods, and his eyes haven't left mine since I started talking. "I've never had a place like that before," he says thickly. "But lately, I think I might be experiencing it for the first time."

My heart beats wildly in my chest, and I take a deep breath. "That's good," I say.

"Maybe I need to buy a ranch out in the middle of nowhere and go off the grid."

"Women are loving cowboys in romance novels lately. They probably love them in real life too." I take a sip of my water. My skin is warm and my vision is blurry from sharing so much personal information with him. "Not that you need help in attracting women, according to the TMZ article I read last night."

"Thinking about me when you're in bed?"

"Dart practice, remember?"

"Wow. You printed off an article about me? Do you want me to sign it for you? Make it out to Maverick's Biggest Fan?"

I flip him off. "I read it on my phone, you asshat. You know what I meant."

"Asshat, huh? You need to stop flirting with me, Red. I'm not that kind of guy." His smile makes me want to throw another napkin in his face, but it also makes my stomach swoop low. "You read romance books?"

"Yeah. They're a nice escape from reality. You're going to make fun of me, aren't you?"

"I'd never make fun of you for liking something. I'd give you shit in different ways."

I frown, unsure of where to go from here. I'm so used to having to defend my reading choices, and his easy acceptance throws me off. "Oh."

"Have people made fun of you for that in the past?"

"It doesn't matter."

"It does if it's important to you."

"Yes," I say, and I tap the edge of the table. "People have made fun of me."

"Well, they suck. If I ever meet them, I'm going to give them an earful."

I snort. "Thanks."

"There's another one of your chortles."

"At least you didn't call it a laugh this time." I wrap my hand around my glass of water and take a long sip. "Your turn to answer the question. What did you want to do when you were growing up? Hockey, right? You probably came out of the womb holding a stick."

"I didn't start playing hockey until I was nine. I grew up in Las Vegas, and ice rinks weren't that popular when I was a kid. Now they have an NHL team and a huge following. That wasn't the case when I lived there."

"Vegas? Really? I took you for a Northeast boy."

He narrows his eyes. "That's an insult, Hartwell. I don't drop my r's like Ethan does. I wanted to be a dolphin trainer. I watched *Flipper*, like, twenty times in a row, and I was obsessed. When he saved Elijah Wood from the shark? Man. That was an elite cinematic experience."

"Did you learn echolocation? I'd pay big money to see a

video of hot shot Maverick Miller trying to talk like a dolphin."

"Nah. There aren't any videos. That would require—"

Darla cuts him off, returning to our table with our dinner.

"I have two grilled cheeses with a pickle on the side." She sets the plates down and drops a stack of napkins between us. "I loaded up on the fries for y'all too. You must have burned a lot of calories today."

"Thanks, Mama D." Maverick smiles at her. "Is it Ray back there cooking tonight?"

"It is. He made sure to put a double layer of cheese on your sandwich for you." Darla pats his head, and I swear he melts under her touch. "Ketchup is over there, and you let me know if you need anything else."

"This looks delicious." I take a bite and moan. "My god."

He eats half the sandwich in one go. Cheese hangs from the corner of his mouth, but he ignores it, powering on through another bite. "Nirvana, right?"

"I see why you come here once a week. I'm going to have to try everything." I wipe my mouth with my napkin and sigh. "I almost forgot I'm supposed to ask you a question."

"Oh." He perks up, and now there's a glob of ketchup on his chin. "Hit me, Red."

"Which of your tattoos is your favorite?"

"The J, obviously, for June. But besides that, I like the hockey stick. It's a cliché, I know, but it was my first one."

"How old were you when you got it?"

"Eighteen. Spring break, my freshman year of college. I was with some friends down in Florida, and I thought, why not? I realized tattoos are a way of telling a story, so I started to get more and more. I'll need to start filling up my right arm soon."

"Which is your least favorite?"

"I should probably say the one on my ass, but I actually like that one."

"You have a tattoo on your ass?"

"Yup." His mouth curls into a smirk. "Want to see it?"

"No, thank you." I break off half the pickle and eat it. "What the hell do you have tattooed on your ass?"

"It's a secret."

"You've slept with half the women in this city. How is the mermaid on your butt not in some online forum?"

Maverick laughs and hits his chest. "A *mermaid*? Shit, that would've been brilliant. It's not a sea creature, but good guess. I might do that on the other cheek."

"I really don't believe you."

"Maybe one day you'll see for yourself."

"Never going to happen, Miller."

"Keep telling yourself that, Red. What about your tattoo? Is it just the one?"

"I have two," I admit. "And I love them equally. I got them at important times in my life, and I don't have any regrets."

He drags his gaze from my face to my arms to my ribs. It's like he's undressing me with his eyes and searching for what might be under my clothes, and it makes me warm all over.

I wonder if he would like what he found.

"Tattooed women are sexy," he says lowly, and even though it's a generalization, it's like he's saying it just to me. No one's called me sexy before, and I scoop up the compliment. "I'm glad you did something that empowered you."

"Yeah." I grab my water and take a long sip. "So am I."

We sink into silence as we enjoy our food, and the longer I spend in the diner, the better I feel.

I might not like him, but I can't deny Maverick has a calming presence. The ability to help me settle in a way I haven't settled in days. For the first time since I joined the Stars and dove headfirst into the chaos, I take a breath.

Darla comes back and leaves a check on the table. "It was good to see you, Maverick." Her attention turns to me. "And it was so nice to meet you, Emerson. I hope you'll come back."

"Emmy," I tell her. "You can call me Emmy. And I promise this isn't the last time you'll see me."

"Good." She touches my shoulder, and a smile sneaks out of me. "Take your time with the bill."

"I'll pay," I say when she leaves, but Maverick bats my hand away.

"You won't. I invited you here." He lays down multiple one-hundred-dollar bills, and I gape at him. "What?"

"That's a lot of money."

"Darla is the guardian to her granddaughter, and she works two jobs to make ends meet. I leave an extra tip whenever I stop by—I won't notice the difference, but she does."

I swear to god my heart skips a beat.

Maverick has surprised me twice today.

He's still that aloof guy who poses for magazines without his shirt on and gets womens' numbers whenever he's out. There's probably a Rolodex in his bedroom of Sandras and Sarahs.

But he's kind too. Soft around the edges with a big heart and enough space for everyone he meets.

I don't know much about him, but I can tell he likes to take care of the people who are important to him. He likes to go the extra mile for those who might normally get left behind.

I wonder what it would be like to see the good everywhere you go. To love and be loved without any hesitation.

I'm not sure I could do it.

"Thank you for tonight. For practicing after the game and bringing me here. It's nice to know I'm not alone," I say.

"Alone?" Maverick frowns and leans closer. "You're never alone, Hartwell. Not anymore. Not when you're part of our team."

This is getting too deep. Too raw and full of emotions I'm not sure I know how to express.

I slide out of the booth. "I should get going."

"Are you going to take a rideshare?"

"I think I might walk and get some fresh air. I'm only a few blocks up the road."

"Will you let me know when you get home?"

I roll my eyes, but a smile sneaks out of me too. It's nice to have someone looking out for me. "Yeah. I will."

Later, after I take another shower and climb into bed with a book, I pull up my text message thread with Maverick.

ME

Home

BANE OF MY EXISTENCE

Excellent.

You good?

ME

I'm good. See you at practice.

BANE OF MY EXISTENCE

Chin up, buttercup (I can say that now because you aren't here to beat me in arm wrestling). The sun will come out tomorrow.

ME

Thanks, Annie.

BANE OF MY EXISTENCE

That's you, Hartwell.

Maybe I should save you in my phone as that from now on.

ME

What am I right now?

BANE OF MY EXISTENCE

Redheaded Assassin. LOL.

ME

At least you find yourself funny.

Better sleep with one eye open, Miller.

BANE OF MY EXISTENCE

Can't wait.

I'll leave the window unlocked.

I don't remember the last time I fell asleep with a smile on my face, but leave it to Maverick goddamn Miller to be the one to do it.

SIXTEEN
MAVERICK

PUCK KINGS

ME

I think we should start a book club.

Might be fun.

RILEY

I'm in. What are we reading?

CONNOR

Huh?

ME

Books. Have you heard of them?

EASY E

Why would we read for fun?

ME

Hartwell told me women love romance books.

Maybe we should read them too.

HUDSON

I read romance books.

EASY E

The fuck? You do?

HUDSON

How else are you supposed to learn what women want in a relationship?

G-MONEY

Who said anything about a relationship?

EASY E

Don't they just want to be fucked?

HUDSON

You two are not allowed to talk to women ever again.

ME

Any recommendations, Hud?

HUDSON

What do you want to read?

ME

IDK. She said cowboys were popular.

HUDSON

I'll report back.

SEYMOUR

Speaking of Emmy, don't you think we need to have a group chat with her in it?

RILEY

Shit. She's not in this one?

HUDSON

No. Thank god.

LIAM

I wish I wasn't in this group chat. She can take my spot.

G-MONEY

That's because you have a stick up your ass.

RILEY

I'll add her.

Riley has named the chat Professional Stick Handlers
Riley has added Redheaded Assassin to the chat

G-MONEY

What happened to Puck Kings?

ME

We have a lady in our midst.

REDHEADED ASSASSIN

What is this?

LIAM

A group chat that goes off at all hours of the day and night. Welcome to hell.

Liam has left the chat
Redheaded Assassin has left the chat
Easy E has added Liam and Redheaded Assassin to the chat

REDHEADED ASSASSIN

I don't want to be here.

EASY E:

You can run, but you can't hide.

HUDSON

Really, Ethan. Just stop talking.

RILEY

Yeah, dude. Next thing you know, you'll be growing a creepy mustache.

EASY E

I'd rock the shit out of a mustache.

ME

Team dinner tonight. 6 sharp at my place!

I love playing in front of thousands of fans in sold-out arenas.

I love scoring the game-winning goal on the road and silencing the haters who were booing me for sixty minutes.

I love signing kids' jerseys and taking selfies with them.

But my favorite part of being a professional athlete is having team dinners on Tuesday nights with the people I adore.

The tradition started when Coach got to DC four years ago. He inherited a shitty team with players who had shitty attitudes.

We were in the middle of a ten-game losing streak.

No one had any pride in wearing their jerseys.

Hell, I even asked my agent to start looking at trades because I was fed up and sick of playing with guys who only wanted to collect a paycheck.

Until one day when Coach told me to invite a teammate over for a meal and gave me one rule: no hockey talk.

I started with Hudson. We were already friends, and I figured he'd be the easiest to talk to.

He brought Thai food. I popped open a couple of beers. We sat in my kitchen and talked about the *Fast and the Furious* franchise for two hours. He came back the next week, and he brought Ethan with him.

Something cool happened.

Relationships formed, and they were deeper than the connection we had on the ice.

I learned that Connor has a brother on the autism spectrum. Riley's dad lost his leg after a house fire. Grant's mom walked out on him and his sisters when he was eight, and Liam is fluent in Spanish.

The guys weren't just my teammates anymore—they were my brothers.

Our dinner group grew to five, then ten.

Eventually, the whole team started coming around. Tuesday nights turned into a chance for us to shut off the sports talk and just be together.

In the last year, we've expanded to other people coming by too. Piper and Lexi joined in, and so did Dallas, Maven, and my other best friend, Reid Duncan, who manages the social media accounts for the DC Titans.

Seymour's girlfriend, Brooke, started making appearances, and the family keeps growing.

Nothing makes me happier than a room full of good food and even better conversation.

"I'm going to make sure everything is set up in the kitchen," I tell Grant and Ethan. They barely look up from the NBA2k game they're playing on my eighty-inch television, and I could be talking to a wall right now. "You guys need anything in the meantime?"

"For you to get out of the way, Cap." Ethan leans to his right to look around me then groans when Grant dunks on him. "Goddammit, you motherfucker."

"You snooze, you lose, E. Get out of here with that shitty defense."

"Be glad I don't unplug that console, you ungrateful shits," I laugh.

I head for the kitchen and grab empty water glasses as I go. We have an early flight to Milwaukee tomorrow, so I'm forcing everyone to stay hydrated.

"Need some help?" Dallas asks, trailing behind me.

"I'm good." I check the foyer to see if anyone else got here while I was handing out drinks. "Thanks, though."

"Why do you keep looking at the door?"

"I'm not." I drop the cups in the sink and grab the two charcuterie boards Seymour brought from the fridge. "I'm being a good host."

"You're being weird."

"I'm not being weird."

Dallas laughs. "Bullshit. You can't even look at me. What's wrong with you, Miller? Don't tell me someone's pregnant."

"*What*? No. *Fuck*, no. I haven't been with anyone in a month, and I always wrap it up."

"A month? That must be a personal record."

I flip him off. "Hartwell might be coming tonight."

"Sweet. Did she say she would be here?"

"No. I reminded her ten times at morning skate that her invitation still stands, but I doubt she'll show up. She'd rather throw a shoe at my head. I wish she would, though."

"You wish she'd throw a shoe at you?"

"No. I wish she'd show up."

"Wait a second." Dallas drops his chin into the palm of his hand and grins. "Do you have a *crush*?"

I stab a piece of cheese with a knife, because it's definitely *not* a crush. "Hartwell and I hung out after our game the other day. She seemed like she could use a friend. Someone in her corner. I get the impression people haven't done that for her in the past."

"You've never been friends with a woman."

"Uh. Yes the fuck I have. I'm friends with Maven. And Piper and Lexi."

"You're friends with Maven because of me, and you work with Piper and Lexi. The only f-word you know when it comes to women is fuck," he says.

"It's not like that with Hartwell. We're not friends, and we're not fucking, either. She can't stand me, and sometimes, she annoys the shit out of me too."

"But you hang out after games?"

"Only because I found her on the ice working herself to exhaustion and forced her to stop and get food. It's not like we're falling in love or some shit like that. She's part of the team, and it would be nice if she were here." I shrug. "That's it."

"I didn't mean to imply anything. Sorry if it sounded that way," Dallas says.

"It's fine." I pull him into a hug. "I don't want her to feel left out, no matter how badly she wants to throw things at me."

"You probably deserve it, Mav."

"Yeah." I grin and think about the six text messages I sent her earlier this afternoon. The ones that were delivered and read but went unanswered. It's a wonder she hasn't blocked me yet. "I probably do."

"Why are you two hugging?" Reid asks. He barely looks up from his phone as he walks into the kitchen and swipes a cracker off the cheese tray. His glasses slide down his nose and a lock of red hair falls into his eyes, but he ignores the distractions for his screen. "And why am I not included?"

"Because you're using your phone even though it's against the rules. No devices at team dinner. Put it away, Duncan."

He grumbles under his breath and shoves the phone in a drawer. "There. Happy?"

"Ecstatic. Do you want a hug?"

"No. I'm too stressed for a hug. I need the girl who manages the Thunderhawks account to stop getting on my last nerve. Do you know what she did today? She changed their handle from @ThunderhawksFootball to @footballindc. They play in fucking *Baltimore*," he groans.

"Okay. And why is this bad?" I ask, missing the point.

"Because now I'm getting notifications for them. Our handle, the one I set up *years* ago, is @dcfootball, and people are confused." Reid glares at the oven like it's the woman he's talking about. "I swear she's doing it to get a rise out of me."

Dallas and I exchange a look, both knowing his feud with the other social media manager is bound to reach a breaking point soon.

"I would too. Your mad-face is cute, Duncan," I say, and I move the charcuterie boards to the buffet table with the rest of the food my teammates brought. "Come and get it, kids!"

There's a stampede to the kitchen. Connor gets shoved into a wall and a stack of napkins goes flying. Hands grab for plates and silverware and the Swedish meatballs Riley brought.

"I'm first." Grant elbows his way to the front. "Youngest ones start the lines. You fuckers are too old to enjoy the finer things in life."

"Absolutely not." Hudson nudges Grant out of the way. "I've given more time to this team, and my knees suck the most. I'm going first."

"I think we can agree that Liam's knees suck the most," Seymour says, and Liam scowls.

I laugh and stand off to the side, watching them all act like idiots. There's more than enough food to go around, but it's fun to see them riled up and competitive over who gets first dibs on the chicken piccata Dallas grabbed from an Italian restaurant on his way over.

Over the loud noise and name-calling, I hear the soft click of a door.

I jerk my head toward the foyer and it feels like all the air is sucked out of the room.

Emerson Hartwell is standing in my apartment, looking like a goddamn knockout.

SEVENTEEN
MAVERICK

I'M STILL NOT USED to seeing her in normal clothes, and it throws me out of whack.

Thank god she doesn't walk around like this all the time. I'd be distracted as hell.

Even right now, someone is trying to get my attention, but I'm not listening.

I'm too busy staring at the leather boots that make her legs look a mile long. The black skirt that hits the tops of her knees and the crop top that shows off her stomach.

"Hey," I say, walking toward her.

"Hey." Emerson tilts her head to the side, and her gaze locks on mine. "What's a girl have to do to get a plate of food instead of getting eye-fucked around here?"

I give her a guilty grin. "I wasn't very smooth, was I?"

"Nonchalance isn't in your vocabulary, is it, Miller?"

"I'm afraid not, Red. I'm not sure I can even spell it. Sorry for objectifying you. You look really good, and I didn't think you would show."

"Is it okay if I'm here?" she asks hesitantly, rubbing the toe of her boot on the marble floor.

"Of course it is," I say right away, not wanting her to feel unwelcome. "I'm surprised, but it's a good surprised."

"Piper sent me eight thousand texts." Emerson shrugs, an unbothered pop of her shoulders, but she's not scowling. I can work with that half-assed enthusiasm. "I admire her tenacity."

"That woman might be small, but she sure is mighty. Grab a plate and help yourself. There's no order to things, and it's pandemonium in the kitchen."

"I think I'll hang out here for a minute and let the madness die down," she says. Her fingers brush along the hem of her skirt and she gives the velvet a little tug. "If that's cool. I don't want to be in the way."

"I could give you a tour while you wait. You're the only one who hasn't seen the apartment. It's nothing special, but I'll show you around."

"Nothing special? It's the penthouse of a luxury high-rise."

"You're right." I slide my hands into the pockets of my black joggers and rock forward. "This place is fantastic and well worth the hefty price tag."

Emerson eyes me. She glances over my shoulder at the mayhem unfolding with our teammates, then bites her bottom lip.

She does that a lot, I've noticed.

When she's deep in thought. When she's not sure how she's supposed to react to something. When she's trying not to smile.

Fuck. I want to make her smile.

"Okay," she finally says. "Only because it's better than standing here and looking like a creep."

"You do remind me of a Peeping Tom. Admit it: You want to know all of my secrets."

"Seeing how you organize your socks might give me some insight into why you're so obnoxious."

"Not sure we have enough time for you to figure that out. Come on," I say, and she follows me without another word.

I lead her into the living room and point out all the features of my apartment—the framed team photos on the shelf, the fancy Barbie dollhouse I bought for June to play with when she comes over. The old mahogany coffee table I purchased from a small shop down in South Carolina, hauling it the five hundred miles back home by myself.

Emerson takes her time and studies every little detail. She stops at the antique clock on the wall. My board game collection and the couch in the middle of the room.

I wonder if I should've fluffed the pillows or thrown a blanket over the back to make it homier. It looks sad right now with the gray cushions against the gray walls.

It's weird to stand here and let a woman pick through these parts of my life I'm not used to showing off. I'm normally stumbling home with my tongue down someone's throat and my hand under their dress. Fingers curled around the waistband of her underwear and trying not to stub my toe as I carry her down the hall.

This is…

I don't know what this is.

"What do you think?" I ask, and that old habit of seeking validation, of needing to hear if someone likes me, is pounding in my chest.

"It's nice." She runs her finger along the wood of the entertainment center and stops at the stack of puzzles in the corner. "You said you like puzzles."

I brighten up. "Look at you paying attention. I love puzzles."

"Is that your favorite thing to do when you're not on the ice?"

"Is that your question of the day?"

"Yeah." Emerson nods. She looks at me over her shoulder,

and the smallest smile curves at the corners of her mouth. "As long as you don't mind sharing."

"We didn't have a lot of money when I was growing up, but there were always puzzles around. The first time I put one together, my brain went quiet. I focused on what was in front of me, and… I don't know. I always feel relaxed when I do one. Which I realize sounds so fucking stupid. I'm a thirty-year-old man who—"

"The things that make us happy are never stupid. That's how I am with plants," she says. "Plants and flowers and gardening. It's a way to turn my mind off."

"Really? I'm going to have to introduce you to Reid later. He loves plants too. You can be botany enthusiasts together."

Her laugh is loud, and I puff out my chest. Stand a little taller like a smug bastard, because I'm finally getting somewhere with Emerson, and that boosts my pride.

The woman has more walls up than a castle. She's determined to keep people out, but I'm dead set on getting in.

"I need to figure out what I want to grow while I'm here." She pivots and walks down the hall. "Winter in DC is harsher than California."

"Not nearly as harsh as Michigan, though," I say, and she stops in her tracks. "I finally watched your tapes. I found some of your high school clips too."

"Only took you a month."

"Better late than never, right? You were good, Red."

"Am I not good anymore?"

"You are. Just not as good as me," I joke, and she flips me off with a middle finger painted in red nail polish. "My room is the one on the right."

"Is there some sort of curse on it? If I go inside, will all my clothes come off?"

"That would be a cool party trick, wouldn't it?" I crowd up behind her and turn the knob on the door. Her breath catches, and I wait for her to elbow my stomach. To tell me to get lost. When she doesn't, I move an inch closer to her. "Your clothes aren't going to come off," I say low in her ear. "I know how to be a gentleman."

Except, all I'm thinking about is her spread out on my bed.

That fiery hair all over my pillows and her fingers gripping the sheets. My hands under her thighs, dragging her toward me, and my head between her legs.

It doesn't feel very gentlemanly.

"Good. I'd hate to have to cut off your dick. Women everywhere would be so disappointed."

"Are you trying to see my dick, Hartwell? You could've just asked."

I swear her ass brushes against the front of my pants, and I start reciting the presidents backwards in my head so I don't get hard while she's pressed against me.

"No," Emerson says. "I prefer men who actually know how to use their stick."

"Professional stick handler, remember?" I say, and I side-step away from her. I need to clear my head. "You can go in."

"Thanks for the permission." She tugs at her skirt again and walks into my room. I do my best not to stare at her ass. "Wow. This is not what I was expecting."

"What were you expecting?"

"Three women in your bed. Bras everywhere. Sex toys on the floor and a sex swing hanging from the ceiling."

I grin and scratch at the taco tattoo on my arm. "Sorry to disappoint. This building's been restored, so a sex swing might make the whole roof collapse in."

Emerson puts her hands on her hips and surveys the bed. Her attention shifts to the doors out to the balcony and the floor-to-ceiling windows that show off the night sky. She hums when she opens my closet and rifles through the jerseys and shirts and suits.

"You have a signed Mario Lemieux jersey?" She yanks it

off the hanger and holds it up to her chest. "How much did you spend on this?"

"Nothing. I met him at an event benefiting Hodgkin's lymphoma a couple years ago, and we started talking. At the end of the night, he gave me the jersey and told me how much he appreciated the awareness I was helping to raise for the disease. I've thought about auctioning it off for charity, but he was my idol growing up. The little boy in me can't let it go, and I'd rather write a check anyway."

She pulls the jersey away from her body and slips it back on the hanger. Her eyes drag from the clothes to me, and she bites her bottom lip again.

"I think I might have been wrong about you," she says quietly. "At least some parts of you."

"What do you mean?" I ask, confused.

"Here I've been, thinking you only care about yourself. Turns out, you're a nice guy."

"That makes you mad, doesn't it, Red?"

"Downright furious." Emerson tucks the Lemieux jersey back where it belongs and moves to the balcony doors, throwing them open. "And I hate these views."

"So do I. They're the worst." I follow her and lean my arms over the metal railing. "You see the Washington Monument over there?"

"Yeah. It's beautiful at night. I still need to do all the touristy things in town. Museums, monuments. There's so much to see."

"I'll go with you. If you want some company," I volunteer.

"That would require spending more time with you." She turns to face me, and her attention hangs on my necklace before she stares past my shoulder. "And that sounds revolting."

"You're surviving just fine right now."

"Because I can escape whenever I want." She rubs her hands up her arms and shivers at the cold breeze that whips through the air. I pull off my hoodie and toss it to her. "What am I supposed to do with this?"

I laugh. "Normal people would put it on and warm themselves up."

She tosses it back to me and shivers again. "No, thank you."

Stubborn fucking woman.

I love that she doesn't give into me like everyone else does.

"What's your favorite food?" I ask.

"Is that your question of the day?"

"Yup. I figured I'd spend the first fifty questions asking you all the boring shit, then we'll get to the good stuff."

Emerson blows out a breath, and I lay the hoodie between us. An invitation to take it, if she wants, because I really can't stand to see the goosebumps on her skin.

"Potatoes," she says around an exhale that sounds tired and heavy. "Mashed. Scalloped."

"Makes sense why the alien babies are half potato. How do you feel about twice baked?"

"My least favorite, but I wouldn't say no."

"You're a carb girl."

"I'm an athlete." Her fingers inch toward the sweatshirt before she pulls her hand back and taps her nails against the railing. "What about you?"

"Pasta. Lasagna, specifically. Had it once a week as a kid, and I never got sick of it." I smile into the night and glance at her. "Don't tell any of the guys I have some hidden in my fridge. I'm going to warm it up when they all settle down."

"Speaking of, I think I'm going to head in and grab some food."

"Too cold out here for you?"

"No." She shoots me a look and turns for the door. Her skirt spins with her and I get a glimpse of creamy thighs. The curve of her quad muscles and smooth skin. "I'm hungry."

"Avoid the charcuterie boards—there are strawberries on them. I'll make sure there aren't any next time."

Emerson hesitates. "What are you talking about?"

"Strawberries?" I repeat. "The fruit? You're allergic, right? The flight to Milwaukee tomorrow would suck if your eyes were all puffy."

Her mouth opens then closes. A deep flush of pink settles on her cheeks, and she grips the door knob with white knuckles.

"Yeah, I'm allergic. I'm surprised you—" She shakes her head. "I'll see you inside, Miller."

I grin when she shuts the door softly behind her.

I managed to not get thrown off the balcony *and* I made her laugh.

Twice.

Hat trick for me.

EIGHTEEN
MAVERICK

"ON THE ROAD AGAIN." I lean back in my seat on the charter plane and stretch out my legs. "People always have such nice things to say about Chicago in November."

Hudson laughs across the table from me. "That's like saying the North Pole has the nicest beaches around. It's going to be cold as hell, and I forgot my beanie at home. It's my lucky one, too, so if things go wrong in tomorrow's game, you can blame me."

"Can I blame you for the other three losses?" I joke, knowing fully well it's not Hudson's fault we've stumbled into a losing streak.

We've all been off lately, but I've been really fucking off.

I've missed open shots on net. I've spent more time in the penalty box this past week than I did the first month of the season. I keep letting my frustrations out on the ice, which puts my teammates at a disadvantage that isn't fair to them.

I'm distracted, some outside force occupying my mind and pulling my attention from the game, but I can't figure out what the hell it is.

I've tried to do puzzles. I've tried to meditate like the team psychologist suggested. I've been getting enough sleep and sticking to the nutrition plan my personal chef put together, but something is still off.

It's irritating the fuck out of me, and I don't like that it's also affecting the team.

"Do you have any plans for the Windy City?" Hudson asks as he taps on his headphones. "You're probably getting into something tonight, right? Grant mentioned a club or a karaoke bar or a karaoke club. The details have slipped my mind."

"I think he was talking about a club that plays the top songs people pick when they sing karaoke, but the idea of a karaoke club could be really fucking lucrative." I turn my phone on airplane mode and slip it in my pocket. "I'm not going, though. I'm just going to chill at the hotel. Why? Do you have plans?"

"Come on, man." He laughs and brushes pieces of blonde hair out of his eyes. "You know my away game tradition consists of croissants from local bakeries and checking out bookstores."

"Hud. Have your traditions ever included a one-night stand?" I ask. I dig deep into my memory, and there's no recollection of him bringing anyone back to the hotel after curfew.

"Nah. You know that's not my thing. I'm a relationship guy." A blush creeps up his neck, and he grins sheepishly. "I'd have no idea how to handle that. You go from talking to hooking up in a couple of hours? What about getting to know them?"

"That's the whole point. You don't get to know them. It's just mindless stuff for you both to enjoy for the night. No names. No personal details. No sticking around."

"I think I'd be terrible at it. I'd be asking her where she sees herself in five years while she's got her hand down my pants." He stares at me, and his sudden attention makes me fidgety. "Speaking of one-night stands, you've been different lately."

"Different?"

"You're not sneaking anyone into your room. You're downstairs at breakfast before all of us, and there haven't been any hickeys on your neck." Hudson leans forward, pulling on my collar, and I bat his hand away. "It's interesting."

I pop a shoulder in a shrug. "I'm putting hockey first and trying to keep us from losing four in a row. I think that win we stole last week was a fluke."

"It's not just right now. It's been going on for a while. Ever since—" Hudson sits up and looks over his shoulder. He rubs his jaw, and there's something on the tip of his tongue he's not telling me. "Anyway. I'm here if there's ever anything you need to talk about. No judgment. I promise."

"I appreciate that, Hud, but I'm fine." I smile. "If that changes, I'll let you know."

"Hi, boys." The flight attendant leans her elbow on my seat and bats her eyes at us. I'm not sure her tight shirt is in line with the airline's uniform standards, but that's above my pay grade. "Can you put your seatbelts on, please?"

"Sure thing," I say, and I give her a thumbs-up. She giggles and flips her hair over her shoulder, hurrying down the aisle. "Wow. Didn't know I was that funny."

"You're not," Hudson draws out. "She wants to join the mile high club with you."

"Fuck, no. There's probably piss everywhere, and I have some standards."

The plane pushes back and taxis out, rolling down the runway until we're in the air and DC turns into a speck behind us.

The flight attendants keep the overhead lights off, knowing that most of us like to sleep on morning flights, but I'm restless.

I can't sit still, and I crane my neck over the seats until I see long red hair ten rows up.

I jump into the aisle and saunter toward the front of the aircraft. I get stopped by Seymour and Connor on the way, answering their questions that no, they sure as shit cannot eat hotdogs for lunch tomorrow before the game but yes, they can have deep dish pizza tonight.

When I finally get to Emerson's row, I grin down at her.

"What are you doing here?" she asks, barely looking up from her phone. It's like she was waiting for me. "The seat belt sign is on, and this is a safety risk."

"Guess I'll have to sit next to you then." I plop down in the aisle seat and shrug out of my suit jacket. "What's up?"

"Really?" She lifts her chin and finally glances my way, a scowl on her mouth. "It's too early to be having conversations, Miller. Do you ever sleep?"

"You were just talking with Piper and Lexi."

"They're my friends."

"Am I not your friend?"

"No." Emerson snorts. "You're my teammate, and there's a big difference."

I frown. "What the hell has gotten into you? You had a great time at team dinner last week. We even got through a meal without you wanting to strangle me, but the only times you've talked to me since have been on the ice."

"I'm not surprised you think everything is about you."

"Why are you so adamant about keeping me out?" I challenge. "Would being my friend really be the worst thing in the world?"

"Yes, it would be. You're obnoxious, and you never know when to stop."

"Wow." I laugh and lace my fingers behind my head. "Tell me how you really feel, Hartwell."

"I've been down this road. I know how being your friend ends, and I'm not putting myself in that position again. I'm glad you consider all of our teammates close pals, but I wish you would stop trying so hard to make me one of them."

I drop my head against the seat and sigh. "Not every hockey player is a bad guy. Some of us have the team's best interest at heart, and that includes everyone getting along."

"And some of you don't understand when to stop pushing," she tosses back, and that stirs up something inside me.

"I'm not pushing you. I'm trying to figure out how to get my left winger to play better, because she missed three shots on goal in our last game, and I'd really fucking like it if she showed up when we needed her." I huff out a breath. "Forgive me if I thought that by being nice to you, by being someone who tries to make you laugh and gets a half-hearted smile from time to time, it might fix that."

Heat burns behind Emerson's eyes when I look at her again. "You haven't shown up either, Miller, and I don't appreciate you throwing me under the bus. This is a *team* sport, and I'm not the only one out there fucking up."

"Exactly. It's a team sport, and here you are, not talking to me. Is that what you want, Hartwell? For me to ignore you? To not give you the time of day? To treat you like we're strangers?"

"Why don't you mind your business and I'll mind mine?"

"Last I checked, my business as captain includes getting the team to play together, and if someone needs to step up, then I'm going to call them out on it."

"Call yourself out, Miller. Stay in your lane and I'll stay in mine."

I roll my lips together.

It's so obvious Emerson is dead set on keeping me at arm's length. If I haven't won her over yet, there's not any hope for us, and I guess the only way forward is to wave the white flag.

"Fine." I pinch the bridge of my nose. I'm irritated. Pissed off and fucking *tired* of trying to convince her to think about me a certain way. If she wants to operate in her own little bubble, that's on her. I'm done trying. "Sorry for bothering you."

Her mouth opens like she wants to say something else, but she snaps it closed and leans her head against the window. "See you in Chicago."

NINETEEN
EMMY

WE GET BLOWN out by Chicago.

As a team, we're off-kilter.

That cohesiveness we had my first week on the Stars disappeared, and it might be my fault.

Frustrations were high during intermissions in the locker room, and when the final buzzer sounded, Maverick stormed out of the arena like a kid who didn't get his way.

The ride back to the hotel was silent, and after a quick debrief with Coach and instructions to be in the lobby at seven tomorrow morning for our flight home, we all went our separate ways.

Connor, Grant and Ethan invited me out to dinner, but I took the room service route. A bowl of spaghetti the size of my head and a glass of red wine in the peace and quiet is so much more appealing than a loud restaurant.

There's also a pint of chocolate chip in the mini freezer, and the only things I plan to do the rest of the night involve a couple of episodes of reality television and the vibrator hidden in my suitcase.

I shovel the last bite of pasta in my mouth and toss my

used napkins in the trash can. I grab my toy from my bag and stretch out on the bed, clicking it on.

I've been wound up tight the last couple of days. From the losses, to not playing well, to the conversation with Maverick I keep replaying in my head, I know a quick orgasm will help relieve the tension I'm holding on to.

I don't know the last time I touched myself, but *god*, it already feels good to turn my brain off and relax into the pleasure. I tease my nipples with the toy then drag it down to my shorts. The vibrations pulse against my clit, and a soft moan slips free.

Before I can sink into the mind-numbing bliss, a knock on my door has me throwing my toy in the air.

It nearly hits the ceiling then lands in the middle of the bed, still humming as I hear a louder knock.

I really can't catch a break.

"Shit." I turn off the vibrator and shove it under a pillow. "Who is it?"

"Open up, Hartwell," a familiar voice says.

I narrow my eyes and jump off the bed, stalking toward the door. I open it and find Maverick standing there, looking obscenely attractive in his gray sweatpants and plain white shirt. The ends of his hair are wet, and there's a small red mark on his cheekbone.

"Can I help you?" I ask politely, three seconds away from slamming the door in his face.

"We need to talk." His dark eyes sweep over the shorts and tank top I slipped into after my shower, and he lets out a shallow breath. "Now."

Maverick squeezes past me without an invitation inside. His hip grazes against mine as he makes his way into my room, and I don't bother arguing with him.

"Why are you here?" I close the door and flip the deadbolt. "Does curfew not apply to you?"

"What the hell happened out there tonight?" He paces

around the small living room and glares at me. "You were slow as shit."

I laugh and push the strap of my shirt up my shoulder. He follows the movement, and his eyes gleam a shade darker. "I guess we're getting everything out in the open, aren't we?"

"You didn't pass to me. Three separate times you went to someone else."

"Because Seymour had the better shot, you selfish ass. Do you make room calls for everyone so you can criticize their playmaking? Or am I the only one lucky enough to be interrogated by you today?"

Maverick stops pacing. He steps toward me, his stride quick and determined. Before I can take a breath, my back is against the wall.

His hands rest on either side of my head, caging me in with nowhere to go, and a spark of adrenaline races up my spine.

"No," he says, and I feel the word everywhere. "For some goddamn reason, I can't get you out of my fucking head."

"And that's my fault?" I whisper.

"You're maddening. Impossible to read." He touches my cheek. Drags his finger down my jaw with exquisite care. "The most annoying person I've ever met."

"Yet here you are, pinning me against a wall." I lift my chin, and our gazes collide. "Why aren't you walking away? You did yesterday."

Maverick blows out an exhale. It sounds like it's pulled from the trenches of his soul. Like he's reluctant to let it go.

"I don't want to walk away," he says lowly. "Not anymore."

"What—" I lick my lips, and he follows that movement too. "What do you want?"

There's a beat of silence, and I wonder if he'll ignore the obvious invitation I've laid at his feet.

Asking him to stay would be the stupidest idea I've ever had, but I've been so lonely lately.

It seems like this moment is inevitable, like everything has been leading to *here* since he invited me back to his apartment the first day we met.

If not tonight, then eventually, and now that he's right in front of me, I really don't want him to go.

"You," he says, and it's so soft, I think I might have misheard him. "Can I have you, Emmy?"

Emmy.

Not Red.

Not Hartwell.

Emmy.

My breath catches. My heart trips and stutters over itself. A little *m* gets carved out in my chest, an incision in a spot no one else has ever found.

Now it belongs to him.

"Yes," I say, and his eyes twinkle as bright as stars in the midnight sky. "You can have me."

Neither of us move.

It's like we're both waiting to see who will give up their power first. Who will call out the other's bluff.

But the next thing I know, his mouth is on mine.

It's rough and messy. A feverish press of his lips. The swipe of my tongue against his. A low sound working its way up his throat when I run my fingers through his hair and tug.

"Jesus," Maverick mumbles.

"I think the time for Jesus has passed," I say.

He lifts me off the ground and splays his hand over my ribcage. His thumb strokes along the underside of my breast, a tortuous drag that makes me want to scream at him.

"Do that again," he tells me.

I pull on the ends of his hair, the longer strands that brush against his ear. His skin flushes a dark red, and he hisses when I leave hot kisses down his neck.

"What?" I ask. "This?"

"Emerson." He presses me into the wall, and I feel him hard between my legs. Long, thick, and absolutely distracting. A painting of the Golden Gate Bridge tips sideways. His hand folds around the back of my head to stop me from stabbing myself on the corner of the canvas. "What are we doing?"

"I don't know." I roll my hips and a sigh slips out of me. I could get off like this: the friction from the seam of my shorts. His fingers stroking my ass. "You started it."

"And you aren't stopping it."

"Because I'm horny and your dick against my thigh is better than the vibrator I shoved under my pillows when you almost knocked down my door."

"Hang on." Maverick pulls back and looks at me. There's a bead of sweat on his forehead, and his pupils are blown wide. "Are you okay with this?"

"The talking? Not particularly. I can think of a dozen other things I'd rather be doing, and half of them involve your fingers."

"What do the other half involve?"

My eyes bounce to the front of his sweatpants, and I lift an eyebrow. "Want to find out?"

His laugh is soft and boyish, and he kisses me again.

This kiss is lazier. A slow, sensual burst of lust as he takes his time with me.

He guides my arms above my head. My legs wrap around his waist. His lips glide against mine, coaxing them open so he can sink his teeth into my bottom lip.

I moan at the sting and quick bite of pleasure. Maverick answers with a pleased hum that rivals a wildfire as it burns its way through me.

"Are we doing this?" He bends his neck and moves his mouth to my shirt. He sucks on my nipple through the cotton, soaking the material until it sticks to my skin in a translucent haze. "Are you ready to admit that you want me, Hartwell?"

"*Fuck.*" I wiggle against him, and he presses my hands harder into the wall.

"That wasn't a yes or no."

"Why not? Maybe your dick will make me hate you a little less."

"I have a nice dick. No complaints, ever." Maverick moves to my other nipple and sucks on the pointed peak. Rolls his tongue over the thin fabric, and heat builds at the base of my spine. "And you could never hate me."

"I hate you more than I hate anyone else," I say, but when he bites the soft flesh of my breast, we both know I'm a liar.

"Is that why you're grinding against me, Red? Why you're getting my sweatpants all wet? Because you *hate* me?"

"Yes." I move my hips in a circle and gasp when the tip of his cock brushes against my clit. "But I'd like you a whole lot more if you got on your knees like a good boy and showed me you know how to use your tongue and fingers for something less annoying than running your mouth. If not, I have no problem making you sit in a chair and watch while I get off from eight inches of silicone."

"Well, shit." His thumb strokes my collarbone then the line of my throat. "Sounds like heaven on earth."

"Rules," I say. I try to break my wrists from his hold, but he doesn't let me budge. "This is a one-night thing."

"It'll probably help us on the ice. We can fuck out the tension between us and be good as new."

"It's only fucking. I don't date hockey players."

"And I don't date period. I've never been with the same woman twice."

"Then this will be easy. It's just sex. You leave as soon as we're finished. We don't speak of this ever again, and we don't let it affect our professional roles."

"Deal. Last time you were tested?"

"Six months ago. Everything was negative, and I haven't been with anyone since. You?"

"Over a month ago. Also negative."

I bob my head in some sort of nod, not sure what else to say.

"Have I finally figured out a way to shut you up, Red?" Maverick murmurs. "A way to keep your smart mouth from running all the fucking time?"

"There are other ways to shut me up, but here we are. Still against a wall when I could be choking on your cock."

He grins, and *gosh*, it's a devastating thing.

Maverick walks us to the bed and drops me on the mattress. From the way his tongue sneaks out of his mouth as he watches me, I know he's going to be thorough when he finally touches me.

He pulls his shirt over his head and tosses it to the side. I can't help but study the lines of his body when he's bare-chested. The artwork on his arm and the dark hair trailing down his torso. The deep cut of muscles across his stomach, and how his silver necklace sparkles under the lamplight.

My throat goes dry.

Maverick Miller is the most beautiful man I've ever seen.

"You're staring," he says, and there's pride in his tone.

My eyes snap up to meet his. "I am not."

"It's okay to think I'm hot, Hartwell. You can tell me about it when I'm on top of you."

"I don't think you're hot."

"Liar." He runs a hand up my calf. His fingers reach the hem of my shorts, and he gives them a gentle tug. "*Fuck.*"

"What?"

"You. I've never gotten to see so much of you."

I pull off my shirt and throw it with his. "So why aren't you looking at me?"

"Because you didn't tell me I could look." His thumbs hook in the waistband of his sweatpants, and he works them down his thighs. "Until you do, I'm just going to stare at your pretty face."

I don't know what I thought sex with Maverick would be like, but it's not *this.*

Him talking about consent when I'm half naked in front of him. His erection pressing against his briefs and my hand dangerously close to slipping into my underwear.

"You think I'm pretty?" I ask, taking a line from his playbook.

"Nah." He breaks into another grin, and there's a pang in the center of my chest. Between my legs, too. "I think you're fucking gorgeous."

"You can look at me," I say, and he steps closer. "If you want."

"I want. More than I've ever wanted anything else," Maverick says, rough and low, and I believe him.

His eyes move away from my face. They drop to my chest and he lets out a noise that sounds like a mix between a moan and a whine. The hand at his side flexes before he adjusts himself over the outside of his briefs.

He licks his lips again, a man starved. "Take off your shorts."

I wiggle out of the flimsy pajama bottoms and kick them away, leaving me in a pair of lacy purple underwear. My toes scrunch against the sheets, and I'm itching to touch him.

Maverick brushes his knuckles against the inside of my thigh, then curls his fingers around my ankles. He tugs me toward the edge of the bed, and I sit up.

"What are you doing?" I ask.

"You said you wanted me on my knees." He drops a kiss to my shin, then kneels on the ground in front of me. "And I've always liked being a good boy."

TWENTY
MAVERICK

I DIDN'T PLAN for this to happen when I knocked on her door.

If I wanted a naked girl in bed with me, I could have answered any of the three dozen Instagram DMs blowing up my phone.

But here I am.

On my knees between Emerson's legs. Leaking in my briefs like a horny fucking teenager when she tips her thighs wide open, teasing me within an inch of my life.

She has to be doing it on purpose.

There's no other explanation for why I'm teetering on the brink of insanity and she's smirking at me.

Fuck.

I can't stop looking at her.

Her tits are pretty and full and the perfect size to fit in my hands. When I reach up and roll a hard nipple between my finger and thumb, she lets out a pleased sigh that goes straight to my dick.

God damn.

The things I want to do to this woman.

There's a list a mile long and not nearly enough time.

I want to wrap my hand around her throat and finish all over her chest. Smear my cum down her stomach and paint a picture. Maybe write out the word *mine* so everyone else stays the fuck away.

I might only have her for one night—an hour at best—but I'm going to ruin her so badly no one will ever measure up to me.

The next time someone kisses her, she's going to wish it were my mouth on hers.

The next time someone touches her, she's going to wish it were my fingers trailing down her body.

The next time someone fucks her, she's going to wish it were *my* cock buried inside her.

"Am I being good, Emmy?" I twist her other nipple, and her back arches off the bed. "Good enough to touch the rest of you?"

"Yes," she rasps, a needy noise from the back of her throat. I can't wait to fuck her mouth and see what other sounds I can get her to make. If she'll gag or moan. Maybe she'll laugh. "Such a good boy. You can touch me wherever you want."

I grin smugly at her praise and move my attention away from her tits. I don't have a lot of time, and I'm not leaving this room before I get a chance to taste her.

I spot something on the underside of her ribs, and I tilt my head to get a better look.

"One of your tattoos?" I ask.

"Yeah." Emerson puts her hand over mine. She guides the tips of my fingers to the shape of an hourglass with half the sand already gone. "A reminder that life is short."

"I like it." I press a kiss to the design and run my tongue over the spot I just touched. She's warm and soft, and I know her pussy is going to feel the same way. "Where's your other one?"

She moves our hands to the top of her underwear. The

purple scrap is made of lace and bows and way too many fucking strings.

"Here." She taps her hip, and I spy a bouquet with yellow and orange and bright pink flowers. A bow tied around the stem that forms a heart. "I like all the colors."

"So do I." I rub my thumb across the artwork. Trace the petals and the basket they all sit in, and I kiss that one too.

"Maverick," she whines, and I blow out an unsteady breath.

Jesus Christ.

I want to hear her say my name like that every day for the rest of my life.

My dick turns rock hard. It takes every bit of my waning self-control to not give myself a quick jerk. To not hold the back of her head and make her choke on my cock like she mentioned earlier.

What is she going to sound like when I make her come? When I make her take every inch?

"And look at this pretty thing." I brush my fingers over the front of her thong. I snap the waistband sharp against her skin and her groan echoes in the room. "Who knew this was under your jersey?"

"I'm sweaty and gross in my uniform and pads. I know no one sees them, but I like to wear something for myself. Something that makes me feel sexy and... and like a woman."

"You're all woman, baby." I pull her underwear taut, wedging the thin material between her pussy lips. "I mean, fucking *look* at you."

"You said you were going to use your tongue." Emerson squirms on the sheet. "Do you need a lesson in female anatomy?"

"I don't think I need any lessons, Red."

"Are you sure about that? I don't see your tongue anywhere near my body."

"I think I'm doing an okay job." I yank the underwear down

her strong thighs and pull it off her legs. I wrap the lace around my wrist, a souvenir I'm absolutely taking home with me, and grin when I see her pussy. Glistening, pink. Wet and fucking ready for me. I use two fingers to spread her open, and I laugh. "You're drenched, aren't you? And I haven't even touched you yet."

She lets out an angry huff. "I'm not drenched because of you."

"Yeah?" I challenge. "Who else has you turned on like this?"

Her grin is dangerous. "Hudson. Grant. Liam. Anyone but you."

I sit up tall on my knees and lean forward so I can kiss her and shut her up. I press my lips to the corner of her mouth and she turns her head, answering me enthusiastically.

Teeth. Hands. The bump of her nose. A moan when I bite that sexy bottom lip of hers and a whimper when I drag my tongue over the mark to soothe the sting.

"Maybe I should stop. Or watch from the chair. I could make you put on a show for me without ever giving you my cock. It's what you get for mouthing off and being a fucking brat." I grip her chin, leaving room for her to pull away if she wants an escape. "I don't fucking share."

"Don't you *dare* stop, Miller," she practically growls. "You know I'm not going to any of their rooms tonight."

She sure as shit isn't.

"How do you like it?" I rock back on my heels and kiss both of her knees. I run my hands up her thighs and spread her legs wider to make room for my shoulders. "Fast? Slow? Soft? Rough?"

"No one's ever asked me that before."

"Never? What kind of assholes have you been with?"

Emerson scoffs but doesn't answer the question.

It's probably for the best.

The idea of someone else having her like this—red hair

everywhere. Pink cheeks and hard nipples. A softness to her movements. It makes something roar inside me.

"I like slow," she finally says. "I like when someone takes their time and lets me enjoy it. But I like it rough too. You don't have to be gentle or careful with me."

"Gentle and careful are the last things I'm going to be with you." I drag my thumb down the column of her throat. I add a little bit of pressure right at her windpipe, and I hum when she doesn't pull away. "I'm going to make a mess of you, Emmy girl."

She shivers. "I'd like that."

"Here's what's going to happen: I'm going to eat you out. Fuck you with my fingers and get you nice and stretched out. Then I'm going to fuck you into the mattress and make you come again—the second time is going to be around my cock. You're going to tell me when you like or don't like something. After, I'm going to ask you my question of the day then tuck you in before you can kick me out."

"You're awfully confident." Emerson blinks down at me with hazy eyes. She looks a little drunk. Totally sexy. "I've never come from sex before, so good luck with that."

I lift an eyebrow, intrigued. "Really?"

"Really. It's always too much dick and not enough hands. Close, but not all the way there."

"Good thing I know how to use all my appendages. We're done talking. I want you to lie back and hold your legs open. Get comfortable, baby, so I can take a good look at that pretty cunt of yours."

She trails her hand up her legs. Grasps her thighs so I can see every inch of her, and I almost forget my name.

My cock aches, but I know if I touch myself, it's going to be game over.

So I touch her instead, dragging a single finger through her slit and pushing inside until I reach my first knuckle. We groan at the same time, and I scoot closer, desperate for more of her.

"Fuck. You're so tight, Emmy," I breathe out, and now *I* feel drunk. Tipsy off the feel of her stretching around me and the sound of her rough exhale.

"I like when you call me that," she whispers, like she's afraid to admit it.

"So do I." I rub the tendons and muscles on her thigh, my thumb stroking higher up her leg. "Can you relax for me? There you go. Atta girl. That's good."

"More." Emerson trembles, and she pulls her knees close to her chest so I can get deeper. "Give me more, Maverick."

I'll do anything when she calls me *that.* When she looks at me with wide eyes and a swollen mouth.

"Say please," I say. She scowls, and I don't care. It's payback for telling me the other guys on the team were the ones to get her wet. "Say please, Emmy, and I'll do everything you want."

There's a war raging in her head, but when she tips her head back, I know I've won.

"Please, Maverick," she says.

"You can do better than that. If you're going to be fucking desperate, you can at least look at me when you beg for more of my fingers."

She lowers her chin. Her eyes are dark, and I'm not sure if she wants to kill me or kiss me.

Probably both.

"Please give me two fingers, Maverick. Give me three fingers and your tongue. Use my toy under the pillows. I don't care what you give me, but give me *something.*"

"Was that so hard?" I ask.

I slip another finger inside her before she can protest anymore. When I get past my second knuckles, I curl them, and she groans.

I love sex, but I love this more.

Going slow.

Learning her body.

Finding the rhythm she likes and repeating it again and again.

"I hate you," she whispers, but she squirms on the sheets. Drops one hand away from her leg and brings it to her tit, pinching her nipple hard.

"Say it again," I murmur. I press down on her stomach with my free palm, my fingers splayed out and stroking her skin. I can't get enough of her, and I want to touch her everywhere. "You know how much it turns me on."

Whatever other taunt she wants to add dies in her throat when I add a third finger at the same time as I lick her pussy and bury my tongue in her.

She tastes like heaven.

One fucking second inside her, and I'm already an addict.

Nothing is ever going to be this good again.

I sneak a look at her, just to make sure she's enjoying herself, and that was a fucking mistake.

She's thoroughly wrecked; a sheen of sweat on her skin. Panting and shaking with parted lips like she's trying to tell me something.

I loop one arm under her and drag her so she's almost at the edge of the bed. I put her feet on my shoulders and dip my head lower, holding her open as I circle her clit.

"Maverick." Her toes curl and dig into my muscles. She grabs at my hair. "Right there."

"I thought I needed a lesson in female anatomy. You still going to teach me, Red?"

"No." She shakes her head frantically, and a bead of sweat rolls down her shin. I reach up and lick it away. "It's good. So good. No one's ever—"

"No one's ever what?"

"Made me come like this," Emerson says, and that makes

me want to burn the fucking world down. "With their tongue on me."

"We're changing positions." I lift her in my arms and crawl onto the bed. She holds onto me, and I drop her near the headboard. "Sit on my face."

"What?" She looks at me like she's in a fog. "What was—I was so close!"

"I'll get you there again." I lie flat on my back, my head against the pillows. "No one's ever made you come like this because you were with boys before. I'm a man, and I told you I like to eat. Now fucking sit."

I don't give her a choice, lifting her up and setting her on my face.

"Fuck," she cries out.

"Open your legs nice and wide. Death by your pussy is the only way I want to go, and I'm not going to stop until you come on my tongue."

She settles into the position and shifts her weight forward. Her legs shake around my cheeks, squeezing my ears, and her breathing turns rough.

I cup her ass cheeks, my nails digging into the swell of her curves, and she grinds against my mouth.

"There you go," I say, and I bite the inside of her thigh. "Take what you need. Use me. Show me how much you hate me."

"I don't," she says, and she yanks on my hair again. "Not when you do that. *Maverick.* I'm going to come. Please. Can I—"

"I've got you." I squeeze her ass impossibly hard. "Come for me, Emmy girl. Let me taste you."

She trembles above me, and I laugh against her clit when she shoves my face deeper between her legs, like she wants to suffocate me.

I don't think she realizes this isn't torture, but paradise.

I can tell the second she breaks. She leans forward and

almost falls over. Her hands hit the wall, bracing herself upright, and she chants my name over and over again through a broken sob.

I'm going to be thinking about that for months.

I don't stop, taking her all the way through her orgasm until her legs loosen their grip and she moves off of me into a heap of tired limbs.

I look at her, and she's even more beautiful now than she was ten minutes ago. I reach over and trace her lips with my fingers. When she opens her mouth, I press down on her tongue.

"Suck," I tell her.

Her eyes flutter open and lock on mine. She sucks my fingers with so much enthusiasm, I go out of my mind wondering what it's going to be like when she sucks my cock. When she finishes, I drag my thumb across her bottom lip and pat her cheek.

"My good Emmy girl," I murmur, and she lights up. Rolls onto her side and looks at me. "Did you like that?"

"Is this the post-orgasm survey?" She gives me a dopey smile, still clearly floating high above the clouds. So fucking beautiful. "The part where I give you feedback?"

"What kind of feedback do you have for me?" I prop myself up on an elbow and run my wet fingers over her tits. "Tell me how I can improve."

"That was—" Her throat bobs. "Nice."

"Nice?" I repeat. "That's it?"

"Satisfactory."

I lean closer to her, nose brushing against hers. "Admit it. That was the best orgasm of your life."

"It was decent enough," she murmurs, and she kisses me. I cup the back of her head and wrap her hair around my wrist, right there with her underwear. "Got the job done."

"Sounds like all that talk about hating me was just bullshit, wasn't it?"

"I like your tongue. And your fingers. That's it."

"What about my cock?" I shove my free hand in my briefs and drop my head back when I think about how tight she's going to be around me. "Do you like that too?"

"I don't know." Emerson sits up and swings her legs on either side of my hips, straddling me. She rubs her pussy over the front of my briefs, and I hiss. "Guess we'll have to find out."

"Condom," I say, but it probably comes out like a garbled mess. She's rolling her hips and I'm seeing stars. Six seconds away from sinking into her right here, right now. "My wallet."

"You carry a condom around with you?"

"I like to be prepared. You should be grateful—otherwise we wouldn't be able to do this."

"That's not true." She climbs off me, and I watch the sway of her hips as she walks to my sweatpants. I stare at the shape of her ass as she bends down, looking at me over her shoulder. "We could just not use one."

I groan. "Don't say things like that. It's going to make me want to do this with you again."

"Too bad." The mattress sinks under her weight, and she kneels next to me. "Once is all you get, pretty boy." My cock twitches at the nickname and my cheeks turn pink. "Oh," she whispers, a mischievous glint in her eyes. "You like when I call you that, don't you?"

"Yeah. More than I'd like to admit." I swallow and grab her wrists, pulling her toward me so she's in my lap. "I do get off on this power dynamic of ours, but right now, I'm the one in control. Take off my briefs, Hartwell, and open your mouth."

TWENTY-ONE
EMMY

I'LL NEVER TELL him this, but Maverick Miller *did* give me the best orgasm of my life.

My body is still humming, and I feel weightless. Blissed out in and in some transcended state.

"Why are you smiling?" Maverick asks, a rasp that makes my nipples turn to points. "Did I do that?"

"I'm not smiling." I squirm on his lap and glance down at him, surprised to find him already looking at me. His skin is tinted pink. His hair is a mess, and there is a mark on the side of his neck where I pressed my thighs into him. "You're delusional."

He grins up at me and cups my cheeks. "You're fucking cute. I wish I had my phone so I could take a picture of you right now and make it my lock screen."

"You just want a photo of my tits."

"Not totally wrong, but I like this more." He adjusts our positions so he can reach up and kiss me. "Seeing you happy," he murmurs against my mouth.

In my twenties, I would've fallen for that line.

At thirty, I know it's a part of this fantasy we've stumbled into.

An hour of pretend before we go back to how we were earlier in the night: quips and barbs and two people who could not be more opposite.

"You'll never get me to smile," I say.

"But I can get you to come on my tongue. Some might say that's better than a smile."

Heat rolls through me at the thought of his hands between my legs. The slick glide of his fingers and the sparkle in his eye when he called me *Emmy girl.*

I'm not well versed in face sitting, but Maverick deserves an A-plus. A gold star for enthusiasm and delivery and audience participation.

"Satisfactory, remember?" I say, and his laugh is a rumble beneath me.

"Nice, I think you said." He pulls down on my bottom lip and presses his thumb on my tongue, just like he did with his fingers. "Are you going to let me fuck you?"

"Yeah," I manage to get out, and moisture builds between my legs. "We're definitely doing that."

Maverick leans back and puts his hands behind his head, a vision of lazy arrogance. My underwear is still wrapped around his wrist, and I wonder if he's going to try to take it back to his room with him.

"Whenever you're ready."

I roll my eyes but hook my fingers in the waistband of his briefs, desperate to feel him without any restrictions between us. I shimmy his underwear down his legs until they loop around his ankles, and my mouth pops open.

His cock is thick and hard. A long length, and easily the biggest I've ever seen. Pre-cum glistens on the head, and a smug part of me revels in knowing he enjoyed getting me off as much as I enjoyed him doing it.

"You absolute asshole," I whisper.

He strokes himself up and down. A dimpled smirk pulls at

the corner of his lips when I follow the bob of his hand. "Average, right?"

"You know there's not a damn thing about you that's average." I rest my palms on his chest and drag my nails down his skin, leaving little half-moon marks behind. "What do you want me to say? That you're not going to fit? Because I'm not sure you are."

"We'll get you there." He lets go of his cock and gives my hip two taps. "Go to the end of the bed and lie on your back."

I move at his command because the man is wielding a fucking *weapon.*

I scoot across the wrinkled sheets and prop my legs up. My neck hangs over the edge of the mattress, and I wait for what he's going to do next.

Maverick climbs off the bed and walks until he's standing above me. He strokes himself, fingers curled around his shaft, and I take a steadying breath.

"Do you still want to choke on my cock?" he asks, and there's a pang in my chest at his question. That he's taking the time to make sure I'm in agreement about something I said off-handedly and not rushing in without asking.

I nod, my eyes set on him. "I do."

"Do you trust me?"

I tip my head farther back, wanting to make my intent clear. "I trust you completely, Maverick."

His grin is stunning, a burst of joy that explodes into a thousand colors across his face.

I've never seen something so beautiful.

This is just sex, my head screams, a reminder I need as he runs his thick cock over my lips. *You're not going to fall for his charm.*

"Open up, Emmy girl. It's time for you to deliver on that promise."

I shiver at the affectionate name and open my mouth wider. Salty pre-cum sticks to my tongue, and I lick him from the base of his shaft to the tip eagerly. I hollow out my cheeks, and when he comes close to hitting the back of my throat, my eyes explode with tears.

"There you go." Maverick rests his large hand around my throat, and my pulse jumps at the pressure he adds. "You're doing so well."

He wipes the tears away from my cheeks with his thumb, and I don't bother to make this pretty.

It's sloppy. Drool hangs from the corner of my mouth and the sound of my gagging fills the room. I don't stop, taking him deeper until he bottoms out, then I cup his balls in my hand.

"*Fuck*," he mumbles, tugging on my hair. "I think that's enough."

"But I haven't choked yet." I put my mouth back on him and swallow. "You can give me more than that, can't you, hot shot?"

"Your compliments really help my confidence, Red." Maverick pulls out of me with a *pop*, and I blink up at him. "Look at you all messy. So beautiful."

"You did say you were going to make a mess out of me." I slip my hand between my legs and tease my sensitive clit with a gentle brush of my fingers. Tasting him turned me on. "What do you like, Maverick? What makes you feel good?"

"You," he says, and he hauls me across the bed until he settles against the pillows. "You're more than enough."

"Do you tell all the girls that?" I ask into his neck as he lies on his back and sets me on top of him, my legs on either side of his hips.

"No." He takes my hand in his and kisses my palm. "I've never told anyone that. You're the only one."

I know I'm in a fog of lust, but I believe him.

I hear the honesty in his words, and that terrifies me.

No one's ever made me feel like *the only one*, but somehow, in a hotel room high above the city of Chicago, I'm suddenly special.

"Condom?" I ask before the moment gets too heavy, and Maverick nods.

He rolls the latex down his length and lines up with my entrance. His eyes lock on mine, and there's a moment where we both hesitate, like the second he sinks into me, we know the dynamic between us is going to change.

"Fuck me," I whisper, and his eyes flash with heat. "Please."

He grips my thighs so tight, I know I'm going to be covered in bruises that match his fingerprints tomorrow. He lifts his hips, and the head of his cock pushes inside me. We groan in unison, and my breath gets tangled in my chest.

"Okay?" Maverick slurs, and he sits up so he can take my breast in his mouth. His teeth bite down on my nipple, and I sigh. "Want to get deeper, baby. Need to fuck you right."

Baby.

I like when he calls me that too.

It feels precious, like I'm adored.

And from the way he looks up at me with his cheek against my chest, I think I might be.

I tip my knees open wide and lower my hips, sinking down on him until the stretch becomes too much. Until I'm so full, my vision goes blurry and a warm and wonderful sensation starts to build in my stomach.

"I can't take anymore. It's too much," I say.

"*Shit.* I'm not even halfway in, Emmy," he says, and he drops his hand between my legs. His fingers touch my clit, and he uses my wetness to rub through the ache.

"Of course you aren't, you asshole," I say around a gasp, and he smiles against the curve of my shoulder.

"We're going to make it fit."

"How? Are you going to chop off four inches?"

His laugh is warm on my skin and his fingers work in a

slow, rhythmic circle that dulls the stretch to tolerable. He's too good at this, and I'm too close to the edge again.

"It's going to fit because this pussy is mine," he says, and the metal of his silver necklace makes me shiver as he cups me possessively. "Can I try again?"

"I want to do it," I say, and I blow out an exhale as I sink lower onto him. "*God.*"

"I love the names you call me," Maverick murmurs, and a laugh sneaks out of me. "That's it, Emmy girl. *Look.* Look at how well you take my cock."

I stare down at where we're joined, the slick slide of his finger and the thrust of our hips to match each other's intensity. He disappears completely inside me, and nothing has ever felt this incredible.

"Harder," I say, and I bend over him, my hands on either side of the pillow. "Fuck me harder, Maverick."

"You can claim you hate me all you want, Red." He slides one hand under my thighs and lifts me off of him, only to slam me back down. "But we can both feel how your pussy clenches around my cock. You love it when I make you come."

I do.

I do love it, and I feel myself teetering near that glorious high again.

I'm climbing closer and closer, and with every bump of his knuckles, every press of the heel of his palm, every tug on my hair and scrape of teeth down my neck, I come dangerously close to screaming his name, loud enough so the whole hotel knows who's making me feel *so damn good.*

"I think I'm going to—" I nod when he kisses just below my ear and sucks on the skin there. His fingers work in tandem with his cock, and I know I don't stand a chance of surviving. "*Maverick.*"

"So good, Emmy." He presses me tight against him, our chests fused together and our limbs intertwined. "Come on my cock. *Please.* I want to feel you."

I don't bother fighting it anymore; I let the wave crash over me. It pulls me out to sea as white-hot ecstasy burns through me.

My legs tremble and my shoulders shake. I squeeze my eyes shut, a failed attempt to preserve some of my dignity as I say his name again and again through the pleasure like I'm praying to him.

"Goddamn. You feel so good," Maverick groans into my hair, and he holds a handful of my ass. "Going to come in you, okay?"

"Yes," I beg, wanting him to reach the ledge with me. "Come for me, pretty boy."

His moan is long and low, and his grip slackens. He pulls his fingers away from me one by one as his legs spasm. A string of curses tumbles from his mouth when he pulses inside of me then stills.

"Holy shit," he pants, flinging an arm over his face. "I think I just got fucked to outer space."

"Where are the alien babies when you need them?" I ask, and he giggles like he's drunk. "You did most of the work." I ease myself off him, and I wince at the emptiness I feel. "I was just kind of there."

"Pretty sure your pussy did most of the work, Hartwell, squeezing me tight like that. Cunt of the year."

"Are you going to give me a medal?" I ask.

Maverick cracks an eye open and turns his head to look at me. "I might need to."

"Well." I blush and curl up on my side, not sure what happens now. "This was fun."

He chuckles and reaches for me, pulling me close. I rest my head against his chest and take a deep breath. "I need ten minutes to recoup, then I'll get out of your hair. If I try to walk to the elevator right now, my legs will give out."

"Ten minutes. I have a pint of ice cream waiting for me in

the freezer, and I'm going to be pissed if I don't get to eat it before I fall asleep."

"What's your favorite ice cream flavor?" Maverick runs his hands through my tangled hair and massages my scalp. An embarrassing sound leaves my body. "That's my question of the day because I can't think of much else."

"Chocolate chip. What about you?"

"Oreo." He yawns and drops his chin to the top of my head. "But I mean, come on. I'm not going to say no to any kind."

"Same." I trace the links on his necklace and sigh, bone-achingly tired and sated. "Are you a dog person or a cat person?"

"Dogs for sure, but I like both. Hudson keeps trying to get me to rescue one from the shelter where he volunteers, but I haven't taken that step yet."

"Why not?"

"I don't know. Doing what we do comes with so many uncertainties; I could get traded. I could sign with a different team in free agency. I don't have a whole lot of experience with animals, but letting a pet get adjusted only to uproot its entire life and move across the country seems cruel. I plan on adopting when I retire, whenever the hell that is."

"Speaking as someone who's been on four teams in six years, there is so much uncertainty." I stretch out my legs and wince at the soreness I feel between my thighs. "But dogs are the best."

"Four teams? Was that by choice?"

"Sort of. I crave change, and staying in the same spot for too long puts me on edge." I pause and run my finger up the line of his forearm. Over the tattoos and all the stories there. "Another was a conflict of interest that resulted in having to leave for another team."

"Your ex was a hockey player, wasn't he?" Maverick asks. I

push up on my elbow so I can look at him, surprised he figured it out. "It's not that hard to put together. You said you don't date hockey players. There was a conflict of interest. That comment on the plane yesterday about being down this road before. I figured it was because of a bad seed along the way."

"Yeah." I swallow. "He was."

"We aren't all terrible." He grins and tucks a piece of hair behind my ear. "Take me, for example."

"You've slept with half the women in this country."

"That is a gross exaggeration, Red, and I haven't been with anyone besides you in over a month."

"Really?"

"Mhm."

"Why not?"

"I don't know." Maverick pulls the used condom off his length and wrinkles his nose. "Been busy, I guess."

"I'm sure you'll get back on the horse soon." I pat his chest. "It's time for me to pee then eat. Which means it's time for you to get dressed and show yourself out, buddy."

"Fine, fine." He curls his fingers around my chin and brings my mouth to his. His lips brush against mine in a soft kiss. "Don't make things weird, Emmy girl."

"You're the one making it weird by calling me that when you're not inside me. I'm going to go back to pretending like you don't exist."

"Just the way I like it. By the time you get out of the bathroom, I'll be gone."

"Good. And leave my underwear." I stand up and put my hands on my hips. "They were expensive."

"As they should be. You deserve nice things." His gaze roams down my body, and he grins.

"What?" I ask, suddenly self conscious. "Why are you looking at me like that?"

"Need to commit this to memory. It's too good to forget."

I throw a pillow at his face and he laughs, reaching for his briefs. "Wait!" I exclaim. "I didn't see your ass tattoo."

"Too distracted by my average length?"

"God, I hate you." I spin my finger in a circle. "Show me?"

"Gladly." He turns around, and there on his right cheek is a peach. Orange and yellow and white, it stands out against his tan skin and the sculpted curve of his backside. "Thoughts?"

"Why the *hell* do you have a peach on your ass?"

"Long story, but I lost a bet to Dallas, who's from Georgia. He wanted me to get the state of Texas, in honor of his name, but that was an automatic no. So, we settled on a fucking peach."

"Wow. A peach on your peach. There are layers to that." I cover my mouth, but my smile is impossible to hide. "You're so weird."

He looks at me over his shoulder. "Made you smile again, though."

"You're dreaming."

"Feels like this whole thing has been a dream, to be honest."

I rub my hand across my chest and bite my bottom lip. "Yeah," I say softly. "Feels like it."

Maverick smiles, and he presses a kiss to my forehead. "Sweet dreams, Red."

An hour later, I'm nearly asleep when my phone buzzes next to me on the mattress. I open it up, bleary-eyed and on the edge of consciousness, and find a message from Maverick.

BANE OF MY EXISTENCE:

Attachment: 1 image

Finders keepers.

It's a photo of him, my underwear in his hand and his teeth sinking into the lace.

I throw my phone across the room, vowing to block his number first thing tomorrow morning.

TWENTY-TWO
MAVERICK

PROFESSIONAL STICK HANDLERS

ME

Closed toed shoes tonight.

EASY E

Can I come shirtless?

HUDSON

No.

G-MONEY

Pantsless?

HUDSON

No

EASY E

We're going to start calling you Daddy soon.

HUDSON

No

G-MONEY

Come on, Hud!!!! We beat Chicago!!! We deserve to celebrate a little!

HUDSON

By taking off your clothes?

Redheaded Assassin has left the chat
Easy E has added Redheaded Assassin to the chat

EASY E

I can play this game all day, Emmy.

Of all the places in the world I could've seen Emerson after we got back from Chicago, an ax-throwing outing labeled team bonding wouldn't have been my pick.

Somewhere with less weapons would've been ideal. A place where she can't throw something at my head if I look at her with bedroom eyes when she shows up in a pair of jeans I already know are going to drive me wild, but I didn't have a lot of say in the matter.

"Are you okay, Mavvy?" Hudson asks. He signs a waiver and hands the clipboard back to the teenage kid behind the desk. "You look a little pale."

"All good. Coach has had some unique ideas in the years that he's been with us here in DC, but this one might take the cake."

"It has something to do with trust. He mentioned we're not playing like we have each other's backs, but that's bullshit. I'd run through fire for you all, and I know you'd do the same for me."

"Of course we would." I look around the lobby and laugh. "What better way to develop trust than by giving a bunch of athletes some alcohol and an ax and seeing which one of us loses a finger first?"

"If it will get us out of our slump, I'm all for it. The game against St. Louis tomorrow is going to be tough. Whoever made our schedule hates us."

"Let's blame Ethan. He slept with some higher-up's granddaughter, and they're definitely fucking us over," I say. "Hey. Have you talked to Hartwell since we got back from Chicago?"

"No. We don't talk outside of practice, and after Coach canceled yesterday's morning skate so we could all have a break, I haven't heard from her. Last I saw her, she was fast asleep against the side of the airplane. She didn't even wake up when we had that rough landing. Must've been tired," Hudson says.

Tired or thoroughly fucked, I think, and I clamp down on my smile.

I saw the way she was walking up the stairs when we were boarding our flight home. When I asked her what happened, knowing full well it was my dick that caused her awkward gait, she flipped me off.

Normally, I would have already moved on after a hookup. I don't give the woman a second thought, but I can't get Emerson out of my head.

Every time I close my eyes, I see her naked and gagging on my cock.

I hear her moaning my name and saying *please*.

I feel her nails digging into my skin.

I've gotten nothing done in the two days we've been back, and I'm starting to think I'm going out of my mind.

She's hands down the hottest woman I've ever been with. I love that she didn't wait for me to give something to her—she knew what she wanted and she fucking *took it.*

It wasn't an act to show me she's adventurous in bed, either.

That's all her, and knowing I can't have her again makes me want her even more.

I blink out of my daydream and clear my throat. "Meanwhile, I hear you breathing and I'm wide awake. I don't miss the days when we had to share a room."

"You don't want to bunk with me again?" Hudson pouts. "I liked our sleepovers."

"Fuck no. I make sure we're on separate floors so your snoring doesn't haunt my dreams."

"Asshole." Hudson shoves my shoulder. "What are you doing after this?"

"Heading home. Why?"

"Riley, Connor and I are headed to the bar up the road for a drink. Want to come and play some pool for a bit?"

"That would be fun. Feels like I haven't hung out with you in forever."

"Because you haven't. Connor is pissed because this prick he played against in college just signed a massive deal with Miami and he's nervous about his own contract extension at the end of the season. Thought he could use some cheering up."

"Are you talking about Perkins? I hate that guy, and I'm in for a few rounds." My teammates file into the small lobby, and their bodies take up too much space. "Is Coach coming to this?"

"Doubt it. He's on dad duty this week."

"Bummer. He could've brought the tyke with him."

"I don't think they let kids in here. Seems like a liability."

"Not any more than Ethan and Grant with an ax," I counter, and I pull out my phone. "I'm going to see where Hartwell is."

ME

Hope you aren't skipping the mandatory team bonding, Red.

REDHEADED ASSASSIN

Miss me, Miller?

ME

Nah. I can still see you when I close my eyes.

REDHEADED ASSASSIN

I have no clue what you're talking about.

I'll be there in a second. The Metro broke down.

ME

It's freezing out.

I have a second vehicle parked in the garage at my place. You can borrow it.

REDHEADED ASSASSIN

No thanks. I don't like owing people things.

ME

Like your underwear?

REDHEADED ASSASSIN

I might kill you for those. They're my favorite pair.

ME

Interesting.

Mine too.

"What's so funny?" Hudson looks over my shoulder. "Did I miss a message in the group chat?"

"Nope." I click my phone off. "You ready to throw some axes?"

Before he can answer me, the door to the building opens. Emerson waltzes into the lobby in a pair of leather pants, boots that come up to her knees, and a sweater that hangs off her right shoulder.

It gives me a nice view of the bite mark I left on her neck the other night, and I grin at the sight of her.

"Is that Emerson Hartwell?" The kid behind the counter stands up, and his stool goes flying. "Oh my god. She's my favorite player in the league. Holy shit. Is she going to come over here? Can I say hi? Will she give me her autograph?"

"Ask her yourself. Hey, Red," I call out, and she glances my way. There's a half a second where I think her eyes sparkle, but then she blinks, and her usual cool indifference settles into place. "Come here. Someone wants to meet you."

She shuffles past the guys who all say hello to her. There are a couple of hugs. A couple of high-fives. She and Ethan do some sort of secret handshake that involves wiggling their fingers and bumping their hips, and I'm jealous of the attention everyone is getting.

"What's up?" she asks when she finally makes it to the desk.

"This is Kevin," I say, looking at his name tag. "He's a big fan of yours."

"Thank you so much."

"Do you think you could—" He gulps down a breath. "Sign something for me? That's not a legally binding waiver?"

"Of course."

She puts her swoopy signature on a personalized piece of paper and poses for a photo, her tongue out and her eyes closed. She looks so carefree right now with her wind-burned cheeks and the tug of a smile on her mouth, and it makes my chest hurt a little.

I nudge her shoulder after she finishes the paparazzi session. "You want to be on my team?"

"I'm with Grant. It would be dangerous if you and I were throwing at the same target. I might accidentally miss and cut off your hands."

"I thought you liked my hands," I say, dropping my voice low so only she can hear me. "At least, that's what it sounded like the other night."

Emerson narrows her eyes. "Don't start with me, Miller. I don't want to regret anything."

"You don't regret it?" I ask.

She pauses and pretends to brush a piece of lint off her sweater. "No. Do you?"

"Hell, no. I had a great time, and from this moment on, I swear to pretend nothing happened."

"You were supposed to pretend nothing happened days ago."

"Whoops." I laugh and take a step back. "Are you busy tonight? Hudson, Riley, Connor and I are heading out to play some pool. Do you want to come?"

She looks me up and down, and I wonder if she's thinking about the way she tipped her head back and opened her mouth. The drool on her cheek and the hand she slipped between her legs, wanting to touch herself while she sucked me off.

Fuck.

"Want to make things interesting?" Emerson asks.

"You have my attention."

"If I score more points than you, you give me back my underwear."

"It'll be a tragedy to part with them, but I'll entertain that option. What do I get if I win?"

"I'll come to the bar with you."

I stick out my hand. "You've got yourself a deal."

I've never heard Emerson laugh so much.

I'm not sure what the hell Grant is saying, but she thinks it's really funny, obviously.

She doesn't think *I'm* that funny, and I wish she did.

"Hey." Hudson snaps his fingers in my face, and I turn my attention back to our lane. "What is wrong with you? You missed an easy throw."

What *is* wrong with me?

I'd love to answer that question, but I wouldn't know where to start.

I don't know why I'm thinking about red hair and a secret hotel room meetup. Purple lace underwear and the feel of a five-foot-ten woman with curves for days in my arms.

It's probably because there's no distance between us. After my usual one-night stands, I can easily erase the memory because I never see them again.

That's not the case with Emerson.

I'm here and she's here, and the more I look at her, the more I remember.

That has to be it.

The only logical explanation for why my thoughts are so goddamn off-kilter.

"What's wrong is I prefer hitting things over throwing things." I stand with the ax above my head and give it a hard toss. It lands in the center of the wooden board, and I pump my fist. "That's what I'm talking about. Hey, Red. How's it going down there?"

"Not well," she calls out, and she drops her head back. "This is bullshit."

I leave my lane and walk over to her, laughing when I see that her ax landed wide right.

"You don't like not being anything but good at something, do you?" I ask.

"No." Emerson stares at the board. "I don't understand the technique. It goes against everything I've been taught as a hockey player."

"But a good way to get out any frustration you might have,

right?" I back off and give her some space. "Try again. Focus on the target. Imagine the board as a net."

Emerson huffs. She lifts the ax in the air and launches it forward. It doesn't hit the bullseye, but it comes closer than her last toss.

"Better," I say. "Nice job."

"I was envisioning your face as the target," she tells me. "Maybe it will help me win."

"You haven't checked the score?" I lift my chin toward the whiteboard we've all been updating as we play. Seymour is in the top spot, and Liam is right behind him. Riley is dead last, the poor fucker, and Emerson isn't doing much better than him. "You can't catch up, which means you've officially lost to me, Red. Looks like you're coming to the bar and I'm keeping—"

"Do *not* finish that sentence," she warns me.

"What are you keeping?" Grant asks. "Did you take something of hers? Stealing isn't cool, Mavvy."

"I accidentally shoved her gloves in my bag the other night when we were in Chicago. They're better than mine, and I want to keep them," I explain.

"Oh." Grant looks at Emerson, and he wrinkles his eyebrows. "What brand are they? Bauer is the only way to go. They're expensive as shit, but if you need a new pair, you should check them out. Make sure you get the Pro series, not the HyperLytes. Those suck."

"Thanks, Grant." She pats his shoulder, and he beams. "I'll keep that in mind since it seems like Miller doesn't understand what ownership means."

"I understand it perfectly. You're the one who doesn't understand Finders Keepers." I wink at her, and she scowls. "Enjoy your last few throws. You might be a loser on the board, Hartwell, but you're a winner in my book."

I hurry back to my lane and ignore the two middle fingers she gives me.

TWENTY-THREE
EMMY

THE BAR CONNOR leads us to is darker than Johnny's.

Smokier, too, and the stench of alcohol from the last forty years hangs in the air.

"We'll grab a table," Hudson says. "Can you get me a beer?"

"Sure." Maverick looks at Connor and Riley. "You boys want anything?"

"A water for me." Riley rubs his neck and closes his eyes. "My back still isn't right from that hit in Milwaukee, and I don't want to do anything to piss off my body before our game tomorrow."

"You haven't gone to see Lexi?" I ask, and even in the dim lighting, I can tell the tips of his ears turn pink at the mention of her name. "She's a miracle worker. My hamstring was acting up last week, and she massaged the pain right out of me."

"I don't want to bother her with something so silly. I'm doing some exercises I found online and using a heating pad. I'll be okay in a few days." Riley smiles. "Thanks for looking out for me, Emmy."

"I'll take a beer," Connor says, and the three of them head around the corner.

Maverick's fingers brush along my hip as he moves from my left side to my right and leans over the bar. "I didn't realize we were going somewhere that's been around since the Stone Age."

"What are you talking about? It's perfect. It reminds me of this bar back home I used to go to with my dad," I say.

"Michiganders don't give a fuck, do they?"

"I was there on Fridays at 3:00 p.m, not Saturday after midnight. He and his friends would get together once a week and talk about all the important stuff going on in the world: MLB spring training. Whether there should be more paid holidays. Which *Jurassic Park* movie is best."

"The only correct answer is the original one," Maverick says. "I'm not a film critic, but I think society can collectively agree that number three is a disgrace to the movie industry as a whole. It wasn't even believable."

"But a theme park with dinosaurs is?"

"Billionaires do weird shit, Hartwell."

"That's my dad's opinion too."

"I like the guy already. Did you participate in these spirited debates?"

"Nope. I ate my cheese pizza, drank my chocolate milk, and listened while they talked for ninety minutes. Gosh, I haven't been there in years. I wonder if it's still standing."

"Who knew you'd be in for a bit of nostalgia when you trudged down here after an ax-throwing defeat? You might end up having fun."

"With Hudson, probably. Not you," I joke, but my mind flashes back to the hotel room in Chicago.

Maverick, telling me he *doesn't share.*

Maverick, with eyes as dark as coal and his hand around my throat.

Maverick, saying *that's so good.*

There's not enough alcohol in this bar to get the sounds he makes when he comes out of my head. To forget how those tattoos look in the moonlight and between my legs.

"You okay?" he asks roughly, like he's thinking about that night too.

"Fine." I look at the liquor selection instead of him. "Do you think this place has olives?"

"If they don't, I brought some." Maverick digs around his black coat and pulls out a glass jar.

I stare at the jar then up at him. "Where did you get those? Do you carry olives in your pocket?"

"I popped into the bodega on our way here and grabbed some."

"Why would you do that?"

"Because I remembered you said you like martinis. Can't make a good drink without a garnish." He sets the jar down and nudges it toward me. "Take them home with you."

I pick up the jar and run my thumb over the label. It's the expensive brand, the one I splurge on once a month when I want to spoil myself.

Knowing he didn't pick the cheap ones makes my heart skip a beat.

"This is for me?" I ask softly.

"Yeah." Maverick frowns. "I didn't think it was that big of a deal when I bought them. It's not a marriage proposal or anything. You can throw them at me if you want. I wouldn't—"

"Thank you," I interrupt him, and his eyes widen. The corner of his mouth turns up in a smile, and the dimple on his right cheek makes me blush. "I appreciate this. It's very considerate of you."

He pretends to tip a hat. "You're very welcome."

"I'll take a gin martini," I tell the bartender when he comes over, and I hold the olives tight to my chest. "Please."

"Three beers and a water for me," Maverick says.

He pulls out his wallet and lays down a couple of twenties, overpaying for the cheap bottles by a mile, and we wait for our drinks.

I tap my fingers against my thigh. He leans his forearms on the ledge of the bar and stares at the football game playing on the television in the corner. It's quiet, and it makes me anxious.

"Are you ready for St. Louis on Thursday?" I ask, feeling the need to break up the silence. It's awkward and heavy, both of us wanting to say something but not knowing what it is. "They're a good team."

I cringe.

A good team?

Who the hell am I?

I sound like I've never talked about sports before when really I spent all afternoon studying the Pelicans' statistics.

"A great team." Maverick rubs his jaw, and there's a line of scruff there. Dark hair he hasn't shaved since his face was buried between my legs, and I wonder what it would feel like on the inside of my thighs. "Back-to-back Stanley Cup champs."

"They're young, aren't they?" I ask, even though I already know the answer.

The average age of the team is twenty-four, but I'm going to keep asking questions if it means Maverick keeps talking to me like he did before he fucked me into oblivion.

"Second youngest team to reach the playoffs, and the youngest team in history to win it all," he tells me. "I like what they're doing out there. There's no superstar on their roster. They've got a lot of talented guys, but one person doesn't outshine the rest. I was hoping that's how it would go here when I got drafted, but we're not there yet."

"This season isn't as bad as the last couple of years, is it?" I take a deep breath and get ready to ask the question that's been on my mind lately. "Have you seen a weakness I could work on that would be beneficial to the team? An area on the ice I can improve in? I'm not dragging us down, am I?"

"What?" Maverick tugs on my belt loop so I can face him, and I wish he'd keep his fingers there. "What are you talking about?"

"I don't know." I play with the ends of my hair, needing a distraction from his intense stare. "You all were playing well the first few weeks of the season. Then I got here, and everything turned to shit. You said so yourself on the plane."

"That is *not* what I said on the plane, and I'd never blame you for things turning to shit. That's how sports work, Hartwell. It's an ebb and flow. You know that."

"We're doing more ebbing than flowing right now. We're drowning."

"The reason we were playing better earlier in the season is because we were in better shape than any of the other teams coming out of the preseason. Coach gives us a regimented strength training plan to follow during the summer, and we all take it seriously. We don't lose a lot of our fitness in the off season, and we're able to steal a few wins right off the bat. Now everyone else is caught up."

"Oh." I bob my head. "That makes sense."

"Is something else going on?" he asks, and he takes a step toward me. "I know we're not friends, but you can talk to me about things."

What if I want him to be my friend?

What if I want to take back everything I said on that plane ride?

"No. Yes." I shrug and try to look past his shoulder, but he's too tall. "After the last couple of games, I've been wondering if I should've stayed in the ECHL. If coming up was a mistake."

"Are you happy, Emerson?" Maverick asks. "Does playing in this league bring you joy?"

"Yes," I say without hesitation.

"Then it wasn't a mistake."

"Now that I'm here and living out this dream, I just... I don't want to love it any less," I confess. "Hockey has been a constant for me, and I don't know what I'd do without it."

"That's how life and sports go. Some days you're frustrated as hell, and some days you want to throw in the towel. But as long as it still makes your heart beat, you have to keep showing up. You don't give up on the things you love just because they get hard."

I grip the counter, and I'm caught off guard by how powerful his words are.

Maverick is right.

I've been feeling that I'm not worthy just because I've been frustrated lately, but that frustration is normal. It comes with loving something deeply, and I refuse to give up on this opportunity.

"I didn't expect a pep talk tonight," I say, and I look at him. "I get in my head sometimes. Thank you for validating me."

"Have you talked to our sports psychologist, Dr. Jenn? She's a great resource."

"No, I haven't. Have you?"

"I have a standing appointment on Wednesdays, whether in the arena or virtually if we're on the road. Being a professional athlete is really fucking difficult, but remember what I told you? You're not alone."

"Yeah." I smile at the bartender when he hands me my drink. I open the jar of olives and drop two in the glass. "It doesn't feel like I am anymore."

"You are *not* taller than me," Maverick challenges.

"I'm an inch taller," Hudson argues. "At least."

"Bull fucking shit! I'm listed at six-four and you're barely six-three."

"I've grown in the last year."

"That's not even possible."

"Boys," I say, and they both whip their heads to look at me. "There's an easy way to settle this. Take off your shoes and stand back-to-back."

"This is going to be good." Riley grins.

"I'm not sure who I want to be right," Connor adds.

"Hudson," Riley says. "Definitely Hudson."

Maverick leaps off his chair, eager to prove a point, and kicks off his shoes. One goes flying in the air and the other hits Connor in the shoulder.

Hudson moves slower. He bends down and carefully unlaces his Converse and sets them neatly to the side.

"You're going down, motherfucker." Maverick rolls his shoulders back and puffs out his chest. "You're the judge here, Red."

"Why am I involved in this?" I ask.

"Because it was your idea." Hudson leans back and stands up straight. "And you're an impartial party. Every other woman in this bar would give Maverick the win so they could sleep with him. You won't do that."

Been there, done that, I think, and Maverick smirks.

"Fine." I finish the last of my drink and stand next to them. My eyes bounce to the tops of their heads. "Hudson is taller."

"*What?* There's no way. Do it again," Maverick urges.

"Sorry, pretty boy. You're not the tallest one on the team anymore."

"I don't believe you." Maverick crosses his arms over his chest. "We're using a tape measure at the arena tomorrow."

"Are you sure you want to use a tape measure?" I ask, and the guys burst out laughing. "You might be disappointed."

"We're going to use every tape measure in the building, and you assholes are going to be wrong." Maverick scoops up one of his high-top Nikes, slips it back on his foot, and looks at me. "Want to play a round of pool?"

I check the time on my phone. It's only eight, and Piper mentioned she was meeting up with some work colleagues tonight. The idea of sitting at home alone sounds miserable, and I'm having fun.

It wouldn't hurt to hang out here a little longer.

"Okay," I agree, and his eyes light up. "One round."

"See you soon," he tells Riley, Connor, and Hudson, and I follow him to the table in the back of the room. "Am I really shorter than him? Or are you messing with me?"

"Hudson was standing on his toes," I admit. "You're still taller."

"I knew it. That bastard is inches shorter than me on a good day." Maverick racks the balls. "Do you want to break?"

"You can do it," I tell him, and I hand him a cue off the wall.

He sinks in a solid and motions me forward. "Have you ever played?"

"No," I say, but it's a blatant lie. My dad taught me when I was six and could barely see over the table. "Will you show me?"

"Sure. Come here."

I maneuver around until I'm standing in front of him. There's barely any room in this corner, but he doesn't back up.

I don't push him away, either.

"What should I do first?" I ask, and his eyes bounce to my mouth.

"Turn around. Face the table," he says, and I spin. "Lean forward."

I bend over the edge, my forearms on the felt and my hips behind me. The curve of my ass brushes against the front of his jeans, and he inhales sharply.

Maverick rests one hand on my waist and the other on the

cue, on top of mine. He crowds my space, his chest against my back, and there's nowhere for me to go.

"Which pocket are you aiming for?"

"The far corner," I tell him. His thumb rubs over my knuckles, distracting me, and I swallow.

"Good choice. Pull the stick back and line up your shot."

I nod. "Like this?"

"Perfect Emmy," he murmurs, and it's like I've touched a live wire.

Every part of me ignites, and I'm electrocuted by the deep rasp of his voice and the heat of his body on mine. His cock presses into me, half-hard, and I'm transported back to Chicago.

His praise and the mumbled words in my neck. The way we slotted together so perfectly and the feel of his body under mine.

"Now what?" I whisper.

"Now you hit it." His mouth brushes against my ear. "Can you do that?"

"Yeah," I breathe out, and I pull back the cue.

Years of playing does nothing to help me. Not when I'm disoriented as hell and turned on by his hands. The ball knocks off the side of the table and spins away from the pocket.

"That was a great try," he murmurs, and the hand on my hip slides across my stomach. It's so soft, I might have dreamed it. "You'll get it next time."

"It's your turn." I look at him over my shoulder, and his eyes are as dark as night. He's watching me, and when I bite my bottom lip, he drops his head back. "Unless you don't want to play."

"I want to play. I want to play very, very badly." Maverick squeezes his eyes shut and taps my hip. I think we both understand that he's not talking about pool. "Maybe this was a bad idea."

"Yeah. Maybe."

I step away from him, but he grabs my elbow and spins me to face him. Our chests knock against each other, and he cups the back of my head.

"What superpower do you wish you had?" he asks, and I blink up at him.

"Why are you asking me about superpowers?"

"Because it's distracting me from thinking about bending you over that table and fucking you into the felt. From sitting you on the edge and eating you out. These are things I'm not supposed to think about, but I am. And it's driving me insane."

"Oh." I lick my lips, and his eyes track the glide of my tongue. "Since we're not talking about *that*, if I had to pick a superpower, it would be flying. What about you?"

"Mind reading," he says around a strangled exhale. "So I could know how much you like my cock."

"I hate it," I say, and his laugh is low. Sexy and infuriating. "Worst I've ever seen."

"Thought so." He cups my cheek and smiles. I don't pull away. "What's your question, Red?"

"When is your birthday?"

"June fifteenth. When is yours?"

"August sixth."

"So you're a—"

"Everything okay over here?" Hudson asks from behind us, and we spring apart.

"Yeah," Maverick answers, almost falling over as he steps away from me. "All good."

"Who's winning?"

"We haven't gotten very far," I say. "I like to take my time and make sure I'm getting the best shot."

"Same," Maverick agrees, and he glances at me. "Being thorough is the only way to do it."

Hudson looks between us and frowns. "What am I missing?"

"Not a thing, man." Maverick clasps his shoulder and walks backwards away from us. "I'm going to hit the restroom. Anyone need anything?"

"Nope," I say, and he disappears.

"You two seem like you're getting along," Hudson says. "Are you friends now or something?"

I drag my thumb along my cheek, the spot where Maverick just touched. "Or something."

TWENTY-FOUR
EMMY

OUR LUCK HAS TURNED AROUND.

After beating St. Louis at home last week, we went on to defeat Calgary and Minnesota.

I scored my first goal in a Stars jersey, and it seems like we've gotten over the slump we had fallen into.

We have a game against Boston tomorrow afternoon, and while the rest of the team is planning to head to the Seaport for dinner, I'm opting for a night in at the hotel to recharge.

"You're not coming?" Piper asks over speakerphone as I scan the menu sitting on the desk in my room. "Lexi agreed to come out, and that girl *never* hangs out when the boys are around."

"Sorry, Piper. I need to shower and stretch, and with an early puck drop tomorrow, I want to catch up on sleep."

"Fine." She laughs at something on the other end of the line. "Text me if you need me, Emmy."

We hang up, and before I can toss my phone on the pillows and power down for the night, it lights up with a text message.

BANE OF MY EXISTENCE:

No dinner?

ME

Do you know everything about everyone?

BANE OF MY EXISTENCE:

I'd like to say yes, but Piper just told us you're bowing out.

ME

I'm tired.

BANE OF MY EXISTENCE:

I'm not going either.

ME

Why not? You always go to dinner.

BANE OF MY EXISTENCE:

Love how you keep tabs on me, Red.

Spicy food makes me sick.

There's a french fry restaurant up the road. They have a dozen dipping sauces.

Want me to place an order and bring it over, Potato Girl?

I stare at Maverick's messages and gnaw on my bottom lip.

I should say no.

It would be a bad idea.

Inviting him over feels like an invitation to hook up again. We had insane chemistry in the bedroom, and as much as I said *just once*, it's going to be hard to ignore that attraction.

But maybe I can try.

ME

Room 517.

BANE OF MY EXISTENCE:

See you soon.

Thirty minutes later, I open the door before Maverick has a chance to knock. I drag him inside and lock the deadbolt behind him, checking the peephole to make sure none of our teammates spotted him loitering outside my room.

"Did you miss me, Hartwell?" Maverick grins and kicks off his shoes. "You're very eager to see me."

"I'm hungry."

"For what, exactly?"

I narrow my eyes and take the bag from his hold. "French fries."

"Weird synonym for my dick, but okay," he jokes.

"You're two seconds away from being banished," I warn him. "And I'm going to keep the food."

"Sorry. I got all the jokes out of me." He peels off his hoodie and drops it on top of his shoes. He walks into the room and looks at the two queen beds. "Please tell me one of these is for sleeping and the other is for stuffing our faces. I want to murder those fries."

"Duh." I shuffle past him and sit on the mattress closest to the door, dropping the food in the middle of the bed. "That's why I put a towel out."

"Smart girl." Maverick sits opposite me and rubs his hands together. "I didn't know what kind of sauce you would be partial to, so I got one of everything."

"*Everything*? What are we talking here? Ketchup? Spicy ketchup?"

"Come on, Red." He chuckles and shakes his head. "We're talking pimento cheese. Roasted garlic. Smoked chipotle. Herbed ranch. Do you want me to keep going?"

My mouth waters. "I want you to shut up and show me all these choices."

Maverick unloads two Styrofoam boxes from the bag.

There's a mountain of fries in the first one, and the second has a dozen individual cups he arranges in a neat line on the towel.

"You first," he says.

"You paid for it. You should start."

"I've been there before, and you should do the honors. Roasted garlic is my personal favorite, but you can't go wrong with any of them."

I pop the top off the cup he points to and dip two fries in the sauce. I shove them in my mouth and groan. My eyes roll to the back of my head and I reach for another handful before I've even swallowed.

"Delicious," I say.

"What was that? I couldn't understand you through the heathen bite you took."

I throw a napkin at him but he catches it mid-air. "Forgive me for being starving."

"Eat up then, Hartwell. I normally put back a large by myself, so it's nice to share the carbs with someone else for once."

I open the cup with pimento cheese and almost melt at the smell. "You don't like spicy food?"

"Nope. Not my thing. I've tried dishes that other people recommend, but I end up sick." Maverick shrugs and reaches into the bag. "I was a PB&J and chicken tenders kid. I've gotten better as an adult, and I make an effort to branch out when we're traveling to try local restaurants."

"You're missing out on so much."

"I know I am. Are you going to do room service for dinner? The fries can't be all you eat."

"Yeah. I was planning on eating a little later. The grilled chicken and veggies looked good." I stand and walk to the desk, picking up the menu and handing it to him. "Do you want anything?"

His mouth pops open, and there's a drop of sauce hanging

near his chin. "Emerson Hartwell. Is this an invitation to join you for dinner? Is the world ending?"

"You brought fries. I can at least return the courtesy of a mediocre hotel meal."

"I'd love to, but I'm going to need a few minutes. Gotta let the spuds settle first."

"How about in an hour?" I sit back on the mattress and lean against the pillows. "Does that work with your digestive system?"

"So kind of you to ask. An hour is perfect." He pops another fry in his mouth and looks at me. "Are you excited for your first NHL game in Boston?"

"Yeah. We get to play in the oldest arena in the league surrounded by the most passionate fans, and it feels like I'm finally finding my groove on the ice." I cross my ankles and put my hands behind my head. "What about you?"

"I fucking love Boston. I always have my best games of the season here."

"Really?"

"Mhm. I feed off the negative energy they throw my way. The fans can boo all they want. I'm still going to score." He wipes his hands with a napkin and chucks it toward the trash can. "I hope you can score tomorrow too."

There's a moment of quiet between us. Out of my peripheral vision, I see Maverick getting comfortable on the pillows next to me. The bed shifts, and I let out a shallow breath.

"Do you think it's interesting that after our night in Chicago, we suddenly go on a win streak?" I ask softly.

"It is interesting," he agrees. I dare myself to turn my chin so I can look at him, and he's already staring at me. "I fuck you, then you score your first goal? Talk about coincidence."

"Yeah. Coincidence." I laugh, and my nipples pebble under my shirt. I lick my lips, and I swear his hand inches closer to my leg over the top of the sheets. "Do you think we should—"

"Do it again?" Maverick finishes for me. "It could be considered research."

"You're into science now?"

"When it comes to your pussy, Red, I'm Bill-fucking-Nye."

It's silly to think that one night together changed the trajectory of our team.

There's no *actual* correlation to his dick, my ability to score goals, and our win streak.

But I'm curious.

"Same rules apply," I say. "You leave as soon as we're finished, and this night never happened."

"Any other demands?" he asks. He reaches out and tugs me toward him, his mouth nearly on mine. "I want to make sure I beat my satisfactory rating."

"Faster this time." I thread his silver chain through my fingers and run my thumb over the links. "And I'd like to wear some of your jewelry again."

Maverick's eyes flash bright with longing, and heat spreads across my skin.

"Maybe my next tattoo will be the word *mine* on the back of my right hand." His fingers dance up my neck and curl around my throat. "So you know who you belong to when you're with me."

"Show me," I whisper. "Show me I'm yours for the night, Maverick."

TWENTY-FIVE
EMMY

MAVERICK CRASHES his mouth against mine with so much intensity, it's like he's afraid I'm going to take back what I said.

I'm not.

I want to be consumed by him.

This kiss is exactly like the first time. Rough. Hot and messy like we're at war with each other, and I sink into the bite of his teeth and the tug on the ends of my hair. The scrape of his nails down my back and the smooth, easy way he moves me so I'm on top of him, one leg on either side of his.

I've missed this.

Not *him*, but intimacy with someone else.

The ache of satisfaction when something feels so good, you want to scream about it. A hand other than your own and the fire that stirs inside you when you reach divine bliss.

I've always been a sexual woman, someone who knows what she wants and isn't afraid to voice it. I've had partners criticize my desires and shrug off the need for bedroom compatibility.

I'm a firm believer that a good sex life—one built on trust, honesty, and respect when you're at your most vulnerable—is important. It tells you things about a person, and what I know about Maverick after just one time is that he can give me exactly what I want.

An hour where I can shut off my brain. A moment in time when I feel beautiful and powerful and on top of the fucking world.

I don't have to be a professional athlete who smiles in front of cameras and busts her ass in the gym and on the ice. Who pushes herself to the brink of exhaustion again and again because it's what's expected of me.

I can be a mindless, boneless woman worthy of the highest pleasure.

"Do you have a condom?" I ask before I kiss the corner of his mouth. "Please tell me you have a condom."

Maverick grips the back of my head and a low laugh rumbles out of him. "Of course I have a condom. I put a new one in my wallet after Chicago. I was feeling optimistic about there being a second time."

"Thank god."

"Probably my favorite nickname you have for me."

I roll my eyes and dig into his pocket. A frantic need pulses through me as I pull out the leather wallet and sort through his credit cards and ID.

I have to have him.

I stop when I see a picture tucked behind his black AMEX.

"You carry around a photo of June?" I ask.

"Yeah." He traces the picture of her with high pigtails and her two front teeth missing, and my heart nearly cracks in two. "I told you she's my favorite person in the world."

"Goddamn you." I fist the cotton of his shirt and give him a little shake. "Why do you have to be so goddamn hot and such a nice guy?"

Maverick smiles. A dimple, a flush of red on his cheeks. "You hate that I'm a nice guy, don't you?"

"I despise it."

"This would be so much easier if I was an asshole, wouldn't it? Then you could pretend you want to fuck me because you hate me, not because I know how to treat you right. Because I know how to treat you like you deserve." His fingers toy with the strap of my tank top, and he drags it down my arm, all the way to my elbow. "We both know two times isn't going to be enough."

"It's more than enough," I say, and his laugh is sin on my skin. "Two times too many."

"All right, Emmy girl. I'll play your game." Maverick plucks the foil packet from behind a wad of cash and chucks his wallet at the wall. "Only because I'm not afraid to admit I want you so damn bad."

Our shirts land in a heap on the floor. My eyes roam down his chest, and I sigh.

"It's really unfair how good you look," I say under my breath.

"I could say the same about you." He puts one hand on the small of my back and the other on my stomach, sitting up so he can suck on my nipple. "I'm usually more of an ass guy, but I could touch your tits all day long."

"I wouldn't be opposed to that." I spread my legs wider, and the head of his cock presses into my shorts. "Touch all you want."

"Did you like what I did last time?" Maverick switches to the other side of my chest. His tongue swirls around the peak of my nipple, and I groan. "Anything you'd change?"

"Now is not the time for a survey, Miller." I close my eyes and reach between us, adjusting the bulge of his length so I can drag myself over it. "*Oh.* I like that."

"Think you can get your first one while you still have shorts on?" He massages my breast, and I rock forward. "I bet you can."

"Why am I doing all the work?" I huff and roll my hips,

searching for the friction I crave. "You have two hands. And a tongue."

"Because watching you try to fuck yourself on me is hot as hell, even though we both know you're going to need more. Three fingers, right? And every inch of my cock."

Words are impossible to find. I blow out a shaky exhale and grind against the fabric of his clothes, a slow swell of pressure building inside me.

"There you go," Maverick whispers, and he brushes a piece of hair out of my face. "Stain my shorts. Make me walk back to my room with your cum all over them."

"I've never—"

"Come on someone's lap before? You do it so beautifully, Emmy girl. *Fuck.* When you're close, I want you to pull your shorts to the side, okay? I want to see you when you come."

I hold onto his shoulders and dig my fingers into his muscles. I'm uncoordinated and off-balance, rotating my hips again and again until I find the perfect angle where the head of his cock pushes against my clit.

My legs shake, trembling in a way that makes it difficult to reach down and move the wet fabric aside.

"Look at that pussy. That's so good, Emmy." Maverick kisses the top of my chest then sinks his teeth into the curve of my breast. I cry out, the stimulation almost too much to bear before he licks over the bite marks with his tongue. "All of it, baby. I want all of it."

I bury my face in the crook of his neck and muffle my moan as I explode in bursts of color. I squirm against him and he lifts his hips a quarter of an inch, rubbing against me so I don't leave anything behind.

Before I can understand where I am or how I got there, my shorts are off and I'm naked on top of him. The air is cool on my sweat-soaked skin, and the world comes back into focus.

Maverick is watching me with one palm wrapped around

his cock. He pumps himself twice before he stops to rip open the condom and roll it down his length.

I sit up on my knees, hovering above him, and our eyes meet.

"Take me to church, Emmy," he murmurs. His hands run up my thighs and squeeze my hips. "Please."

"I didn't think you were a religious guy," I whisper, and I sink down on him in a bleary fog.

"I'm not." Maverick bites the soft skin near my shoulder as I take him another inch deeper, and my breath catches in my throat. "But I imagine you're what heaven feels like, so I'm a converted man."

The only sound in the room is the gentle slap of his hips meeting mine until I'm fully seated on him. Until I'm full and warm and drunk on the shape of his smile and the flash of heat in his eyes.

He takes his time snaking his left hand up my body, touching and teasing me until he reaches my neck. He closes his fingers around my throat, tighter than last time, and I give him a silent nod that tells him it's okay.

"You're incredible," he says, thrusting into me.

"You're saying that because your dick is inside me."

"I've thought it since the first time I saw you."

"You're lying."

"Am not." Maverick lifts me off of him in a single swoop and lays me on my stomach, my ass in the air. "I've thought about your curves. Your legs. All your strong muscles and your razor-sharp wit, and I've been dreaming about you for days. *Fuck*, Emmy. You're perfect."

Perfect.

I'm *perfect*.

Another word no one's ever called me, and I hold it close to my chest.

He slams into me, and I lose my mind. It's possessive.

Claiming, and exactly what I wanted. Maverick is unrelenting, thorough, and he touches me everywhere he can reach.

His movements turn ragged, and a soft groan tells me he's close. He reaches around my hip and presses on my clit with his thumb.

I look at him over my shoulder, desperate to see more of him, and I wish I hadn't.

He's beautiful, with his hair sticking up in all directions and his parted lips. With labored breathing and the pink marks on his skin that are going to turn into little purple bruises.

All because of me.

"See something you like?" he asks with a sly grin.

"No." I shake my head. "Not a damn thing."

"I love it when you lie." He tips his head back toward the ceiling, and the muscles in his arms strain. "How close are you? I'm hanging on by a fucking thread."

"Close. Just keep doing—*fuck, Maverick*. Right there."

"One more, Emmy girl. Give me one more."

I hate that my body responds to him.

I hate that a second orgasm sneaks up on me, his name a moan on my lips.

I hate that I smile when I hear him follow me over the edge, *Emmy, Emmy, Emmy* a whispered prayer in my ear as his legs shake and his hands fall away from my body.

Maverick collapses on top of me in a daze. I roll out from under him and try to catch my breath.

"If that doesn't help me have a good game," I pant, "then nothing will."

He wraps an arm around my waist and pulls me against his chest. "We better both get hat tricks. Top Ten on ESPN."

"We might have used up all our energy." I twist onto my side and look up at him. His eyes are closed, and for half a second, I think he might be asleep. "We didn't think this through."

"There was a study on endorphins and female athletes," he mumbles. "They said sex aided their performance."

"Who is they?"

"I don't know." He waves a lazy hand in the air. "Them."

I huff out a giggle. "Them is very smart."

"Very smart," he agrees. "You have to ask the question of the day. I'm spent."

"And I'm not? Two orgasms, Miller. I could fall asleep standing up."

Maverick opens one eye. "Did I earn another satisfactory?"

"Acceptable," I tell him. "Don't get too cocky."

"It's always good to have room for improvement."

Nothing about his performance needs improving, but I keep that to myself.

"What's your biggest fear?" I ask.

"Wow. Getting deep with the psychological questions after I got deep in you. I like your style, Red."

I grab a pillow from behind me and hit him square in the jaw. "I'm not playing your game anymore."

"Don't ruin my pretty face!" Maverick hugs me tight and kisses my collarbone. "I'm only trying to make you laugh. Did it work?"

"No," I say, but I clamp down on a smile.

"My biggest fear is the ocean. I love pools and lakes and going to the beach, but the ocean terrifies me. It's too big and too unknown. I barely put my toes in because I'm afraid some sea creature is going to snatch me away."

"That would be a sucky way to go. Imagine an eel getting you."

"What's your biggest fear?" he asks.

"Snakes. I can't even see one in a movie. I'll have nightmares for days." I shiver. "God, they're disgusting."

"So don't leave a rubber snake out to scare you? Got it."

Maverick trails his hand down my arm then back up. "If you could live anywhere in the world, where would it be?"

"Somewhere warm, like a private island in the Caribbean. But I'd also want to have a summer home in England. Is that allowed?"

"Of course it's allowed. It's our game. You can have as many houses as you want."

"Where would you live? A city, I bet. You strike me as a big city guy with Prada peacoats and Armani suits."

"Nah. I'd like to live in the mountains. Crisp air. Wide open skies. No neighbors for miles. It would be heaven."

"Really?" I prop my chin up on his chest and touch his cheek. "That's a surprise."

"No one wants to be predictable, Red. Where's the fun in that?" Maverick yawns. "I know I said ordering food sounded like a good idea, but I'm going to head back to my room. I'm exhausted."

"Same. Rain check on dinner?" I ask, and he smiles.

"Definitely." He untangles our limbs and climbs off the bed. He pulls off the used condom and ties it in a knot before dropping it in the trash can. "Do you have your alarm set?"

"Yeah." I stretch out my legs and sigh. "Thanks for a good night."

"Right back at you. We'll see the results of our experiment tomorrow."

"What happens if we win again?"

"I guess we'll have to fuck a third time, just to be sure," he says, putting on his clothes.

"And if we lose?"

"Is it really losing if we fuck away the disappointment?"

I laugh and nudge his thigh with my foot, pushing him toward the door. "Good night, pretty boy."

Maverick bends down and kisses my forehead, just like he did the last time we were together. His lips linger on my skin, and my heart skips a beat when he's slow to pull away.

"Night, Emmy girl. Sweet dreams."

TWENTY-SIX
MAVERICK

SLEEPING with Emerson twice accidentally turns into a third time (on a warm night in Florida) then a fourth (in New York City after the heater in her room stopped working).

Around our teammates and on the ice, everything between us is exactly the same.

She still rolls her eyes at me and acts like I'm the biggest pain in her ass. I still try to make her laugh and am smugly satisfied when I get half a smile out of her.

When we're together behind closed doors, it's fucking *electric*.

I've never wanted someone the way I want Emerson—repeatedly.

Consistently.

Every second of every day.

The best part?

We keep winning, and as a superstitious motherfucker, I need to find a way to convince her this needs to be an every night thing.

We head into early December with an eight-game win streak. I'm playing the best hockey of my career, and the league hit me with a no-notice drug test last week.

I almost called the commissioner to tell him I don't need performance enhancing drugs when I'm having the best sex of my life, but I figured that would open up a line of questioning I really don't want to answer.

"Finish your warm-ups," Coach calls out. "We're starting in five minutes."

I stretch my hamstring and grimace at the tightness in my leg. It's been sore since I fucked Emerson against the window with the Empire State Building behind us two days ago, and I'm trying my best to keep it loose so no one asks why I'm limping.

Worth it, though.

I scan the rink, looking for her red hair and her snarky smile, but I can't find her anywhere.

She's usually the first one on the ice, and after six weeks on the team, she's never been late.

I grab my phone from my duffle bag and fire off a quick text to her.

ME

Knock knock.

Who's there?

Not Hartwell.

Not Hartwell, who?

Not Hartwell, because she isn't at practice.

Are you alive, slacker?

"Is there something going on in your life that's more important than practice, Miller?" Coach asks. I look up, and half the team is staring at me. "Do we need to revisit the personal devices policy? I could put it in a picture book. Will that help you understand it better?"

My cheeks flame, and I throw my phone back in my bag

before he can yank it out of my hands and read the incriminating messages before the stupid knock-knock jokes.

The ones where I tell her I'm still thinking about her. The photo of her in the shirt she stole from me in Miami, sprawled out on her bed with her hand between her legs.

I should probably delete that, but she looks so damn hot.

"Sorry, Coach. It's Hartwell. She's not here," I say, and the rink goes quiet.

Grant freezes midway through his groin stretch. Liam lifts up his mask. Ethan pulls off his gloves, and Riley drops his stick.

"What do you mean she's not here?" Coach asks.

"She's usually twenty minutes early, but I can't find her," I say.

"Holy shit," Seymour says. "I knew something was off when I got on the ice. What if she was murdered? I've been listening to a lot of true crime podcasts lately, and over seventy-five percent of the women knew their killers."

"I can't even kill a spider. How are people out there murdering other human beings then sitting down at the breakfast table like it's not a big fucking deal?" Connor shivers. "That creeps me out."

"What if the Metro crashed? Oh, hell. Maybe she got pushed onto the tracks. That happened at Federal Triangle last week," Ethan says.

"Sometimes she runs to the arena," Grant tells us. "She might have gotten kidnapped."

"All of you need to stop." Hudson looks at me, and he's the only one being rational right now. "Did you call her?"

"Can I?" I ask, and Coach sighs.

"Fine," he says, and I know I have eight seconds before he confiscates my phone for good.

I scramble for my bag. My palms are clammy, and when I call her, it goes straight to voicemail. I try two more times, and there's still no answer.

"She's not picking up," I tell the guys, and someone gasps.

"Try Piper," Liam grumbles.

I find her contact info in my phone, but it goes to voicemail too. "No luck there either."

"What if someone hurt *both* of them?" Grant asks. "This could be sabotage."

"Enough with the dramatics." Coach rubs his forehead. "Do you know where she lives?"

"With Piper, but I don't have an address."

"I'm not supposed to give out this information, and if I find out you did anything with it besides check and see if she's okay, I'll suspend you," Coach warns me, then he thumbs through his phone.

"Do you have a lot of secrets on there, Coach?" I joke, trying to lighten the mood, but my heart won't stop racing in my chest.

"Don't push it, Miller. She's in Garden Villas on Connecticut Ave."

"What?" I frown. "Are you sure?"

"Eleventh floor. Number seven."

"What the hell? That's next door to my place. I could throw a rock at her window."

Did I hear any sirens when I left my place an hour ago?

Was there caution tape outside her building marking a crime scene?

Fuck.

Where the hell is she?

"Go," Hudson tells me, and I'm already halfway off the ice.

I tear through the locker room like a bat out of hell. I drop my skates on our logo, and I put my shirt on inside out. I'm still tugging on my shoe when I hop into the players' garage, calling her another time without any luck.

I nearly rip off the door of my Mercedes and head for

Emerson's apartment, yelling at the traffic that keeps me from doing less than fifty when I really want to do one hundred.

The entire drive through the city, I keep calling her, and she still doesn't answer.

Panic claws at my throat. I almost leave the keys in the ignition when I park in the visitor's spot at her complex. A bright piece of paper taped to the elevator tells me it's out of order for the day, and I curse under my breath.

I head for the lobby. After a ten minute conversation with a security guard and convincing him I'm the same Maverick Miller he watched on TV a few nights ago, he finally points me toward the stairwell.

I climb all eleven flights faster than I've moved my entire life, and when I get to Emerson's apartment, I lean against the wall, huffing and puffing.

"Hartwell?" I call out, knocking loudly. I press my ear to the door and listen. It's silent on the other side, and I bang again. "Emerson? Piper?"

I hear a faint groan, and I freeze.

Mother fucking shit.

Is she hurt?

Is there someone with her?

Why the fuck did I come here alone?

"You have six seconds to tell me not to break down this door," I yell.

When I don't get an answer, I run my shoulder into the barrier until it busts open.

"Goddammit," I groan.

I stumble inside and nearly fall across the hardwood floor. Pain shoots up my arm, and it's worse than getting slammed into the boards during a game.

"Pull it together, Miller," I grumble, and I shake out my shoulder.

I step into the foyer and scan the apartment, searching for

any signs of violence. I grab a candlestick off a table and hold it in front of me.

"Hello? Look, if this is some hostage situation, I'll give you my credit card and you can go wild, all right? Just leave whoever is in here alone. I have a weapon."

There's a noise from down the hall, and I take off. I see a room to my right, and I hold the candlestick above my head, ready to attack. I push the door open and find Emerson with her head in the toilet.

"Maverick?" She lifts her chin, and I stop in my tracks. "What are you doing here?"

She looks horrible.

Her eyes are red-rimmed and her skin is pale. Her hair is knotted on top of her head, and there's dried vomit in the corner of her mouth. I toss the candlestick in the sink and move toward her.

"What's going on? What happened?" I ask, and she wipes her forehead with the back of her hand.

"Food poisoning or something equally horrific from a sandwich I got at LaGuardia airport." She winces, and her whole body shudders. "Terminal kiosk. Never again." She leans over the toilet and hurls into it. "God. I hope that's the last of it."

"You look like you've been hit by a truck."

"That might be the nicest thing you've ever said to me."

"Nicer than calling you gorgeous when you're on top of me? I need to step it up."

"Maybe not." She smiles weakly. "I'm fine. Really. You should go."

"Bullshit. Where's Piper?"

"Out of town visiting family."

"That explains why she didn't answer my call. How long have you been like this?" I ask.

"I don't know." Emerson closes her eyes and tips her head

back. I dart forward and catch her before she can knock her skull against the wall behind her. "I don't know what day it is."

"It's Wednesday."

"Wednesday." She cracks an eye open and looks at my workout clothes. Her lips part into an O, and there are tears in her eyes. "Shit. *Shit.* I missed practice."

"Don't worry about practice, Red. We'll cross that bridge later. I'm here. How can I help?"

"You don't have to help."

"I don't have to do anything, but I want to. Tell me what you need."

Emerson blinks, and I wait for her to argue. To push back and tell me to get the hell out, but she doesn't. She sighs and gives me a small nod.

"I need a shower, but I'm afraid to stand up."

"Easy enough." I pull off my shirt and throw it toward the door. "I happen to love showers."

"You just want an excuse to take off your clothes, don't you?" Emerson murmurs, and I wrap my arms around her.

"You know me well," I whisper in her ear. "Get naked, Hartwell."

"I'm disgusting, and I smell," she argues.

"And? I've seen you sweat your ass off at practice and with blood on your jersey. This is nothing."

"It's too much work."

"Arms up then, darlin'. I'll do it for you."

Emerson grumbles, and I fight back a smile when she slowly lifts her arms. I hear her say something that sounds close to *asshole* and *pushy* under her breath, but I consider it a win.

She shivers, and I rub my hands down her arms. Her skin warms under my touch, and the sigh she lets out is the best thing I've heard all day.

"I'm going to take your shorts off then pick you up, okay?"

I ask, wanting to make sure we're on the same page. She's out of it, a half second late with her reactions, and the last thing I want is for her to think I'm taking advantage of her. "It's only to put you in the shower."

"Stop flirting with me."

"You'd know if I was flirting with you." I brush my lips over her shoulder and kiss her neck. "This is nothing."

I shift out from behind her and lean her carefully against the wall. I run my hand up her shins and straighten out her legs, tugging the flimsy shorts down her hips and thighs.

"I hate these things," I say.

"What did they do to you?"

"They're distracting. I've gone years without something pulling my attention from the ice. Then you show up, and I can't focus on anything except your sleepwear."

Her smile is soft and subtle. "Sorry. I'll start wearing cargo pants to bed."

"You're not sorry at all."

"No." Emerson reaches out and traces my tattoos. Her fingers move across the taco shell on my bicep and the fern down my forearm. "I'm not. The shower is behind you, by the way."

"Figured it was. I just wanted to keep looking at you."

"You said I look like I got hit by a truck."

"Doesn't mean you're not beautiful," I say. "Why didn't you tell me you weren't feeling well? I would've been here the second you called. You wouldn't have had to spend hours all alone with your head in the toilet."

"You would've?"

"I already broke the door down once. I'd do it again."

"You broke down the door? For me?"

"Yeah. Might have fractured half the bones in my arm in the process, but I'll survive. I'll get you a new one, by the way."

She rubs her thumb up the inside of my wrist and closes her eyes. "I might need to start calling you Superman."

"Easy, Hartwell. You're going to give me a complex."

"I would've called if I realized what was going on. One minute I was fine, and the next I was puking my brains out for hours on end. I don't know where my phone is, and moving through the apartment sounds like hell."

"You'll let me know next time, okay?"

She grumbles again. "Fine."

"Stubborn woman." I stand up and scoop her into my arms. "I'm not letting you take a shower—you can't keep your head upright. How about a bath?"

"I haven't taken a bath in years."

"Really? I love baths."

"You do?"

"Hell yeah. I light some candles, put some Epsom salt in there, and set up my iPad with an episode of *Ted Lasso*. It's my favorite way to unwind after a hard workout."

A quiet laugh slips out of her, and I love that fucking sound. I want to make her laugh again. "I'm picturing you with battleships and rubber ducks."

"It's fun to pretend to be a war general." I pull back the shower curtain and turn on the faucet. "How hot do you like your water?"

"Scalding," she says.

I wait for the water to warm up before I set her in the tub. "Too hot?"

"No." Emerson groans and leans back. "It's perfect."

"Where's your shampoo?" I ask, and she gestures to the shelf stacked with bottles. There's nearly a dozen. "Christ. You use all of this stuff?"

"Not all the time. Just occasionally."

"It's like a salon in here."

"You really don't have to do this, Miller."

"Shut up, Hartwell." I pick one up and grab the shower head. She moans when I wet her hair, and I massage her scalp with my nails. "What will it take for you to relax?"

"That," she breathes out. "That feels like heaven."

It feels like heaven for me too.

I love when she's riled up. I love when there's a blaze to her words and fire in her tone. But I also like her like this.

Quiet.

Soft.

So fucking pretty with droplets on her eyelashes and her mouth curling around a pleased sigh.

Everything about the moment is intimate. I've never touched a woman without the promise of sex as the end result, but with her, I like it.

I like the way she tilts her head so I can wash and condition the ends of her hair. I like the way she sinks further into the tub the longer I kneel next to her.

I wonder what it would be like to do this every day.

"Thank you," I say, and her eyes flutter open. "Thank you for letting me help you, Emmy. Thank you for letting me be here. You can tell me to go whenever you want and I will, but I want you to know this is exactly where I want to be. I've got you."

She laces our fingers together and squeezes my hand. "Thank you for coming. I'm not… this is—"

"I know." I smile and put the shower head back in place. "It's a one-time thing. Our little secret. Tomorrow you can be the ass kicker you normally are, and no one has to know."

"You think I'm an ass kicker?"

"The best of the best. I'm going to put you in bed then bring you some food. You need some protein and carbs. What do you want? Soup? Toast? Rice? A whole plate of mashed potatoes?"

"The living room is fine. You don't need to go into my room."

I pull the plug on the tub. "Why are you being so secretive about your room?"

Emerson swallows. "I might have wet the bed, and there's definitely vomit on my pillows."

I stare at her, and that fear from earlier is back. "You could've died."

"I wouldn't have died. I can take care of myself. I made it to the bathroom, didn't I?"

"For fuck's sake, woman." I lift her out of the tub and wrap her in a towel. "No one is saying you can't. I want to help, Emmy. *Let me help*. Share the load with me. You don't have to carry it alone."

I keep her in my arms and grab the candlestick from the sink, marching toward the living room.

I take mental notes of everything I need to get done: a new fucking door. Clean sheets and bland food. A gallon of water and a thermometer to make sure she doesn't have a fever. A message to Coach and the boys to let them know she's okay.

"Why are you holding a candle?" Emerson asks into my shoulder.

"Remember when I broke down the door? I thought someone was being held hostage, and this was my weapon of choice," I say sheepishly.

"Piper is going to be very confused."

"It'll be fixed by tonight." I set her on the couch and pull a fuzzy blanket up to her chin. "Don't move an inch, Red. If I see you crawling like a goddamn worm, I'm going to haul you over my shoulder and tape you to a chair."

"I bet I'd move faster than you," she mumbles, and she rests her head against the cushions. "Even if I was wiggling."

"You're delusional."

"Maverick?" she says. Our eyes meet, and my chest puffs out at the sound of my name. "Thank you for being here. Thank you for taking some of the load from me."

"You're welcome, Emmy girl. Get comfortable. I'll be back soon."

Emerson nods and closes her eyes. Her breathing turns shallow, and she's asleep within seconds.

Before I can think twice about what the hell I'm doing, I drop a kiss to her forehead and get to work.

TWENTY-SEVEN
EMMY

IT'S dark outside when I open my eyes, and my chest presses against something firm.

I take a second to get my bearings, and I realize the nausea from earlier has subsided. I'm relaxed, and a bone-aching bliss settles over my body in a way I don't ever remember experiencing.

I stretch my arms and turn my head to the side, and I find Maverick next to me.

There's a pillow crease on his forehead, and his hair is rumpled beyond belief. One of his hands sits on my hip, long fingers splayed out over the curve of my thigh and the bottom of my tattoo. He's shirtless, fast asleep and breathing heavily, and in all the moments I've known him, this is my favorite one.

I stare at him, and the last few hours come rushing back to me.

The hair washing and the door he knocked down.

Waiting for him to put clean sheets on my bed and carrying me to my room.

The soup he spoon-fed me and the water he made me drink.

I rub a hand over my chest, an ache nudging its way behind my ribs as I watch his eyelashes flutter and listen to his soft exhales.

He dropped everything for me.

He helped put me back together and stayed to make sure I was okay all because he *wanted* to.

No one's ever been so nice to me before, especially when I've felt small and uncomfortable and nothing like myself, and that's disorienting.

There's this magnetic need to touch him, and I don't fight it. I cup his cheek and run my thumb along his jaw. I study the planes of his face. The hook of his nose and the way it looks like he's smirking, even when he's unconscious.

Beautiful man.

Stubble pricks my palm, and I smile when he turns his head and nuzzles into my touch.

"Are you awake?" he rasps, a tired slur from the back of his throat. The fingers on my hip stroke across my skin, and it almost feels like he's trying to write out a word. "Or am I dreaming?"

"Definitely dreaming," I murmur, scooting closer to him. "What time is it?"

"Don't know." He rubs his eyes and reaches behind him to turn on the lamp with his free hand. He taps his phone and I see a photo of him and June wearing face paint and sticking out their tongues. "Eight."

"Why didn't you wake me up?"

"You were burrowed under the covers like a bear in hibernation. It was cute." Maverick pinches my cheek. "I had to squeeze in here and see if you were that tired, or if the bed is that comfortable."

"Both. It's Piper's mattress, and when she told me she spent four grand on it, I nearly had a heart attack."

"It's nice." He elbows the pillows and tries to fluff them up. "But not as nice as mine."

"How much did you spend on yours? Five grand?"

"Close. Six."

"Doesn't surprise me. Come to think of it, I remember the toilets in your apartment being made of gold."

"Joke all you want, but my physical therapist tells me my back muscles are in great shape. The mattress was worth the investment." He yawns and pulls me away from his body. His eyes bounce over my face and down to the front of the T-shirt he must have slipped me into. A line of wrinkles forms between his eyebrows, and I decide I don't like it very much when he's not smiling. "How are you feeling?"

"Better. I kept the food and water down, so I think I'm on the mend."

"Good. I'm going to make you drink another glass of water before you go to sleep for the night. Your skin was clammy, and you were severely dehydrated."

"I think hurling up every liquid and piece of food you've put in your body will do that to you." I sigh. "Was Coach pissed I missed practice?"

"No. I told him you were violently ill, and he said you're not allowed back until you can keep your dinner down."

"That'll be tomorrow."

"Debatable. You're going to have to get cleared by the team doctor first. The boys were happy to hear you're okay too."

"They were worried about me?" I ask.

"Yeah. Well, to be fair, they thought you were hacked up into a million pieces by a serial killer while getting shoved onto the Metro tracks, so to hear it was food poisoning was a huge relief," Maverick says.

"You all are weird."

"We are, but we're your weirdos. The good news is you should be back to a hundred percent before the holiday gala in two weeks. It's our biggest fundraiser event for charity, and the donors are going to be psyched you're there."

"Don't remind me. An auction for a lunch date with me sounds like hell. I'm probably going to end up eating KFC with some creepy guy named Bartholomew."

"Know a lot of Barthalomews?"

"No. But they're probably lurking out there."

"I won't let that happen, Red. I'll throw a couple thousand into the pot to keep you free from any finger-licking dudes."

"Glad to know you're a man of the people. Are you—" My phone rings, and I untangle my legs from his. I look under the pillows and on the bedside table. "Where the heck is my phone?"

"Here." Maverick unplugs it from the charger next to his, handing it to me with a frown. "Grady? Who the hell is Grady?"

"*Shit.* You cannot say a word." I snatch it out of his hands and answer, scooting to the edge of the bed so I can have some space. "Hey."

"There you are. I called you four times yesterday, and you didn't answer," Grady says on the other end of the line. "Are you alive?"

"I'm alive, but barely. I was sick," I tell him. "Vomit, everywhere."

"Food poisoning?"

"Yeah."

"That's the worst."

"It was miserable. Anyway, I'm sorry I've been missing your calls and texts. November was hectic with sixteen games, and I've been busy to start this month too." Behind me, Maverick snorts, and I flip him off. "How are you? I miss you."

"Miss you too. Are you feeling better?"

"I am, yeah." A hand wraps around my waist and rubs across my stomach. I tip my head back to get closer to him and let out a shaky breath. "How are things in California?"

"Fine. Jeremey got sent to the AHL, so that was good news."

"When will it be your turn?" I ask, and Maverick's fingers move up my skin. He pinches one of my nipples, and I hold back a groan. "You're just as good as any of the guys in the AHL."

"I know I am. It's easy to get frustrated about when I'll get my chance, but I keep my head down and play the best that I can."

Maverick's other hand brushes over the front of my underwear, nudging my thighs apart. He presses against my clit, and the palm under my shirt moves to my neck.

I cover my mouth and squeeze my eyes shut, so close to crying out his name.

"You're number one in my book," I tell Grady, but it's muffled.

"You okay, Em?"

"I think I might get sick again. Can I text you tomorrow? I need to catch up on my sleep, so it's going to be an early night for me."

"Sure. Love you, Emmy. Talk to you soon."

"Love you too, asshat," I say, and I end the call. "You're a goddamn menace, Miller."

"You took a call from another guy while you're in bed with me. I had to remind you who filled you up three nights ago. When were you going to tell me you're fucking someone else?" His lips ghost down my neck. He sucks on the spot on my shoulder that drives me wild, and I lean against him. "And *love*? Emerson Hartwell. Who are you?"

"He's my best friend." I squirm when Maverick rubs a slow circle over my clit. "And look who's talking. You probably have a line of women waiting at your apartment."

"Hang on." His hands fall away from my body and he lifts me into his lap. "What are you talking about?"

"What are *you* talking about?"

"You're not sleeping with him?"

"With *Grady?*" I burst out laughing. "He's like a brother to me. I saw his dick once, and it was traumatizing."

"Are you sleeping with anyone else?" Maverick asks.

"Are *you* sleeping with anyone else?"

"No. You're the only woman I've been with lately."

"I am?" I straddle his hips and look at him. "You haven't brought anyone to your hotel room? Or your apartment?"

"Between our hookups and the text messages you send me, when would I have time to bring someone to my hotel room? You ride my cock so well, Red, and I can't keep my eyes open after you're finished with me. I don't have the physical capacity to fuck someone else, nor do I want to."

"We've never talked about exclusivity or if we were sleeping with other people. I just assumed based on your past that you're not a one-woman kind of guy."

"I wasn't before, but you're taking care of me just fine, Emmy girl. Fucking yourself on my thigh? Making me watch you use your fingers before you finally let me touch you? Those pictures of you in my shirt?" He bumps his nose against my chin and nudges my attention to him. Our eyes meet, and I inhale a sharp breath. "I don't need anyone else when I have you."

My heart hammers. That same ache from before settles in my chest. I'm too warm, too overwhelmed by the gentle consideration of the press of his hands. How his words sink into my skin and stay there, a key in a lock.

It's entirely too intimate a conversation to have, but I'm desperate for it.

"What does this mean?" I whisper. "You don't date. I don't date hockey players. Are we—" I break off and reach for his necklace, tugging on the chain. "Is there a label for this?"

"Friends with benefits who are exclusive?" Maverick suggests. "Orgasm sharers who don't get off with anyone else?

Teammates who fuck then play together on the ice and help their team lead the Atlantic division without any bullshit like emotions and feelings? You're enjoying this, right?"

"God, yeah," I say before I can stop myself, and his smirk is proud. He's gloating, and I hate it. "This is the most fun I've ever had with a guy. As long as we're both on the same page, why not keep doing what we're doing?"

"Can I propose something?"

"Possibly."

"We don't just fuck when we're on the road. I'm literally in the building next door. Think of all the fun we could have on our days off. Plus, I'm superstitious as shit. It would be in the best interest of the team."

"I'll consider it," I say, because it *does* sound like fun. "Anything else?"

"We keep our arrangement between us. None of the guys need to know. It's easy right now, and the more people that find out, the more it'll complicate things. I don't do complicated."

"Deal." I stick out my hand, and he shakes it. "I can't believe you were jealous."

"Seems like I've been jealous a lot lately. Your phone calls with friends. The secret handshakes you have with some of the guys." He topples us backward onto the pillows and holds me close to his chest. "I want that too."

"You get me here, though. I'm not going home with any of them."

"Let's keep it that way. And this is my favorite place."

I yawn and close my eyes, snuggling into his arms. I'm not usually a cuddler, but there's something about Maverick's embrace that makes me want to stay awhile. "You'd like Grady. Hudson reminds me of him. Eternally optimistic. A nice guy."

"Who doesn't love a nice guy?" He runs his fingers

through my hair and I hum in appreciation. "I'll have to meet him one day."

"We'll see about that. Whose turn is it to ask a question? I can't keep track."

"You can ask first. What do you have for me?"

"What did you study in college? Did you graduate?"

"I didn't. The chance to enter the NHL draft presented itself, and I took it. When I was in school, I wanted to get my degree in biology."

My eyes fly open. "*Biology*? That's surprising."

"*Surprising?* Wow, Hartwell. You thought I was a dumb jock, didn't you?" he asks, and he digs his fingers into my ribs. I shriek and try to wiggle out of his hold, but he doesn't give me an inch. "I was great in school. Straight-A student, fuck you very much."

"It's just an unusual subject," I say, and he finally relents, letting me go. "I don't know anyone who studied biology."

"Now you do." His smile hits me straight between the legs, and I want to smother him with a pillow. "What did you study?"

"I got my degree in communications. If the whole hockey thing didn't pan out, I wanted to work in PR. Thankfully my skills on the ice came through. I'd hate having to talk to people all day."

"People are the worst, aren't they? Okay. My turn." Maverick rubs his jaw, deep in thought. "What's something you want to do before you die?"

"Go to Antarctica. It's a once in a lifetime trip, and to see the glaciers and miles and miles of landscape no human has ever touched would be incredible. And I want to see the penguins too, of course."

"That's a good one. It's too predictable if I say I want to win the Cup, isn't it?"

"You're going to have to think outside of hockey."

He's quiet for a minute, and when he talks again, it's softer.

A dream he's dreamed a thousand times and is finally sharing with the world. "I'd like to set up my own charity and create scholarships for kids who might not have a roof over their heads. Yeah, I want to see the world and travel and spoil the people around me, but my legacy doesn't mean anything if I don't share the resources I have with those who get overlooked and might need a little extra help."

I cradle his chin in my hand. "That's a wonderful idea."

"I'm talking with my lawyer about distribution of wealth and a lot of other legal words that go way over my head, but I think we're going to get the ball rolling on it next season. It'll be a special milestone anyway—my tenth year in the league."

"You have a kind heart, Maverick, and it's special that you want to share it with so many people."

"Shucks. You're really inflating my ego over here."

"For once it deserves to be inflated."

"How are you feeling? Do you want to try to eat anything else?"

"No. I think I'm ready to go to sleep for the night. I'm still so tired. Thank you for all your help. You nursed me back to fantastic health. Ten out of ten, would recommend your puke-cleaning services again."

"Will you text me if you need anything or if the nausea comes back? I can be over here in three minutes. Two if I run."

"That's about as fast as you do other things."

"You're a little shit." He climbs off the bed and pulls on his shirt. "Need anything else before I head out?"

There's a moment where I think about asking him to stay.

To lie back down and curl up next to me until morning, but I'm not sure where that falls on the fuck-buddy scale or if I'm even allowed to have it.

I shake my head instead, shoving the invitation far, far away. "I'll see you at practice tomorrow."

"You'll see me at the arena tomorrow. Whether or not

you're going to practice is up in the air." Maverick bends down and kisses my forehead. He tucks a piece of hair behind my ear and smiles. "Bossing you around is fun."

"Don't get used to it." I pull the covers up to my chin. "Night, pretty boy."

"Night, Emmy girl," he says, and he leans against the door of my bedroom, watching me until I fall asleep.

TWENTY-EIGHT
MAVERICK

"I HATE PLAYING video games with you guys." Reid tosses his controller on the couch and pushes his glasses up his nose. "You use your athletic capabilities, and I bring nothing to the table."

"It's *Grand Theft Auto*, not real life sports. Athletic skills don't mean shit when you're driving a car through the streets of LA," I say. "At least you're better than those twelve-year-old kids we went up against in Halo. It would've been real embarrassing if we lost at capture the flag."

"We won capture the flag because you told the kids who you were, and they screamed for eight minutes." He scratches at his red beard and leans back against the cushions. "Not because we played better."

"A win is a win," Dallas says as he pops onto his feet. "You all are staying for dinner, right? Maven and June are eating over at her dad's place, and it's been ages since we hung out just the three of us."

"An eighty-two-game season is a hell of a lot more intense than an eighteen-game season," I tease. "Some of us are busy."

"We have the best record in the league, and I've already

kicked two game-winning field goals, so you can fuck off," Dallas says.

"Hockey is still the harder sport."

"God." Reid groans. "Not this argument again."

"I think my absences are forgivable given I've been in three different time zones in the last two weeks, but count me in for food tonight," I say, ignoring him.

"You've been home plenty and we still haven't seen you." Reid grabs his phone and scrolls through his social media apps. "You posted that you went to Georgetown Cupcakes the other night, and we didn't get an invitation."

I did go to Georgetown Cupcakes the other night, but it wasn't for me. Emerson told me she hadn't had a chance to try the famed bakery yet, so I picked up a half-dozen treats on my way to her apartment.

I got creative with the frosting from the red velvet cupcake, licking it off her chest and stomach before feeding her the rest of the dessert while her legs were wrapped around my neck and her fingers were in my hair.

The text messages from Dallas and Reid and the rest of my teammates are going unanswered, but it's hard to respond to them when Emerson invites me over, drops to her knees in the foyer, then sucks me off with my jeans around my ankles.

I crave her, and it's getting hard to keep my hands to myself when we're around people. I'm horny all the time, and I feel like I'm back in high school when she straddles my lap and kisses me until my lips are swollen.

The sex is top tier, but it's not just the physical stuff I'm enjoying.

Some nights when she sneaks into my hotel room, we lounge on the bed in robes and talk about our upcoming games or our favorite movies. We won't touch each other besides a quick kiss or the graze of a finger against a thigh, but it feels right.

It's fucking *fun*, and while I know I should be more accessible as a captain and the best man in an upcoming wedding, it's practically impossible to stay away from her.

"Sorry, buddy. Next time I'm on a late-night snack run, I'll make sure to stop by with a delivery," I say, shooting him a smile. "How's the season going? And the woman you're in love with?"

"I do not *love* her," Reid counters, not bothering to look up from his phone.

Dallas snorts. "Are you sure? You talk about her an awful lot."

"She annoys me to no end, and if I ever meet her, I'm going to give her a goddamn earful," he says. "I get it. She's good at her job. The videos she posts on social media get thousands of likes, and even people who aren't football fans follow the accounts. I just wish she would tone it down. It's making me look bad."

"Maybe you should step it up," I say, and I pluck a handful of grapes from the grazing board on the coffee table. "How's wedding planning going, Dal?"

"Good. Maven told me she found a dress, and I'm tempted to cancel the fancy party so I can see what she looks like in it tomorrow." He sighs dreamily, and Reid pretends to gag. "I'm the luckiest bastard in the world."

"You really are. That woman is incredible. Mark my words, Lansfield. If you ever do anything to hurt her, I'll come for you," I tell him.

He waves me off and heads for the kitchen. "I leveled up," he calls out. "I'm not going anywhere."

"We need to plan his bachelor party," I say to Reid when we're alone. "Their wedding is next fall, so maybe summer?"

"Sure. Things will be slow at work, and I'll be able to get away for a few days without any issues. What do you want to do? A cruise? An island filled with women? Somewhere we can play a round of golf?"

I wrinkle my nose. "Women are not a requirement."

"Since when?"

"Don't know. Today?"

Reid stares at me and narrows his eyes. He reaches out and pulls the collar of my shirt to the side, inspecting my neck. "You don't want women, but you have a hickey? Something you need to tell us, Mav? I hope you know we're not going to judge you."

"I do know that, but it's not what you're thinking." I scoot away from him and use my hand to cover up the marks Emerson left behind. "I'm, uh, sort of friends with benefits with someone, and we agreed not to sleep with anyone else."

"How does one become *sort of* friends with benefits? It's either all dick, or no dick, right?"

"Valid point. I'm definitely in a friends-with-benefits arrangement with someone, and I'm not sleeping with anyone else."

"Dallas," Reid barks out, and I jump. "Get in here."

"What the hell is going on?" Dallas stands in the entryway wearing a pink apron and holding a flowered spatula.

"Maverick has a girlfriend," Reid says.

"I don't have a girlfriend. I have a fuck buddy," I clarify. "There's a big difference."

"Hang on. Is that why you haven't been texting in the group chat and June's been asking where you are? Because you're sleeping with someone?" Dallas asks.

"We don't need to make it a big deal. We're just two adults who fuck each other. It's no different from what I've done in the past with the dozens of other women I've been with."

"You never sleep with the same woman twice," Reid points out. "Why this one?"

I shrug. "Because she's fun and smart and I have a good time when I'm with her. Neither of us is looking for anything serious, and our schedules line up well enough to ensure we'll both get what we want out of each other before moving on with our lives. It's a mutually beneficial setup."

"Wow. I never thought I'd see the day," Dallas says. "Maverick Miller is locked down."

"I am not locked down. There aren't any flowers or poems or anything like that. It's just sex."

Reid scoffs. "Until it isn't."

"What does that mean?"

"It means there's always some sort of emotion associated with a physical relationship. It might just be sex right now, but eventually, one of you is going to fall for the other, and things are going to get messy."

I laugh. "Trust me. That is not going to happen. The woman likes me for one thing, and one thing only."

Except when I woke up with Emerson in my arms the night she wasn't feeling well. She was staring at me with an expression I've never seen from her before, and it felt… important. Like I had a purpose and she was glad I was there, just as much as I was happy to be there helping her.

I haven't seen it since, though, so it must've been a sleep-deprived and utterly spent glance of appreciation after I watered her plants, replaced her door and cleaned her up.

"I don't know why you act like dating is the worst thing in the world," Dallas says, leaning against the wall. "It's exactly what you're doing now but with other fun stuff."

"Like wearing matching pajamas? Sounds fucking lame."

"My daughter picked those pajamas out, you asshole." He huffs and points the spatula at me. "Just you wait. That's going to be you one day, and I'm going to give you so much shit."

"Dream on, Lansfield."

My phone buzzes in my pocket, and I see fifteen notifications from the team group chat I've ignored over the last hour. There's another message on my screen from Emerson, though, and I grin when I slide my finger across the screen.

REDHEADED ASSASSIN

Busy tonight?

ME

Why? Miss me, Red?

REDHEADED ASSASSIN

Only your dick.

ME

Thought so.

Three dots show up then disappear, and I wait for her to answer.

REDHEADED ASSASSIN

Am I allowed to say yes?

ME

Yeah, because I miss you too.

I am busy tonight. I'm hanging out with Reid and Dallas.

REDHEADED ASSASSIN

Gotcha.

ME

How are you feeling?

Can I bring you anything?

REDHEADED ASSASSIN

I'm better. I think all the puke is behind me, thank goodness.

ME

Glad to hear it.

What are you doing tomorrow night?

REDHEADED ASSASSIN

I'm getting dinner with Piper, Maven and Lexi.

ME

Look at you having a girl squad!!

Sounds like a good time, but bummed I won't see you until our flight to Toronto the day after tomorrow.

REDHEADED ASSASSIN

Think you'll survive?

ME

You tell me, Hartwell. You're the one who texted first.

REDHEADED ASSASSIN

Blocking you now.

ME

XOXO!

"Why are you smiling?" Reid asks. He tries to take the phone from my hands, but I'm forty pounds heavier than him and easily knock his arm away. "Is it *her*?"

"It's no one," I say. "Mind your business and grab the controller. We're playing another game."

"The deflection tactic. I'm onto you, Mav."

My phone buzzes again, and I sneak a look at it while Reid gets the next round of *GTA* set up.

There's another message from Emerson, a single black heart emoji that has me grinning like an idiot the rest of the night.

TWENTY-NINE
EMMY

"GREAT WIN, Y'ALL!" Grant yells. "We're going out tonight, and I will not accept no for an answer!"

I throw my bag under the bus and shiver. "It's freezing, and my legs are killing me."

"Come on, Emmy," he whines. "It's like the good Lord blessed us with an afternoon game on a Saturday. There's plenty of time to rest up before coming out. Hey, Lexi! Isn't it better for lactic acid buildup to move around after you exercise?"

She looks up from her phone. "Do you want the scientific answer or the easy-to-understand answer?"

"The easy answer," Connor jokes. "Grant barely got through a year at FSU."

"FSU is a great school, and I only lasted a year because the NHL called so I could help your sorry asses," Grant says fiercely, and he shoves Connor's shoulder. "You can talk science all you want to me, Lex. You know I like when you use really big words."

"It's funny that he thinks he can understand big words," Maverick murmurs, his lips brushing against my ear and his hand at my waist. "How are you feeling after the game? Any nausea or dehydration? What about lingering symptoms from when your head was in a toilet?"

My heart thumps steadily at his questions and the way he's checked in on me every day since he found me with food poisoning in my apartment.

Maverick sends me texts in the morning and again at night, asking if I need anything. He hangs around at the end of practice and waits for me to give him a thumbs up before he leaves.

It's ridiculously nice, and telling him *thank you* doesn't seem like enough.

"I'm good." I squeeze his arm. "I felt great out there today."

"You looked great too. Are you going to come out with us?"

"You're going?"

"Thought I would. It really was a great win, and celebrating sounds like a good time."

"I wasn't planning on it. A hot shower, a glass of wine, and a warm dinner in my pajamas sound way more enjoyable than loud music and three hundred people."

"What if I make it worth your while?" He trails his fingers down my shoulder. "It would be fun. An excuse to touch you out in public, and no one would know I've already been inside you."

A club is my idea of hell, but I don't doubt Maverick's ability to change my mind.

Dark corners and loud music. A hand on my waist when our teammates aren't around and standing close so we don't get separated.

It's risky, but he makes me want to break the rules.

"Okay," I say, and his lips pull up into a smile. "On two conditions."

"Name them," he says right away.

"I get my favorite ice cream at the end of the night, and

you give me a piggyback ride on the way back to the hotel when we're finished dancing."

"One pint of chocolate chip and having your legs wrapped around me? Done and done." He hops onto the bus and offers me his hand so I don't slip on the icy steps. "You're making this too easy."

"We'll see if you're still saying that when you're exhausted and climbing up the hill outside our hotel."

His pinky hooks around mine before he drops his hand away and plops into a seat. "I can't wait to see what you're going to wear tonight."

"Don't get your hopes up. It's just something I threw in my bag." I scan the open spots on the bus and decide to sit next to Maverick. "I'll probably look like a troll."

"You could never look like a troll, Red."

"Grant." I turn around, and he pops his head up. "What time are we going?"

"You're coming, Emmy? Holy crap. A road win against a divisional rival. My favorite person on the team is healthy again, not murdered, and joining us at the club. Can today get any better?"

"Hey. I thought I was your favorite person on the team," Seymour says, and Grant rolls his eyes.

"You got demoted weeks ago. I'm thinking we'll meet at nine. It gives everyone time to chill so we can rage until dawn. Three days off after this—we're going *hard*."

"Our flight is at six." Maverick yawns. "You can't rage past that."

I rifle through my purse and try to find my phone. "Can I invite Piper?"

I got an earful when she got back from visiting family, a twenty minute speech in the living room about how next time I need to call or text her the second I feel sick, and I've missed her.

"The more the merrier." He looks around the bus until he

finds Lexi, and he lights up. "Did you hear that, Lex? The girls are coming out tonight. Will you come too?"

"Say please," she says, and I swear I see hearts in Grant's eyes. "And maybe I'll think about it."

"Please come." He drops to his knees in the aisle, and Hudson steps over him to get to his seat, shaking his head. "I'll get you whatever kind of drink you want, and I'll make sure no creeps hit on you."

"Does that mean *you* won't hit on me either?" she asks, and the bus breaks out into a chorus of *ooh*s.

"Kids these days." Maverick yawns again and scratches the cut on his cheek. "They don't know when to stop."

"Says the leech," I toss back, and he grins.

"I love the nicknames you have for me, but I'm partial to *god*. Particularly when you're on top of me."

A flush creeps up my neck, and I'm glad none of our teammates are paying enough attention to listen to our conversation.

"I might call you Satan next time, just to keep you balanced."

"Don't care what you call me." He wraps his ankle around mine and drags me toward him with the strength of his leg until our thighs are touching. "I like that there's going to be a next time."

I've never had a friend with benefits before, but Maverick is a good starting point. There are no messy emotions or hours of waxing poetic about feelings and relationship expectations.

It's sex however we like it, whenever we want it, and I secretly love that he can trade barbs with me and make it feel like flirting.

I also love that he touches me when he's not supposed to, little stolen moments when no one else is watching because he can't keep his hands away.

It's nice to be wanted.

"Are you sure you still want there to be a next time?" I ask quietly. "You saw me when I looked like literal garbage."

"Doesn't change a thing."

"And you're okay with being exclusive and only sleeping with each other?" I rub my forehead and wince. "Sorry. I shouldn't be talking about this right now. The night I was sick is a little hazy and—"

"Hey." Maverick's fingers wrap around my wrist, and he smiles. "I'm more than okay with it. I meant what I said—you're enough, Emmy, and what we're doing right now makes me happy. Vomit and all."

My heart flutters dangerously in my chest. "It makes me happy too."

"Look at us." He grins. "Two happy people."

"Speaking of happy people, you might have a fight on your hands one of these days." I look over my shoulder and see Grant talking Lexi's ear off. Two rows back from them, Riley watches their conversation with hunched shoulders, and I want to give him a hug. "Something to keep in the back of your mind as captain."

"Hm?" Maverick's eyes are closed. He's half-delirious and ready for a nap. "What are you talking about?"

"Grant is flirting with Lexi. Riley clearly likes Lexi. I'm not sure Lexi likes either of them."

"Grant likes Lexi?"

"Yup."

"And Riley likes Lexi?"

"It's the most obvious thing in the world."

"It is? Huh. I never noticed."

"How did you not notice?"

"I don't know." He shrugs, and his fingers dance over my knee. "Guess I've been too busy looking at you."

The bass at the club is so loud, my eardrums might burst.

The ten of us who walked the half mile to the club in downtown Toronto got escorted to a VIP section on the second floor with thick curtains along the wall and plush leather seats.

The drinks started flowing the second we sat down, and they haven't stopped in the ninety minutes we've been here. A string of men and women have come by, trying to get our attention, but no one pays them any mind.

Not even Maverick, who, when our conversation was interrupted by a horde of women in dresses with plunging necklines that screamed his name and asked for an autograph, didn't take his eyes off me.

I don't know how our teammates haven't figured out that we can't stay away from each other. It helps that the majority of them are on the dance floor. The rest are so past tipsy, they won't remember a damn thing from tonight.

"Having fun?" Maverick whispers. His breath is warm on my skin, and he toys with the hemline of my dress. He inches it higher up my thigh, and I shudder. "God, you look fucking incredible, Red. Every guy in here has been staring at you since the minute we walked in."

"Thank you." I cross my legs, and my dress rides up another inch. Maverick tracks the motion and licks his lips, heat behind his eyes. "And it's tolerable. The company is decent."

He grins, and *god*, I want to kiss him right now. I want to tip my chin up and brush his mouth against mine. Drag him to a dark corner and let him run his hands all over my body.

"You want another drink?" he asks.

"A drink would be nice," I say.

He glances around us. When he doesn't see anyone we know, he drops a quick kiss to my cheek and slides out of the booth. "Be right back."

I watch him work his way to the bar through the throngs

of people. Three different women try to get him to talk to them, elbowing each other in attempts to get closer. He gives them a polite nod then moves down the counter, chatting with the only male bartender there.

I know he's not going to kiss someone else while I'm around, but it's amazing how seeing him ignore the stunning clubgoers makes me happy. I expected that playboy side of him to sneak through. A grin. A wink. A flirtatious hand on someone's body when he slipped past them.

There hasn't been any of that, and when he turns around and his eyes meet mine through the crowded room, his smile turns softer. Something secret and something only I know. It's the one I get to see late at night, a leg hooked over his shoulder and his laugh against the inside of my thigh.

He gives me a goofy wave and proudly holds up the drinks. I try to roll my eyes, but I smile instead, a silly, giddy sensation sweeping me away all because of his damn dimples and laser-sharp attention.

"Oh my god." Piper collapses onto the seat next to me and I glance away from Maverick. "My feet hurt."

"Why do you look so happy?" I touch her pink cheeks and laugh. "You're burning up."

"I just danced with some guy from Italy, and he was *very* handsome. I asked if he could come to our gala with me next week, but he told me he has to fly back to Europe tomorrow." She pouts. "Bummer."

"There will be other Italian men. Do you already have your dress?"

"Yes! It's pink and floor-length and *very* fancy." Piper giggles and reaches for my empty drink. "Oh no. Where did it all go?"

"I drank it all, believe it or not. Maybe you should eat something, Piper."

"A burger sounds great." She closes her eyes and sways to

the beat of the music. "In-N-Out. Don't they have In-N-Out here?"

"I think that's just a West Coast American thing."

Piper groans. "Damn geography. Dammit all to hell."

"What does she want?" Liam asks from across the table, and I jump.

I don't know when he sat down, and he's watching us with a tense jaw and a flicker of irritation behind his eyes. I can't believe the guys got him to come out tonight, but Grant said something about a gentleman's code, like I understood the meaning.

"She's hungry. I'll take care of her. Maybe we can find somewhere that's open and I—"

"I've got it." He cuts me off gruffly and stands up, towering over us with his six-three, two-hundred-pound frame. The man is a freaking brick wall. "You want something to eat, Pipsqueak?"

"What?" She blinks and her mouth pops open. "Did you just make up a nickname for me? I thought you weren't capable of human emotions. Just twenty-four-seven grumpiness." She slaps a hand over her mouth and her cheeks turn even redder. "Oh my god. Pretend I never said that."

Liam's lips quirk, the hint of a smile on his face, and he holds out his hand. "I know somewhere good."

"You're not going to murder her, are you?" I ask, and he snorts. Either the world is ending, or I'm more drunk than I thought.

"Murder isn't my thing." He waits for Piper to take his hand, and when she does, he moves so carefully, you'd think he was holding onto something fragile. "I'll text you if I need anything," he says, and they disappear down the stairs.

"Was that Liam?" Maverick asks, two glasses in hand. "And *Piper*? What the hell is going on tonight?"

"Not what you think." I take the drink he offers me. "He's going to get her a burger."

"Liam never does anything for anyone." He tucks a piece of loose hair behind my ear. "Do you want to hang out up here?"

"No." I swallow half my martini before setting it down on the table and standing up. "I feel like dancing."

"Yeah?" His eyes follow the bob of my throat and linger on my lips. "Is that an invitation, Red?"

"If you can find me out there, Miller, you can do whatever you want to me," I say, and I saunter away to the sound of his groan.

THIRTY
MAVERICK

EMERSON IS KILLING ME.

The curves of her tight ass and the glow of her skin under the lights are more intoxicating than the liquor I've been sipping all night.

I wasn't kidding when I told her every man in this club has been looking at her since the minute we walked in.

Some of our teammates have looked at her too.

I saw the way Connor stared at her hips when she walked up the stairs to the VIP section. I didn't miss Ethan widening his eyes when she sat down and crossed her legs.

I want to shout at them all that she's mine.

Mine, mine, mine and to *back the fuck off.*

Fuckers.

I give Emerson a head start in our game of hide and seek. We both know I'm tall enough to see over the crowd and she's sly enough to make me work for it, and I can't wait to fucking play.

By the time I count to thirty, I've had enough.

It's loud downstairs, and I push through a wall of people. I spot her off to the side, almost tucked away in a corner, her back to the room and dancing by herself.

I take a second to admire the way she moves and the dangerous swish of her silver dress that barely covers her ass. She's impossible to look away from, and there's some hypnotizing drug in the way she lifts her arms above her head and shimmies to the beat of the music.

I close the distance between us. "There you are," I say. "What do I get for finding you?"

"Stalking me, Miller?" she asks, but I'm distracted by the sway of her hips and her long hair that hangs down her back. Her tits and the thin sheen of sweat on her arms and the top of her chest. "Seems like you can't stay away from me."

"Isn't it obvious? I'm fucking addicted to you." I press my cock against her ass, and her breath stutters. "This is what you do to me."

I need to touch her, and if that means pretending to dance to EDM music to get away from our teammates so we can have a moment to ourselves, then so be it.

"What are we doing?" she asks when I band my arm around her waist and pull her toward me.

"Letting loose after our win."

Emerson hums. Her dress rides up her ass, enough for me to see the underside of her cheeks, and I groan.

Christ.

I'm hard, and I know she can feel me. I can practically see the smirk on her blood-red lips, like she's proud that she's the one turning me on.

"I haven't let loose in a while." She rests her head in the crook of my neck, and I brush my nose against her throat. "This could be fun."

"You're safe with me." I drop a hand to her thigh and squeeze the bare skin I find there. "If you want to get wasted, I'll keep an eye on you. If you want to take eight shots, I'll make sure you get to bed safely."

"And if I want to dance with someone else?"

"I'll break his fingers."

"I'm not yours, Maverick," she says, and *fuck me*, I love when she say calls me that.

"You're not? Who made you come last night?" I ask, and my grip tightens around her. "Whose name did you say this morning when I had my fingers inside of you? Kind of sounds like you might be mine, Red."

She lifts her chin and I turn my head to look down at her. Some of the makeup around her eyes is smudged from the warm temperature in here, but she's so goddamn beautiful.

"What if I asked you to touch me?" Her voice is low, and my dick throbs in my jeans. "Would you do that?"

"Yeah," I say roughly. I move my hand up her thigh, and her feet press against mine to widen her legs. "I'd give you anything you want. Even if you don't ask for it."

Her mouth pulls into a smile. It's half wicked, half dangerous. The good kind of trouble I keep finding myself falling into, again and again.

"For a hockey player, you don't have a lot of rhythm on the dance floor," she says over the noise, and I bury my face in her neck.

Her skin is hot, and I can smell traces of her soap. It's the hint of summer and the edge of ecstasy. I inhale because I'm a fucking goner, and I drop a kiss right above her collarbone.

"Because I'm too busy trying to hide my boner in the middle of the dance floor," I say.

"It's a good thing it's dark, then." Her shoulders shake with laughter. "I didn't know this kind of music turned you on."

"Not the music." I drag my hand higher, and my pinky brushes against her underwear. I want to find out what color it is tonight. "You."

"I'm right here." Her hand folds over mine. "Maybe you should do something about it."

I've never touched someone in public.

Not like this.

But something about Emerson makes me want to be irresponsible.

My heart races at the thought of being caught. I brush my thumb over the front of the lace under her dress, and she gasps.

"You like that?" I ask. "I know you like when I get right into it, but do you like to be teased too?"

"Yes." She exhales, and her chest rises and falls. "Only when you do it, though."

I crowd her space and nearly fold my body over hers so no one can see her. So no one can watch me move the wet fabric aside and run two fingers over her entrance. "Fucking hell, Emmy. You're already drenched."

Emerson hisses. She arches her back into my chest, and she wraps an arm around my neck to keep me in place.

I want to laugh, because she's out of her mind if she thinks I'm going anywhere else besides deep inside her tight pussy.

"You like when I call you that, don't you?" I say into her ear. Her breathing turns rough, and she gives me a quick nod.

"Yes." She grips the ends of my hair, trying to hold onto something steady. "Yes, I do."

"Emmy." I rub my thumb against her clit, and her moan hovers between us. "My sweet Emmy girl…" I slide one finger inside her at the same time I run my free hand up her neck. My thumb strokes over the pulse point in her throat, and she grinds into me. "…who loves when I fuck her cunt in front of everyone. The whole team could see us. Maybe I'll make them watch so they know you're mine."

"*Maverick*," she whines. "I need more. Please."

"Two?" I ask, and when she nods, I work a second finger in her. "Deep breath, baby. You can take it, can't you?"

"Of course I can take it. I take your cock, don't I?" she challenges, and I laugh.

"You might be my favorite person in the world."

A bead of sweat rolls down her cheek, and I lick it away. Every inch of her skin turns red, and I blow on her neck to keep her cool.

Emerson closes her eyes. She's using me—I'm here for her pleasure and her pleasure only, and it's the hottest thing I've ever experienced.

"What else do you need to get there?" I ask.

"More," she begs, and her grip on my hair turns rougher. "Can I have three?"

"I told you that you can have anything you want," I say, and when I slip another finger inside her and feel her stretch around me, I have to squeeze my eyes closed to stop myself from losing control. "Fuck, Em. This is doing it for me."

Emerson turns to face me. My fingers slide out of her before she guides me back in while moving her other hand from my hair to the front of my jeans. She traces my erection through the denim, a soft touch that makes me buck my hips like a needy fucking asshole.

"No guy has ever finished in their pants for me before," she says, and there's a dare behind it.

"You know I always like to be the first and the best." I drop my head back and groan when she cups me, her thumb stroking me up and down. "Emerson. Seriously. If you keep doing that—"

"I'd like to see it." Her other hand wraps around my wrist and she picks up the pace of my fingers, urging them in and out of her. "I'd like to see you fall apart."

"After you." I curl my fingers, and she gasps. I open my eyes and smile at the blush on her cheeks and the pointed nipples through her dress. "That's my girl. I told you you're safe with me. Let go, Emmy. Let me see how pretty you are when you come."

Her breathing changes. I bend down and kiss her temple, her cheek and her neck. She tightens around me and tells me she's close. I circle her clit until she moans long and low, her body shuddering against mine as the music thumps around us.

I coax her through the high, whispering in her ear how good she is. How beautiful she is and how much I like being here with her. And when she unzips my jeans and slips her fingers inside of my briefs, stroking me and jerking my cock, pleasure builds at the base of my spine.

"Emmy," I say, shuffling us to the back corner of the club. I put a hand on the wall to hold myself up. "I'm—"

Her thumb swipes over the head of my dick, and I lose it.

My vision turns dark and my limbs get heavy. I groan, nothing but satisfaction in my bones and a goddamn mess in my pants.

"Fuck. *Fuck.*"

"Give me all of it, pretty boy."

I whimper, some desperate sound I'll be embarrassed about tomorrow. But right now, she's still holding me, still stroking me, drawing every bit of pleasure out of me that she can.

"Shit. *Shit*, Emmy," I pant. I think I'm about to topple over. "God damn."

"Did you like that, Maverick?"

I swallow down a gulp of air. "I haven't finished like that since I was fourteen," I admit.

"That's hot." She kisses me again and runs her tongue across my lips. "You're such a good boy doing what I ask. Look at the mess you've made."

Goddamn.

My body is an inferno, and I whine at her praise. I pull my fingers out of her and bring them to her mouth.

"Open up," I say. "Want to watch you suck them clean." Her lips part, and I press my fingers down on her tongue. "How do you taste?"

"Good. But you'd taste better."

I grab her chin and kiss her, a promise of what else is to

come tonight. We might be done here, but I'm just getting started with her.

"Want to head back to the hotel?" I ask.

"And do what?"

"Sex. Lots and lots of sex," I say. "Then we can go from there."

"Okay." She looks down at the front of my jeans, and there's a cute little smirk on her mouth. "I was going to ask if we could get food but—"

"I'll order you one of everything off the room service menu. The ice cream too."

"I need to clean up first."

I take her palm and wipe her fingers on my shirt, not giving a shit about the stain. "There. Problem solved."

Emerson links her hand in mine and drags me toward the door. "Let's go, pretty boy."

Outside, I bend over and pat my shoulders. "Climb on. Someone asked for a piggyback ride."

Emerson jumps on my back, her legs around my waist and her face in my hair as we walk down the sidewalk in the freezing cold. When we get back to the hotel, I fuck her twice, once in the bed and the other against the wall.

We stay up until two in the morning eating french fries and grilled chicken and a bowl of ice cream. When she sneaks out of my room just before sunrise, I kiss her one more time, thinking this one-woman thing doesn't suck at all.

It's really fucking fun.

THIRTY-ONE
EMMY

"DAMN, EMMY." Piper whistles. "You look fantastic. Give me a spin so I can admire the whole outfit."

I laugh and twirl in the foyer of her apartment, showing off my form-fitting gown and the stiletto heels I paired with the forest green dress.

"I figured I had to pull out the big stops for the important donors," I say.

"You did not miss, woman. My god. Look at your ass. I might need to get out of the media booth and onto the ice if it's going to give me a backside like yours."

"Hush." I swat her arm with my black clutch, but I can't help smiling at the compliment. "Is our ride almost here?"

"Yup. Lexi and Maven are meeting us in the lobby. Traffic is always a nightmare at these things. If we're going to be stuck in a gridlock, we might as well be stuck together in a limo with champagne."

"A limo? How did you pull that off?"

"I didn't. Maverick did." Piper's smile is sly. "Is there something you need to share, Emmy? A reason why the notorious playboy and star right winger hasn't been spotted with a woman in months and is sending fancy cars to the apartment?"

I pretend to be interested in my silver earrings and shrug. "I don't know anything about Miller's personal life. What he does off the ice is his own business."

Except, it's become my business too.

The lines have started to blur since our conversation about exclusivity.

I keep getting tangled up in him, and I can't find a way to stop.

I'm not sure I want to.

I went to his apartment twice last week, and he snuck over to my place yesterday while Piper was at the grocery store. It was rushed and frantic as he slid his large hand over my mouth and told me to *be quiet.*

"Someone's been through media training," she says. "That's the equivalent of *no comment.* And the only people who say *no comment* are the ones with a lot of comments."

"I don't have anything to say."

Piper opens the closet door and rifles through the hangers until she finds her black peacoat. "If you're getting good dick, I'm happy for you. And definitely not jealous."

"Oh, my god." I burst out laughing. "Please never say *good dick* again."

"So, it's bad dick?"

"No one is getting dicked."

I feel bad lying to her, but Maverick and I agreed to keep this between us.

As much as I want to gossip with her like we're back in high school and talking about crushes and the hottest guys in our grade, I hold it in. I lock it away in a compartment I'll only let myself open when I'm alone.

"That's a shame." She sighs. "Someone should be getting dicked."

"Hear, hear," I agree, lifting an imaginary glass. "Should

we get going? Knowing this ride is going to be on Miller's dime, I think we should take the long way there."

Piper loops her arm through mine and grins. "You're damn right we should."

We meet Maven and Lexi downstairs and spend fifteen minutes fawning over each other's outfits. Our hair, our shoes, the diamond necklace Maven shows off—a gift from Dallas to match the diamond on her ring finger.

I'm warm and smiling when we slide into the limo and pop open the first bottle of champagne. I haven't had a sip of alcohol yet, but already, there's this bubbly, fizzy excitement in me. That rush you get when you're with people who make you feel good.

It's hard to make friends as an adult, and it's almost impossible with a schedule like mine. Friendship with them is easy, though. Every time we're together, I feel more and more like I'm a part of something special. Like I want to stay in DC for longer than the season and make a name for myself here, not just with the Stars, but with these women too.

"There's a note from Maverick." Lexi grabs the card sitting on the small table to her left and clears her throat before reading it aloud. "'To the four best women in the league—thank you for all you do. You deserve your name to be shouted from the rooftops.'"

"Aw, Mavvy!" Maven puts her hand over her chest, and my own heart skips a beat with his generosity. "I love that man so much. He's such a good guy."

"We might as well open the second one, right? Since he's paying and all," I say, and I reach for the next bottle.

The girls are distracted, speculating about who might be bringing who as a date tonight, but my attention snags on the small paper hiding behind a set of martini glasses.

I turn it over and find messy handwriting and a scribbled note.

EG—

I HOPE YOU'RE THE ONE WHO FINDS THIS.

IF NOT, I'LL DENY ANY INVOLVEMENT.

DON'T TELL THE OTHERS, BUT YOU'RE MY FAVORITE.

CAN'T WAIT TO SEE YOU TONIGHT.

I REALLY HOPE YOU'RE NOT WEARING ANY UNDERWEAR.

—PB

I read it a second time, and my cheeks hurt from smiling. I should toss the secret note in the trash, but I tuck it in my purse instead, wanting to keep it safe for reasons I can't quite figure out.

I can see the swanky hotel where the gala is being held from two blocks away. It's lit up in big, bright lights, and there's a red carpet rolled out like we're sports royalty.

Photographers stand in a line, snapping pictures of the players as they arrive, the flashes of cameras eager for a peek at the NHL's hottest team right now.

"Wow," I whisper as I step onto the sidewalk. "This is incredible."

"The events team likes to make a statement." Piper waves to someone up ahead, and Maven and Lexi climb the steps toward the building. "I'm pretty sure they blow their annual budget on this night alone."

"Now we can really celebrate. Is the auction as awful as I think it's going to be?"

"No. It's all very tame. Most of the time the guys will bid on each other if things turn awkward. Two years ago, this woman wouldn't leave Hudson alone. She kept trying to get his attention and upped her bid throughout the night so she'd be the one to win a lunch outing with him. It went well past friendly, and it made Hud really uncomfortable. Maverick swooped in and ended up donating a hundred grand, and they went on a bromance date to the planetarium at the Smithsonian."

"It's not nice to talk about people behind their backs, ladies," Maverick's deep voice says, and goosebumps sprout on my arms. "Even if you are complimenting me."

I take a second before turning around.

I really don't want to embarrass myself or have a physical reaction to seeing him out in public.

I don't want to give him that satisfaction.

Maverick sent me a selfie earlier, a sideways shot where I saw a pair of cufflinks. Polished shoes and tailored slacks that hug his body.

There was also the curve of his signature smirk, and the top two buttons of his shirt were popped open, showing just enough skin to make out a hickey on his neck. The red is fading to purple, and it made me want to leave another one next to it.

I blow out a breath, spin, and immediately want to throw my heel at his face.

Goddamn him all the way to hell.

I've seen him in suits and ties walking into games, but this is different.

He's sexy. The picture of every woman's fantasy wrapped up in a six-foot-four hunk of a man wearing a tuxedo and bowtie.

Moisture pools between my legs, and there's a swooping sensation low in my stomach. Liquid heat settles in my blood the longer I stare at him. My nipples harden under my dress, pointed peaks I know he can see, and as much as I'd like to blame it on the wind or the cold or anything else, we both know it's because of him.

"Hi, Mav." Piper gives him a quick hug. "Thank you so much for the limo."

"Anything for my favorite ladies. Did you all have fun?"

"We had a blast." She smiles and squeezes his arm. "You look nice."

I want to laugh.

Maverick Miller looks so beyond nice.

"So do you, Piper," he says, but he's not looking at her.

He's staring right back at me.

There's molten-hot awareness behind the darks of his eyes and the curl of a smile on his mouth. He licks his lips, a slow drag of his tongue reminiscent of a man starved, and it feels like he's running his tongue over every inch of me.

The jut of my hip. The inside of my thigh. The swell of my breast and across my stomach as he nudges my knees apart, ready to feast.

"Are you all right, Hartwell?" Maverick asks, and he tips his head to the side. "You look a little flushed."

I think I'm going into cardiac arrest.

"I'm fine." I fix the strap of my dress and his gaze flashes a shade darker. I wonder if he's undressing me with his eyes like I'm doing with him. "You do look nice, Miller. Glad to know you clean up so well."

"I'm going to head up," Piper says, turning for the stairs. "I'll see you inside, Em."

"Will you save me a seat at your table?" I ask.

"Sorry, Red. It's assigned seating, and you have a spot next to me," Maverick interjects. "But I'll make sure you have a good time."

"I'll come and visit," Piper promises, and she blows me a kiss. "Don't stay out here too long. It's freezing."

Funny.

I feel like I'm on fire.

"I'm right behind you," I assure her, and when she disappears into the crowd, I look back at Maverick. "Did you bring a date with you?"

"I did," he says, and I don't know why my heart sinks to the floor. "She's about yea high." He holds up his hand to his hip. "Likes to talk a lot. Definitely knows more about the Stars than I do and would put me to shame in a trivia match." At my confused expression, he laughs. "I brought Rachel. The girl from—"

"The arena tour," I finish for him, and my heart leaps back up to my throat. "You did?"

"I thought she…" He trails off, the rest of the sentence hanging unfinished. He shoves his hands in his pockets and looks up at the night sky. "She deserves to be here."

I reach out and touch his bicep, right where I know the tattoos of a cluster of stars sit. "Can I meet her?" I ask, and his smile is a shot to the center of my chest.

"She's sitting with her parents, so I'll make sure to bring her by the table. She'd love to see you." Off to the side of the crowd, someone calls out his name. "Save me a dance, Red. If I don't get my hands on you tonight, I think I might die."

"We'd hate to see that." I pat his chest and step past him, swaying my hips as I walk up the stairs. "You've turned into a liability since you stole my favorite pair of underwear, Miller. You should know I'm not wearing any tonight."

His mouth goes slack, and I grin all the way to my seat.

THIRTY-TWO
MAVERICK

WATCHING Emerson all night has been torture.

Her knee brushed against mine when we were listening to Coach's opening remarks, and I swear it was like she was on top of me.

Her fingers grazed up my thigh when she stood up from the table to use the restroom, and I forgot where I was for a few minutes.

No underwear.

A dress that hugs her curves.

A cocky little smirk that tells me she thinks she's winning whatever game it is we're playing.

She really is a redheaded assassin.

People have been vying for her attention since the minute she walked into the ballroom, and I can tell she's close to tapping out.

Her eyes bounce to the exit every few minutes like she's planning an escape. She keeps trying to step toward the buffet line, and I haven't seen her take a bite of food all night.

It's time to intervene.

I push back my chair and shrug off my tux jacket, making a beeline for Emerson. I work my way around the crowded dance floor toward her. I get stopped a handful of times by some of our corporate sponsors and season ticket holders. They tell me how much more fun it is to cheer for a team who's winning, and I laugh when I'm supposed to laugh.

I shake hands with all the important people who pay a lot of money to come and see us play, but the whole time, I keep an eye on her.

When I finally break free from a conversation about the All-Star team this year, I make a pitstop at the buffet line. I load up on chicken tenders and a helping of mashed potatoes. I shove a stack of napkins in my pants pocket for good measure—I've seen how the woman eats. She's going to make a mess, and it'll be the cutest thing in the world.

"I'm so sorry to interrupt." I slide up next to Emerson and rest my free hand on her lower back. "I need to steal my winger for a second. There's an urgent matter involving stick lengths, and her opinion is very important."

"Oh." The reporter—Stewart, his name tag tells me—widens his eyes. "That sounds important."

I nod, really wanting to sell this. "It's gravely important. Thank you so much for being so understanding, Stewart. I'd love to send you a jersey."

"Wow, really? That would be wonderful." He fumbles in his pocket and pulls out a business card. "Here's my contact information."

"I'll have our merchandise folks get in touch with you on Monday. Thanks, man." I pat his shoulder, and he beams. "You're a good one."

"Nice talking to you, Stewart. Have a good rest of your night," Emerson adds, and I guide her to a table tucked behind a speaker and a huge potted plant. No one should bother us over here. "Stick lengths, huh? Please tell me that's not a really corny innuendo, Miller."

"It could be." I drop my voice and brush my knuckles over

her bare shoulder. She shivers, and I want to touch her everywhere. "You look incredible in that dress, Red."

"Thank you. I don't get a chance to wear clothes like this often, and I wanted to take advantage of it."

"You should." I point to the empty chair, and she drops in it. I hand her the plate and napkins and sit beside her. "You wear business casual to the arena anyway. Why not wear a ballgown every once in a while?"

Emerson pops a fry in her mouth then licks the salt from her finger, and I've reached a new low in life: I'm officially jealous of a fucking appendage. "I wish it were that easy."

"It's not?" I frown and drop my elbow on my thigh, staring at her. "Enlighten me."

"I don't want to make this a whole sexism thing, but women are held to such a double standard. I wear a skirt to the arena that shows off my legs, and people call me a slut. I wear a jacket and a buttoned-up shirt, and I get called a prude. I'm sure when pictures of tonight make the rounds online, people are going to think I'm a bad role model for young girls just because you can see my cleavage."

"I, for one, am all for the cleavage. In fact, I think there should be more of it. Better yet, take the whole thing off. Preferably in my bedroom."

She smiles at me. There are four hundred people are here, and she's picking me to give out her smiles to.

I'm the luckiest bastard in this room.

"I appreciate your commitment to the cause." Emerson takes a bite of a chicken tender and sighs. "It's exhausting. Being a professional athlete is hard enough, but then there are comments under every one of my posts criticizing me. Why am I wearing makeup? Who let me leave the house in that outfit? How many guys on the team have I fucked? There aren't any of those comments under your photos."

I grab the leg of her chair and drag her closer to me. Our

thighs press together, and I don't bother to pull away. I want her right here.

"I'm sorry you have to go through that, and I'm sorry for joking about something that's not funny. I had no idea that was happening, and it's bullshit that people even say that kind of stuff in the first place. You're a role model no matter what you wear. Look at the arenas—not just ours, but the ones on the road too. Hundreds of girls are wearing your jersey. They look up to you because of how good of an athlete you are, but also because you're a kind person who goes out of her way to show her appreciation for the fans who show up for her. Take tonight. You talked with Rachel for twenty minutes and made her whole year when you could've been schmoozing with the rich guys who help pay our paychecks. What you wear on the outside isn't going to change what's on the inside, and that's a beautiful woman."

"Wow," she says, and I'm surprised when she reaches over and laces her fingers through mine. "That was the hottest thing I've ever heard."

"I'm not just saying that so I can slip my hand under your dress later."

"You can, by the way."

"Oh, I'm planning on it. I'm going to lose my mind otherwise. But I'd say the same thing even if I didn't get to bury my head between your legs. I mean it, Emmy. Every word."

"I like when you call me that," she whispers. "I like when you call me Red and Hartwell, but I also really like when you call me Emmy too. It doesn't sound the same compared to whenever anyone else uses my name."

"Yeah?" I swallow thickly, the tension between us slowly climbing. It's taking everything in me not to pull her into my lap and kiss her senseless, but I settle for resting our joined hands on her thigh. "Then I guess I'll have to keep doing it."

It's fucking reckless to be out in the open and acting like

this, to be touching her and drawing circles on her knee, but I want her to know she's perfect. That she could show up to games in a burlap sack and I'd still think she's the most incredible person.

I've been thinking about it more and more lately, and it's confusing me.

I know why I'm sexually attracted to her; there's her sarcasm and that dry wit. Her quick one-liners and how easily she makes me laugh. The softness she shows when she lets her guard down and the way her eyes light up when something makes her happy.

I just don't understand why I'm not bored of it yet.

I've always found it hard to stay interested in one person. I get antsy. My attention wavers after a few hours, and I'm ready to move on. I've been with plenty of women who are kind and sweet and funny. They check all the boxes other men are looking for, and I've never cared.

I care with Emerson, though.

I care a whole lot, and I don't know what the fuck that means.

"Are you okay?" She squeezes my hand and looks at me. "You disappeared there."

"Sorry. I was lost in my thoughts for a minute."

"Were they good thoughts?"

I look at her with her pretty dress and pretty make up, the twinkle in her eye and the half smile on her lips. "I was thinking about you." I swallow. "They were the best thoughts."

She touches my cheek, and her smile grows to a beam. "I'm glad."

"Do you want to dance?"

"To Justin Bieber? Is that even possible?"

"Anything is possible if you believe." I stand up and tug her to her feet. "Let's go."

"Hang on." She holds onto my shoulder and kicks off her heels. "Those were killing me. I have a blister on my pinky toe that's going to hurt when I wear my skates tomorrow."

I drop her hand as we walk through the crowd, but I can feel the heat of her body behind me.

Just as we make our way onto the dance floor, the song turns slower. Emerson purses her lips and lifts an eyebrow.

"Did you plan this, Miller?" she asks. "I bet you slipped the DJ a twenty."

"I'm innocent, I swear." I hold out my palm, an invitation there, and she glances around. I know she's worried about what people might think, but we can chalk it up to the spirit of charity. A captain and his teammate dancing together for one song in the name of raising funds for the local food bank and community outreach projects. "I'll be on my best behavior."

"Fine." She closes the distance between us. One of her hands settles on my shoulder, and I rest my palm on her lower back. "But if you step one toe out of line, you're going to be in big trouble."

"I promise," I say, sinking my fingers into the smooth fabric of her dress. "You haven't asked your question yet tonight."

"Because I asked first the other night," she says, and her chest almost presses into mine. "It's your turn."

"I just hit you with the Uno reverse. You're up."

"Do you want kids?"

"Wow, Hartwell." I laugh and rub my hand up her arm. "You're putting me through the wringer, aren't you?"

"Sorry. It's obvious you love June, and you did so well with Rachel tonight. I didn't know if that's a role you'd want to have."

"I'm not sure, to be honest," I answer, keeping my voice low in case people are listening. "I never saw myself in a position where I would have kids, so I've never considered it. I really enjoy being an uncle and hanging out with the young fans who come to the games, but I can't say for sure if I want them for myself. It's not a no, but a maybe."

"I think you'd make a great dad. You have one of the kindest hearts, Maverick. And there are plenty of people out there who need that joy you give."

Her praise makes my skin itch, like I'm not sure I'm worthy of it.

Kids means a commitment and a commitment means forever and... *fuck.*

Could I do that?

My own parents couldn't. Who's to say I won't turn out exactly the same way?

"What about you?" I ask around a rasp, and I clear my throat. "Do you want kids?"

Every time I peel back a layer of her, more appear. She's never mentioned her mom, and I'm wondering if that's because she's closer to her dad, or if her mom isn't in the picture anymore. I'm not sure I'll ever learn the answer.

"I could go either way," Emerson tells me. "I see all these happy families on social media and wonder if that could be me too. Then there's this louder part of me that knows how much I love my job. I love that I get to live out my dream, and right now, that's my focus. Maybe that makes me selfish, but until I close this chapter, I'm not ready to move on to the next one."

"You'd make a great mother, if that's something you decide you want to do."

She snorts. "I'm not sure I would. I just said I want to put myself first. Isn't parenthood supposed to be the most selfless job on the planet?"

"That doesn't mean you would be bad at it. You're self-aware, and that's important."

"I didn't expect my question to turn into something so deep. Can you lighten the mood, please?"

I dip her in my arms and the ends of her hair brush along

the floor. She looks up at me, and I can see the smile she's trying to fight. "Boxers or briefs?" I ask, and her sharp laugh surprises me.

"On who? You or me?"

"Me, obviously."

"Briefs." Her eyes bounce to my slacks, and her gaze heats. "I like that they don't hide anything. I like to see what I'm working with."

"Do you like what you see right now, Emmy girl?"

Emerson drags her attention to my mouth and lingers there. "Yeah," she says. "I like it a lot."

"Wanna head to the coat closet? I've done enough socializing. If I don't sink inside you soon, I will die."

"You're not dramatic at all." She rolls her eyes, but when I put her back on two feet, she gives my arm a tug. "Come on, Miller. Bring the potatoes with you too."

"I knew food was one of your kinks," I say, and we slip away from our teammates without anyone so much as batting an eye. "But, in the spirit of honesty, Red, I have to tell you something."

She glances at me over her shoulder. "What?"

"I did pay the DJ to play a slow song, and it was a lot more than twenty bucks. You've looked gorgeous all night, and I wanted a minute with you for myself. I guess that makes me selfish too. Something we have in common."

"How much did you pay him?"

"A thousand bucks. And I would've paid him a thousand more."

"You're absurd."

"You like it," I toss back.

This time when she smiles at me, I feel it in the center of my chest. There's a hollow part behind my ribs where I've never felt an ache before. It spreads through me until everything boils down to a single entity: her.

"Yeah," Emerson whispers, and I've never loved a word more. "I do."

When she yanks me by the belt loop and pulls us into the closet, there's a small, lingering voice in my head that tells me I might be in serious fucking trouble.

THIRTY-THREE
EMMY

"ARE you sure you don't want to come out with us?" Piper asks. "It's New Year's Eve!"

"I know, but after the loss the other day and our road trip coming up, I need a night in." I slip a shopping receipt into my book to mark my spot and stretch out my legs. "You're going to that new club downtown, right?"

"Yeah. I really want to have someone to kiss at midnight. Even if it is a stranger." She looks at me in the mirror and pouts. "I really can't convince you to come, can I?"

"Nope. I have some ice cream in the fridge, I'm going to open a bottle of wine, I'm reading a romance book that's making me kick my feet. What more can you ask for?"

"I'm only letting you off the hook because I started that book too, and I had to force myself to put it down. I know it's fictional, but it's making me believe in love again. Is that silly?"

I climb off the couch and walk toward her. "It means you know that kind of love is out there, and you're worthy of it. There's nothing silly about that, even if the words are make-believe. They can be real to you."

"Gosh." Piper fans her face. A tear slides down her cheek, and she wipes it away with her thumb. "I'm going to cry, and I told myself I am not allowed to cry this year."

"You are allowed to cry, but you're not allowed to cry over shitty men. They don't deserve your love and attention, let alone your tears." I wrap my arms around her in a hug and hold her tight. "I'm so proud of you. This is going to be your year. And what better way to kick it off than by finding the hottest man in the place and sticking your tongue down his throat?"

"Thanks, Emmy." She laughs into my shoulder and gives me a squeeze. "I might sleep at Lexi's tonight depending on how late we stay out. We might only last an hour then stuff our faces with Taco Bell."

"A Crunchwrap Supreme is never going to fuck you over. I support that decision." I pull away from her and pat the top of her head. "Have fun. Tell Lexi I say hi, and text me if you need me. I'll keep my ringer on just in case."

"You'd interrupt your sleep for me? I know how much you hate someone waking you up before your alarm goes off."

"You're not someone, Piper. You're my best friend."

"Damn you, Emerson Hartwell," she curses at me, grabbing her purse. "I'm leaving before you mess up any more of my makeup."

"I love you too," I call out, laughing when she makes a heart with her hands before she shuts the door.

I flip the deadbolt in place, and head back to the couch. I read for the next hour and a half, growing tired and letting out a yawn as the time on the clock stretches closer to midnight.

When I shut my book and stand up, my phone buzzes on the coffee table. I pick it up, expecting it to be Piper letting me know she forgot something, but I'm surprised to see a message from Maverick.

PRETTY BOY

Happy almost New Year's!

How are you spending the big night?

ME

Lounging around with a book. I'm about to have a bowl of ice cream then head to bed.

What are you doing? Are you at some fancy party on a yacht?

Instead of an incoming text, my phone rings with a Face-Time call.

Maverick's contact photo—the one he took at practice last week of him shirtless and holding eight hockey sticks above his head—flashes across my screen.

A small smile works its way across my mouth when I answer.

"There she is," he says, and he waves at the camera. There's a bruise on his cheek, a purplish red spot from when he got punched in the jaw during our game on Saturday. "Hey, Hartwell."

"That doesn't look like a yacht. Are you celebrating by yourself?"

"No way." He tilts his phone down, and June is sitting in his lap. She's painting the nails on his left hand, and they're wearing matching party hats that say HAPPY BIRTHDAY! "I have my best girl with me. She's giving me a makeover."

"What color did you go with?"

"Pink. It's her favorite," he says, and the camera pans back to him. "Are you home alone?"

"Yeah. Piper and Lexi went to a club. They invited me, but I'm tired. Plus, the thought of putting on real clothes sounds absolutely miserable."

"Do you want to come over and celebrate with us? We also have ice cream, so you wouldn't have to abandon your plans."

"And champagne," June adds, and I laugh.

"Champagne, huh? Are you being a bad influence, Miller?"

"Me? Never. The kid version is grape juice, but I have the adult version too. Come on, Red. You're right next door. You can be here in five minutes. No one should start off the New Year alone."

Suddenly, the apartment is too empty. That quiet I craved is too loud, and I feel unsettled and restless. A change of scenery sounds like the perfect idea.

Maverick sounds like the perfect idea.

"Okay," I say, and his whole face brightens. His eyes crinkle in the corners, and his smile could light up a whole room. "Let me brush my hair and change. I'll be there soon."

"Who cares what your hair looks like? Get your butt over here." Maverick flashes the camera to his thighs and the joggers that hug his muscles. I salivate a little, a natural reaction to seeing a man in gray sweatpants. "We're keeping it casual."

"Not all of us look that good in sweatpants."

"Wear a pair and let me be the judge of that. I'll give you a thorough inspection."

I roll my eyes, but I'm already halfway to my room and yanking off my thick socks. Unraveling my hair from its messy bun and opening my dresser drawers. I knock over a stack of folded laundry, and I leave it on the floor, making sure to grab the small gift bag sitting on my bedside table.

"I'll be there in ten minutes."

"You can do better than that, Emmy girl. Make it eight."

"Do I get a prize if I win?"

"Yeah." His eyes gleam. "A midnight kiss."

Never one to back down from a challenge, I flash him a smile. "Deal."

I make it to his apartment in seven minutes and thirty-two seconds.

Maverick opens the door before I can knock, and I'm immediately handed a party hat.

"Required dress code." He snaps the band around my chin and drags his fingers down my jaw. "Well done, Red. I'm proud of you."

I blush at the praise and distract myself by shrugging off my coat. I add my boots to a pile of shoes, and I smile at the little pair of Nikes on top of the stack.

"Where are Dallas and Maven? How did you end up on babysitting duties?"

"I volunteered. They're doing a dinner and champagne toast at the Four Seasons, and I got them a room for the night. They've been busy with their seasons and wrapping up the holidays, so I thought they deserved a little time to themselves tonight."

"That was kind of you."

He pulls me toward him and rests his hand on my hip. His thumb strokes down the inside of my thigh, and I sigh. "I like your sweatpants."

"The host was adamant. He's obnoxious."

"Sounds like it." Maverick cups the back of my head and urges his mouth to mine. The kiss sets my nerve endings on fire, and I feel like I'm floating high above the clouds. "Thanks for coming over."

"Thank you for having me. I, uh, brought you a present. It's a thank you for placing the highest bid for lunch with me at the charity gala auction. Now I don't have to eat a meal with any creeps."

"A present?" He smiles and takes the bag from me. "You didn't have to do that."

"It's nothing big. It's silly, really. Something stupid and—"

"Can I open it?"

"Of course you can."

Maverick plucks the tissue paper from the bag and pulls out a box. "A puzzle? Wow. Thanks, Emmy."

"I got one with fewer pieces so you and June could put it together." I shake my head. "I told you it's silly."

"No way. I'm adding it to the collection. I can never have enough puzzles, and this one is perfect."

"I appreciate the auction bid, but we don't have to actually go eat lunch anywhere."

"What if instead of going to lunch with me, you went with Rachel instead?" he suggests. "The money is already going to a good cause, and I'd like her to go in my place."

"That…" I nod, lost for words. "I'd really like that."

"I'll get in contact with her parents, and we'll set something up."

He holds my hand and guides me to the living room where June is sitting on the couch. She swings her legs back and forth, enthralled by the celebrations on the television.

"June Bug? Do you want to meet my friend Emmy?"

"Yes," she squeals, jumping off the couch and running my way. "Wow, Uncle Mav. She's really pretty."

"Did you pay her to say that?" I ask him.

"Nope. That's all her." He bends down and picks her up, holding her against his side. "She is pretty, isn't she?"

"I like your hair," June tells me. "It looks like a fire."

"Thank you." I smile and touch one of her pigtails. "I like yours too."

"Are you going to kiss Uncle Mav at midnight? Mommy and Daddy said you're supposed to kiss someone special."

"I'm not sure. Do you think I should kiss him?"

"Yes! Uncle Mav is the best."

My eyes meet Maverick's, and he's looking at me with an unreadable expression on his face. It's stuck somewhere between happy and confused, like he can't quite figure out what he's feeling.

I can't figure out what I'm feeling either, because seeing

him with a kid in his arms and loving on her does something to my insides.

It makes an image of five, ten years down the road pop in my head. A big house with a big yard. Bikes in the driveway and Maverick on a porch, his arms crossed over his chest and the world's most beautiful smile.

"He is the best," I agree, and I shake the daydream away.

"Do you want a drink? She's barely going to make it past midnight, and I'm going to put her to bed as soon as the ball drops."

"Are you drinking?"

"Nah. I stay sober when I'm watching her. My little monster can be a handful, and I like to have my wits about me when I'm in charge." Maverick tickles June's sides, and she screeches. "But I wouldn't have it any other way."

I watch the two of them, and instead of feeling like an outsider, I feel included. Part of their little group when June reaches for me and Maverick hands her over. When we sit on the couch and he drapes his arm around my shoulder, pulling me close. When we get to the five-minute countdown and June bounces on my lap.

I'm exactly where I'm supposed to be.

"June Bug, do you know what a resolution is?" Maverick asks, and she shakes her head. "It's when you pick something you're going to try to do for a whole year. It can be something big or something small. Like, my resolutions are that I'm going to try to cook more meals at home and do one in-person volunteer outing a month."

"I want to learn to ride a bike," she declares. "Crystal brought her bike to show and tell and it's pink."

"Whoa." Maverick pops his mouth open in surprise, but something tells me he's heard this story before. "A pink bike? How cool is that? We'll have to talk to the bosses, but I'm sure they'll be on board. You'll be zipping around here in no time, kid." He nudges me. "What about you, Red? What's your resolution?"

"I want to start thinking about making DC a permanent stop. I want to find an apartment and go to the same coffee shop on the weekends. I want to try out the farmers' market when the weather gets nice. I want to enjoy where I am and not look for the next thing for once."

The words rush out of me, and until he asked, I wasn't sure *what* my resolution was going to be.

I didn't think I had one.

Seeing the way my friends are living their lives, though, makes me want to give it a try.

It's scary to think I'm going to root myself somewhere and leave a piece of myself behind… but I'm ready.

"Yeah?" Maverick's smile rivals the sun, and I want to bottle it up. Keep it for when my days get dark and gray, a reminder of how much good is left in the world. "I really like the sound of you being around long term."

"That doesn't mean that we have to continue our arrangement or anything," I add, because I don't want him to get the wrong idea. Like I'm doing this for *him*.

"And if I want to continue our arrangement?" he asks, soft enough so June can't hear us. "What if I want to figure out how you take your coffee? See what plants you buy for your place and make fun of you for sleeping with eight blankets?"

I lick my lips. "I'd like that very much."

"Good. I'm glad we're on the same page."

"Ten!" June yells, and I glance at the television. Confetti falls from the sky, and "Auld Lang Syne" starts to play. "Nine! Eight!"

"Happy New Year, pretty boy," I whisper, and he rests his hand on the back of my neck. His touch is an anchor on my skin, and I blow out a breath.

"Two! One! HAPPY NEW YEAR!" June yells, and she blows on a streamer.

"Happy New Year, Emmy girl," he murmurs low and rough, and he crashes his lips against mine. It's brief, hardly anything like we do when we're together in bed, but that same bolt of electricity runs through me. "I think this is going to be the best year yet."

THIRTY-FOUR
MAVERICK

"JUNE IS ASLEEP. She wanted me to tell you she really liked you, and she can't wait for you to come back and hang out again soon." I lean against my bedroom wall and smile at Emerson. "You got the stamp of approval, Red."

"I'd hate to let her down," Emerson says from my bed, her legs hanging over the edge of the mattress and her feet almost on the floor. "Guess I'll be back."

"We'd like that very much."

She taps her phone on my bedside table and stands up. "It's late. I should get going."

"What if you stay?" I blurt. "It's cold, and I know you're right next door, but everyone's going to be stumbling home drunk and messy. I don't want something to happen to you."

"We don't do sleepovers," Emerson says slowly. "We never have."

"What if we did tonight?"

In all the times we've fucked, we've always gone back to our own rooms after a few minutes of cuddling.

I'll kiss her forehead. She'll run her hand up my chest. There's a moment where we both pull apart, a string cut in two and the natural end to the intimacy.

I don't want that tonight.

I want her right here.

Emerson bites her bottom lip. Her eyes bounce to the door behind my shoulder then to the stack of pillows next to her.

"Okay," she says, and I almost pump my fist in the air. "Only if you set an alarm so I can sneak out before June wakes up. I don't want to be held responsible for having to give a lecture on the birds and the bees."

"Deal." I lock the door and pull off my hoodie. "Do you want some clothes to sleep in? You can borrow one of my shirts. I want to see what you look like with my name on your back."

"When are you going to wear my name on *your* back?"

"I'd love to make that happen, Red." I rifle through my dresser and find an old practice jersey, tossing it to her. "Wear that one."

"Thanks."

Emerson pulls her shirt off, and her tits bounce free. I blow out a breath when she stands up and takes off her sweatpants, leaving a pair of boy shorts she's been hiding all night behind.

"Those are pretty," I rasp, staring at the pink lace. "I like that pair."

"You do?" She slips on my shirt and turns in a slow circle so I can admire her backside. The muscles in her hamstrings and calves. Her ass cheeks and smooth skin. *My fucking name* stretched over her shoulders, and I might come from the sight of that alone. "Is the rest of me pretty?"

"So fucking pretty, baby. I like that you have nice things." I shimmy out of my pants and switch my briefs for a pair of loose boxers, my eyes never leaving her body. "I like that you spoil yourself and buy what you want. It's sexy."

"I don't have the contract you do, but men have been intimidated by what I make from playing and the few brand partnerships I have. They don't usually like that I'm tall or that I could beat them in arm wrestling. They don't like the blisters on my hands or when I look sweaty and gross." She tips her head to the side, and our gazes meet. "Not you, though. You like all those things."

"I love those things." I swallow and take off my shirt, leaving it in a pile with the rest of our clothes. "I told you that you've only been with boys, not men. Men want you to spend your hard-earned money. They want you to wear those heels, Emmy girl, because you look like a goddess in them."

Emerson sits on the bed and opens her thighs. Her underwear is wet, a small damp spot on the front I want to lick and taste. "You should fuck me in my heels one day."

I tilt my head back and groan. My cock jumps in my boxers, and my hand flexes at my side. *Fuck*, I want to feel her shoes around my waist. Pressing into my back as I press into her.

"I'd like that," I say, feeling dizzy as I watch her lean back on her elbows and offer herself to me. "Next time we're on the road and you wear that little leather mini skirt. I'll fuck you in that."

"Keeping tabs on my outfits, Miller?" Her smile is soft at the corners, and she reaches for me. "Is that one your favorite?"

"Yeah." I turn off the lamp by the bed and scoop her in my arms, shuffling across the California king until we're in the middle. "I'm a sucker for your legs. Fuck what the prudes think."

"Noted." She rests her cheek on my chest and yawns. As much as I want to pull her on top of me and fuck her, I can tell she's exhausted. "What's your question? It's the first one of the year, so it has to be good."

"Will you tell me about your family?" I ask, brushing her hair with my fingers. "You didn't go home for the holidays, did you?"

"Oh." Emerson is quiet for a minute, and she stiffens in my arms. "No, I didn't."

"You don't have to talk about it if you don't want to. You never owe me an answer."

"It's complicated. My dad played hockey in college, and when he and my mom were trying for kids, he really wanted a boy. When I was born, my mom was determined to steer me toward any other sport. Ballet. Figure skating. I even tried water polo and rowing. I kept going back to hockey, and she resented it," she says.

"Why?"

"She always wanted a daughter, and I think she had this idea in her head where we'd go shopping together and get our nails done and I wouldn't be around sweaty teenage boys. I do like to do those things, but I like to hit the puck too. I'd come home with black eyes and bruises on my body and she'd be so angry. She and my dad argued a lot—there was a lot of blame. A lot of yelling. Eventually, they got divorced. Sometimes..." Emerson trails off.

"Hey." I brush a piece of hair away from her face. "You don't have to tell me if you don't want to."

"No. It's not that. It's just... I carry this weight with me. I think it's my fault. Maybe I should've just done something else to make her happy. It's why I walk around with this chip on my shoulder; I feel like I have to constantly defend my decisions."

"No way," I say fiercely. "That's not how being a parent works. You were doing things that made *you* happy, and she should've been happy for you too."

"She remarried and has three perfect daughters who wear dresses and go shopping with her and don't have bruises all over their arms from getting shoved into the boards during a game." She sighs. "She got what she wanted, and I guess I did too."

"What about your dad?"

"He got hurt," she says softly, and my heart drops to my feet. "A freak accident at a beer league game a decade ago. Broken cervical vertebrae. He's paralyzed from the waist down."

She sniffs and buries her face in my neck. I don't know what to say. I don't know how to comfort someone who just shared the most tragic part of their life with me, because telling her *it's all right. It's going to be okay* sounds like a load of fucking bullshit.

But I want to make it okay. I want to take her pain and carry some of it for myself, so she doesn't have to do it alone.

"I'm sorry," I whisper, and I stroke her hair. I rub her back and hold her tight to my chest. "I'm so sorry he had to go through that."

"It's not your fault." She looks up at me, and her bottom lip quivers. I wipe away a tear and kiss her forehead. "I go home during the summer, but it's hard to get away for more than a day during the season. When I'm there, everything moves a little slower, and I never want him to feel like I'm rushing through my time with him."

"I'm glad you still get to see him. I bet he's so proud of you."

"Proud is an understatement." Her laugh tickles my skin. "He tells everyone I play hockey. People at the grocery store. The guys at the gas station. He owns about fifteen of my jerseys, and he has a weekly rotation."

I smile. "He sounds awesome."

"He's the best. Despite everything he's been through, he sends me a text every morning saying 'great news! Today is the best day of your life!'" She laughs. "I didn't inherit his optimism, but I go along with it anyway."

"What are you talking about? You're the most optimistic person I've ever met," I tease, and she pinches my ribs. "Thank you for sharing him with me."

"What about you?" Emerson asks. "There's nothing on your Wikipedia page about your family. I've checked."

"Stalking me, Hartwell?"

"It's called curiosity, Miller."

I hum. "You won't ever find anything on my Wikipedia page. I pay a lot of money to keep it that way."

"You do?" She frowns. "Why? You're not that private a person, are you?"

"No. I, uh, grew up in foster care," I say, and her eyes widen. "I aged out of the system."

"What?" Emerson sits up. She crosses her legs and stares at me. "Are you serious?"

"Yeah. I don't remember a lot about my childhood. I know my dad wasn't very nice to my mom. There was lots of yelling and things getting thrown. My childhood psychologist told me my mom was fighting a lot of mental health battles; postpartum depression and anxiety. Bipolar disorder. The best thing for my future was foster care."

"You never found a home?" she asks softly.

"No. Nothing ever worked out. I went through eight different families before I aged out, and by then, I was grateful to be out. I didn't want to get my hopes up only to be sent back." I take her hand in mine and kiss her knuckles. "People ask why I sleep with so many women, and I think it's because I just want to be fucking wanted. They know what they're getting into because I'm very honest about it—it's only for the night. Sex and no attachments. They might claim they want to date me, that they want something long term, but we know it's only for tickets and money and fame.

"One-night stands soothe that need to be wanted, to have someone who wants to keep me, even if it's only for a few hours. This way, I get to control things. *I'm* the one who leaves, not them. That probably makes me a horrible person. My therapist tells me sex can't be my coping mechanism forever, and I'm starting to understand why. The older I get, the more I have this deeper desire to be wanted for real. To find someone who wants to keep me—not Maverick Miller the hockey player, but Maverick Miller, the fuckup kid without a family who tells jokes so no one knows he sometimes feels dead inside. And not just for the night, but for a long time. It goes against everything I've wanted up to this point, and it confuses the ever-loving fuck out of me."

"Oh, Maverick," Emerson whispers, and she climbs into my lap. Her hug is grounding, and when she rocks me in her arms, my nose stings. I blink away tears, and I hide my face in her hair. "You sweet man. You're the furthest thing from a horrible person. You have a gentle soul that's been beaten up and broken through no fault of your own. I'm so sorry anyone's ever made you feel like you weren't worth keeping for more than a night. You are and you're wonderful and… and one day, when you want to settle down, you're going to make someone really happy, and they're never going to leave. You know why?"

"Why?" I ask, keeping my face hidden.

I'm afraid to look at her. To show her this stripped-down and broken side of myself I've never let anyone else see. Not even Hudson or Dallas or Reid have cracked open this part of my shell. I guess I shouldn't be surprised that Emerson's the person to do it; she's heard so many of my secrets, this is just another we're adding to the pile.

"Because you love everyone fiercely. You put your whole being into the people you care about, and a woman is going to come along who sees that. Who knows what a gift you are, and it will be an honor for her to fall in love with you. She'll protect your heart, and it's going to be okay."

I've never imagined my future, but for a second, I do. I look one year, five years, ten years down the road and try to get a glimpse into who that person might be, but all I see is red hair.

Green eyes.

A wicked smile and a whispered *pretty boy* in my ear.

Oh, fucking shit.

My eyes fly open and I pull away so I can look at her. Emerson is staring at me, and I don't know what to do.

I don't know what to *fucking do* because this is my *fuck buddy* not my *fucking forever buddy*. But the idea of fucking her forever doesn't scare me when it normally would, and I think I might be having a stroke.

"Hey." She touches my cheek and frowns. "Are you okay?"

No.

Yes.

I don't fucking know.

Am I staring at the woman whose finger I'm going to put a big fucking ring on someday?

Am I going into a tailspin because I never talk about this shit and she's the one I'm talking about it with and it's tricking my brain into thinking we're going to have a life together?

"I'm fine," I get out, and I know she doesn't believe me. "Thank you for listening to me. I know it doesn't have to be said, but if you could not run off and tell—"

"My lips are sealed. I promise."

I'm done talking. I'm done with feelings and confusing emotions.

I want her.

I want to fuck her like I always do and get back to the normal that we do so fucking well.

I take off her shirt and bring my mouth to her chest, sucking on her nipple. I slip my hand between her legs and nudge her thighs open, hissing when I find her wet and tight and ready for me.

"Fuck, I want you, Emmy," I say into her neck, and I lick a hot swipe of my tongue up her throat. "Can I have you?"

"Please," she begs, and she tugs on my boxers. Her hand wraps around my cock and she strokes me with determined pumps. "I need you, Maverick."

"Let me get a condom." I reach for the bedside table, but her fingers curl around my wrist. "What's wrong?"

"Can you fuck me without one?" she whispers, and my skin burns. "I want to feel you."

I take a deep breath and try to shove all the smart and rational thoughts to the front of my brain, but it's fucking difficult when she takes my other hand and rests it flat on the bed. When she lifts her hips and sinks down, fucking herself on my fingers.

"*Goddammit*," I groan. "Are you—what do—"

"I'm on the pill," she says. "I take it every day."

"Are you sure?" I let go of the drawer and wrap my hand around her neck. "You have to be one hundred percent sure, Emmy, because when I sink into you and fuck you raw, that's it. You're mine for good. I'm not sharing you with anyone else. It's my cum that's going to fill you up. It's my cock that's going to take care of your pussy. I'm going to have you wherever the fuck I want, and I'm a needy man, baby. I'm going to need you a lot."

Her throat bobs, and her eyes blaze with desire. She rolls her hips and moans. "No one fucks you like I do, do they? That's why you keep coming back to me. I'm the only girl you've ever been with more than once because you can't get enough of me, can you?"

White-hot pleasure rips through me when she grips my cock and runs her thumb over the slit. She rubs pre-cum across the head, and I'm already seeing fucking stars.

"I can't get enough of you," I agree, and she strokes me all the way to the base. Up, then back down, and I'm panting like I've never been touched before. "I'll never get enough of you, baby."

"I'm sure. I'm sure, Maverick, and I want you to fuck me like I'm yours."

Everything turns blurry after that.

Mine.

I ease Emerson onto her back and climb on top of her. I bend her legs until they press into her chest and I grip her thighs. I tease her with my cock, rubbing her clit until I'm covered in her wetness and she's begging me to take her.

And I do.

I slide inside her, and this, *this*, is fucking heaven. The way she feels warm and perfect around me. How she clenches around my cock and groans when I hit the perfect spot.

It's fucking—rough and primal and claiming in a way I've never claimed anyone else.

But it feels different too.

I notice it when she takes my hand in hers. When our eyes meet mid-thrust and she smiles. When I try to pull out but she asks me to come inside her, a shyness to her words that's never been there before.

After, when we've cleaned up and she's in my arms, it's there again.

I never really felt like I had a home. But with Emmy next to me, I think home is wherever she is.

A place I'd like to stay forever.

THIRTY-FIVE
EMMY

THERE'S a knock on the door of the bathroom I'm getting ready in.

The Dallas Wildebeests, like every other NHL team, don't have a female locker room in their arena. I've had to make do with the companion restroom in the hallway that leads out to the ice.

I hate it.

I hate that all my gear is spread out on the floor.

I hate that I don't have a spot or an area that feels like mine.

I hate that I have to drape my jersey over the hand dryer while my teammates get eight-foot-tall cubbies where they can hang their uniforms and keep them looking nice.

I hate that it smells like pee, and I hate that I'm separated from everyone else.

"Someone is in here," I say. I check the hair tie around my braid and make sure it's secure. "I'll be out in a second."

"Emmy? It's Piper. Can I come in?"

I unlock the door and step back so she can slip inside. "Hi."

"Hi." She wrings her hands together and stares at the floor. "I have to tell you something."

My mind immediately goes to Maverick. An injury. A trade. A suspension for something stupid he said in an interview just now.

There's a pile of bricks in my stomach, and every muscle in my body stiffens.

"What's going on?" I ask, and my heart rate kicks into overdrive.

"The Wildebeests just handed us their final roster for the game." Piper brings her chin up and looks at me. "They called up Cole Meyers from their AHL affiliate, and he's playing tonight."

The world stops spinning.

I grip the edge of the sink so hard my knuckles turn white. My breath stutters in my chest, and I almost topple over.

We all have a relationship we wish we could take back. The one we'd do over and warn our past selves to steer clear of.

Cole Meyers is mine.

I met him when we played for the ECHL's Nashville Bulls four years ago. He was a late-season addition, a trade acquisition from Philadelphia, and I was immediately drawn to him.

He's the kind of guy everyone likes. His personality dominates a room, and he's always the center of attention. A crowd favorite and a real charmer, he knows how to make people laugh.

His blond hair makes him look like he belongs out in California catching waves instead of being on the ice, and with blue eyes and a kind smile, I fell for him.

I fell for him *hard.*

I'd dated other men before, but I thought Cole was going to be the one.

Everything was great our first year together. We fell into a routine between practice and games and picking out plants for my apartment. I talked about him moving in. He talked about rings. A wedding in a field or a ceremony on the beach.

The stupid things we say when we're in love.

After a stretch of games where his performance was off and he had trouble controlling his temper, he got moved to the second line, then the third.

I took his spot as a starter, and that's when all hell broke loose.

In front of people, we were fine. A perfect couple living out their dreams.

When we were alone and no one could hear him, it was a different story.

You know Coach only moved you up because he wants to sleep with you, not because you have any actual talent.

The only reason you have a position on this team is because management likes your tits.

Did you know there's a running joke in the locker room about who you're going to have a gang bang with? Sometimes I tell our teammates I'll sneak them over when you're asleep. Maybe let them lift up your shirt and take a peek.

Bile rises in my throat.

I don't know why I stayed another six whole months after that.

Maybe I got caught up trying to justify his behavior. Maybe it became so normal to hear those things, I started to think they were true.

It wasn't until I watched him give his number to a fan at one of our games that finally broke me out of that horrible spell. I wanted out, and two weeks later, I was in San Diego.

"When did this happen? Last I checked, he was in Utah."

"He was, until the Wildebeests lost a winger after a Christmas ski accident that left him with a broken arm, and Cole got called up." Piper steps toward me. "Are you okay?"

No.

I'm not okay.

A month after I landed in San Diego, I found out he had been promoted to the AHL.

There was so much relief. I'd never have to see him again. I wouldn't have to skate past him and tune out the things he said under his breath. I could pretend that part of my life never happened.

But now I'm going to see him again in front of twenty thousand fans.

God.

"Does he know I'm playing for the Stars?" I ask, which is a stupid question, because *how could he not?*

The media attention hasn't quieted down since I joined the team. Anyone who's watched a sports network in that time has seen a picture of me in my Stars jersey.

Even Cole.

"Yeah. He, um, was giving an interview in the tunnel and said he doesn't understand the hype around your mediocre performance."

Some things never change.

"Of course he did." I rub my forehead and sigh. "Do I have any options here?"

"Do you want to play?"

"Yes," I say right away. "I'm not going to let him take this away from me."

"From a media standpoint, I can tell you the easiest thing for you to do is to not engage with him unless it's totally necessary. Ignore what he says—you know he's going to try to start some shit. Keep your head down and play your game." She pauses. "As your friend, I would tell you to give him hell."

"I can do that." I roll my shoulders back and fix my pads. "I'll be okay."

"I know you will be. You're so strong, Emmy. I'm sorry I had to be the one to tell you, but I figured you'd rather know now than be surprised when you get on the ice."

"I do. I appreciate you looking out for me, Piper." I scoop

my helmet off the floor and buckle it around my chin. "I need to get to the tunnel."

"The boys are out there. Are you going to tell them?"

I don't want to, but I think I have to.

"Yeah." I nod and chew on my bottom lip. "I'm going to tell them."

"I'll be in the stands." Piper squeezes my elbow. "And I'll be here after the game if you need anything."

"You're the best kind of friend." I hug her. "Gosh, I love you."

"I love you, too, Em. Now go kick that fucker's ass."

I open the door. The tunnel is crowded, and my teammates are all waiting to head to the ice.

Connor and Grant knock their skates against each other. Riley is listening to something Lexi is saying, and I've never seen someone nod so many times. Liam is staring at the wall, mumbling under his breath and biting his jersey like always, and Hudson and Maverick are in the corner, talking each other's ears off.

When Maverick spots me, his eyes light up. He breaks out into a smile, and he lifts his hand in a wave.

I try to laugh, but it comes out more like a grimace. He frowns and walks toward me, scooting past Seymour and Ethan.

"Hey. What's wrong?" he asks.

"Nothing."

"Bullshit."

I tip my chin to look up at him. "I just found out my ex is playing for the Wildebeests tonight. I wasn't expecting it, and I'm kind of freaking out."

"Is this four-inch-dick dude?"

"Yeah."

"Bad breakup?"

"Something like that."

Maverick steps closer. He crowds my space, eyes holding

mine. "Did he lay a finger on you?"

"What?" Hudson asks from my left. "Who put a finger on her?"

"Someone hurt Emmy?" Ethan pulls off his gloves. "Who the fuck was it?"

"Hell, no. We ride at fucking dawn!" Grant yells, and Seymour pats his shoulder.

"Maybe we ride in the next ten minutes, G."

"My ex who I played with in the ECHL. He moved to the AHL, and the Wildebeests called him up to play tonight," I rush out, telling them all the truth.

"Did he hurt you?" Maverick asks, lethally low.

"No. *No*. He wasn't nice, but he never put a finger on me."

"What did he say? What did he do?" Maverick yanks off his helmet and tosses it at the wall. There's so much intensity behind his eyes, I almost stop breathing. "Tell me, Emerson."

"He said a lot of things... That the only reason I got anywhere on the team was because my old coach wanted to sleep with me. That I was only signed because management liked how I looked. He joked—" I shake my head. I can't finish the next part.

"What. Did. He. Say?"

"He joked that he was going to let my teammates come over and do what they wanted to me while I slept. That I was going to be passed around the locker room so everyone could have their fill." A sob bursts out of me. "I'm sorry. I don't know why I'm crying. I don't want to make this weird. I promise I have control over my emotions."

Out in the stands, the fans scream in anticipation of the game. The starting lineup music begins to play, but inside our tunnel, it's deathly quiet.

"Come here," Hudson says, the first to speak, and he pulls me into a hug.

I sink into the comfort of his embrace, and it feels good to be held by someone I look to as a brother. To know he has my back and he's here for me, tears and all.

"I'm going to kill him," Maverick whispers. "I'm going to rip each one of his limbs from his body until he's nothing but a pile of fucking bones."

"What position does he play?" Hudson asks, and I wipe my eyes.

"Left winger. I replaced him on the starting line, and that's when things went south."

"That's our girl," Seymour yells, and I'm close to bursting into tears again.

"We're going to take care of him," Ethan says, and he puts a hand on my shoulder. "We've got your back, Emmy."

"Yeah," Grant adds. "You're ours now."

"If he comes within four feet of the goal, I'll shove my stick down his throat," Liam says, and from him, it's the equivalent of a love poem.

"You all really don't have to—"

There's a tug on my arm, and Maverick pulls me toward him. He cups my cheek and drops his head so his forehead presses against my helmet. "Do I need to remind you about the things we have to do and the things we want to do?"

"No." I swallow. "I remember."

"And you also remember that I take care of what's mine, right?" he asks, lower this time.

"Yes," I whisper. "I do."

"Good."

He pulls away and looks down the hall. Coach Saunders is walking our way, and he stops in his tracks when he sees us all huddled together.

Maverick grins, and there's nothing sweet about it. "You might want to call the commissioner and start apologizing, Coach. We're going to be in a heap of fucking trouble when we're finished here tonight."

THIRTY-SIX
MAVERICK

I'M NOT A VIOLENT GUY.

I get into the occasional fight during games, a tussle where I throw off my gloves and get down to business, but most of the time, it's for shits and giggles. Something to rile up the crowd that doesn't have any real bite behind it.

Today, though, I'm on a warpath.

Cole Meyers is my target, and I'm not going to stop until I've broken him into a thousand pieces.

The rest of the guys feel the same way. I see it in their eyes as we take the ice for warmups. Disdain rolls off of them when they look at the Wildebeests bench, and I know tonight is going to be a fucking bloodbath.

I half-ass my stretches near center ice. It's pointless to spend my normal amount of time getting my body loose and limber—I'm not going to be in the game long enough to care how my legs feel.

Cole skates up to me and gives me a wide grin. "Miller," he says, like we're best fucking friends. College bros in the same fraternity who partied together, and it makes me sick. "Nice to meet you."

I'd love to put my hands around his throat. Wring his neck

until he was out of air and couldn't breathe. And when he begged for mercy, I'd only press harder.

"And who are you?" I bend down to fix my laces. Anything is better than looking at his stupid face.

"Cole," he yells over the music. "Cole Meyers. I got called up for tonight's game. It's my first time in the NHL," he says proudly, and I hum like I give a shit.

"Congratulations," I toss back.

Passed around.

Everyone could have their fill.

I don't care if he said it as a joke.

Whether it's locker room bullshit he's tossing around because he's trying to be fucking funny.

This man is a predator and the scum of the earth, and I can't wait to end him.

I take a breath and scan the rink, trying to calm down and ignoring the fucker in front of me. I spot Emerson finishing her stretches and talking with Hudson.

He's making her laugh, telling some elaborate story with his hands. I smile when her shoulders shake and she tips back her head, her laughter echoing across the ice.

There's not a lick of jealousy when I look at them. I don't want to pull him away from her or act like an idiot so I can get her attention.

All I am is really fucking grateful.

I'm grateful for his cool demeanor and the way he's keeping her company. I'm grateful he's making sure there's a smile on her face. I'm grateful when he glances over at me and gives me a single nod, telling me it's okay.

"You all are having a good year," Cole says, and I realize he's been talking for the last fifteen seconds. "Playoff bound probably."

"Looks like it."

"My AHL team has been shit this season, and I really hope I can stay with the Wildebeests long-term. The AHL is filled with a bunch of has-beens, so it's nice to be around some real athletes."

My eye twitches.

Real athletes, like we don't all play the same fucking sport.

I'm proud of myself for not already pummeling this fucker to the ground, but I have to be strategic.

Punching him in the face unprovoked before the game starts will get me arrested. As soon as the whistle sounds, though, anything goes.

I'm going to butter him up. Let him think I'm on his side with his holier-than-thou act, then pull the rug out from under him. Surprise him with a twist he'll never see coming.

"Good luck out there tonight," I say, and Cole blinks at me. He's so delusional, he thinks I'm being sincere. "You're going to need it."

The horn on the arena clock sounds, and I skate toward my teammates. We form a huddle, and I sling my arms around Ethan and Grant's shoulders.

"I know each of us has a personal vendetta going into this game, so I'm not even going to bother with the lecture about staying focused. However you want to take out that frustration is up to you, but know that I support you. I have your back. We'll be spending a lot of time in the sin bin, and that's fine by me," I say.

"Can I say something?" Emmy asks, and I nod. "I'm not a woman who likes when people do things for her, and I'd never ask you all to defend my honor or anything like that. But knowing you have my back means a lot to me. I'm so lucky to play next to you all every night, and I wouldn't want to call anyone else my teammates."

"We love you, Emmy," Grant yells, and he tries to jump in her arms. Her skate slips out from under her, and they both go tumbling to the ice.

"Pile on," Ethan says, and other guys join them like we just won the Cup.

"Hey," I say. "No getting injured before the game. We have business to take care of."

"What's your plan tonight, Cap?" Hudson murmurs, nudging my my side.

"The only thing I have planned, Hud, is that I'm going to spend fifty-eight minutes in the locker room after I get tossed, and you all are going to have to play without me."

"When Emmy told us all of that…" He trails off and shakes his head. He's always been sensitive, a guy with the utmost respect for women. I saw the horror in his eyes when he heard about her past, and it looked like he was going to be sick. "I don't know what I want to do."

"I guess we need to decide if we care about a loss or not. We're three weeks out from the All-Star Game, and we're sitting pretty at the top of our division. Third in the east, but we're only two games off Boston for the top spot. I know what my answer would be and—"

"Forget the win. This goes past hockey. This is personal," he says, and he glances at me. "More so for some of us."

"What are you talking about?"

"I saw the way you reacted when Emmy repeated what her ex said. I saw how you wanted to comfort her. You don't have to tell me what's going on with you two, but I've been playing behind you for years. I can read you like a book, Mav. She means a lot to you."

"Yeah." I swallow and watch Seymour pull her back on her skates. "She does. That's why all bets are off."

"That's what I thought." He clasps my shoulder. "Let's give this asshole hell."

"Get him," I scream at Ethan from the bench, and he rams Cole into the boards so hard the glass shakes.

The crowd boos, asking for a penalty, and I know Ethan is flipping them off under his glove.

Five minutes of game time, and this dude's been brutalized ten times. I almost feel bad for him, but then I see Emmy skate past me, and I think it's not nearly enough.

Coach whistles, and I jump back on the ice, charging toward the puck. I catch a pass from Hudson and take off toward the goal on a breakaway. Out of the corner of my eye, I see Emmy open on my left.

"Red," I yell. I pass to her and block the Wildebeests player on her heels, bumping him out of the way with my lower half. "Go!"

Emmy gets a burst of speed, and as she approaches the goal on a breakaway, she pulls back, a beautiful snap shot that sends the puck straight into the net.

It's the same maneuver she did on me all those months ago when we had our first skate together, and my chest feels impossibly tight.

"Yes!" I scream, wrapping my arms around her and pulling her against me in a hug. Hudson crashes into us and Riley joins too. "That was perfect, Hartwell."

"What a shot, Em."

"Fuck, that feels good." She laughs and wipes a bead of sweat from her cheek. "The nerves are gone now."

"Thatta girl," I murmur, and she fists the bottom of my jersey. "You're incredible."

"Thanks for the assist."

"Told you I was going to work on it." I grin when she shakes her head. "You all are going to have to finish it from here. I'm done being a nice guy, and I'm ready for some carnage."

"Are you sure about this?" Emmy asks.

"Never been more sure of anything in my life, Red. I'll be watching the rest of the game from the locker room." I look at Hudson. "Think you could start a fight for me?"

"You want *me* to start it?"

"I know you're not an instigator, but I'm going to be the one to finish it."

Understanding dawns, and he gives me a firm nod. "You've got it, Mav."

The crowd is antsy. Their team is losing, and as someone who's lost a lot of games in his career, I want to give them something to be excited about.

The play progresses past center ice, and Ethan has the puck. Hudson hangs back, and as Cole starts to advance forward, he sticks out his skate and trips him.

Cole hits the ice face first, and the fans scream. He springs back up, ready to duel, and Hudson drops his gloves faster than the blink of an eye.

I give them a second to go at each other, and I have to give Hud credit. As a dude who never, ever dukes it out with anyone, he's holding his own.

I skate up next to them and shake off my gloves, grabbing Cole by the back of his jersey.

"What the fuck?" he yells, and he stares at me with wild eyes. "What the fuck is your problem?"

"You want a list?" I punch him square in the jaw, and his face whips to the side. "Let's start with Emmy."

Cole tries to smack my shoulder, but I'm bigger than him. More athletic with more experience, and he doesn't get close. "That whore? Who's she fucking to get the starting role this time? Is it you, Miller? Your buddy Hayes? Or maybe both of you."

A referee tries to grab me, but I use my size to my advantage and shrug him off. The fans in the front row of seats beat on the glass, a faint noise I barely hear because my next punch lands right in the middle of his face. Blood spurts from his nose, and I grin. Adrenaline pulses through me, and I haven't felt this alive in years.

"Let me tell you something about Emmy, you small-dicked

piece of shit. In fifteen years when she's being inducted into the Hall of Fame and you're a nobody who's never accomplished anything in this sport, your kids are going to be talking about her." I yank on his collar and pull him closer, making sure he catches every word. "You're going to have to buy them her jersey, and you'll tell them about the time you let her get away because you couldn't stand the thought of being with a woman who was a better athlete than you. But guess what? She's mine now, motherfucker, and I'm not going to let you disrespect her anymore." My fist connects with his teeth, and I laugh when he whimpers in pain. "You want more? I can keep going."

Cole breaks free from my hold and manages to throw a punch that hits my right eye. I stumble backward and grab his arm, tugging him down to the ice with me. I kick my legs free and flip us over, straddling him and cracking my knuckles.

I aim for his nose again. "That's for saying she only has a job because she sleeps around." I go for his jaw next, and something pops in his cheek. "That's for saying you'd let your teammates touch her." I move to his forehead and deck him there. "That's for making fun of the books she likes to read." My final blow is to his eye, and I hope I break his eye socket. "And that's for getting to her before me."

Chaos unfolds around us. Two refs try to pull me off, but it's another Wildebeests player who yanks me away from Cole and slams me down. I get punched in the nose, and the copper taste of blood stings my tongue. A whistle blows, and Hudson is in front of me, helping me to my feet.

Cole lies motionless, his eyes closed and blood trailing down his face.

Good.

I kick his leg as I skate toward the locker room, already knowing my punishment.

I look toward the bench and see Emmy, her mouth half-open and her eyes wide. I grin at her, and before I head into the tunnel, I make a heart with my hands and hold it up to her. She tucks her chin and hides her smile.

Being on top of Cole helped me realize something.

I don't want her as a teammate or someone I fuck multiple times a week.

I want her as so much more—a partner. A girlfriend. My best friend.

I don't know if we lose the game or not.

I really don't fucking care, because I've already won.

I have her, and she's the greatest prize of all.

THIRTY-SEVEN
EMMY

GRADY:

Maverick didn't show Cole any mercy, did he?

When were you going to tell me you two are dating?

ME

We are not dating.

GRADY:

You're doing some extracurricular activities, that's for sure.

And they're probably horizontal.

ME

I'm never answering your texts again.

GRADY:

Classic Emmy deflection!

Must mean it's true.

THE VISITORS' locker room is chaos after the game. Grant sneaks me in, and the boys are acting like we won the Cup.

Someone filled Coach in on why we played so aggressively, and even though he's not acknowledging his star player and three other guys getting tossed, there's pride in his eyes when he drags Maverick to a small alcove to debrief.

"We have a lady in our midst," Ethan yells. "No one drop your drawers, and keep everything covered."

"That was worth playing shorthanded," Riley says. He wipes his forehead with his jersey and grins. "My legs are on fire, but I liked seeing those fuckers get decimated."

"How are you doing?" Hudson asks, patting the spot next to him on the bench. "Proud of you for scoring that goal."

"I'm good." I smile and stretch out my legs. My skates are heavy on my feet, but I can't be bothered to take them off. "I have all this adrenaline, and I feel like I could play another three periods."

"Don't tell Coach that. He'd find a way to make it happen." He laughs and nudges my shoulder. "Hey. I'm sorry you had to deal with someone so shitty from your past. I can't pretend to know what that's like, but you're our friend now. If someone isn't treating you right, you let one of us know. We'll take care of it."

"By starting a brawl?" I take his hand in mine and squeeze. "Thanks, Hudson. You're the sweetest guy."

"Mav was smart to make sure the fight went down like that. A regular tussle wouldn't have worked, and I'm impressed he lasted so long without decking that douche in the face."

I bite back a smile. "I'm surprised too."

I know why he made Hudson kick things off: the third-man in rule.

The first player who joins a fight already in progress automatically gets ejected. Maverick had nothing to lose.

A single punch wouldn't have worked. It was obvious he wanted to go in for the kill.

And, *gosh*, he did.

I've never seen so much blood. I've never been so turned on, and I've been questioning my sexual preferences since he got ejected.

Watching Maverick punch the ever-loving shit out of Cole was hot as hell, but the icing on the cake was when he was escorted off the ice. He looked back at me, bloodied and bruised, and smiled.

Fucking *smiled*, and mouthed, *I'd do it again.*

I know he would.

"Listen up," Coach says, and the locker room quiets down. "Good win. Obviously tensions were high, but we got the job done. That shows me not only that we can play under pressure, but we can also play when our number one guy isn't on the ice. This is a team sport, and you all showed heart tonight. We've got a game against San Antonio the day after tomorrow, then we get to head home. We'll celebrate the victory, but let's not lose focus."

"Thanks for stepping up tonight," Maverick adds. He scans the room, taking his time to look each of our teammates in the eyes. "I know my behavior doesn't reflect the values of our team, and I'm sorry I put you all in a position to play a couple players down."

"Bullshit," Grant calls out, and everyone laughs. "Don't give us the media answer, Mavvy! Tell us how you really feel!"

Maverick glances at Coach, who sighs and gestures for him to keep talking.

"Fuck Cole Meyers," he practically growls. "Fuck him straight to hell. This wasn't just about heart. This was about trust and having each other's backs, which we do. Those assholes learned that if you fuck with one of us, you fuck with all of us. We weren't playing like this back in late October, and to see that growth tells me how great this team is."

He's made a lot of speeches, but I've never seen him embody the role of captain more than he is right now. There's dried blood on his face, and his cheek is swollen beyond belief, but I know every single person in this room would repeat the last two hours and thirty minutes over again.

"I don't want any posts on social media," Coach warns us. "Nothing about the fights or taunting the Wildebeests players. My phone is already blowing up, and I'm sure the commissioner will be calling soon to hand out punishments." His eyes flick over to Maverick. "I'll be shocked if you're not suspended."

"Like I give a shit." Maverick shrugs and pulls off his jersey, chucking it toward his locker. "I'll match the fine with a donation to charity."

I wonder if he donates to foster care housing in DC. After what he told me on New Year's Eve about his childhood, I've been thinking nonstop about the ways he gets involved in the community.

It makes me want to get involved too, and the next time we're alone, I want to ask him if I can join him in his volunteer work.

"Hit the showers. We're flying to San Antonio tonight, and we'll do a late-morning skate tomorrow so you all can catch a breather," Coach says, and he looks at me. "There's a small shower room down the hall, Emmy. The arena staff said they unlocked it for you to use."

"Thanks." I smile. "It'll be nice to be clean on the plane for once."

"I know it doesn't change anything at the moment, but I'm working with our arena manager to get something set up for you at home. Something that's not a supply closet."

"I appreciate it, Coach."

The guys start to head for the showers, and Hudson squeezes my knee.

"You good?" he asks, and I nod.

"Yeah." I glance across the room and find Maverick staring at me. "I'm good."

"Thought so." Hudson unlaces his skates and pops to his feet. "I'll see you on the bus, Em."

I wave at him and pull off my jersey, tossing it in the pile of sweaty clothes with my shoulder pads. I grab an ice pack from the first aid kit and trudge toward Maverick, watching him drop to one of the benches in the corner and hold out his hand.

"Hey," I say.

"Hi." He looks around, and when he doesn't see any of our teammates or coaching staff, he puts his hands on my waist. "You played great out there tonight."

"Thank you." I press the ice pack to his right eye, and he hisses. "You're going to be bruised for days."

"Worth it." He tilts his head back and looks up at me. "I know actions speak louder than words, but I promise I will never, *ever*, treat you like your ex did. I want you to feel safe with me and—"

I rest my hand in his hair and rub his scalp, cutting him off. "I feel a lot of things when I'm with you, Maverick, and safe is always one of them," I whisper, and his mouth twists into a smile.

Maverick squeezes my hips. "What else do you feel?"

"Is that your question of the day?" I ask.

"Yeah." He nods and grips the waistband of my pants with strong fingers. "It is. I really want to know."

"I feel powerful. Beautiful." My fingers move to his cheek, and he relaxes under my touch. "Like I can do anything I set my mind to."

"You're all those things and more. You really can do anything, Emmy."

"How do I make you feel?" I whisper, and when he grins, I see dried blood on his teeth. The remnants of the fight, and how he stood up for me, left behind. "Will you tell me?"

"You make me feel important." Maverick's thumb brushes over my stomach and I shiver at his touch. "I know I still have skates on my feet and just beat some guy to a pulp, but you make me feel like I'm more than a hockey player. And it's never been like that before. You make me feel like I have a purpose."

"You're so much more than a hockey player. Remember how I said you have a kind heart? Tonight is the perfect example of that."

He snorts. "I basically committed assault, but it's okay because I'm paid twelve million a year to score a couple goals."

"That's not what I mean. You're a man who cares deeply about people, and to know you feel that way about me…" I shake my head. "Thank you."

"I care about you more than I've ever cared about anyone else, Emmy," he murmurs, and my heart explodes in my chest. "And I'd get decked in the face all over again if it meant seeing you smile."

There's something else I want to say, but I can't find the words. It hangs on the tip of my tongue and sits there until the guys start to file back into the locker room, towels around their waists and their hair wet.

It echoes in my head when I hand Maverick the ice pack and take a step back, putting distance between us so no one starts to ask questions. I think after tonight, though, they wouldn't care.

"I'll let you get cleaned up," I say. "I'll see you on the bus."

"Hey." He reaches out and wraps his fingers around my wrist. He squeezes once and looks up at me. "Are you okay?"

"Yeah." I nod, and that feeling is back, more persistent than ever. "I've never been better."

THIRTY-EIGHT
EMMY

"I'M SO glad you're here," Piper loops her arm through mine as we ride the elevator up to Maverick's apartment. "Team dinner is my favorite part of working for the Stars, and it's not even an official thing."

"I've come to the last six dinners," I say. "And it's really only for Riley's meatballs."

"In any other context, that might sound very different." She giggles and rests her head on my shoulder. "What a wild week, huh?"

It's been an exhausting whirlwind.

Maverick and Cole's fight made headlines on the national news. It's all every sports network can talk about, and *SNL* even did a parody of it over the weekend.

Social media has been flooded with comments from people trying to figure out what caused him to get involved in the first place, but no one's gotten it right.

Maverick earned a two game suspension for an illegal check to the head, and he didn't bother to negotiate the punishment with the union.

"I'm good," I say. "I might have slipped an anonymous tip to the admins of the r/hockey thread on Reddit and given them proof of Cole acting like a sleazebag. It's been fun to watch people drag him. I think the weirdest part about it all is now that I've seen him, it feels like a weight has been lifted. I don't have to dread it because I've already crossed that hurdle, and everything else from here on out is going to be easy."

"Liam told me some of the things that Cole said to you." Piper takes my hand and squeezes tight. "He's a vile creature, and if he *ever* plays another game in the NHL, I will make sure his name is desecrated on our broadcasts."

"You're the best. My feisty little fighter." I kiss her cheek, and we stop outside Maverick's door. "I didn't know you and Liam talked."

"We don't," she says, but her cheeks turn red. She busies herself with tucking a piece of hair behind her ear and fixing the hem of her skirt. "It was mentioned in passing."

I hum and push down on the doorknob, leading us inside the busy penthouse.

Team dinner has become my favorite part of being on the Stars too.

I've played on a lot of different teams and seen a lot of different dynamics, and no one has the trust and cohesiveness that these guys do. It's so evident those bonds have impacted their playing, and now we're getting close to the All-Star Game with the best record the team has had in years.

"Half the girls are here," Grant yells, and Connor and Ethan wave from the couch.

"Hey." Hudson greets us and gives us each a quick one-armed hug. "Where are your other two?"

"Maven is on her way with Dallas, and Lexi isn't coming. She has a date," Piper says, and Riley looks up from his video game controller.

"A date?" he asks. "With who?"

"A guy she met at her Pilates class. She didn't seem too excited about it, though," I add when his face falls, and Piper and I exchange a look.

"Oh." Riley glances back at the TV. "Good for her."

"Anyone want a drink?" Hudson asks, and we walk into the kitchen where Maverick is busy setting up the line of food.

I haven't seen him since we got home from our road trip, and my heart races at the sight of him.

He glances up from a veggie tray and smiles at me. There's still a bruise on his cheek, just under his eye. His nose is still swollen, and his hair is a little longer than usual. There's something about his features that tell me he's exhausted, but he's still gut-wrenchingly gorgeous.

God, I've missed him.

Not just his hands and his fingers and the corner of his mouth I like to kiss right before he comes.

I've missed *him.*

His jokes and his laugh and how he holds me close to his chest before we fall asleep. We've graduated to more regular sleepovers, and I've missed the way he looks in the early morning light with a pillow crease on his forehead. A little drop of drool on his cheek. Bleary eyes and wandering touches.

"Hey, Piper," he says, and he walks around the corner of the island to give her a hug. He moves to me next, and when he wraps me in his arms, the weight on my shoulders eases.

I didn't realize how much I needed him until he wasn't there, and excitement sparks in my chest as he rests his hand on the small of my back and doesn't pull away.

"Hi, Emmy girl," he murmurs softly.

"Hi, pretty boy."

"Did you have a good day?"

I nod into his shirt, the threadbare cotton that smells like cedar and apples and the hint of chocolate. "Better now."

"Me too."

I missed you. I missed you. I missed you.

I pull away. "Do you need any help?"

"Nah, we're all good. I'm going to call the masses in here

in a minute. You should grab a plate before everything gets picked over," Maverick says.

"You all and your appetites."

"Says the girl who eats three pints of ice cream a week," Piper teases. "I swear our freezer is just a Ben and Jerry's stash at this point."

"Boys! Dinner's ready!" Maverick yells, and there's a stampede of feet.

"Dammit," I curse, grabbing a plate and moving to the front of the line. "A little warning next time, Miller?"

"I gave you plenty of warning, Hartwell. I said a minute. You know how long that is, right?"

"Do *you* know how long that is?"

"I have excellent time management, and I haven't had any recent complaints." He pops a grape in his mouth and points to the charcuterie board. "No strawberries tonight, so you're good to take whatever you want."

There haven't been strawberries since the first time I showed up all those weeks ago, and still, it does something to my insides when he tells me it's all clear. It makes me feel gooey and warm and like a giggling teenager who has a crush on the hottest boy in school.

"Thanks," I say, and Grant barrel rolls past me on the floor to cut in front of the line. "Watch out, Everett. I will step on you."

"That's not a threat, Emmy." He grins and pops onto his feet, taking the slice of pizza I'm reaching for. "It would be an honor."

"I don't understand this game." Piper groans and flops back on the couch, frustrated. "I'm passing the football but my other player isn't scoring."

"Because you also control the other player." Liam folds his

big hands over her smaller ones on the controller. "You have to switch between them."

"Like this?" She moves the joystick forward and gasps when the player on the screen moves forward too. "I did it!"

"That's great, Piper," he tells her, and she beams up at him.

Maverick leans over, and his thigh presses into my knee. "Do you feel like we're interrupting something by being here?" he murmurs, and I nod.

"I do. In ten seconds, I'm going to say that I need another drink. You're going to offer to get me one, and we'll leave them alone."

"Why would I offer to get you a drink? You've gotten the last three all on your own," he says, and I sigh.

"You're not actually getting me a drink. It's just to make them think you're getting me one."

"Oh." His grin is wide, and he knocks his knuckles against mine in a fist bump. "Got it."

I roll my eyes and smooth out my skirt. "I'm going to get another drink. I'll be right back," I announce.

"I'll get it for you, m'lady," Maverick says. "I need another water anyway."

We head out of the living room and down the hall. Instead of turning for the kitchen, Maverick guides me toward his bedroom. We pass the floor-to-ceiling windows, and I see some of the guys out on the balcony enjoying an unseasonably warm late-January night. They're laughing and playing a competitive game of cornhole that has Connor throwing a beanbag at Riley's head and Hudson arguing about board placement.

God, I love these boys.

"You have the ultimate party apartment. Are you hiding an eighteen-hole putt putt course anywhere?" I ask.

"It's on the roof. I haven't shown you?" he jokes, and he opens his bedroom door.

"Not yet." I pull him toward me, standing up on my toes so I can kiss him. He smiles against my mouth and cups the back of my head. "I really wanted to do that. I've missed you."

"Fuck, I've missed you too." He kicks the door closed with his foot and moves us toward the bed. "I've been so busy with disciplinary hearings and meeting with Coach to assure him I'm *not* turning into a raging lunatic on the ice. I'm sorry I've been so absent."

"Just a regular lunatic," I say, and he tosses me onto the mattress. "And I forgive you."

"Sleepover tonight?" he asks, crawling over me and bending down to kiss my neck.

I sigh and lift my hips, desperate to feel more of him. "I can't. I came with Piper, and she'll think it's suspicious if I stay. How about tomorrow night?"

"No can do. I have a tux fitting with Dallas and Reid for the wedding, then we're grabbing dinner."

"What about the tux you wore to the gala? You looked good in that."

"Did I?" Maverick runs his hand up the inside of my thigh, and my nipples harden under my shirt. "Everyone knows you need a different tux for different occasions."

"Sorry I'm not up to date on all my tux wearing rules."

"So no sleepover tonight or tomorrow night? Guess that means I'll have to have you right now."

"With everyone outside?"

"Would that be okay?"

"Yes," I whisper. "But I'm not sure I can be quiet."

His eyes sparkle with mischief, and he hooks his thumb in the waistband of my underwear. He drags the red thong down my legs and holds it in front of me. "I know how to fix that. Open your mouth."

I inhale sharply, understanding the meaning. My lips part,

and he pushes the lace in my mouth, patting my cheek when I clamp down on the underwear.

"There you go," he says. "You look perfect, Emmy girl." I squirm at the praise, and he scoots down my body. Maverick pauses at my chest, that wicked gleam still behind his gaze. "Hold up your shirt, baby. Let me see those pretty tits."

My hands shake as I lift my shirt to my chin. A wave of pleasure starts to build low in my belly, an awareness that anyone could walk in at any time and see me like this—half naked, wet. Already trembling on the sheets at the thought of what's to come.

He tugs on my bra, the cups pushing my breasts up and into his mouth. His tongue laps at my nipple and he hums against my sensitive skin, making me moan around the thong.

No man has appreciated my body like Maverick does. There's no race to get to the final product; he likes to take his time and savor every inch.

He's turned me on by touching parts I've never thought were sexy before—my shoulder blades. My calf. The time he got me off just by using a vibrator on my chest and stomach. He's meticulous on the ice and even more meticulous in bed. When he knows I don't like something, he tries something new, not stopping until I'm a proud owner of three new orgasms.

I've been naked in front of him dozens of times, but when he moves from my chest to my skirt, hiking the denim up to my waist and leaving me exposed on his bed like his own personal plaything, white-hot heat rolls through me.

"I can't take my time with you like I want," Maverick says, and he lies on his stomach between my legs. "If we spend too long in here, someone's bound to find us." He spreads me open with his thumbs, and I try to close my knees, embarrassed. "None of that, baby. Let me look. It's been too long, and I want to see your perfect pussy up close." He rubs the inside of my thigh, and when I relax, his grin is proud. "There you go. That's my girl."

I hate not being able to talk to him, but I love getting to watch him. His pupils are blown wide and his cheeks are pink. He lets out a soft groan that matches my own when he gently presses two fingers inside of me, the thumb of his other hand working my clit in slow, lazy circles.

"That feel good?" he rasps, and I nod. "You can be as loud as you want, Emmy. They're not going to hear."

I sink into the sensation of him. Of the curl of his fingers and when he adds a third. The surprise when he lifts my hips and presses his thumb between my ass cheeks, a spot he's started to really, really like. One of the guys laughs outside the window, and a jolt goes through me like I've been electrocuted.

"You liked that," Maverick says with awe. "The way you just clenched around my fingers—I can't wait to feel that around my cock."

I whine when he swirls his tongue and I groan when he buries it inside me, replacing his fingers and sending me to the brink of ecstasy faster than I've ever gotten there before. I reach down and tug on his hair, warning him that I'm close, and he looks up at me with sharp eyes.

"I'm not stopping," he says. "I'm not stopping until I taste every drop of you." His palm slides across my stomach, pressing down, and I lift my hips again, grinding into him. "That's it, Emmy girl. All the way for me, baby."

I tip over the edge, a free fall that has me groaning so loud, my throat goes dry. My eyes prick with tears and my legs spasm, and I ride the high until my mind goes blank.

When I come back to earth, Maverick touches my cheek. "Get on your knees," he says. "All fours, facing the window."

It takes me a second to get in position, my brain slow to catch up to the rest of my body. I lean forward, my elbows against the crisp sheets and my ass in the air. Maverick runs his hand along my curves and rumbles out an appreciative hum. He parts my cheeks and kisses the left then the right, and my face burns bright red.

"Your ass is next," he says, voicing something I've been dreaming about myself. "We'll work up to it, but I've been wanting to fuck you there since the first day I saw you in those skin tight leggings of yours."

I nod, a frantic bob of my head that has him laughing and brushing his lips against the back of my neck. I hear the glide of his sweatpants down his legs and I look over my shoulder, finding Maverick with his hand wrapped around his cock.

I love seeing him like this; so close to letting go and losing control. Hunger in his eyes and flushed skin. Disheveled but sharp determination to his movements.

He brushes the head of his cock against my clit, dragging it across my entrance without pushing inside. I whimper and rock back to him, asking for what I want.

"Needy thing," he laughs, and his grip on my hips is rough.

I take a steadying breath knowing what comes next, but I'm still not prepared for the way he slides inside of me. The feeling of fullness and the stretch to accommodate his thick length.

Maverick gives me a second to adjust, and when I reach behind me to run my nails down his thigh, he sinks all the way into me.

"*Fuck*," he exhales. "Look how well you take me, Emmy girl."

His hips snap into mine with quick thrusts, and I match his rhythm and intensity. We move like we've done this a thousand times, anticipating each other's needs before we ask for them.

Maverick brings his hand to my throat, that delicious pressure settling around my windpipe. I tip my head back, and he presses a kiss to my forehead.

"This isn't going to last long. One week without you, and it feels like I haven't fucked before in my life." He bends over me, his bodyweight heavy on my back, and his hand moves to my clit. "I want you to scream when you come this time, Emmy. Can you do that for me?"

I nod, that swell building again. I know Maverick won't let himself finish first, the selfless bastard, and I want to get him there almost as much as I want to get there myself. I bite down on the lace and close my eyes, the stimulation too much.

Our bodies work in unison. Sweat rolling down his chest and clinging to my back. A mouth on my shoulder and a thumb pressing into where I'm most sensitive. It's frantic, both of us knowing we're working on borrowed time.

The second orgasm rushes up my spine, a blaze of fire on my skin. I scream, not because he told me to, but because it feels *so fucking good*, and I almost collapse on the mattress.

Maverick follows me, five more thrusts before I feel the warmth of his release deep inside me. The jerk of his legs and the long, low groan from the back of his throat.

"Emmy," he says. "*God.* You're going to take it all, aren't you?"

I do.

Every drop, including the cum that trails down my leg. He wipes his fingers through it then presses it back into me, an intimacy I've never experienced before.

With gentle care he rubs my shoulders and rolls me onto my back. He massages my cheek and my mouth opens willingly. Maverick pulls the underwear out and kisses me like there's no tomorrow.

"Hi," I whisper, and his eyes twinkle.

"Hi," he whispers back, and his nose brushes against mine. "Are you okay?"

I nod, something warm and fuzzy pressing against my ribs with his quiet consideration. "Never better."

"Good. I don't want to, but I should clean you up."

"Yeah." I yawn and stretch my arms above my head. "I really don't want the guys to see me like this."

"Absolutely not. My eyes only." He scoots off the bed and holds out his hand. "You want to take a shower?"

"I think that would make what we did in here really obvious." I smile and fix my clothes. "Can I have my underwear back, please?"

"Nope." He jumps into his sweatpants and shoves the lace in one of his pockets. "It's mine now."

"You can't keep stealing my underwear, Miller. I'm not going to have any left soon."

"That's the point, isn't it?" He grins. "Question of the day?"

"Asking me to come up with questions after you've fucked me isn't fair. I can't think straight." I groan and stand up, my legs a little wobbly. "We're going with the bare minimum tonight: does pineapple belong on pizza?"

"Fuck, no," he answers right away. "Please tell me you agree."

"I do. What's your question?"

"What's the best popsicle flavor?"

"Wow. We're all over the place tonight." I laugh and make sure my skirt is buttoned. "Orange."

"Incorrect. Grape is where it's at."

"You are so weird," I say, and I walk toward the bathroom door to clean up.

"You love it," Maverick tosses back, and for one terrifying second, I think I might.

THIRTY-NINE
MAVERICK

ME

Whose jersey are you wearing for Heroes and Legends night?

It's so nice to not have to dress up in a suit and tie. We need to have some more of these next season.

REDHEADED ASSASSIN

No one's. My dad told me he'd disown me if I picked a favorite, so I'm being neutral and not wearing one at all.

Are you wearing your Lemieux jersey?

ME

Nope. Someone else tonight.

REDHEADED ASSASSIN

You can't wear your own jersey, Miller.

ME

Try and stop me, Hartwell.

"HEY, BILL." I whistle at the retro Gretzky jersey he has on. It looks decades old, and I'm jealous as hell. "Damn. Is that authentic?"

"It is." The security guard turns around and proudly shows off the memorabilia. "It's from his rookie season."

"Shit. I would've loved to have seen him play back then."

"I saw him in his first year and knew he was going to be special. I thought the same thing about you. Still do."

"Nah, man." I shake my head. "You can't do that. I'm nowhere near as good. I've been in the league almost half the time as he was, and I don't have anything to show for it. No Stanley Cups. No game sevens, and no playoff experience. We're not on the same playing field."

"Wins don't mean everything, Maverick. You're the same kind of leader. You have that same kind of passion for the game. That's the stuff that matters more than goals and assists."

"Come on, Bill. You're making me all emotional, and I have a game to get ready for."

"Sorry." He gives me a sheepish grin. "Who are you wearing? I can't see under your jacket."

"It's a surprise." I wave and head for security screening. "All I'll tell you is it's my favorite player to date."

I throw my phone and keys in a bowl and make small talk with the officer standing at the metal detector. He picked one of my jerseys for tonight, and I happily sign the back of it for him.

I whistle as I walk down the hallway toward the locker room, a lightness in my step.

Everything's been so *good* lately.

I got to play in the All-Star Game and competed on the same team as some of the guys I went to college with. Our schedule for the second half of the season is lighter than the first, which leaves me optimistic about our playoff chances.

Emmy has been over almost every single night this week, and when we had a road game in Phoenix two days ago, we spent the afternoon walking around downtown in a pair of baseball hats, soaking up the sunshine.

I know it's not dating, but it's exactly what dating would be like.

Dallas was right—this other stuff is really fucking fun.

We sleep together and eat meals together. We hang out when we're not at practice or on the road. She calls me when she's watering her plants, and I call her when I'm at the grocery store. Sometimes we chat for ten minutes. Sometimes it turns into an hour.

It's like we're stuck in the murky middle between friends with benefits and boyfriend and girlfriend, and I think it's time to have a talk with her. I don't know if she wants to keep going down this road of constantly being in each other's lives, but I do. And I want to put a label on it so there's no confusion.

"Smile, Mavvy," Maven calls out, and I grin as she snaps a couple photos of me in the players' hallway. "Take your coat off so I can see who you're wearing, please."

"So bossy." I shrug off my jacket and drape it over her arm, turning around so she can see the name stitched on the back. "What do you think?"

"Oh, shit." She laughs, and her camera clicks two dozen times. "You're going to break the internet."

"What?" I face her and frown. "Fuck. Did I do something wrong?"

"No, sweetie. You did something very, very right. It's always the girl wearing the guy's jersey, not the other way around. This is so cool."

I glance down at the jersey I ordered two weeks ago—an XL Stars jersey with Hartwell's name and number on the back in our hometown white. I've had the idea since they announced the themed night, but I didn't want her to think I was wearing it as a joke or to poke fun at her.

"Do you think she'll like it?" I ask, suddenly nervous about how she might react. Emmy doesn't strike me as a grand gesture kind of woman, and I really hope I'm not overstepping some invisible boundary we've put up. "I have a spare jersey in my locker I can change into."

"She's going to love it," Maven assures me.

"Is she here yet? I tried to come in early so I could see her before we dress."

"No, but it should be any minute now. She rides with Piper, and they have this weird habit of rolling up at exactly the same time every night."

"Thanks, Mae." I bend down and kiss the top of her head. "How's my June Bug?

"We went shopping for her flower girl dress the other day, and you're going to die when you see it." She gives me a sly smile. "Speaking of June Bug, a little birdie told me you had a special visitor for New Year's."

"I might have," I say. "We—"

I hear her before I see her.

Emmy's voice travels down the hall, and I look over my shoulder.

One second the hallway is empty, then I blink, and she's there. Red hair everywhere. A white turtleneck and pinstripe pants with a matching vest. A gold necklace around her neck and leather sneakers that make me go weak in the knees.

"Fucking Christ," I murmur under my breath.

"I heard that," Maven says, and I flip her off.

It's been months of seeing her in business casual, in pretty dresses and different pairs of heels, and my heart still skips a goddamn beat at the sight of her.

I think I might have a chronic condition brought on by Emerson Hartwell.

"Hey, Mae," Emmy calls out, and she waves. "Miller?

What are—" She stops in her tracks and blinks at me with those green eyes. Her gaze hovers on my shoulders then snaps to my face. "What are you wearing?"

"Hm?" I keep my back to her and shrug. "I don't know what you're talking about."

She stomps across the hall, and it takes everything in me not to laugh at her feistiness. She tugs on my sleeve.

"This is my jersey."

"Is it?"

"Maverick. What are… Why are you wearing my jersey?"

"Because it's Heroes and Legends night. You're my hero, Hartwell, and you're definitely going to become a legend. You already are, but technically I don't think we can classify one season in the NHL as legendary. Kind of bullshit if you ask me. Also, I distinctly remember you asking when I was planning on having your name across my back, so here we are."

"Why… I—" Her fingers trace the block letters and the number seventeen then trace them again. "The only person who's ever worn my jersey is my dad."

"And the eight thousand fans out there," I say.

"I mean another athlete. One of my peers."

"Men in other leagues wear women's jerseys all the time. That trend should start in the NHL too, don't you think?"

"This might be the most romantic thing anyone's ever done for me," she whispers.

"You deserve nice things, remember?" I glance to the side and see that Maven and Piper have disappeared. I didn't even notice they left. "It's a fucking honor and a privilege to play beside you. There was never any doubt about who I wanted to represent. It's you, and it's always going to be you."

"Are you just talking about the jersey?" Emmy tips her chin up. "Or something else?"

I crowd her space and put my hands on the wall, bracketing her head. "Do you want me to be talking about something else?"

"Yes." She bites her bottom lip. "I do."

I take a deep breath. This isn't where I expected to have this conversation, but I'm not going to complain. The sooner we have it, the better.

"I want more with you, Emmy. I want to come home to you every night and I want to take you out to dinner in the city. I want to hold your hand on the sidewalk and I want to kiss you in the rain. I want all that shit they talk about in the movies. I'm going to be honest with you, though. I don't have a fucking clue how to be in a relationship or how to be a boyfriend, but I'm going to learn. I'm going to try, and you're the only person I'd ever want to try with. This isn't just sex to me, and it hasn't been for a while. If keeping it casual is the only way I get to keep you, then so be it. But I think you want something more too."

Her nod is slow. "I want that. I want you to wear my jersey and let me wear my heels. I want you to come food shopping with me and give me an eight-minute lecture on why almonds are better than pecans."

"They are," I say firmly, and she touches my cheek.

"That's why I like you so much. You're so passionate about the things that are important to you, like almonds. Who the hell gets excited about almonds?"

"I do, because they're good for you. They've got vitamins and minerals and all that other stuff we're supposed to eat every day." I take her hand in mine and kiss the inside of her palm.

"Enough almond talk."

"Is that a yes to… to being whatever comes after fuck buddies?"

"I think they usually call that boyfriend and girlfriend. Dating. Acting like idiots because we can't keep our hands off each other."

"Yes." I bob my head. "Yes to all of that."

Her smile is soft and pretty. "It's okay if you don't know

what you're doing. We're definitely going to mess up, but we can mess up together and it doesn't matter. I'm going to get mad at you for wearing mismatched socks. You're going to get mad at me for not laughing at your jokes. We'll give it a try and see where it goes."

"This conversation is not what I had planned when I put your jersey on."

"What did you have planned?"

"I was ready to hype you up and tell you all the reasons why I'm going to buy one of your jerseys in every color. I had your stat line ready to go."

"I can be difficult sometimes, Maverick. I know I'm snarky, and the last thing I'd ever want is for it to come across as ungrateful for something that's so nice." Emmy pauses to take a breath. "I want you to know when you do things like this—" She gestures up and down my body—"I struggle to find the words for how it makes me feel. Thank you seems too small, and I'm working on being more outwardly appreciative of your kindness. Inside I'm..." She pops a shoulder and tucks her chin to her chest. "It gives me butterflies, and I feel lucky that I'm the one you're giving your time to."

"I know how you feel, Emmy." I rest my hand at the back of her neck. "I see it when you smile at me. Which is a lot, by the way."

"No, it's not," she challenges, and I grin.

"You're smiling right now, Red. You've got these little wrinkles around your eyes, and they're the cutest damn thing. They make me want to stick around for a while."

"How long?"

Forever.

"Until you get sick of me."

"I'm not sure I'll ever get sick of you," Emmy admits. "You're my favorite person in the world."

"Funny. You're my favorite person too."

The door down the hall opens, and she scoots out of the

cage I have her in. Grant gives us a big wave, and Emmy waves back.

"Sup, G?" I ask, and we exchange a high five. "You good?"

"Yeah, I'm good. Oh, *shit*, Cap. Is that Emmy's jersey? No fucking way. That's fire." Grant pulls out his phone and starts to record a video. "Check out the drip from Maverick Miller tonight, y'all. He's rocking an exclusive Emmy Hartwell jersey complete with custom high-top Nikes."

"I don't know what half of those words mean," Emmy says.

"Neither do I." I stick my tongue out at the camera. "I'm going to head to the locker room and dress. You all should too so we're not late and stuck skating laps before the game."

"Yes sir." Grant gives me a salute and heads down the hall, talking to his followers.

"See you out there?" I say to Emmy.

"Yeah." She nudges me as she passes. "And later tonight, I want you to fuck me wearing that jersey."

I groan and put my head against the wall, embarrassed by how much her smirk turns me on.

FORTY
EMMY

"WHOEVER DECIDED to pair wine and pizza together is a genius." I take a giant bite of my slice of pepperoni and wash it down with a sip of red. "This was a great idea, Lexi. Thank you for doing it on a night when we don't have a game the next day so I can really enjoy."

"I needed some friends to commiserate with. I had the worst date last night, and I don't want to see another man ever again." Lexi tops off Piper's glass and leans back on the couch. "They all suck."

"What happened?" Maven asks. "And how did you meet this one?"

"At the grocery store. We both reached for a package of oranges. He made a joke. I laughed. And that was the last time he made me laugh. I didn't tell him I'm an athletic trainer, and we went to a sports bar for dinner. A basketball game was on, and the female sideline reporter was interviewing Colton Clark—you know that guy from Orlando? Anyway, this man turned to me, looked me dead in the eye, and said, *I really wish women would stop talking about things they know nothing about.*"

Piper gasps. "He did not."

"Swear on my life. I sat through the meal because I'm too nice of a person, but I blocked his number the second I left. It's so frustrating. Where are all the good men?" Lexi groans. "I'm thirty-one. There aren't any winners left."

"This is why I'm staying far away from dating. I downloaded an app on Saturday night just to poke around and see what's out there, and I deleted it within minutes. Two separate people asked me to come over and sit on their face." Piper blows out an irritated huff. "Being thirty and divorced sucks, and I wish I could find the man of my dreams by running into him on the sidewalk."

"That stuff only happens in the movies." Maven pulls a clump of cheese off her pizza and pops it in her mouth. "Not to sound like a bitch, but I'm so glad I have Dallas. I remember the headaches of dating, and they are not fun. I have enough horror stories to fill an entire book."

"I once had a guy tell me he wanted to be referred to as King in the bedroom," I say. "I thought I was transported back to regency London."

"The audacity. Can you share your perfect fiancé with us, Mae?" Lexi asks. "I don't even need a physical relationship, just someone of the opposite sex to have a civilized conversation with every now and then."

"I wish I could, but he can barely handle me and June. I'm afraid of what it's going to be like when she's a teenager. Add in three more women, and he'd probably run off in the night and never call again."

"No way." Piper throws the end of a breadstick across the table. "That man is a saint, and he's obsessed with you."

"Seriously obsessed," I agree. "He gets this dreamy look whenever he talks about you. When you come into a room, he lights up. It's cute."

"You want to talk about dreamy looks? How about Maverick and the way he was staring at you the other night when he wore your jersey to the arena? The tension in that hallway was insane." Maven sets down her wineglass and rests her elbows on her thighs. "Did you know he waited there so he could surprise you?"

I swirl my drink around and blush. "No. I didn't."

It doesn't surprise me, though.

That's who Maverick is, I'm learning.

In the week since we put a label on our relationship, he's been perfect. It's such a cheesy and stupid word to use, but it's true.

He bought me flowers and cooked me potatoes three different ways for dinner. He answers my texts almost the second they go through, and after I told him I was craving a sweet tea, he went to four different stores until he found the brand I like.

I tried to tell him he doesn't have to do those things, that this isn't an all or nothing arrangement, but the man picked up one of my romance novels, flopped on my bed, and told me he was learning how to be the perfect boyfriend by reading my books.

For having the reputation of a playboy who never spent more than a couple of hours with the same woman, he's nailing this partner thing.

I'm doing my best to keep my guard down with him. I've stopped anticipating when something might go wrong, and my trust in him grows every time he smiles at me.

He's nothing like the men in my past. I know that, and the more time I spend with my hands in his hair and his lips against my forehead, listing all the things he adores about me, the closer my heart comes to falling out of my chest.

"I have a confession," I admit. "But it cannot leave this room."

Maverick and I haven't talked about sharing our relationship with other people, but these women are my friends. They've shown me so many bits and pieces of themselves over the last couple of months—the good parts and the messy ones too—and I really want to gush about him for a second.

"Swear," Piper says.

"On my life," Maven adds.

"Your secret is safe with us," Lexi agrees.

"Maverick and I are sleeping together," I blurt out.

"*What?*" Maven yells. "I thought you only kissed on New Year's!"

"You kissed on New Year's? You said you were staying in!"

"Is that why he came into the athletic trainer's office the other day and complained about a sore hamstring? Because you two tried a new sex position?"

"Oh my god." I bury my face in my hands. "I take it all back. I hate that man, and I've never seen him naked."

"We want details." Piper pulls my hands away and grins. "All the details."

"It's been going on since November and—"

"*November?* That's months ago!"

"Time flies when you're getting fucked," Lexi says, and I can't help but laugh.

"Who initiated it?" Piper asks.

"He did. Maybe I did. I don't know, it was a blur. One minute we were arguing in my hotel room after a game, and the next he was kissing me against the wall."

I think back to that night, the excitement that rippled through me and the way he tasted for the first time. I felt that same giddiness this morning when he bent down and kissed me before slipping out of his bedroom to hit the weight room before practice.

"Damn, that's hot," Lexi says.

"It was only meant to be a one-time thing, but it happened again. Then again and again. The sex turned into sleepovers and hand holding and feelings I kept trying to avoid, but he's impossible to resist. The other day we decided we didn't want what we're doing to just be physical. We're dating now, and I'm…" I take a deep breath. "I'm so happy."

"This is so much to unpack. I *live* with you," Piper says. "How did I not know this was happening?"

"We've been smart about our sneaking around, and a lot happens on the road. As for the night he wore my jersey… " I trail off and hold back a grin. "I understand why guys go feral when they see their girls in their clothes. It was the hottest thing in the world."

"Can I ask the question we're all wondering? How is he in bed?" Lexi asks, and Piper squeals.

I blush. "I'm not going to get into detail, but all the rumors are true. Size. Satisfaction level. Selflessness. Everyone else I've been with has been doing it wrong up to this point."

"And the multiple orgasms?"

"The truest of true."

"I need another glass of wine," Piper says. "You lucky bitch."

"What comes next?" Maven asks. "That man has never been in this situation before, and I'm curious what you all are planning to do."

"Take it day by day, I guess. My contract is only for this year, and Finn is eventually going to come back from his injury. I'm not sure there will be a spot for me on the roster long-term, and that's a little scary. I'm usually a runner and always looking for the next thing, and it's been fun to slow down and enjoy the now. To not worry about the future and what comes next. That's what I'm doing with Maverick, and it's kind of perfect," I say.

"Why am I crying?" Piper wipes her eyes. "It's so good to see someone so deserving of love finally receive that love."

"Blame it on the alcohol," Maven says. "That man once told me he'd rather die than ever settle down. I knew it was going to take a special girl to rein him in, and it was."

Lexi grins. "What he needed was someone who wouldn't put up with his shit, and that's definitely Emmy."

I laugh. "Slow down there, everyone. We don't need to be tossing out the L word just yet."

"Maybe not. But he's head over heels for you. We can't help who we love, and if you're going to fall in love with anyone, he's the best choice," Maven says.

"Yeah." I rub a hand over my chest. It feels like a piece is missing there, like Maverick's taken a part of my soul and tied it to his. "He is."

"A toast." Maven lifts her glass in the air. We all follow suit, and she smiles. "To the good men with good dicks who treat us right. And to the good dicks out there who haven't found their way to us yet. May they hurry up and get here so everyone is happy and satisfied."

"Hear fucking hear," Lexi says, and we knock our drinks together.

For so long, I've felt like I was alone. Chasing after something I couldn't quite reach and running until everything in me ached.

When I'm in Maverick's arms, I think I've finally put my feet on the ground. I think I've found someone who might help heal that loneliness that's followed me for years.

FORTY-ONE
EMMY

PROFESSIONAL STICK HANDLERS

EASY E

Did you see that NBA player get suspended for life for betting on games?

Wonder if any of the guys in the NHL are doing that.

LIAM

The only thing they bet on is when you're going to stop talking.

CONNOR

Ouch. Goalie Daddy with the sick burn.

LIAM

Don't call me Daddy.

GRANT

He's not calling you Daddy. The internet is. That video the social media team uploaded of you biting your jersey went viral, and you've been dubbed GD.

PRETTY BOY

Wait a second. I used to be Puck Daddy. What happened to that nickname?

HUDSON

No one called you that besides yourself.

PRETTY BOY

That's not true! There was a whole message board about it!

EASY E

Sorry, Mavvy. Grumpy gills Liam has taken your spot as favorite Stars player.

ME

I'd vote for him.

RILEY

Same.

PRETTY BOY

Some friends you are.

"We're playing in Detroit next week. You must be excited to be in front of a hometown crowd." Maverick props up on his elbow and smiles at me. There's a hickey on his neck, just below his ear, and his shirt is on inside out. "Who's coming to see you? There's going to be a whole Emmy Fan Club, isn't there?"

"No." I rub my thumb up his arm and lean forward so I can kiss his tattoos. The cherries might be my favorite, and I kiss those twice. "My mom never comes to my games, and it's difficult for my dad to travel."

"With the wheelchair?" he asks, and I nod.

"Yeah. There's a lot of stress involved with getting places, and Detroit is too far of a drive for him to make. The seating in the arena isn't very ADA friendly either, and don't get me started on the extra security measures he has to go through."

"Has he ever seen you play?"

"He was at all my high school games, then once or twice in college. He didn't get to see me in the ECHL." I shrug and gently nudge Maverick onto his back so I can rest my head on his chest. He smells like the banana bread we tried to make in the kitchen earlier before we gave up and ate a whole bag of chocolate chips. "I send him game film and he watches it, though. He has no problem telling me when I should've taken the open shot instead of recording an assist."

"Half the time you pass, you should've taken the open shot," he agrees, chuckling as he wraps his arms around my waist. He buries his face in my hair, and his heart beats under my cheek. "What if we were able to get him to the game?"

"How would we do that? Lansing is one hundred miles from Detroit. It's not like we're going to make a pitstop on the team bus."

"I've been doing some research." Maverick reaches for his phone and hands it to me. "Password is 3669."

"Why are you telling me your password?"

"So I can keep holding you. You're so warm."

I punch in the digits, and there's a website displayed on his screen. "What's this?"

"You can rent wheelchair accessible vans. I thought we could drive to Lansing before morning skate, pick him up, bring him to the arena so he can watch the game, then take him home after. We don't fly out until Friday morning, so there's plenty of time."

"Hang on." I sit up. My eyes bounce from the phone to him then back to his phone. "What are you—Maverick. This is so thoughtful of you, but he can't be alone during the game. I mean, he can. He's cognitively sound, but if he needs to use the restroom or get some food, it's better if someone is with him to offer some assistance. Navigating crowds can also be a nightmare."

"I remember you mentioning that." Maverick sits up and kisses my forehead. "I talked with Coach, and I have no problem not dressing so I can hang out with him. Or, if you're comfortable with it, Hudson's dad is going to be in Detroit for the game. Duke is a great guy, and he's familiar with helping folks who use wheelchairs. Hudson's mom used one before she passed, and I bet he'd be comfortable accompanying him."

I take a deep breath and try not to cry. It feels like the wind just got knocked out of me, and my fingers curl around his navy sheets.

"You would sit out a game just so you could spend time with my dad?" I whisper. "Why would you ever do that?"

"It's important to you. I know how much it would mean to you if he were there. It would make you happy, and if we're being honest, I really want to meet the man who helped bring my favorite spitfire girl into the world."

"We're less than six weeks out from the playoffs, and we could lose without you in the lineup. Do you want to take that risk?"

"I love your confidence in me." His grin is gentle, and he reaches for me. "We're five games ahead of Orlando in our division, and we're only trailing Boston by a half game in the East. Unless things go to shit, we've got the home advantage for the playoffs locked up. If I sit out, Grant could have some experience in the first line. It's a win-win for everyone."

I don't know what to say.

My mind is a whirlwind, a mess of sounds and feelings and emotions I've tried so hard to fight and keep away, but a single word slips through and echoes loudly amongst all the noise.

Love.

Love, love, love.

I think I might love him a little bit.

A whole lot, actually, and I don't know when that happened.

Somewhere between the Thai food he started ordering for me after practice when I'm craving something spicy and the questions he scribbles down on Post-it notes and slips under my door at the arena, I went and fell head over heels for the one person I swore I was immune to.

I don't think I ever stood a chance with Maverick, though.

It was inevitable right from the start.

Oh, god.

This is terrible.

Horrific.

Possibly the best thing that's ever happened to me.

I *just* told the girls it was too soon to throw that word around, but it's so painfully obvious that's what this is.

It's why being in his arms feels so right. It's why I'm steady and settled when he's next to me. It's why his touch calms and grounds me.

I love him.

"Hey." Maverick cradles my cheek. "What's going on, Emmy girl? Did I do something wrong? It wasn't too much, was it? Shit, I'm sorry. I didn't mean to—"

"No. *No.*" I sniff and wipe my nose with the back of my hand. The last thing I want is for him to think he messed up when he's so *right.* "It's such a kind thing to do, and I'm having a difficult time processing it."

"Oh." His nose bumps mine, and I lift my chin. His eyes are bright and twinkling, like the pretty stars in the night sky outside his window. "That's okay. You take as long as you need, Emmy girl. Can I do anything to help?"

Stop being so nice to me.

Love me back.

Stay with me forever because I'm terrified of what might happen if you go.

"Can I keep hugging you?" I ask.

"You can hug me all you want." Maverick shuffles us around until I'm in his lap and my cheek is against his shoulder. His hand slips under my shirt and rubs soft, soothing circles on my back. "Is this the part where I say I'll never let go?"

"Please don't compare yourself to Leo. He was my childhood crush, and you're not him."

"But I'm your adult crush, right?" he teases, and his lips are heaven on my skin.

"You're something," I say, and a confusing, prickly sensation sits at the base of my spine. "Thank you, Maverick. This really is the nicest thing anyone's ever done for me, and I'm so excited he's going to see me play."

"You deserve all the nice things, Emmy girl, and when you're with me, I'm going to give them to you."

I love him.

"What about when we get to Detroit? The guys will realize we're missing, and I'm sure they'll have questions."

"Hudson will notice, but he's too smart for his own good. And so what if they all realize it? I'm not going to hide that we're going to get your dad. If you're comfortable with it, I'm comfortable with it."

There's a lump in my throat, and I nod. "Okay."

"Okay? Is that a yes that we can bring him to the game?"

"Yeah." I bite my bottom lip, and a smile sneaks through. "It's a hell yes."

Maverick whoops and pulls us back onto the pillows. They're like little clouds under my head, and a laugh bubbles out of me.

"I'll talk to Hudson about Duke helping out, then I'll book everything so we can get the ball rolling."

"Do you have him on speed dial?"

"Basically. Hudson and I bonded right away when he was drafted. He's close with his dad, which means I've become close with his dad. Duke's been the father figure I never had. I like to pretend he likes me more than Hud, and it's so fun to give him shit."

"You're a damn menace, Maverick Miller." I sweep a lock of dark hair across his forehead. "I'm glad you have someone like that in your life."

"Me too. I underestimated the pressure of being the number one draft pick and the attention that comes with being a professional athlete. It's not just hockey—it's learning to manage money and hiring people I trust and advocating for myself. Saying no without feeling guilty about it. I'd love to start a league mentorship program where veteran players can partner up with rookies who might need some guidance to help them navigate this new life. That's what Duke did with me."

"You have so many brilliant ideas." I touch his temples and massage the warm skin above his eyebrow. He lets out a happy sigh and closes his eyes. "Can I ask you a personal question you don't have to feel obligated to answer?"

"You can ask me whatever you want, Emmy. I'll tell you anything."

"Have either one of your parents reached out to you since you got drafted? I know hiding your past from the internet is probably easier than hiding yourself from people who might have been in your life before."

"Ah." Maverick's fingers dance down my arm and hold my hip. "No, they haven't. I waited for a call my rookie year, and nothing came. It's motivated me to play harder, though. I want to be the best I can be at this sport, and knowing one of them might be watching me adds fuel to the fire."

"That's how it is with my mom. I told myself the only way it would be worth losing my relationship with her is if I was the best of the best. Now I'm in the NHL, and I know it was all worth it."

"We've been through some shit, huh?"

"I guess we have. But maybe that's why we work so well."

"I love when you flirt with me, Emmy girl."

I love you.

I love you, I love you, I love you.

"Thank you again for finding a way for my dad to be there," I say, because once isn't nearly enough. Not for something this kind and this thoughtful. "He's going to be so excited to meet you."

"Of course he is. I'm me," Maverick jokes, and I press my fingers into his ribs.

His giggle is high-pitched and contagious, and as night stretches to early morning, the two of us fall asleep in each other's arms, and I think this is what it means to be truly happy.

FORTY-TWO
MAVERICK

"WHOSE IDEA WAS it to come here on our day off?" I look around the lobby of the fancy workout studio. "We already do plenty of stretching."

"Pilates isn't just about stretching. It has other benefits," Hudson answers, balancing on one foot. "It helps with muscle control and flexibility. It can also increase your lung capacity and helps your concentration."

"What the hell are you, a pilates spokesperson?" I hold on to the wall and stretch my hamstring. "Is this one of those pyramid schemes? Blink twice if you need help, Hud."

"He's being a good friend," Emmy chimes in, and she fixes her ponytail high on her head. "Lexi just got certified, and what better way to show she's an incredible instructor than by bringing DC's hockey boys to her first class?"

"Lexi should get paid more for being an athletic trainer. Then I wouldn't have to support her while wearing tights," Liam grumbles, a scowl on his face and his arms crossed over his chest. It's a good thing we're the only ones here, otherwise his pissy attitude would turn away any potential clients.

Piper tilts her head. "They aren't tights, Liam. They're leggings, and there is a big difference between the two. I thought you'd prefer them to the big pads you wear on the ice. These let you move freely."

"I'm comfortable in the pads. I feel like I'm showing off my dick in these. You can practically see my nuts."

She looks him up and down. "At least it's a nice dick."

Liam, the man who could strangle someone with a flick of his wrist, fucking *blushes*. "Thanks," he mumbles, and I've never heard him sound so sincere.

"This isn't being recorded, is it?" I ask. "I did a hot yoga class once and it was terrible. I had to pay the lady five thousand dollars to delete the live stream so my downward dog pose wasn't seen by a million people."

"You're going to be fine." Emmy taps my arm and her fingers drag across my shirt. To anyone watching us, they wouldn't be able to see the way her touch lingers on my shoulder. But I can feel her reluctance to pull away, and that makes me grin. "You're probably going to be a pro, just like you are at everything else."

"Nothing like an ego boost to start the day."

"Don't worry, Cap. Pilates is a breeze," Grant says. He's decked out in an athleisure outfit and looks like a total tool. "Lots of moms do it."

Emmy lifts an eyebrow. "So, because moms do it, it's easy?"

"I didn't mean it like *that*," he says, backtracking.

"How did you mean it?"

Grant looks at me, panic-stricken, and I shrug. "You did this to yourself, kid," I say, and his cheeks turn dark red.

"Just… you know. It's not black belt karate."

Emmy hums, and I have to fight back my laughter at the wicked gleam in her eye. "We'll see how you're doing in thirty minutes. Do you know what pelvic floor muscles are?"

"Um. No. Should I?"

"This is going to be fun," she says, turning to Piper and diving into a conversation about the pair of socks she's holding up that look different from what the rest of us have on.

"Is it mean to say I hope Grant gets his ass handed to him?" I ask Hudson, and he grins.

"No. He needs to learn a little respect. You were the same way at that age."

"I'm better now though, right?"

"Much better, Mavvy. And you didn't show up in a matching tracksuit. That says something."

"Hey, I have a question for you," I say, dropping my voice low. "I want to get Emmy's dad to the game in Detroit in a few days, and he uses a wheelchair. She said he'll need some assistance in the arena, and I thought Duke might like to hang out with him. I bought a suite so they would be comfortable with plenty of space to stretch out. I wanted to run the idea by you before Emmy told her dad about the plans."

"You're doing all of this so her dad can watch her play?"

"He hasn't seen her in a Stars jersey yet."

Hudson rubs his jaw and stares at me. "You like her, don't you?"

"Of course I like her. She's our teammate. I like all of you."

"I don't mean like that, Maverick."

I cut my gaze away. How do I tell him Emmy is all I think about? She's the first thing on my mind when I wake up. At night, when she's curled up next to me, I'm still thinking about her. I close my eyes, and she's there.

I like her so much, it hurts when she's not around. I'd do anything to make her happy, and when she smiles at me, I feel like the luckiest guy in the world.

"Is it that obvious?" I ask.

"To some of the other knuckleheads? Not at all. But we're best friends, Mav. I know that fight with her ex wasn't just because you wanted to have a dick measuring contest. You were standing up for her because you care about her. More than you care about anyone else."

"Yeah." I run my thumb over my bottom lip, a smile starting there. "I like her a lot, and she likes me too."

"Has Maverick Miller finally become a one-woman man?"

"I never thought this would happen, but here I am. Off the market and happy as fuck. We have a good thing going, and that's why I'm doing all of this. It's important to her, which means it's important to me."

Hudson grins, and he claps a hand on my shoulder. "No more one-night stands? No more collecting numbers from random women every time we go out? Times have changed. I'm happy for you, man, and I'm sure Duke would love to help. I just have to mention the word *suite* and he'll be all for it."

"Tell him his favorite son hooked him up. I don't want you to get all the credit."

"Boys," Emmy calls out, and we turn our heads. "Do you want to socialize all day, or are you going to come and join us?"

There's a weird pressure in my chest when I stare at her.

It's almost like I can't breathe, and it only gets worse the longer I look. The sensation expands behind my ribs and takes up all the space in my head. When her mouth curls into a small smile, it makes me wonder if she's feeling it too.

"That's your girl?" Hudson asks.

"Yeah." I grin, and there's an arrow lodged in my chest. "That's my girl."

"What the fuck?" I groan, throwing an arm over my face. "These should be called torture devices, not pilates reformers. It's not natural to bend like this."

"My abs have never hurt so badly." Grant whimpers and

rolls onto his stomach. The leather mat under him is stained with his sweat, and he's more disgusting now than after a game. "This is cruel."

"I swear to god I tore my hamstring doing those lunges. Who would've thought moving your leg out and back in would hurt so damn bad?" Ethan asks.

"I don't see what the problem is." Hudson puts his hands on his hips, and a bead of sweat rolls down his chest. He ditched his shirt before we started, and the fucker isn't even breathing hard. "You lunge. You hold. You pulse. You repeat."

"Says the suck-up who looks like he's been going to classes for years," I gasp, swallowing down a lungful of air.

"I have," he says. "I also haven't had an injury in my career. Call me a suck-up all you want, but my body loves me."

"I actually hate you." I groan again and climb off the machine. "Is there a hole in my shorts? I heard a rip during those leg lowers."

"The only hole is the one in my heart. I've never been in so much pain." Grant reaches for me, and I hold his hand. "Tell my sisters I love them, and don't let Ethan take my Xbox X. Give it to charity."

"All right." Lexi claps, and I jump. "We're going to get into side lying heel presses. We'll start on our right, and I want you to remember to engage your core muscles."

"We're not done?" Riley is on the verge of tears, and somewhere behind me, someone sniffs. "We've been in here for hours."

"It's been thirty minutes," Emmy says over her shoulder, and our eyes meet.

Her cheeks are red and her hair is damp. She also lost her shirt, and her bright-pink sports bra is distracting me.

Fuck, she's beautiful.

She's always beautiful, but when she's showing off her

athletic capabilities, she's fucking gorgeous. Strong, fierce and determined. Reaching for a goal and going after it.

I've spent the entire class watching the way she moves her body. It's exactly how she is on the ice—graceful and powerful. She did the positions that almost wiped out the rest of the team with ease.

"I'd prefer thirty minutes in hell over thirty more minutes of this." I rub my legs and arms. Muscles I didn't know existed are already aching, and I have no clue how I'm going to survive morning skate tomorrow. "Christ, Lexi. You're going to create an army of soldiers."

"Is it too much?" She frowns and looks around the room. Half the guys are sprawled out on the ground, and the other half have their hands on their knees, huffing and puffing. We're all in the top one percent of body compositions and made of lean muscle that makes shoving someone into the boards easy, but we can't keep up with the brunette who barely comes up to my chest. "I went too hard on you all, didn't I?"

"No, you didn't," Seymour says, and besides Emmy and Hudson, he's the least affected by the grueling workout. Even Piper looks like she's struggling to stand. "We're just weak as shit. This is cross training we should be incorporating into our routine. Maybe we can add it in once a week."

"I take back everything I said. Emmy and Lexi, I'm sorry. This is not easy. In fact, this is the hardest thing I've done in my whole life. I'd rather spend an hour doing dryland training than sit here for fifteen more minutes," Grant says. "But you know what? None of us are quitters, so we're going to dig deep for another thirty minutes and finish this workout strong."

"You really don't have to." Lexi pauses the music playing over the stereo system. "I don't want to injure anyone so late in the season. Coach would be pissed at me."

"You're not going to injure us, Lex. We all know our

bodies damn well, and if anyone is in actual pain, they'll bow out."

"Are you sure?" she asks, and Emmy nods.

"Positive. This is going really well, and your instructions are clear. You have Liam doing that mermaid stretch so well, it's going to help when he's in goal."

Liam grunts in agreement. "True."

"Okay. Tell me if you need a break, and we'll stop."

"Want to make a bet, pretty boy?" Emmy whispers, and the rest of the guys climb back on their machines.

"What are the terms, Red?"

"If you make it through the rest of the workout without stopping, you get to do whatever you want to me tonight."

"And if I stop?"

"I get to do whatever I want to you tonight."

"It sounds like I win either way."

"Are you sure? I might want to tie your hands above your head. I might want to blindfold you too."

I lean forward and give her a slow grin. Her breathing hitches, and I touch my thumb to her cheek. "Either way, I'm with you," I murmur. "That's a win in my book, and I think you like it when I win, Emmy girl."

"Yeah." Her throat bobs, and her eyes stay locked on mine. That pressure is back, and this time, I welcome it. "I think I do."

FORTY-THREE
MAVERICK

"ARE you sure it's okay I stay over?" Emerson takes off her sweater and jeans and exchanges them with one of my old T-shirts. "We've never had a sleepover before a road trip, and I don't want to mess up any of your pregame rituals."

"The only pregame ritual I have these days is touching you. Besides, we don't play until the day after tomorrow. There's plenty of time to make sure my routine is right." I pull back the sheets and pat the spot on the bed next to me. The pillows have started to smell like her shampoo—citrusy and flowery like on a warm summer day. "Please stay."

"Okay." Her mouth twists into a pretty smile. I know she's trying not to look too excited, but I see the cute little wrinkles around her eyes. The way she hurries over to the mattress and plops down next to me. She wants to be here just as much as I want her here. "Only because you said please."

"I can be very persuasive." I open my arms and she nestles into my embrace, her head on my shoulder and her hair all over my bare chest. I sigh at the press of her body against mine, her skin still warm from the shower we shared after we cooked dinner and split a bowl of ice cream. "Where does Piper think you are tonight?"

"Oh." Emmy hides her face. "I may or may not have told the girls we're seeing each other," she admits. "There was wine and pizza, and everyone else was sharing parts of their lives. I wanted to share something, so I kind of let it slip that we've been sleeping together for months and now we're dating."

"I don't care that you told them." I smile and trace the freckles on her shoulder. I spell out the word *mine* and add a little heart at the end. "I've been wanting to shout from the rooftops that you're my girlfriend for a while now."

"You're not allergic to that word, are you? Do you understand what it means?"

"Says the woman who told me she doesn't date hockey players. I know what that word means. It means I'm yours and you're mine. You make me happy, and I hope I make you happy too."

"You make me happy," she says softly. "You make me happier than anyone else ever has."

Pride swells in my chest. It takes everything in me to not grin like a total idiot, and it feels like I'm flying. "I can't lie and say I've ever looked forward to going to Detroit, but I am this time. Are you excited to see your dad?"

"I am. I'm also nervous. I want him to have a good time, and I want to play well. But then I know I won't be too mad at myself if I *don't* play well, because he's still going to be proud of me no matter if we win or lose. It takes some of the pressure off." Emerson tips her chin to look up at me, and I kiss her forehead. "Does that make any sense?"

"Perfect sense. At the end of the day, him being there is more important than the outcome of the game." I rub my palm down her arm and smile. "But we're going to win."

"You really might be the most confident hockey player I've ever met."

"Trust me, it's a curse." My hand falls to the middle of her back, and I sigh again. I don't know what kind of magical powers Emmy has, but whenever she's in my arms, I'm totally at peace. "We're all set with the van. I convinced Coach to push morning skate back to ten thirty, so we can leave around six, grab your dad by eight, then be back in time to ride the team bus to the arena."

"Do any of the guys know you're coming with me to get him?" Emmy asks, her sharp green eyes watching me.

"Hudson does."

"Does that bother you?"

"What? That he knows you and I are spending time together?"

"Yeah. That's not something you usually do." She lifts a shoulder. "I don't want you to be uncomfortable."

"I've done a lot of things with you, baby, that I haven't done with anyone else. One of my best friends finding out about our relationship doesn't make me uncomfortable. In fact, I'm excited about it." It's my turn to shrug. "I was serious when I said I want to hold your hand in public and show you off. Now there's one less person to hide it from. Hudson is all for it. He said he's happy for me, and that's pretty damn cool."

"Be honest." Her fingers loop around my silver chain and give the jewelry a gentle tug, urging me closer. Our mouths are inches apart, and I brush my nose against hers. "How terrible is it to not be single anymore?"

I pull down on her bottom lip with my thumb then cup her jaw. I'm so fucking desperate to touch her. "I would say I wish I had gone off the market sooner, but that means I wouldn't be with you and… I don't know. Not to get all cheesy and shit, but you were worth the wait. I like learning how to do this with you. I like learning that you hog the covers and have to sleep with one leg on top of the sheets."

"It balances out my body temperature," she argues, and I grin. "You're smiling at me. I like it when you smile at me."

"You used to hate it."

"Not so much anymore. Is it silly to say I'm excited for you to meet my dad? I've never introduced him to any of my boyfriends before, and I'm glad that you're the first."

"How the tables turn. Five months ago you would've laughed in my face if I asked to meet your dad. Now look at you. You're *grinning*, Red."

She swats at my chest and I curl my fingers around her wrist. "I am not."

"You're a terrible liar. What's your question of the day?"

"We've done so many of these, I'm afraid I'm going to run out of things to ask soon." Emmy sighs. "Can you go first tonight?"

"Sure. What are you most proud of in your life?"

"I miss when we talked about birthdays and favorite colors. Now we're getting into the real deep stuff."

"I mean, I could ask your opinion on time travel instead."

"I don't even know how to begin to answer that." She wiggles in my arms and closes her eyes. "I think I'm proud that I haven't let the noise surrounding the sport I love get too loud. I wasn't sure I was going to last in this league, not because I doubted my capabilities as a player, but because of the outside factors that tried so hard to get me to fail. The social media comments. The signs at away games telling me I don't belong on the ice. I proved them wrong, and I found a place where I want to stay for a long time, with a person I want to be with. That's never happened before."

"I'm proud of you too. I don't know if I say it enough, but *fuck*, Em. You remind me why I fell in love with skating."

"Thank you. Now you have to tell me what you're most proud of."

"Not killing Cole Meyers," I say, and she snorts. "I'm serious. I was ready to end that motherfucker with my bare hands, and I would've strangled him, if I had the chance. It's a shame the refs got involved."

"I can take care of myself just fine, I have been for years, but watching you stand up for me… I felt like I was yours for the first time. Like I had someone who would be by my side, no matter what."

I write the word *mine* with her freckles again. *Mine, mine, mine.*

All mine, for as long as she'll have me.

I hope it's forever.

"You are mine," I tell her, and it sounds like there's something else trying to sneak through.

Something I swallow down and replace with a kiss to the corner of her mouth, then the spot below her ear that earns me a pleased groan and a gentle roll of her hips. I switch our positions and ease her onto her back, my hands on either side of her head. Her hair is spread out on my pillows like wildfire, and when her eyes lock on mine, I think lightning strikes.

"Show me," Emmy whispers, and her fingers find the tiny space on my bicep without any tattoos. The lone square of my skin that hasn't found a permanent piece of art yet. I swear she writes out her name with pink nails and a hot press of her mouth. "Show me how much I'm yours."

Time skips ahead after that. There are clothes, then there aren't. I touch her everywhere and she touches me. I kiss her as I sink inside her and she threads her hands through my hair when she comes, the quietest little laugh at the back of her throat.

After I clean her up and burrow my face in the back of her neck, it still feels like I'm forgetting to tell her something, but I don't have a goddamn clue what it is.

FORTY-FOUR
MAVERICK

EMMY IS the spitting image of her dad.

Alan Hartwell has the same fiery red hair and green eyes. The same long arms and long legs, and the same snarky smile I can spot from a mile away.

When we park in the driveway of an old craftsman with a covered porch and big windows, I jump out of the driver's seat and follow Emmy toward the wheelchair ramp that leads to the front door. She bends down to hug her dad, and I hang back so they can have a moment together.

"Hi, Dad," she says.

"There's my girl." He runs his fingers through her hair, and when she pulls away, she wipes her eyes. His attention darts over to me. "And who is this?"

"Hi, sir." I step closer and extend a hand for him to shake. "I'm Maverick. It's great to meet you. Emmy has told me a lot about you."

"Has she?" Alan looks over at his daughter and grins. "I haven't heard a thing about you."

"Did you pay him to say that?" I ask, and Emmy smirks.

"A hundred bucks."

"Good god, Red. You could've bought me dinner with that."

"Says the twelve-million-dollar man."

Alan bats my hand away and pulls me into the same hug he gave Emmy. "It's nice to meet you, son. Thank you for making the drive to see me."

"Who doesn't love Michigan in February?" I ask.

"I'd offer to give you a tour, but we're on a time crunch," Emmy says.

"Next time I'm going to have you show me this bar where you ate your pizza and sipped on chocolate milk." I glance at Alan. "And I agree with you on the *Jurassic Park* debate, sir."

"I like him already."

"You're going to be up front Dad, and I'll sit in the back. The van isn't as nice as Maverick's Mercedes, but he drives it just fine."

"A Mercedes?" Alan asks. "What model?"

"A G-Wagon. It's not very practical for the city, but I bought it with my first paycheck when I was young and stupid and didn't have a financial adviser. I don't want to part with it now."

"That's a nice car. I never had anything that fancy, but I did have a bright red Mazda Miata back in the day. I loved to zip around in that thing."

"I have no clue what any of these cars are," Emmy says.

"I'm disappointed. Stick with me, Red, and I'll teach you." I check my phone and gesture to the car. "Do we want to get going? I don't mean to rush us, but you know Coach is going to be pissed if we're late for the bus."

"Shoot, yeah." Emmy looks at Alan. "Do you need anything from inside, Dad? I can grab it."

"I have a bag on the kitchen table if you don't mind getting it and locking up," he says. "And the plastic bag with my medication on the counter."

"Want a hand?" I ask, and she nods.

"That would be great. Thanks." She kisses her dad's cheek and leads me into the entryway. "Welcome to teenage Emmy's home."

"I like it." I smile at the tall plant in the corner and the pictures on the wall. "How long did you live here?"

"A couple years in high school, and he's been here ever since. It's been remodeled since his injury. I was only making seventy thousand dollars when I was in the ECHL, so this contract with the Stars has been really helpful in planning out some long-term adjustments I'd like to make. I've also thought about buying a new house that's accommodating to what he needs, but I'm not sure I can get him to part with this place. It's finally home to him."

I rub a hand over my chest.

I'd like a home one day. A place where you feel the years of memories. No matter how much money I throw at an interior designer to make it more comfortable, my apartment has never been like that.

I feel it when I go to Maven and Dallas's place, though. There's love and warmth and all the shit that comes with feeling happy and settled, and *fuck*, I want that.

I've never wanted it before, but now that I have a little of that with Emmy, I want more. I want all of it.

A wraparound porch with rocking chairs. A play set in the backyard I put together myself and a redhead watching me from the window. A fence and a bedroom we fall into together every night. Rings and cribs and *goddammit*.

How the hell do I make that happen?

"Hey." Emmy touches my elbow. Her fingers press into my jacket, and I sigh. "Are you okay?"

"Yeah." I nod and wrap my hand around hers. "Never better, Emmy girl."

"A suite?" Alan looks around the private box above center ice. "This is too nice for a guy like me."

"Maverick." Emmy puts her hands on her hips, and I love how her leather pants hug her legs. I shouldn't be staring at the curve of her thigh, but it's hard not to. "This wasn't necessary."

"I know it wasn't. But I wanted Alan to have the best experience tonight, and what better way to do that than give him the VIP treatment?"

"You make saying no almost impossible." Emmy huffs and glances at the dark wood walls and leather couches. "It is really nice. I've never been in a suite before."

"Thank you, son. This is a wonderful surprise," Alan says.

Son.

The pride that word brings me.

I'd like to find a way for him keep calling me that, because I like how it makes me feel.

Like I can accomplish anything I set my mind to.

Like I have someone who cares about me and wants the best for me.

Like that void of wanting a permanent father figure is filled.

"Don't mention it." I put my hands in the pockets of my dress slacks and smile. "I'm on a quest to make everyone's dad like me more than they like their own kids. Upgrading you to a suite is just the start of my plan."

"I can't stand you," Emmy says, but there isn't any heat behind it. "I'm going to check in with the guy at the elevator and make sure he knows you're here, Dad. I'll be back in a few minutes."

"Let me know if you need anything," I tell her. "We can go down to the locker room after."

"Thanks." She squeezes my arm and heads for the door. I watch her walk away, and when she looks back and smiles at me, I grin.

Alan clears his throat, and I jump, sheepishly running my hand through my hair. "Hudson Hayes's dad, Duke, will be here in a few minutes," I say, breaking the silence. "He's fairly quiet like his son until the game gets going, then he's the most enthusiastic fan I've ever seen. If you need anything, he'll be happy to help."

"I'm sure we'll get along just fine. Is Hudson one of your friends?"

"Yeah." I sit on the couch across from him and stretch out my legs. My quads are tight from being in the van for so long, but I'd do the long round trip drive again. "All my teammates are great, but I've connected the most with Hudson. If I needed anything, he'd be there in a second to help. I'd do the same for him."

"That kind of friendship is special, especially in sports. It's hard to know what the future holds as an athlete, and to have someone in your corner you respect and trust is important."

"Emmy told me you played college hockey. Where did you go? Michigan?"

"I'm a Boston College boy. Had the time of my life playing there."

"Ethan's from the Northeast. He went to BC too," I say.

"Richardson? I like that guy. He's a scrappy center, isn't he?" Alan asks.

"And a total pain in my ass," I joke, and he laughs.

"How are you feeling about tonight? You're getting into the last stretch of the season. I'm sure the pressure is amping up."

"It is. I feel good, though. Detroit has been sneaky the last couple of weeks. They went from out of the playoff hunt to the seventh spot in the East, and you don't do that without grit. We have to keep our eye on them, especially as the season winds down. I have a feeling they're going to sneak in as a Wild Card, and I sure as hell don't want to play them with the kind of momentum they've had as of late."

"If I have to root for anyone besides my hometown Blades, I'm glad it'll be Emmy on the Stars." Alan smiles. "You've had a good career in DC."

"Thank you, sir. It's not as good as I would've liked, but we're getting there. The last few months have been a game changer for us, and your daughter has played a big role in that. Emmy is a talented athlete, and we're lucky to have her on our team."

"She's good, isn't she? I remember when she got her first pair of skates. After she figured out how to make it around the pond behind our house without falling over, I couldn't pry her away from the ice. I knew then she was going to be a special player."

"Very special," I agree.

"How long have you been in love with her?" Alan asks, and I blink.

"Pardon?"

"How long have you been in love with my daughter?" he asks again, and the room feels like it's a thousand degrees.

"Um. I'm not..." I clear my throat and look at the door behind him. I wonder if I can escape and make up an excuse for my disappearance. A sudden illness forcing me to evacuate the premises immediately. It wouldn't be a total lie. My skin is clammy. I feel nauseous, and there's sweat on my forehead. I wipe it away with the back of my hand. "We're not—"

"You're clearly something if you're going to all this effort for her old man. It's definitely not to impress her; she's already smitten with you too."

"She is?" I ask. I can see it in her eyes and the way her hand always finds mine, but it's nice to hear it from someone else. "That's good to know."

Alan grins. "I didn't mean to put you on the spot, and it's okay if you haven't figured it out yet. Sometimes it takes us a while to put a word to the feelings we have."

I scratch my ear.

Love?

Do I love her?

What the hell does love even mean?

I've only ever used that word with my friends, but I don't feel that way about Emmy. It's deeper, like someone reaches into my chest and squeezes my heart whenever she's nearby. I get warm and tingly when she touches me, and every time she laughs, I swear to god I'm floating.

Is that *love?*

"I, uh, care about her very much," I mumble. I've never been more confused, and all the wheels in my head have decided to turn at the same time. *Love. Love. Love.* I say it a dozen times, and I'm still not sure. "I like her a lot."

"Like who a lot?" Emmy asks, and she looks at me from the door.

Love.

I love her?

The blood drains from my face and I pinch the bridge of my nose.

Oh, god.

I love her.

I fucking love her.

I love her, and I'd do anything for her.

There's no way she loves me back, is there?

Except… when she looks at me, she brightens up. Her smile is wide and her eyes twinkle.

That has to mean something, right?

"You," I say. "I was telling your dad how much I care about you. How important you are to me."

"Oh." Her smile matches the one she gives me late at night. When she's half asleep and curled around me, refusing to let go. "I care about you, too, pretty boy."

I huff out a laugh and stand up. "We've got to head out, sir, but we'll see you after the game," I tell Alan.

"You two play hard out there. And take your time with

finding the words, Maverick. She's worth the wait," he says with a wink.

"Why do I feel like you two have a secret?" Emmy asks, and I drape my arm around her shoulder.

"Maybe we do, Red, and one day I'll tell you all about it."

I love you, I think, when we head to the locker room.

I love you, I think, when we celebrate her goal in the first period.

I love you, I think, when we win the game and she jumps in my arms.

I love you, I think, when she rests her head on my shoulder in the hotel elevator after we get back from dropping Alan off in Lansing.

I love you, I love you, I love you, I want to scream.

When she kisses my chest before we fall asleep, I think she loves me too.

FORTY-FIVE
EMMY

PRETTY BOY

I miss you.

ME

I'm out with Hudson right now.

PRETTY BOY

The fuck?

ME

Our dads are best friends, so now we're best friends.

He needs a new personal chef, so I'm wingwomaning for him at a cooking class.

PRETTY BOY

… Are you fucking with me?

ME

Open your door and find out.

MAVERICK DRAGS me into his apartment before I have a chance to knock. He pins me against the wall and puts his hands on either side of my head.

"Hi, Emmy girl," he murmurs.

"Hi, pretty boy." I touch his cheek, and he melts against me. "How was your afternoon off?"

"Better now that you're here." He kisses my forehead and smiles. "You really did go to a cooking class with Hudson, didn't you? Did you have a good time? Where are my leftovers?"

"There weren't any leftovers to bring, but I thought I could give you something else to eat." I pull at the tie of my trench coat, the fabric opening and showing off the lingerie I have underneath. "If you're hungry."

Maverick takes a step back, looks me up and down, and groans. "Christ, baby. You're a fucking vision."

I shrug out of the jacket and it pools at my feet. I ordered a sexy red set the other night when I was at Lexi's. The girls told me Maverick would go crazy if he saw me in the outfit, and from the way his eyes are blown wide and his cheeks are turning pink, I'd say they were right.

"Do you like it?" I ask, toying with the straps.

"Yes," he rasps. "Please don't tell me you wore that when you went to your cooking class."

"I did. Under my other clothes, so it was my little secret." I pause and arch my back off the wall. "Maybe I'll start wearing it to the rink too. A special blue set that matches our jerseys."

He scoops me up, lifting me off the ground and marching down the hall to his bedroom.

"I'm going to have to come into your locker room before every practice," he says in my ear, and he kisses my throat. "Just to see what surprises you're hiding."

"It's sweet of you to call my storage closet a locker room." I reach down and cup his length through the front of his athletic shorts. He's hard already, and I smile when he shudders under my touch. "And it's funny you think I'm going to let you in there."

"Why? Don't want me to see all the pictures you have of me taped up on your wall?"

"You're so full of yourself."

"What if I beg?" Maverick bends his head and grazes his teeth down my neck. "What if I beg like a good boy, Emmy?"

"Maybe," I breathe out. "That could persuade me."

His laugh is beautiful, and he kicks open the door to his room. He drops me on the edge of his bed and stares at me, his mouth half-open and his hands flexing at his sides.

"You're beautiful," he says. "I can't believe I get to have you. I can't believe you're mine."

When we're together, it's an inferno. Hot, quick, a race to see who can get the other off first. Sometimes we barely make it into the bedroom, choosing a counter or a wall or a chair instead.

Now, though, it's different. It's slower, like Maverick is trying to savor me. Trying to preserve it in his memory. And when he drops to his knees in front of me and nudges my legs open, a gasp works its way free from my chest.

I love watching him when he looks like this. Raw and needy. Glazed eyes and his chest rising and falling so quickly, you'd think he sprinted here.

"Have me," I whisper, and his gaze flashes with heat.

Love me, I want to say too, but I keep that to myself. I swallow it down, because when Maverick leans forward, kisses the inside of my knee, I almost forget my name.

"How wet are you?" he asks, and his mouth presses against the front of my underwear. "Soaked, I bet."

I hook a leg over his shoulder, and his grin is smug. "Find out for yourself."

"You're so pretty like this, though. I don't want to take this off you."

"Then fuck me in it." My fingers curl around his comforter, and I squirm, desperate for him. "I don't care what you do, just do *something*."

"Now who's begging?" Maverick hooks his thumb in my underwear and pulls it to the side. He hums, and I drop my head back. "Fucking look at you."

"Less looking. More doing, Miller."

"Yes ma'am." One finger presses inside me, and I groan. "There you go, baby. That's what you want, isn't it?"

"Yes," I whisper, grinding into his hand. I roll my hips, searching for what I want, and he rewards me with a second and third finger without me having to ask. "*Maverick.*"

"The way you say my name drives me fucking wild." His left hand folds around my leg, keeping me in place. I feel him crowd my space, the bump of his shoulder against my knee and the soft cotton of his shirt against my stomach. "This is my meal, isn't it? I've been a very good boy, Emmy. I've earned a taste, haven't I?"

"*God*. Yes. Just—"

He cuts me off with his tongue, a teasing circle against my clit that has my hips lifting off the mattress and my fingers pulling on the ends of his hair. His moan vibrates against me, a deep sound that makes me wrap both legs around his neck, giving him nowhere to go.

"Heaven." He licks a hot swipe of his tongue over my entrance. "Fucking heaven. Let me die here, Emmy girl."

"If I don't come, you just might," I grit out, and his chuckle is an imprint on my skin.

"Guess it's time to show you my best work." Maverick slips his fingers out of me, and I whine at the loss. He drops my legs from his shoulders and works my underwear down, tossing them away. "Hang on, needy thing. I'm going to take care of you."

He presses on my clit with his thumb, and my eyes flutter open to find him looking at me.

"I want to watch you," he mumbles, his gaze bouncing to every inch of my body. "Want to watch you fall apart."

A string inside me tightens. It grows taut when he holds me open, his tongue replacing his fingers and driving me wild.

I get what I asked for—it really is his best work. The rhythm I like and the way he gets me there; thoroughly and completely, his mouth never stopping and his touch never wavering. Maverick stays latched to me until my legs shake and my skin burns.

"Maverick," I whisper. "I'm going to… please don't stop. Right there. That feels so good."

"Never, Emmy," he says roughly against me. "I'll be here forever."

I know the *here* he's talking about is between my legs, but for half a second I pretend it's a metaphor for something else.

By my side. With me. Loving me back and growing old. Bliss explodes in my blood, and I cry out, a hand on the back of his neck so he can't pull away.

"All of it. I know you have more, baby." Two fingers inside me and a palm on my stomach, and a second wave hits. "That's my girl. There's what I asked for. Doesn't that feel good?"

I groan and ride the pleasure until my vision sparks with blurry colors. When the sensation subsides, I lift my arms above my head, trying to find air, but Maverick doesn't give me a second to breathe.

"I'm not done with you." I blink, and his shirt is already off. He steps out of his sweatpants and walks toward me, a hand around his thick cock and his eyes on me. "Sit up, Emmy, and open your mouth. Get it wet, and make it messy."

I press up on my elbows and part my mouth. He rubs the head of his cock against my lips and smiles when my tongue sneaks out and licks away the pre-cum I find there.

I put my hand on him, my fingers curling around his erection and my mouth widening so he can get deeper. He hits the back of my throat, and I stare at him, silently telling him I can take more.

Maverick pulls down one of the cups of my bra and pinches my nipple. His touch dances up my chest to my throat and his palm settles around my neck.

"Talked to my tattoo artist yesterday." He bucks his hips forward, and I groan against his cock. "I have an appointment next week. I wasn't joking about putting *mine* on the back of my hand. I want to see it every time I touch you. A pretty necklace for my pretty girl."

I press my thighs together, moisture pooling between my legs at the thought of him putting a permanent piece of me on his skin. I nod, wanting to convey how much I like the idea, and he grins bright and beautiful.

I pop him out of my mouth and stroke his length. A drop of drool hangs on the corner of my lips, and he reaches out, wiping it away with his thumb.

"Wet. Messy. Perfect," he says.

"And yours," I add, scooting back across the mattress toward the pillows. I relax against the headboard and tip open my legs, touching myself where he was before. "Come and take what's yours, Maverick."

He moves lightning quick, on the bed in a flash and straddling my hips. He holds the back of my head, fingers threading through my knotted hair and bringing his mouth down to mine.

"There's nothing I want more." Maverick lines himself up with my entrance, and glances up at me. "Okay?"

"Yeah." I rub my hands down his arms and leave nail marks on the curve of his muscles. "It's always okay with you."

He kisses me at the same time he thrusts forward and fills me. Maverick swallows down my moan, a soft bite to my lower lip to help me work through the stretch.

"I've got you," he says, forehead against mine and a bead

of sweat on his cheek. "God, Emmy. I can't believe I get to have you like this."

"You're just saying that because you're eight inches inside of me." I gasp when he lifts one of my legs, holding it against his side and sinking another inch deeper. "*Fuck.*"

"Trying," he grits out, and a laugh bursts from me. "Your cunt is so fucking tight, it makes it difficult to want to do anything but sit here and enjoy."

I grab his ass, urging him to move, and our bodies fall into synchronized movements.

It's rough, with his hand at my neck again and his mouth leaving little pink marks on my skin, but it's tender too.

Gentle in the way he flips us so I'm on top of him, one leg on either side of his hips as I sink onto him and control the pace.

Reverent in how he holds my cheek and smiles up at me, his hair a mess and my heart almost bursting out of my chest.

"Remember when you said you're the only woman I've ever fucked twice because I can't get enough of you?" Maverick asks, taking both of my breasts in his hands. His thumbs brush over my nipples, and a stuttered exhale leaves my body. "You were right, Emmy. I'll never get enough of you. I'll never get enough of your body and the way it fits perfectly with mine. I'll never get over your brilliant brain and wonderful heart. I'm going to have you until the end of time, and it's going to be just as good as right now, baby, because you're perfect for me."

I love you, I almost scream. *I love you so fucking much*, I almost yell, and I show him all the ways by fucking him hard. By kissing him until he's panting my name, until he's asking if it's okay to come inside me, until his legs are spasming and his cock pulses, the warmth of his release making me tip over the edge with him.

I collapse on top of him and he holds me tight. When he

pulls out of me, he nudges me on my back and pushes my knees apart, taking a spot on his stomach between my legs.

"What are you doing?" I ask.

"Want to see what you look like full of my cum. Want to see what it looks like when you're mine."

Heat creeps up my skin from my toes to my cheeks. Maverick uses his thumb to spread his release over my pussy, and in a moment where I should feel exposed and vulnerable, I feel nothing but adored.

"Emmy," he says, and it sounds like it's been pulled from somewhere in his soul. "I—" He licks his lips and kisses my calf. He taps my ankle and laughs. I want to laugh too. "You really are my most favorite person in the world."

"The feeling is mutual." I reach for him, and he adjusts our positions so I'm in his lap, the place where I never want to leave. "Will you tell me about the first time you saw me?"

"You mean the day when I hit on you and mistook you for a fan, and you called me out for being arrogant?"

"Yeah." I play with his necklace and smile. "That day."

"I thought you were hot. Which sounds so superficial, because you're so much more than hot, but *damn* I was admiring your curves."

"You did a lot of eye-fucking," I agree, and he pinches my side.

"Can you blame me? My weakness is tall, athletic women, and you fit that bill pretty damn well, Red. Something weird happened, though. You know I've been with plenty of women, but when you talked to me… it was like my heart skipped a beat. My hands were clammy and I had trouble breathing. It had never felt like that before."

"And then I kicked your ass on the ice."

"We have different memories about what happened next."

"I had seen photos of you, but I wasn't prepared for meeting you in real life. You made me *furious*, but I thought you were the most attractive man I had ever laid eyes on. I still think that." I brush away some of his sweat-soaked hair and smile. "You're also so much more."

"Tell me," he pleads, and I know it's his need for validation sneaking through. His need to be wanted."Tell me what else I am."

"You're smart. You're so kind. I've never met anyone as kind as you. I love that you can get me to laugh so much. That cockiness isn't arrogance. It's confidence, because you know how hard you work to be the best friend. The best athlete. The best lover. Sometimes I think about how lucky I am to have a man like you in my life and I—" I have to squeeze my eyes shut so I don't look at him as I say this next part. "It makes me wonder what I did to deserve someone so wonderful. It makes me think I might finally be good enough to have earned something so… so lovely in my life."

"Emerson. Look at me, please."

I open my eyes. His gaze meets mine, and I feel the power of it behind my ribs.

"You are enough," Maverick says. "You are *more* than enough, and you're so far out of my league, it's not even funny. I… you…" He shakes his head, clearing his thoughts. "Every day I'm going to show you just how enough you are."

"And I'm going to show you every day how wanted you are," I say softly. "How wanted you are for being *you*, not your paycheck or your stat line. I've never wanted anyone the way I want you, Maverick."

I love you.

I love you so fucking much.

We don't say anything else to each other, but we don't have to. The silence is perfect.

Completely and totally perfect.

FORTY-SIX
MAVERICK

COACH

Can you give me a few minutes after practice?

I want to talk to you about something.

ME

I swear I didn't leave trash on the ice. That was Ethan, and I already made him pick it up.

COACH

It's not about that.

It's about a possible trade.

ME

Oh. Sure. See you soon.

BRODY SAUNDERS IS A BLUNT GUY. He's never sugarcoated anything, and the fact that he didn't mention specifics in his message other than a possible trade has me nervous as fuck.

"Hey." I drop into the chair across from him in his office and try to smile. "How's Olivia?"

"She's good." He turns around the photo of his nine-year-old daughter. "Her princess birthday party was a success. Thanks for her gift, by the way. She loved the stencils and sketchbook you sent."

"Don't mention it. My friend's kid is in a big art phase, and I thought Livvie might like all that creative stuff too."

"She does. I can't keep up with all the supplies she asks me to buy." Coach laughs and leans back. "That girl has me wrapped around her damn finger."

"You wouldn't have it any other way, would you?"

"God, no." He pauses and looks at me. "Look, I'm going to cut to the chase about why I asked you to come by. I got a call from Toronto this morning about a trade, and I'm considering taking it."

With three days to go before the trade deadline, I'm not surprised. Teams are always trying to wheel and deal all the way down to the wire, and our win streak and comeback season makes our players more desirable.

"Who is it?" I ask.

I'm not sure he's going to tell me—that kind of information typically stays in the boardroom, not with the captains. But I'm really fucking intrigued.

"Justin Harper," he says, and my mouth drops open.

He's the best winger in the league, a two-time Stanley Cup winner at only twenty-five. I've admired him from the second he was drafted, and we've been casual acquaintances since playing on the same All-Star team three years ago.

"Do it," I say. "I don't care who it is. That's a big fucking move. We get him, we go to the postseason and win it all."

Coach pauses. "They want Emmy."

I stare at him, and he starts to turn blurry. Everything around me is fuzzy, and there's a ringing in my ears. My throat closes up, and I try to gulp down a breath.

"Emmy?" I repeat.

"Yeah." Coach scrubs a hand over his face and groans.

"Who else?"

"Finn when he's healthy again, and a first round draft pick."

They're basically giving Harper away, and it's a steal of a deal.

Every manager in the league would take it in a heartbeat, and it feels like this meeting is more of a courtesy than asking for my opinion.

"Fuck. Okay. What—" I swallow, but that lump in my throat won't go away. "How are you feeling about it?"

"I'm torn. We have something really good going on right now. Is it worth blowing it up to take a chance on a maybe? On something that looks good on paper but might not be the best thing long term?"

"Respectfully, Coach, it's a maybe who has won *two* fucking Stanley Cups."

"We can get there with this team. I know we can. I've seen the improvements we've made, and I know if we keep our core players together, we're only going to get better. But who's to say an offer won't come up for someone else in the offseason and they'll run with it? Money talks, and teams have a lot of cap space to work with this summer. Hell, I'm surprised you haven't run. Losing is really fucking hard. This season is better, but coming up short sucks."

I'm not surprised I've stayed.

This team has become my family. The brothers I never had and the attention from authority figures I've always craved. I'd never fucking quit on them, even when we're in the depths of hell.

With the Stars, I'm not just the number on my back or a piece to move around. I'm *Maverick*, just like Hudson is Hudson and Emmy is Emmy.

Fuck.

Emmy.

"I think we need to decide if the short-term benefits outweigh the long-term goals," I say, and my voice cracks. "Why do they want to get rid of him? Is something happening behind the scenes that the media hasn't gotten a hold of yet?"

"Not that I've heard. Toronto knows Harper is looking for a big contract, and they don't have the resources to give him what he wants. They also see the appeal of Emmy with her size and speed. Finn could be the best player this decade once he's healthy. He's young. He's smart. If he's on your team, you're getting at least ten more wins a year. They'd recoup the loss of their star while adding more versatile players to their roster."

"I don't know what to say, Coach. Six months ago, it would've been a fuck yeah, and I wouldn't have wasted another breath. But today? Today I really want to say no."

Coach stares at me, and he looks tired. Like the weight of the world sits on his shoulders, and you couldn't pay me to have his job.

"I'm going to ask you something. Man to man. Brody to Maverick, like we're shooting the shit at a bar, not coach to player. And I want you to answer honestly."

I nod, already knowing what's coming.

"Are you and Emmy involved?"

I finally take a real breath, and his question makes me want to burst out laughing.

Involved seems like the smallest word in the dictionary to define what we are.

Is that the way to describe the person I look forward to seeing every day? Is it the word to use to talk about the woman who makes me smile even when I'm tired and sore and angry after a bad game? Is it the way to tell people that when I look at her, I see the sun and the moon and all the fucking stars?

It seems so insignificant, because what I feel for her is

bigger than the sky. The whole fucking planet. You could go all the way to outer space and there still wouldn't be enough ways to show her how much I adore her.

But I also know my role as captain.

The job I'm paid to do and people rely on me for.

I've never let my personal feelings come before my professional ones, but *fuck* it's hard when it hits so close to home.

"Yes." I clear my throat. "We're involved and…" I shrug and stare at the corner of his desk. There's a piece of wood missing, and I wonder where it ended up. "I care about her. A lot."

Coach hangs his head. It feels like I've disappointed him, and it tastes bitter on my tongue.

"I thought so. I noticed the chemistry between you two has amped up, but I didn't want to assume anything. It's been getting a little more obvious lately, though, and that game against the Wildebeests sealed the deal. I had to ask."

"Am I in trouble?" I mumble, and there's a pressure behind my eyes that wasn't there before. "I'm sorry."

"Maverick," he says gently, and I look up at him. He's smiling now, and I'm so fucking confused. "You're not in trouble."

"I'm not?"

"No. There's no precedent for this, and to be honest, I was waiting for it to happen. You push each other to be better, and your relationship on the ice probably mirrors what's going on off the ice as well. It's exactly what you'd want in a partner, and I'd never send her away because of your feelings. I want to make myself very clear that this doesn't have anything to do with you."

"Okay." I run my hand through my hair and try to act like I'm composed. Calm, cool, and collected. "Speaking from a captain's perspective, you have to do what's best for the team, Coach. You're not in charge of what happens behind closed doors. If you think this trade is something we need to seriously pursue, you have my support."

I'd never stand in the way of Emmy's career. She's been worried about what her role on the team might look like when Finn gets back next season, and Toronto would be a guaranteed thing for her.

More money. More opportunities for endorsement deals. A chance to help her dad fix up his house to make it more accessible.

I'd be an idiot to even consider asking Coach to let her stay.

"I know how difficult that must be for you to say, and I appreciate the support." Coach pinches the bridge of his nose. "This would be a lot easier if we were talking about fantasy drafts, not people we care about."

"You have a fantasy team?" I ask, and he grins.

"I do. I pick you first every time."

"Shucks, man." I put my hand over my chest, and the tension I'm feeling loosens half a degree. "You're too good to me."

"I need to mull all of this over. I need to look at lines and who would fill that other roster spot we'd lose. There are a couple AHL guys who could get us through the season, but that's a risk in itself. I'll let you know what I'm leaning toward in forty-eight hours."

"That's fine." I bob my head and wring my hands together. "Can I ask a favor?"

"Sure."

"Can I be the one to tell Emmy there might be something in the works? She's someone who likes to move around, but DC is a place she'd really like to stay. I don't want her caught off guard."

"You can tell her." Coach smiles again, and he reaches across the desk to shake my hand. "You're a good man,

Maverick. It's an honor to be your friend and watch you grow up."

He might think I'm a good man, but right now, I feel like I'm about to be the asshole of the year.

FORTY-SEVEN
MAVERICK

ME

Are you guys free?

PLANT DADDY REID

Yeah

DADDY DALLAS

I am.

HUDSON

Just left the weight room. What's up?

ME

I need help.

It's half personal, half professional.

I feel like I'm drowning.

Don't know what to do.

DADDY DALLAS

My place. Now.

Maven and June are out for the afternoon. We can have some privacy.

You remember the address, Hud?

HUDSON

I do. I'll be there in fifteen.

PLANT DADDY REID

I'm already on my way.

I PACE across the floor in Dallas's living room. My mind is running a mile a minute and my heart is sitting somewhere between my chest and my throat.

"Okay." I stop in front of the coffee table and chug the beer Dallas popped open for me. Thank god we don't have practice tomorrow, because depending on how this conversation goes, I might need something stronger. "Okay."

Dallas, Reid and Hudson sit on the couch, watching me. None of them have said a word, and I think they're waiting for me to make the first move.

"I—there's…" I scratch my ear and run my hand through my hair. "She—" I shake my head and look at Dallas. "How the fuck do you do this every day?"

"Do what, exactly? Talk in broken sentences and make no sense? I sure hope I don't do that every day."

"I meant with Maven. How do you tell her how you feel every day? Do you just fucking say it?"

Dallas blinks. "Are you in love with my fiancée?"

"*No*. God, no. Fuck." I laugh and tip my head toward the ceiling. "That would probably be easier than all of this."

"It's like we're playing a drunken game of charades," Reid grumbles, and he pushes his glasses up his nose. "Start from the beginning, Mav."

The beginning would be a hotel room in Chicago where I kissed Emmy for the first time.

It feels like a lifetime ago.

"Right. Well. Emmy and I are sleeping together. It's a little more than sex, though. We're dating, actually, and Coach just told me she might get traded. I—there's this tightness in my chest when I think of what it would be like if she's not here and I think I might… I don't know… how do…"

Dallas grins. He stands up and looks down at Reid and Hudson. "We know what this is, right?"

"Easy diagnosis." Hudson leans back on the couch and smiles. "I've suspected it for a while now."

"Does he really not recognize it?" Reid asks.

"First timer," Hudson says. "We have to cut him some slack."

"Nothing like the first time," Dallas agrees.

"Dude. It's only happened to you once," Reid argues.

"So? I can still say it," he argues.

"Can someone please tell me what the fuck is going on? Am I having a heart attack? It feels like I might be." I rub my hand over my shirt. "Why is it so hard to fucking breathe?"

"You love Emmy," Dallas says, and I blink at him.

"That's what her dad told me, and I thought maybe I might but… I've never been in love with anyone. How can I be sure?" I press the heels of my palms in my eyes and sit on the floor. "I need a definition. Something to go off of."

"Do you think about her all the time? Miss her when she's gone? Feel better when she's around and would do anything to make her smile?" Dallas asks.

"Yes," I rasp, and I'm pretty sure the room is spinning. "All of that."

"Does your heart beat faster when she holds your hand? Do you look for her in a crowded room?" Reid presses.

"He definitely does. You should see him at the rink. He's constantly searching for her," Hudson says, laughing. "I counted the other day. Seventeen times during a two hour practice he was watching her instead of the puck."

"Holy shit," I whisper. "I love her. I fucking love her."

"Welcome to the club," Dallas says. I open my eyes, and he's standing over me, holding out his hand. He helps me to my feet and pulls me into a hug. "Love is the fucking best."

"What am I supposed to do with this information?" I ask into his shirt.

"Tell her, probably," Reid suggests. "That tends to work best."

"I can't tell her." I shake my head. "I don't want to push her away. She's already going to fucking Toronto. What if she doesn't love me back?"

"Bullshit," Hudson says, and I glance up at him. I've never heard him so passionate, not even after our biggest wins and toughest losses. "That woman loves you back. She looks at you all the time, Mav. You don't see it half the time, because she's much better about hiding it than you are, but I'll catch her staring at you, and her eyes get all bright. There's this little smile she has when she sees you, and it's the cutest fucking thing." He pauses and rubs his jaw. "I say that platonically. Please don't kick my ass."

"I'd never. Okay, so, what? I just go to her apartment and say, *hey, by the way, you might be in Toronto this time next week, but, surprise! I love you!* How does that work?"

"Back up. The trade. Coach told you about it?" Hudson asks, and I nod.

"Yeah. Her, Finn and a first round draft pick for Justin Harper. There's no way he doesn't take it."

"Shit," Dallas says. "Harper is a good player. I'm not saying Emmy isn't good, but—"

"But she doesn't have his experience. I know. Trust me. I get it. Coach said he's taking forty-eight hours to decide, but he told me I can give her a heads up. And I have to give her a heads up."

"Okay. Here's what you're going to do." Reid rubs his hands together, and this is where he shines. Logistics. Planning how scenarios might pan out. "You're going to go to her place right now—I don't understand why you're still here. You're going to tell her the bad news, which is about the trade, first. Then you'll move to the good news. You'll tell her how much you love her—and you have to use those exact fucking words, Mav. You can't be ambiguous about this. Tell her point blank exactly how you're feeling, and propose a solution. Alternating weekends between here and Toronto. Buying your own place there where you can stay when you're in town so she doesn't feel like you're crowding her. Giving her a key to your place here so she knows she can trust you even though she's in a different country." He pauses to take a breath. "And then she's going to tell you how she feels too."

"How… what the fuck, Duncan?" I stare at him. "Where has this relationship knowledge been?"

"Here the whole time. But you're a dumb asshole who thought he wasn't going to fall for his friend with benefits. How'd that turn out?"

I flip him off and look at Dallas and Hudson. "Do you guys agree? You three are the most relationship-oriented people I know, so I'm trusting your advice."

"Reid's right," Hudson says. "If you want to be with her and you're willing to put in the work, telling her is going to be the best decision of your life, man. Especially when she says it back."

"I remember when I told Maven I loved her for the first time. I was scared shitless, but everything worked out exactly how it's supposed to," Dallas adds.

"Am I allowed to be pissed off? I told Coach the team comes first, but I'm so fucking angry. I'm angry that the first time I care about someone like this, she might slip away. I'm angry that I didn't show her how serious I was about her early on. I wish I hadn't fucked around for months, because now that I'm here, I don't want to lose any more time with her."

"Go," Hudson says. "Go now. Stop worrying about all that shit you can't control and go tell her how you feel. The longer you stand here with us, the less time you get with her. She might be leaving, Mav. You want all the seconds you can get. Trust me."

"Yeah." I nod and pull out my phone, finding our text message thread and hitting her contact info. "I'm going to call her."

The phone rings, and the guys watch me. I'm not sure Dallas has blinked in nearly a minute, and when Emmy picks up, I almost jump.

"Hello?" she says.

"Hey, baby," I say. "What are you doing?"

"I bought some plants at the farmer's market on my way home from practice, so I'm arranging them with all the other horticulture that's taken over Piper's living room. Where are you?"

"I'm at Dallas's."

"Is everything okay?"

"Yeah." I nod again, even though she can't see me. "It will be. Can I come over? There's something I need to talk to you about."

"That's awfully vague."

"I'd rather do it in person."

"Jesus, Maverick," Dallas hisses.

"That is *not* what I said to do," Reid whispers, and I ignore them.

"Oh." Emmy clears her throat, and I hear shifting on the other end of the line. "You can come over whenever. I'm not doing anything tonight."

"Sounds good. I'll be there in a few." I hang up and look at my best friends. "Well?"

"As someone who's slept in the hotel room next to you and

heard you hooking up with more women than I can count, you've never called someone 'baby'. Not like that." Hudson gently shoves my shoulder. "You lovesick idiot."

"I haven't?" I ask.

"Nope. That was a first, and it was so cute, I think I'm going to be sick."

"Stop making fun of me. I'm going to get going. Wish me luck?"

"You don't need luck." Dallas tugs me into a hug, and two other sets of arms wrap around me. "It's going to be fine."

"I sure as shit hope so. I don't know what I'm going to do if she doesn't say it back."

"She's going to say it back," Reid tells me. "Just relax."

"Go get your girl, Mav," Dallas says.

"I hope she knows she's our girl now too," Hudson adds.

"I love her," I say again. "Let's fucking do this, boys."

FORTY-EIGHT
EMMY

I'M PANICKING.

Maverick has never sounded so anxious before. There was a crack in his voice, like he was fighting to keep a secret bottled inside. He was out of breath, and I think he might have been terrified to call me.

I don't know what that means.

I'm preparing myself for him to tell me something awful.

He's going to break up with me.

He's sick.

My dad got hurt and he wants to tell me the news so I don't turn hysterical.

Waiting for him is torture. I stare at the clock on the microwave and watch the minutes tick by, wondering where the hell he is.

The knock comes fifteen minutes later, and I sprint to the door, throwing it open and finding Maverick on the other side.

"Hi," I whisper, and he steps into the foyer.

"Hi." He wraps me in a tight hug and kisses the top of my head. "I missed you so fucking much."

I melt into him, believing that if he had news he desperately had to tell me, he would've already said it. That gives me hope that maybe this is all a misunderstanding.

"I saw you two hours ago." I rub my hand up and down his back and across his shoulders. *God*, I love touching him. "What's going on?"

Maverick untangles our torsos and threads his fingers through mine. "Let's go to the living room."

I let him guide me down the hall, and I memorize the back of his head. The dark hair that's a little longer on his neck than it was a month ago. The small bruise barely hidden under the collar of his shirt, a mark left behind from our game the other night when he got checked into the boards.

My beautiful, beautiful man.

"You're scaring me," I say, and his thumb glides over the inside of my wrist. "Can you please tell me what's going on?"

"I'm sorry. I don't mean to scare you, Emmy. I want to talk about this where we're comfortable." He tugs me onto the couch and pulls me flush against his chest. "I'm going to tell you a piece of information I'm not technically supposed to tell you, but I've been given permission to do it anyway. I want you to listen to all of it before you say anything, okay?"

"Okay." I take a deep breath. My heart hammers like a drum, and I nod. "Go ahead."

"Coach pulled me into his office after practice and told me you're being considered for a trade."

My stomach bottoms out. I adjust my position on the couch so I can look at him, and I blink. "What?"

"You, Finn Adams, and a first-round pick for Justin Harper."

"*What?*" I repeat, because that's an absurd offer. "Why would they ever do that? It's basically giving away a star player for free."

"They see your size and speed as an asset, and Finn, when he's healthy—which he will be soon—is a great athlete. A first-round pick gives them something for the future, and it dumps the contract of a player who's already paid his dues with a team and brought them exactly what they wanted."

"Hang on. Justin plays in Toronto." My brain is slow to catch up, and I shake my head. "That would mean I would leave DC?"

"Nothing is set in stone," Maverick rushes to say. "Coach said he's taking forty-eight hours to think it over, and I know he's going to do what's best for the team. He, uh, knows about our relationship, and I told him not to make any decisions on my personal behalf."

I nod and stare at the floor.

I want to be disappointed, but that was the captain thing to say. I would've done the same thing in his position.

"Maybe Toronto would be good. Staying still isn't in my blood, and if I get too comfortable, my playing might be affected. I can't lose sight of my goal."

"Don't say that." He scoots closer to me, knee pressing against mine. "Don't run from me, Emmy. I don't want you to go. I want you here with me."

"That's the reality of being an athlete, isn't it? One of us is always going to be somewhere else." I bite my bottom lip and shrug. "It's impossible for us to ever really settle. Not until we retire, and god knows how long that will be. Five years, at least. Maybe ten? That's a long way away."

"I'll retire if that's what it takes to be with you," he says.

I laugh even though it's not funny.

He'd never do that.

"Why would you give up the sport you love?"

"Because I love you more!" he shouts, and my mouth parts. His chest heaves and he closes his eyes. Surely I didn't hear him right. "I'm sorry. I don't mean to yell, but you need to hear it. I love you. I love every part of you, and that won't change whether you're here or there. I told you early on I'd find a way to track you down, and I would. I *will*, baby, because I fucking love you. I'm going to be on a plane to see you every day I can. I'll buy a place up there so I can have somewhere to stay without invading the life you create for yourself. We'll figure the rest out as we go. I know we will, because I. Love. You."

He punctuates the last three words, and it punctures my heart.

Love.

Oh my god, he loves me.

I love him too.

I've loved him for so long.

Longer than I thought was possible or rational or believable, but I love him, I love him, *I love him*.

"Do you really?"

"I do, but don't think you have to say it back. I just wanted you to know. If you go to Toronto, I'm going to be there every weekend. You'll come here and we'll make it work, Emmy, because that's what two people who care about each other do."

"I love you too," I whisper. "I love you so much, Maverick. I didn't mean what I said. I want to stay here. I want to be where you are. If that means commuting back and forth between Toronto and DC, so be it. I'll do it. I'll do it gladly because I love you, and I'd rather have you from a five hundred miles away than not have you at all."

"Can you—" his throat bobs, and his hand trembles when he wraps his fingers around my thigh. "No one's ever loved me before—not like this—and I would really like to hear you say it again."

I put both of my palms on his cheeks. I stare into his eyes, and there's so much hope there. "I love you, Maverick Miller. I love you so very much, and I'll tell you as many times as you like."

"Fucking hell." He kisses me, and it's nothing like the kisses we've had before. There are so many other words behind the press of his mouth and the gentle glide of his tongue. "I love you. I fucking love you, Emmy girl, and I'm going to say it every day. Probably a hundred times a day, because I don't want to stop. I love you. I love you, baby."

I laugh and wrap my arms around his neck. His skin is warm and soft, and I can't wait to see what it feels like in fifty years. When there are wrinkles where his muscles are and after his hair turns gray.

"How long?" I ask. "How long have you known?"

"Your dad pointed it out to me."

"My *dad*? When?"

"When you stepped out of the suite to talk to the security guard in Detroit, he asked how long I had been in love with you. I thought it might be true, but when Coach told me about the potential trade, I spiraled. I imagined my life without you in it and I hated the idea of not having you around. I went to Dallas's, and that's where it all became clear. I think I've loved you for a long time, though. I just didn't know how to say it."

"When you told me you would drive with me to pick up my dad, that's when I knew. I fought it off before, but in that moment, I knew you had my heart." I touch his necklace and tug him closer. "I'm scared though, Maverick."

"Scared of what? Talk to me. Tell me."

"Of this. Of us. Of the distance and of falling so hard for you. I've done it before, and I don't want to end up broken like that again. I'm not sure if I could put myself back together if that happened with you."

"If you fall, I fall, baby. I'm so far gone for you, Emmy, and it's okay to be scared. I'm scared shitless too, but there's no one I'd rather be scared with." His hand settles on my stomach and his thumb traces my ribs. "We'll come up with a plan. The season is almost over, and we'll have all summer to do whatever the hell we want. We can take a trip. We can spend days in the apartment not doing a goddamn thing. We'll go to Michigan and visit your dad.

You can show me where you grew up, and it's all going to be okay."

I think my heart might crack in two.

I've heard this before—the promises. The pretty picture of a perfect future. There's always been a hesitancy to believe it, but with Maverick, I really think it could come true.

"I'd like to do all those things," I say, and his face brightens. I've never seen him look so happy, and even with so much uncertainty on the horizon, it makes me smile too. "I want to do everything with you."

"Everything, huh?"

"I'm trying to be romantic for once in my life."

"Sorry." Maverick grins. "Tell me again how much you love me."

"Nope. You lost your chance, buddy."

"Come on." He sticks out his bottom lip and I reach out, pulling it down with my thumb. "I'll beg."

"You know I like you on your knees."

"I'll go there whenever you—"

His phone rings and cuts him off. He scrambles for it, yanking it out of his pocket and sighing in relief when he sees the name. "It's just Dallas. I thought it might've been Coach."

"You can answer it."

"Nah. I'll call him later. I got a whole lesson on love from him, Reid and Hudson, so they know now. I'm sure the rest of the boys will find out soon, since apparently you stare at me when we're on the ice."

I gape at him. "I do *not* stare at you, you conceited man." I press my fingers into his ribs, and he giggles. "Take it back."

"Don't shoot the messenger." Maverick dodges my attack and stands up, hauling me over his shoulder. He smacks my ass and I grab a fistful of his shirt. "Where's Piper today?"

"Doing something at the rink," I say. "Why? Do you have plans for me, Miller?"

"Lots of plans, Red. I'm going to stare into your eyes. Say

all that ooey, gooey shit I thought I hated, but with you, I can't say it enough. Then I'm going to—"

His phone rings again, and he stops us in the hallway, halfway to my bedroom.

"Answer it," I say gently, and he keeps me in his arms as he pulls out his phone. "Your friends want to talk to you, and that's okay, Maverick."

"It's not my friends. It's Coach."

"Oh."

"Why the *fuck* is he calling me? He said he'd let me know in forty-eight hours."

"Answer it," I repeat. "I can handle it. Really."

"I know you can, baby." He sets me down, and his gaze meets mine. "We're going to be okay. I promise we're going to be okay."

"Yeah." I nod. "I know we are. We'll figure it out."

His shoulders sag when he answers. "Hey, Coach. Yeah. Okay. Right. Yeah, I'll tell her. No, man. It's fine. You don't need to—mhm. Right. Okay, thanks. See you tomorrow."

"Well?" I ask, and from the look in his eyes, I already know what he's going to say.

"There was a lot of interest in Harper, and management had to act quick." His throat bobs, and he tucks his chin to his chest. "They approved the trade pending physicals, and ESPN already picked up the story. The Stingrays want you in Toronto in three days."

"Three days." I scrub a hand over my face and nod. "Okay. Well. That's that."

"At least you can come to team dinner tomorrow," he says, and that soothes the ache. I'll get to be with my favorite guys one more time. "And I'll help you pack a suitcase."

"Thank you." I rest my cheek on his shoulder and sigh. "I can't believe I found the place where I'd be happy to stay forever, and now I have to leave. I guess it's my fault for finally planting roots somewhere."

"You're planted with me, Emmy girl, and we're going to have roots everywhere. Here. There. Wherever our friends end up. We're stuck together now, and we'll take this one step at a time."

"I know the guys will have heard about the trade by tomorrow, but I want to tell them in person at dinner. And I want to tell them about us too."

"We can do that. We can tell the whole world, if you want."

"Let's start with the team first. Then we'll go from there."

He squeezes my hand. "We're going to be okay, baby."

"Yeah." I smile, and for the first time since he told me I could be leaving, I believe it. "We're going to be just fine."

FORTY-NINE
EMMY

GRADY

I'm not great with geography, but I'm pretty sure Toronto is closer to San Diego than DC is.

Right?

ME

I think it is.

I have so much to catch you up on.

The trade. Moving (again).

Maverick.

GRADY

Interesting.

A few months ago you told me nothing was going on between you two.

How the tables turn......

"I CAN'T BELIEVE you have to go to Toronto." Grant groans. "That fucking sucks. It's cold there. Don't they have moose? Moose can be deadly."

"A lot of things can be deadly, Grant." Hudson pats his shoulder. "But if I had to pick between Emmy and the moose, I'd take Emmy."

"When do you leave?" Riley asks.

"I'm flying out the day after tomorrow. If everything comes back clear with my physical, I'll be good to play in less than a week," I say.

"Want me to break your kneecap, Em, so you have to stay?" Ethan chimes in, and I laugh.

"Thanks, E, but I'd prefer to keep my knees intact." I tuck my feet under me and smile at the guys. They're all gathered in front of me on the floor in Maverick's living room, and it feels like I'm doing story time at a library. They're hanging onto my every word, and even Liam is leaning against the wall and listening. "This might be my last team dinner as a member of the Stars, but you can't get rid of me that easily. I'm still going to be here on the occasional Tuesday, and we might see each other in the playoffs."

"Oh my god. *No*, Emmy. I could never shove you into the boards," Grant says. "I won't do it."

"She'd shove you right back," Connor interjects, and Seymour nods in agreement.

"Are you going to get a place?" Hudson asks. "There's only a month and a half left in the regular season."

"No. They're going to put me in a hotel for the time being. My contract is only for the season, so if they offer me an extension, I'll start looking for a more permanent place." My eyes flick over to Maverick. He's watching me from the entryway with a giddy smile on his face. "Or maybe somewhere between DC and Toronto."

"Speaking of that, there's something we want to tell you all," Maverick says.

He reaches out his hand, motioning me forward, and I climb over Connor and Grant to get to him. Ethan tries to hold my ankle, but I shake him off.

"What's happening?" Riley whispers.

"I don't know. It better be something good," Grant whispers back, and I'm going to miss seeing which of them wins Lexi's heart. "We paused *Madden* for this. Emmy's announcement was worth it, but you never know what Cap has up his sleeve."

"Glad to know where I stand." Maverick snorts and drapes his arm over my shoulders. He looks down at me, and his dimpled grin is as bright as I've ever seen it. "Doing okay, Emmy girl?"

"I'm doing great, pretty boy."

"Do you want to tell them, or should I?"

"Fucking shit." Ethan stands up. "Please don't tell me you're leaving too, Mav. Oh, god. The whole team is being split up, aren't we? Next thing you know, Liam's going to be in fucking Phoenix complaining about how hot it is. Seymour's going to be in Montreal, and Grant will be in Europe because he failed to make a new roster."

"I hate the heat," Liam grumbles.

"Whoa, fuck you." Grant launches a pillow across the room and it hits Ethan in the face. "If anyone's going to Europe, it's you. Your face-offs have been shit the last two games."

"I can't go to Montreal. Brooke is pregnant, and her whole family is here." Every single pair of eyes settles on Seymour, and he grins. "Oh, right. Surprise! I'm going to be a fucking *dad*," he says, and the room erupts into cheers.

"God, I'm going to miss this chaos," I whisper, and Maverick laughs.

"Are you sure? I've heard rumors that Toronto is a little more subdued. They won't have the bond we do, and they definitely won't have a Grant or an Ethan."

"Six months ago, I would've been grateful for some peace and quiet. I'm used to it now, though, and I love the noise."

"I love you," he murmurs, then he kisses my forehead.

"Whoa. What the fuck was that, Cap?" Connor blinks, and everyone's heads turn our way. "Why are you kissing Emmy?"

"Yeah. So." Maverick rubs the back of his neck, and his cheeks turn pink. "We're, uh, dating. And not in a casual way. It's more of an *I love you* way? Which I know I've never experienced before and I'm still kind of figuring out the ropes so I don't fuck this up, but I'm happy. We're happy, and we wanted you all to know. You're our family, and we don't want to keep it a secret anymore."

"Emmy," Grant whispers. "Blink twice if you need help. I've always wanted to be a hero."

"Touch her and die, Everett," Maverick says, and I've never heard something so hot in my life.

"I love him too," I tell them. "I didn't come here expecting to fall for another hockey player, and I certainly didn't expect for it to be Maverick. I'm glad it was him though, because he's picked me up in a way I've been searching for but haven't wanted to admit for a long time. I'm not the same person I was when I got to DC, and I think that's a good thing. All of you have played a part in that change, and I can't thank you enough for opening your hearts to a prickly woman who just needed to learn to trust again."

"For fuck's sake." Ethan wipes his eyes. "Are you determined to make me cry tonight, Emmy?"

"We love you too, Em. Not in the way Cap does, obviously, but you're always going to be a part of us. That's not going to change just because you're five hundred miles away," Riley says.

"You can be prickly around us all you want," Connor chimes in. "God knows we already deal with Liam's prickly ass. What's a little more?"

"Thanks, guys." I rub my hand over my chest and smile. "I hate that I have to leave, but this isn't goodbye."

Maverick turns his cheek and buries his face in my hair. "Enough with all this sad shit. We're going to be here next week and the week after. Emmy will be back soon, and even though it might feel like everything else is changing, this isn't going to change. Grab a beer, turn on Madden so I can watch Grant get his ass kicked, raise a toast to Seymour being a goddamn father, and let's have some fucking fun the rest of the night."

Everyone moves around the living room, filtering to the kitchen and out to the balcony. Grant and Ethan fight over a controller, and Liam pats Seymour on the back, a rare smile sneaking onto the goalie's face when he looks at a sonogram photo.

It hurts to leave a place I love so deeply with people I care about, but I know there's always going to be a spot for me.

I rest my head on Maverick's chest and stare at his phone as he thumbs through his social media accounts.

"You have five hundred unread messages?" I ask.

"Yeah. I don't want to look at them." He yawns and scratches his cheek. "Most of them are phone numbers or photos from women. Opening them seems like an invitation, and I don't want there to be any blurred lines or mixed signals when it comes to the communication I have with fans."

"What kind of photos?"

"Use your imagination, Red."

"Does that actually work?"

"It used to." Maverick shrugs. "That's embarrassing to admit, but it's the truth. Validation, remember? They gave me what I wanted, and I gave them what they wanted."

"How did you pick who to answer? There are eighteen

messages just from tonight from women in DC. Did you open them all and pick the hottest one?"

"Sometimes. Men are visual creatures, Em. You know it doesn't take a lot to get us going, and when I was a guy in my mid-twenties who could buy anything I wanted, a picture of a nice rack and the promise of a blow job was enough to do me in."

"And now?" I ask.

He's never given me a reason not to trust him, and I'm still going to trust him from five hundred miles away. I want to hear it, though. The selfish part in me wants to know it's me and me alone for him.

"And now I don't need any of that shit. I'm happier at thirty than I was at twenty-four, and back then I thought I was on top of the world. I could open all five hundred of those messages, and none of them would bring me the satisfaction that you do right now, Red. You look fucking divine in my shirt, and I can't wait to take it off of you." He tosses his phone onto the pillow and rolls on top of me. "My password is the same as it was when we used my phone to search up vans for your dad, and it's never going to change. I have a past, but I have a future now too, and that future is with you. If you ever feel uneasy, I want you to look at all those unread messages and know that you're enough, baby. I'll take a night in with you over a night out with anyone else any day."

"Wait a second." I hook a leg around his waist, and his hand skates up my thigh. His thumb brushes over the front of my underwear, and I arch my back off the mattress. "Your password is 3669."

"It is."

"That's my name. Why are you using my name as your password?"

"Is that your question of the day?"

"It is."

"I use your name as my password because I'm fucking

obsessed with you, Hartwell. Have been since the minute I laid eyes on you."

"You're a menace, Miller." I lift my hips to meet his, and he shudders out a breath. "Maybe one day we can pretend like we don't know each other. I'll send you a picture of my chest and see how long it takes you to respond. You can try to pick me up with the moves you used to use when you were America's hottest playboy. It'll be fun."

"Impossible. I could never pretend like I don't know you. You're my favorite girl."

FIFTY
EMMY

I WAKE up the morning I'm leaving for Toronto wrapped around Maverick. My face is buried in his chest and his arms have me in a tight hold I can't escape from. I would never try to escape, though. Not from this kind of happiness.

"Morning," he says, rubbing my back. "How did you sleep?"

"Not very well," I admit, tipping my chin up and staring at him. "How about you?"

"About the same. I think I spent half the night watching you like a creep." His smile tugs on the corners of his mouth, and he tucks a piece of hair behind my ear. "I know you only have a few hours before you need to head to the airport. I'm sure you want to say goodbye to Piper and double check that you have everything packed, and I don't want to get in your way."

"I want to spend them with you. There's actually something I was hoping we could do before I left."

"I sure hope it involves your ass. You did so good last night, baby."

His appreciation of my body in the early morning light makes me blush. So does the thought of tangled sheets and the gentle encouragement and soft praise he whispered in my ear as he helped me relax and work up to two fingers.

That's it, Emmy.

Look how well you take me.

You're doing so well. I've never seen something so beautiful.

"Stop talking about my ass," I murmur without any bite behind it, and his hand strokes my backside.

"It's hard not to. Have you seen the thing? Okay, I'm sorry. Enough of the jokes. What do you want to do before you leave?"

"Can we go to the rink? I haven't skated in a few days, and I want to take some shots on goal. It'll be like the first day we met."

"A little nostalgia." Maverick grins. "That sounds like the best way to spend the morning. We don't have practice today, so it'll be empty. You can enjoy a quiet arena without any of the knuckleheads being obnoxious."

"What if I want you to be obnoxious? What if I want you to give me the same attitude you did back then?"

"You mean when I was flirting with you?"

"You told me that was not flirting."

"Yeah. I lied." He laughs and eases me out of his arms. "I've been flirting with you for a long time, Red. Keep up."

"You are the most impossible man I've ever met."

"And yet here you are. Naked in my bed and head over fucking heels for me."

"Yeah." I smile and straddle his waist, pinning his arms above his head. "Here I am."

"I swear to god if you pull another deke on me, Hartwell, you're going to be in big trouble. You've got me out here looking like a fucking rookie," Maverick yells across the ice, and I grin.

"It's not my fault you fell for it." I skate a lap around the opposite goal and tap the puck with my stick. "Oldest play in the book."

"I'm thinking about what you're wearing under your jersey."

"You know what I'm wearing. You saw me put it on."

"I did. And now I want to take it off." His eyes gleam. "Give me your best effort, Red. You know I'm a big boy who can take it."

I bite back a response. I know he's trying to rile me up. He's trying to get under my skin the way he got under me before we left his apartment, one hand cupping my breasts and the other slipping between my legs.

An hour on the ice, and my body is covered in sweat. Neither one of us is giving the other an inch, and I *love* that we can go back and forth like this. I love that he's not letting me score and I love that I'm not going easy on him.

Maverick defends the goal like his life depends on it. I go through trick shot after trick shot, firing the puck left, right, and center, hoping to sneak a score through his knees.

He's had months to study how I play, and he makes more stops than he did the first time we went at each other. I'm at a disadvantage but I don't give up, hitting the puck again and again until my arms feel so stiff, I know I'm going to be sore for days.

"Baby," he pants, keeling over and gasping down a breath. "We need to stop."

"Tired, Miller?" I skate up next to him and touch his shoulder. "I can keep going."

"I know you can. You're a machine." He pulls off his gloves and tugs me toward him, his helmet resting against mine. "But you need to leave for the airport soon, and I want time to shower with you."

"You drive a hard bargain." I smile and loop my arms

around his neck. "Fine. We can go. As long as you admit defeat and tell me I won."

"You did not win."

"Your save percentage was less than seventy percent."

"Better than the first time I had to defend the goal from your talented ass." He pinches my butt, and I laugh. "I want to show you something before we go."

"What is it?"

"Come on."

Maverick holds my hand across the ice, heading for the tunnel to the locker room. He leads me carefully down the carpet, stopping at a door that's labeled Audio and Visual Equipment.

"We are not making a sex tape," I say.

"Aw, come on, Red."

"I'll send you all the videos you want, but I draw the line at using an NHL team's video equipment to film me giving you head."

"That mouth of yours." He rubs his thumb across my bottom lip. "The things I want to do to it."

"Is that why we're going into a closet?"

"Not quite. Close your eyes, Emmy girl."

I listen to him, my eyes snapping shut and my palm on the wall. There's a jangle of keys and the turn of a lock. The door creaks, and Maverick nudges me forward.

"Is this some sort of trap?" I ask.

"Give me one more second." I hear the flip of a light switch, and the closet grows brighter. "Okay. Open."

I blink and look around me.

The room that used to hold old video footage from decades back has been moved, and I'm staring at a small locker room.

A *real* locker room, with lots of space, bright blue walls and a door marked SHOWERS.

There's a vanity along the left side, complete with a big

mirror and a stool. There's a cluster of leather chairs in the far corner and a small table between them with a vase full of sunflowers.

On the right side of the room is a row of cubbies, with fresh wood and a long bench. Hanging from the rack is a single jersey.

Mine.

"What—" I swallow and look around, my head on a swivel. "Maverick. What is this?"

"It's something Coach and I have been working on for a while now. It took forever to get the permits we needed to add piping and all that shit, so we were a little behind schedule. You deserve a spot to call your own. Even though you won't be using it, it's still yours. The next woman we have on the team can utilize it, and it'll be here when you're in town for an away game."

"Oh my god." I run my finger along the framed photo of the team Maven took after practice one day. Maverick is on Hudson's back. Grant and Ethan are giving each other bunny ears. I'm standing front and center, my hand on my forehead and my eyes bright. "You did all of this for me?"

"Yeah." He shrugs like it's no big deal. "I thought it would make you happy."

"I've always wanted something like this. Thank you for giving it to me."

"We're not done." Maverick guides me to the bathroom door, swinging it open and smiling when I gasp. "A tub and a shower, which is a luxury we don't have in the boys' locker room. Don't tell anyone, but I'm going to sneak in here after morning skate to soak for an hour."

There's also a hairdryer and hooks on the wall for towels. More flowers take up space on the double sink, and it's obvious someone spent a lot of time and effort into making this look as good as it does.

I can't wait for the little girls who watch the games and

wear my jersey to see this. I can't wait for Rachel to see this. It gives me hope that one day women in sports everywhere will be treated as equals by their peers.

"It's perfect," I whisper. "I love it so much, Maverick."

"Good." He squeezes my hand. "I'm sorry we didn't have it ready for you sooner."

"That's okay. Just knowing you put all this energy into creating something for me…" I trail off and glance up at him. "I love you so much."

"I love you too. And even if you aren't here, your legacy will be. We're naming it the Hartwell Room."

"You cannot do that."

"Already did. There's a plaque on the wall above the door, and you can't take off a plaque. It's bad luck."

"*Maverick*."

"*Emerson*. Don't argue with me on this. You're not going to win."

"Fine." I bite my bottom lip and lean forward to kiss his cheek. "Thank you."

"Thank you for letting me take care of you." He unclips my helmet and tosses it on one of the chairs. "Thank you for letting me be by your side."

Maverick and I don't share a drawn-out goodbye when he drops me off at the airport.

He already has plans to be in Toronto next week over the three day stretch when the Stars don't have any games. I promised to call when I got to my room, and as I shove the door open and drop my bags on the floor of my new home away from home, I sigh in relief.

Today has been long. Good, but *long*. I'm exhausted both mentally and physically, and I can't wait to rinse the airplane off me and talk to Maverick before I head to my physical first thing in the morning.

I pull out my phone and send him a quick text.

ME

Just got to my room!

PRETTY BOY

How was the flight?

ME

Not bad. The guy next to me didn't eat an onion sandwich this time, so that was a plus.

PRETTY BOY

An onion sandwich? Sounds disgusting.

ME

You have no idea.

What are you doing?

PRETTY BOY

Come and find out.

I frown and read his message twice.

ME

Am I supposed to understand what that means?

Maverick doesn't answer, and I walk toward the beds, trying to decipher his riddle. Something catches my attention out of the corner of my eye, and when I look up, I scream.

Maverick is sprawled across the mattress with his hands behind his head and his feet crossed at his ankles.

"Took you long enough," he draws out, giving me a lazy grin.

"What… what the fuck are you doing here?"

"Come on, Emmy girl." He swings his legs over the edge of the bed and stands. "You didn't think I'd let you spend your first night in a new city all alone, did you?"

"How—when—did you teleport here?" I look around, wondering if I'm hallucinating. "I am in Toronto, right?"

"You are." His dimples pop, and his laugh is soft and sweet. "I took a private jet. Being rich as fuck comes in handy sometimes. Like when you want to fly to a different country two minutes after your girlfriend walks into the airport."

I gape at him, trying to find something to say, but not a single word comes out.

"Come here, baby," he says, breaking the silence, and I run to him.

I jump into his arms and he spins me around, his hand at the small of my back and his mouth warm on my cheek.

"This is the best surprise," I whisper, and I pull away to look at him. "What are you going to do about practice tomorrow?"

"Coach is giving me a personal day. He said it's a trade-off for not having to read about my personal affairs on gossip websites anymore. Positive reinforcement for keeping my dick in my pants in public. I'll go back to DC Friday morning, and then it's only a few more days until I see you again. It's going to fly by."

"I'm overwhelmed." I sniff and shake my head. "I never doubted you, not for a second, Maverick Miller. But this is next level."

"Flying to see my girlfriend isn't a chore, Emmy girl. It's a privilege, and just more nice things you deserve."

I see a lone tear hanging on the end of his eyelashes and kiss it away. "You feel like a dream."

"Look who's talking." He rubs my shoulder. "I booked another room in case you wanted some space to unwind without me breathing down your neck."

"The last thing I want from you is space. You're not going anywhere, pretty boy."

Maverick drags me to the bed, and we collapse onto the mattress in a mess of limbs. "I love you, Emmy girl."

"I love you, too, and you're going first with the question tonight."

"Easiest one ever." He beams. "How do you feel about letting me bug you forever, Red?"

I roll my eyes, but I can't help but grin from ear to ear. "I can't wait."

EPILOGUE

ONE YEAR LATER
Emmy

THE CIVIC CENTER is exactly the same as the last time I saw it.

The carpet in the players' hallway is the same.

I can smell the same popcorn and roasted almonds that used to make my mouth water during games.

The security team is the same, and even the music blaring from the speakers is on a loop I know by heart.

I guess the only thing that's changed around here is me.

There's familiarity to it, and even though it is brief, it's good to be home.

"There she is." I look over my shoulder and see Hudson charging toward me in his pads and jersey. I laugh when he scoops me in his arms and spins me around. "I've missed you, my sweet Emmy."

"I saw you last week," I say. "You slept in our guest room. I brought you an extra blanket because the apartment was too damn cold. You were suffering from a food coma, remember?"

He sighs into my hair, and I don't know if it's because of me, or the memory of the food he inhaled that night.

The food, probably.

"Like I could forget. Piper's brownies were delicious. They even got Liam to smile, and that asshole hasn't laughed since 1997." Hudson sets me down carefully and squeezes my shoulder. "I mean I've missed you around here. Are you sure you don't want to come back and play for the Stars again?"

"It's not you, it's me, Hud. I could never turn down the chance to be the franchise player for the NHL's newest expansion team, even if they are called the Baltimore Sea Crabs." I shudder, not used to a mascot that has claws. "I'm still waiting for them to come into the locker room, take my jersey away and say, *Surprise! You fell for our silly little joke.*"

"If they did, someone else would come knocking. There's a line, in fact, and we're number one. Your boyfriend is a determined man, and he wasn't happy when we lost the bidding war for you."

"He's a big boy. I see him enough at home, and some space to live our separate lives is nice. It makes his jokes funnier when I don't hear them three times a day." I look around, surprised by how quiet the tunnel is. On game day, it's normally buzzing with people, but it's eerily silent right now. "Where is he, by the way?"

"No idea," Hudson says. "Last I saw, he was using the shower head in the locker room as a karaoke microphone."

"God." I can't help but smile at the image of Maverick with shampoo in his hair, crooning some dreadful song and annoying the hell out of his teammates. "I love that man."

I'm as head over heels for him as I was when I told him I loved him for the very first time. We've had our ups and downs like any couple, and now ours also involve playing for different professional sports teams.

After the trade went through with Toronto, I finished out the season with the Stingrays. I even got to face off against

Maverick and the Stars in the first round of the playoffs, but we got swept, 4-0.

He likes to hold it over my head.

Last offseason, my agent got a call about the expansion team that had just been approved for Baltimore. They were interested in building their roster with lottery picks and more seasoned veterans from around the league. When they offered me a four-year, twenty-million-dollar contract, there was no way in hell I was saying no.

The money is nice—it would be ignorant of me to disregard how lucky I am financially—but signing with the Sea Crabs also meant coming home to the place Maverick and I created together. An apartment big enough for all our friends, just outside DC. It's a forty-five minute drive to the arena, and only twenty minutes from the Civic Center.

There are big windows with lots of sunlight for my plants. A bedroom for when my dad comes and visits and a room we painted bright pink that's reserved for June.

Maverick built a bookshelf for all my books, and every night we're under the same roof, he lies next to me and reads over my shoulder, like there's nowhere else he'd rather be.

He's the best thing to ever happen to me, and I've never been so happy in my entire life.

"I love that man too." Hudson kisses the top of my head, and I smile. "I should head to the locker room. It was good to see you, Emmy."

"Come by this week. I'm learning to make cheesecake, and I need a taste tester."

He groans. "Don't tell Mavvy, but you're my favorite."

"I'm definitely going to tell him. He really needs to bring his ego down another notch or two." I lean in for one more quick hug "See you on the ice?"

"You'll see me." He gives me a mischievous smile. "Real soon."

"Okay, weirdo." I laugh and wave, turning for the visitors' locker room.

I can't make it ten feet before Piper comes charging toward me, waving her hands above her head and looking like a bird.

"There you are," she says, and she tugs on my sleeve. "I need you on the ice."

"You know I'm not with the Stars anymore, right?"

"Of course I know that. The media wants a photo of the two Mid-Atlantic teams doing a ceremonial puck drop before they open the doors to the fans," she explains, hustling me toward the rink I know so well. "It's sold out tonight."

"I'm not even dressed. I'm in street clothes."

"That's okay. It's just a quick photo op, then you can get back to it."

"Fine," I sigh. "But only because I love you."

When we get to the ice, I spot Maven sitting on a piece of rolled out carpet, her camera in her hands. Maverick stands next to her, his hair slicked back and the ink of his tattoos visible under his short-sleeved shirt. He's not in his jersey yet, and he looks up when he hears me approaching.

"Hey, Emmy girl." He grins and holds out his hand.

"Hi." My eyes bounce to his chest where his newest tattoo is hiding. He got it done two weeks ago, *Emmy's pretty boy* spanning across his heart in my handwriting. "What are you doing here?"

"Promotional photo. They thought it would be good press for us to pose for a face off photo, and clearly they wanted the most attractive people to participate."

"I don't see Grant anywhere," I tease, and he kisses my forehead. "And I'd kick your ass in a face-off."

"You're so goddamn cute when you don't know what you're talking about, Red." His thumb strokes the waistband of my slacks, and I shiver. "You having a good day, baby?"

"Better now. I heard you were singing karaoke in the locker room."

"I was. I'm in a good mood. It's a beautiful day. I get to play an exhibition game against my favorite girl in the world and spend the rest of the time on the bench admiring her ass. What can beat that?"

"Not a lot of things." I wrap my arms around his waist and rest my head on his chest. "I guess we should get this photoshoot started."

"Any time you're ready would be great," Maven calls out, and I laugh.

"Sorry to keep you waiting, Mae." I pull away from Maverick and grab two sticks, tossing one to him. "How do you want us?"

"If you'll stand over there, Emmy, and face the scoreboard, that would be great. And Mavvy, over here, please. We'll do a back-to-back photo first."

She puts us in the positions and clicks her camera. Maverick pinches my ass and I laugh, batting his hand away.

"Thanks for that cute PDA. That's perfect. If you'll face each other, I'm going to add the puck."

I turn around and find Maverick on his knee. "Why are you tying your skate? Don't tell me you ruined a good photo."

"I'm not tying my skate."

"What are you doing on the ground?"

"Because I have to ask my question of the day, and it's easier from down here."

I frown at him. "Are you having a stroke?"

"No." He grins, and both dimples on his cheeks pop. "Do you remember when we first started playing this game?"

"I only agreed because it got you to leave me alone, but somehow, I haven't been alone a single day since."

"Funny how that worked. It's almost like I was playing the long game. Come here, Emerson," he says, and my skin prickles. He never uses my full name, not anymore. I close the distance between us, and he takes my hand in his. "I asked you to play because I thought it would be a way to get to know you better. To push past the walls you had up and force you into liking me."

"I think Stockholm Syndrome is finally setting in."

"You're such a smartass," he mumbles under his breath, but his grin stays locked in place. "I thought we'd ask each other the most random shit and get bored of it after a few weeks, but I kept asking and you kept answering. Those questions where we showed parts of ourselves to each other, and, over time, we fell in love."

"Yeah." I match his smile, and he rubs his thumb over my knuckles. "We did."

"There came a point when the purpose of the game changed for me. I started asking more subtle questions. Things you haven't picked up on, which is mind-blowing, because you're the smartest person I've ever met. I've been waiting very, very patiently for today."

"Today?" I wrinkle my nose. "Today specifically?"

"Yup. Five hundred questions, remember? Today is lucky number five hundred."

"You've been keeping track?"

"What do you think those sticky notes with all those tick marks on the fridge are for?"

"I don't know," I say, and it feels like something important is happening. "An orgasm count?"

"I've given you a shit ton more than five hundred orgasms."

"Have you?" I tap my cheek. "I'm not sure about that."

He laughs. "I love you, Emmy. I love the fire in your heart. I love your stubbornness. I love that you don't let me win things easily, and I love that chip you have on your shoulder. I haven't had a bad day since I met you, and we're going to keep having good days, baby, for a long time."

"I love you too." I cup his cheek and run my fingers down

his jaw. He's growing a beard, and I didn't think it was possible for him to get any hotter. "I love you so much, those three words don't feel like enough. I love you more than I did yesterday, which is insane, because I didn't think that was possible."

"Anything is possible."

"Like dancing to a Justin Bieber song?"

"Fuck yeah."

He reaches into his pocket and pulls out a box.

A velvet box, with hinges on it.

"What is that?" I whisper.

"I had to save the best question for last, didn't I?" Maverick opens the box, and there's a diamond there. It's brighter than any ring I've ever seen and exactly what I would've bought myself if he had given me the choice. "Emerson Rose Hartwell. Love of my life. The most badass hockey player I've ever had the pleasure of being teammates with. My sweet girl and my dream woman. Will you marry me?"

I fling my arms around his neck, and we go toppling backwards. Maverick laughs and brings his mouth to mine, a soft brush of his lips that has me gripping his shirt, needing more.

"You didn't answer me," he says, and I kiss him like there's no tomorrow.

"Is my answer not obvious?" I brush a tear away. I blink and see Maverick crying, too, the stupidest smile on his face. "Yes, *of course* I'll marry you. I'd be the luckiest girl in the world."

There's a cheer behind me, and all the Stars players are skating toward us.

Hudson blasts a confetti cannon and Grant holds up a shirt that says *she said yes to the biggest dick in the world!* Ethan and Seymour have a sign with nearly a hundred signatures on it, and Piper is crying so much, Liam has to drag her across the ice with his stick.

Even the grumpy goalie has a smile on his face.

Dallas is trying to keep June from skating toward her uncle, and Reid is shoving his phone in his jeans, giving us his full attention. Lexi and Maven hold hands and jump up and down, and I see my dad waving from a suite above center ice with Duke and Grady next to him. All of my favorite people are in my favorite spot, and I don't think I could dream up a better moment if I tried.

"You're not just marrying him, you know," Ethan says, and he slides next to me. "You're getting all of us."

"A package deal," Riley adds, and he kisses Maverick's cheek. "A twenty-two for one."

"I like those numbers." I squeeze Connor's hand and wipe my eyes. "There's no promotional photo, is there?"

"Nope I just had to get you on the ice in a way that wasn't totally suspicious." Maverick slips the ring on my finger and runs his thumb over the diamonds. "Mine."

The word matches the tattoo on the back of his hand, and it's my favorite piece of art he has on his body.

"I've always been yours." I hold up my palm, and the ring sparkles under the arena lights. "You just want to show me off."

"Maybe I want you to show me off," he says, and I roll my eyes.

"That does sound like you. I'm going to tell people the biggest dick shirt doesn't refer to your actual dick size. Just your attitude."

"Whatever keeps you talking to me for the next fifty years," Maverick says.

"I have to ask my question of the day."

"Don't tell me *you're* going to propose to *me*. I've always wanted a really shiny ring to match my necklace."

I take his hand in mine and kiss the tips of his fingers. The rest of our friends start to break away and give us a minute alone, heading for the locker room or smiling for photos.

"I'll get you a shiny ring, pretty boy."

"What's your question, Emmy girl? Is it how badly you're going to kick my ass tonight? Because I'd like to see you try, baby."

"The ring is pretty permanent, but what about something that belongs to you that will go with me to the grave?"

Maverick lifts an eyebrow. "What are you hiding, Red?"

I pull my collar down and show off the tattoo I got yesterday afternoon. The dark letters spell out *mine* in Maverick's handwriting just above the swell of my breast where his fingers like to touch when he's holding my neck.

"It matches yours," I whisper. "I want everyone to know."

"Fucking Christ," he groans, reaching out to carefully trace the letters. "As if I couldn't love you any more, you go and get a part of me tattooed on you."

"Do you like it?"

"*Like* it? I'm ten seconds away from dragging you to the locker room and putting you on your knees. Maybe the next one you get can be my name. I want to claim all of you, Emmy girl."

I bite my bottom lip to keep from smiling.

That's already in the works.

"You think very highly of yourself."

"Would you have it any other way?"

"No, pretty boy." I kiss his hand and drag him onto the ice. "I sure as hell wouldn't."

COMING SOON

The DC Stars will be back with more stories soon! Be on the lookout for:

Hudson's book (a single mom, roommates story)

Liam's book (a grumpy x sunshine, fake dating, teach me story)

Coach Brody Saunders' book (a forbidden relationship, age gap story)

ACKNOWLEDGMENTS

This is always the hardest part of the book, because this story wouldn't be what it is without the help of some incredible people.

First, thank you for reading. I appreciate any amount of time you gave my words, and I'm grateful you picked up Maverick and Emmy's story. I hope you loved them like I do. If you did, I'd be grateful if you left a review on Amazon or Goodreads. Positive reviews do wonders for indie authors like myself!

Thank you to my beta readers who saw this manuscript in its rough stages. Thank you for your feedback and for helping elevate the story.

Thank you, Kristen, for your proofreading skills and flexibility. I always appreciate your feedback.

Thank you, Britt, for the time and care you put into these words. I know I've said it over email, but I have to say it again: this wouldn't have been possible without you. Your dedication to bringing this book to life makes me emotional. I cannot thank you enough for your patience, and you are a joy to work with. I'm so grateful for you.

Thank you, Chloe, for a BEAUTIFUL cover! I can't wait to see what the rest of the series is going to look like.

Thank you, Ellie (@lovenotespr) for handling ARC signups/cover reveals/everything! You are superwoman!

To Mikey and Riley: you two are my favorites, and I love you more than words.

Lastly, to the book community. Thank you for your reviews, your comments, your messages screaming about my characters and the enthusiasm you have for authors. You make this fun, and I feel grateful I get to call this my life.

ABOUT THE AUTHOR

Chelsea Curto is a flight attendant who lives in the Northeast with her other half and their dog. When she's not busy writing, she loves to read, travel, go to theme parks, run, eat tacos and hang out with friends.

Come say hi on social media!

instagram.com/authorchelseacurto
amazon.com/author/chelseacurto
tiktok.com/@chelseareadsandwrites

ALSO BY CHELSEA CURTO

D.C. Stars series

Face Off

Love Through a Lens series

Camera Chemistry

Caught on Camera

Behind the Camera

Off Camera

Camera Shy

Boston series

An Unexpected Paradise

The Companion Project

Road Trip to Forever

Park Cove series

Booked for the Holidays

Made in United States
Orlando, FL
24 July 2024

49506576R00264